SONG

OF

ECHOES

R.E. PALMER

FrontRunner  Publications

DEDICATION

For Bern, Tim and Neve.

ACKNOWLEDGMENTS

A huge thanks to Erin Kahn, Amy Buckle, Janet Allmey and Pat Marum for reading the drafts and providing valuable and honest feedback. I really appreciate your time, commitment and ongoing support.

Amy Buckle has an excellent book blog which can be found at www.amybucklesbookshelf.co.uk

A large version of this map is available to download and
print at www.frontrunnerbooks.com/map.html

1. Pillars of the Sky

Of all tales, the tragic fate of the Three Maidens alone can bring a tear to the eye of even the hardest of souls. It is told, the Gods at the dawn of time grew weary of their work, leaving the young world unfinished. As the Gods slept, their daughters ventured into this land eager to visit the promised new realm. But to their dismay, the rising sun on that first morning exposed only chaos. Undeterred, the Maidens took it upon themselves to complete what their fathers had forsaken. With voices pure, they sang of their desire for order, giving rise to the Song of Creation. With each verse, hills, rivers, trees, and lastly, glistening blue seas emerged from the shapeless mass.

The Maidens then rested on the soft grass to admire the wonders they had created. But the world appeared yet empty and silent. More verses they sang, bringing forth birds, fish and land-bound creatures to inhabit the abundant forests, meadows, rivers and oceans to the delight of the Maidens. And, of all those they brought into the world, it is said they cherished the songbirds the most.

But unbeknown to them, their voices had carried to the ears of one who could not tolerate beauty, desiring instead the disorder of the unmade land. Far beneath the surface, the Evil One stirred. The ground trembled as he rose from his throne and climbed the stone steps. In the many days it took to ascend, the Evil One fashioned the guise of a fair face to conceal his hatred of the Maidens' song. And so it was in this altered form he greeted the daughters of the Gods. At first, they were wary of the new arrival not of their making. But his silken words eased their doubt, as in their innocence, they could not perceive the devious nature of evil and chose not to heed the songbirds' misgivings. Thus, the Maidens were deceived and accepted the offer of this stranger, seemingly wise and fair, to enhance their creation. Yet, once the Evil One had gained full knowledge of their song, and could endure the pain of its purity no more, he struck. Of the centuries of torment and vile acts the Evil One inflicted on the poor Maidens, the tales do not tell, for no mortal ears can suffer to hear of such dark deeds.

Not satisfied with their corruption alone, the Evil One moved to bring the sky crashing down upon the world to destroy the work of the Maidens. Too late did the Gods rise from their slumber. Little choice did they have but to sacrifice the rolling hills of the middle lands to thwart the Evil One's desire. With immense force, the Gods drove the east hurtling into the west, forming a colossal mountain wall to shore up the falling sky.

As the jagged peaks erupted forth, the Evil One fled, seeking the sanctuary of his underworld realm to bide his time. Too weak to pursue their foe, the Gods made the mighty mount of Caranach to seal for eternity the gateway to his domain.

With the land saved, the Gods sought their daughters in vain. Distraught and driven to madness, they failed to notice the pleas of the songbirds and, in their sorrow believing them dead, abandoned the world never to return.

Alas, for the Maidens, the tale does not end there, but few have the strength of character to listen to the very end. While the Evil One plots his return from beneath the mountain, the daughters of the Gods yet live. Fearing their defilement would bring shame upon their fathers, they had hidden beneath the thick ice far to the north. But still the Evil One's will holds sway, forcing their ruined throats to shriek new verses of his making, befouling the unfinished song to serve his own purpose. What the Maidens' spring brings into the world, the Evil One's winter withers away. That formed by the pure, first verses of the Song, the Evil One's cunning lures those that follow to spoil. And still the corrupt verses flow. To this day, those wandering the wilds at night, despair at the Maidens' desperate wails carried by the bitter winds blowing in from the north.

Of the mountains, Caranach still stands, forcing the fabric of the night sky to such a height the falling stars, snared, and dislodged by its towering peak, burn out long before they scorch the earth. But while the people take heart in its magnitude; gales, driven rain, and ice will, over time, wear down a mountain. And the Evil One waits, aiding the elements, pounding the foundations with his great hammer, shaking the earth to open the deep fissures and topple Caranach.

Of the discord sown by the Evil One's verses, the full tale cannot be told, for the echo of the Song reaches all dark corners of the world, stirring hatred in the hearts of an ancient enemy long believed vanquished.

Toryn nudged the fence post with his foot. 'Well, that part of the tale's not true.'

'What you say?' Jerrum joined him at the top of the ridge.

Toryn looked at the younger man and pointed to the post. 'Look, it's not moving.'

Jerrum frowned. 'I don't get it. Should it?'

Toryn laughed. 'No, of course not. Just thinking about the Three Maidens and the mountains. If the story was true, that post should roll towards Caranach owing to its weight buckling the land's crust.'

'Oh, I see.' Jerrum picked up the post. 'But look, if you put it over here it would roll' — he stepped back and scratched his head — 'but not towards the mountains.'

Toryn took it from Jerrum. 'Doesn't matter, I wasn't

being serious.'

'Oh, I see.' Jerrum's eyes narrowed. His face turned pink.

'But I'm serious about keeping your eyes on the trees. Hamar reckoned a wolf was howling in the night.'

Jerrum spun around. 'I thought you were joking.'

Toryn nodded at his bow, leaning against the wheel of the cart. 'Why do you think I brought that?'

'Aren't we going to practice?' Jerrum searched the line of trees. 'Can't say I've ever seen a wolf around here.'

Toryn snapped his hand like a wolf's jaw and growled. 'Want to take the risk? Just keep your eyes open and grab my bow if one comes out of the wood.'

Jerrum's face turned orange. Toryn glanced behind. The sun shone, large and red, from between the low cloud and dark horizon. For weeks the heavy clouds had clung to the sky, defying the breeze to move them along and make way for spring. Toryn turned and stood on his toes. His heart leaped. Above the treetops, far to the north—east, the faint snowy crest of the mountain reflected the evening rays. He came as often as he could to the ridge to gaze upon Caranach's peak, his only contact with the world beyond the borders of his home. As a child he had spent hours perched in the highest trees to gaze at the mountain and plot his escape from the village. But now, in his twenty—first year, climbing was out of the question and the trees would soon outpace him and take away his lifelong friend. He gestured towards the peak. 'Good to see it again.'

Jerrum squinted over the trees. 'Your eyes must be better than mine. All I can see are clouds.'

Toryn pointed. 'Over there. It's a peak, a snowy one, so I guess it might be mistaken for a cloud.' He kept his eyes on Caranach. 'Wish we could visit more of the land beyond the fences.'

Jerrum wrinkled his nose. 'Not for me. Bad enough knowing there's a wolf in the woods, but it's them other creatures I'd rather not meet.'

Toryn turned away and trudged back to the cart to collect more fence posts. He called over. 'Surely you don't believe all Hamar tells you?'

'About dark creatures? Yes, I do, because I hear them at night. Besides, you believed the old man about the wolf.'

'That's different. They're for real. But nothing else to worry about ever comes near here. Why would they? Not much to be had.' Toryn tugged the next post from the back of the cart. 'Don't you want to travel? See the world and all its mysteries?'

Jerrum took the stake from Toryn. 'Not for me, even if we were allowed.' He tutted like a man three times his age. 'No, I'm happy staying put, knowing all I want to know, thanks.' He shivered. 'I don't want to be dragged off to some smelly cave by a cobtroll, and I certainly don't want to be swallowed up whole by a stinking, slavering droog.'

Toryn grinned at the farmhand. 'As I said, don't go believing everything the old boy tells you. Half the time he's pulling your leg.' He checked the sun sinking in the west. 'Right, I reckon we've just enough light to set three more stakes.'

Jerrum peered over Toryn's shoulder. 'Talking of the old man, here he comes.' Across the field, Hamar swayed from side to side as his bent legs struggled with the thick mud sticking to his boots.

Toryn nodded towards the approaching figure. 'Then I reckon we've just enough time to drive in two more before he arrives and tells us we should have finished by now.'

Jerrum sniggered. 'Shall I fetch the bow? Even I could take him down from here.'

Toryn laughed as he handed the second post to Jerrum and tucked the third under his arm. He checked Hamar's progress. 'Better get a move on. He's faster than he looks. Beats me how he keeps going at his age.' They headed back up the ridge. But Toryn's mind was elsewhere, and his eyes instinctively wandered back to the pink-tinged mountain.

He had dreamed of scaling its peak since the day he first heard the name of Caranach on his mother's knee. Her stories of the world beyond their borders both fascinated and frightened him. Many a night he had lain awake in his bed, scared the demons would escape from beneath the gigantic mountain. He chuckled at the young Toryn who had become anxious the day his father and Hamar dug the footing for the new barn. He had begged them not to go too deep in case they disturbed the beasts below.

'What you smiling about?' Jerrum stopped at the fence.

'Nothing.' Toryn placed his post on the ground. 'Here, pass me that one.'

His mind went back to the day the foundations had been dug. That night, he came down with the Winter Fever and his troubled dreams had conjured up strange creatures threatening to haul him down to their underworld. He had tossed and turned until the soft voice of his mother singing drove them away, allowing him to sleep.

He shrugged. 'Let's finish this.' He paced eight steps from the last post and pushed the next into place. 'Hand me the sledgehammer.' He took it from Jerrum, hoisted it above his head and slammed down on the post. It sank easily into the soft earth. He raised the hammer again and stumbled back as he fought to bring it under control.

Jerrum held out a hand. 'Do you want me to do it?'

Toryn reset his stance. 'No!' He held up a hand. 'Sorry. Didn't mean to shout. No, thanks, I can do it.' He tried once more, this time swinging and striking the post. Satisfied it would hold, he bent to catch his breath before taking the next from Jerrum. He measured another eight steps, knocked in the post with the handle, and planted his feet ready to drive it home. As he lifted, the mountaintop caught his eye again.

With a brisk pace and pleasant weather, Toryn calculated he could reach the range in around three days, given the chance. But that was unlikely. Instead, he would have to settle with making the journey in his head. Under his bed, he kept an old map Hamar had given him when he was ten, saying, *'Take this, but don't tell no one.'* Toryn spent hours poring over its wiggly lines, careful not to let the candle wax drip on the map's worn cloth. The jagged peaks of the Kolossos Mountains, resembling the spine on a half-starved cow, dissected four of the Five Realms. To the south of the mountains, the mighty Foranfae Forest spanned much of the breadth of the realm of Farrand. And lastly, on the southern border of the forest, sat the fortress city of Archonholm. The great citadel was the seat of their leader, the Archon. His courage alone had saved the realms in the dark days as he fought bravely to repel the Golesh invasion from the south.

Yet Toryn's eye was forever drawn to the celebrated Caerwal Gate, an immense structure sealing the pass. Should it fall, the way would open to the hostile hordes, eager to seize the lands and free people of the north. Even as a child, Toryn was not spared the chilling tales of the Golesh, as they laid waste to the southern realms, enslaving those unfortunate to survive the onslaught. Beneath his bedclothes, Toryn had tried to push the ever-present threat from his mind by planning adventures in the world of the map. He imagined stepping into the faded cloth to explore the known lands. But always his curiosity got the better of him as he envisaged what lay in the blank areas of Hamar's map. To the north, beyond the abandoned Draegelan Trench, the frozen lands of Nordruuk remained mostly a mystery. And what had become of the Lost Realms at the bottom of the map, none could tell.

Toryn struck the post home. But still the mountain beckoned. He recalled the route suggested by Hamar. He would spend the morning navigating the winding paths through the neighboring woodlands, then stop to eat lunch while dipping his tired feet in the cool waters of Tam Ford. Late afternoon would bring him to the edge of the trees. Here he would snare a rabbit and cook it over his campfire while watching the lofty peaks of the approaching range catch the last of the evening sun. Under a starry sky, he could stroll across the wide grasslands, avoiding their sporadic settlements as he could not be sure how the occupants would react to a stranger in their midst. At midnight, he would take a late supper of bread and cheese, then rest to prepare for the next day.

Toryn would be on his way well before dawn to cross the gentle foothills. But the sun could not warm his face until well past midday when it finally climbed above the lesser peaks of Kinderach and Lugnach. Come the afternoon, he would search for a course to the lower slopes of the great mountain. The Kolossos Pass was not open to the likes of him. Toryn would have no chance of evading the eyes of the vigilant watchtower keepers, thus denying him the straightforward route. But he did not want to take the easy pathway; he welcomed the hardship. The sheer cliffs of the Kolossos range rise impossibly high from the earth, throwing down their challenge to a mere man to venture on their slopes. But in his heart, Toryn knew he was no simple man. He would be equal to that challenge, finding his way between their walls to earn the right to climb Caranach. Once at the summit he could stand and survey the entire world and—

'Watch out, he's almost here.' Jerrum nodded towards the old man approaching the ridge.

Hamar stopped for breath and called up. 'Thought you'd have finished the job by now.'

Toryn winked at Jerrum. 'Told you.'

Hamar completed the last few steps and stood puffing gouts of vapor through his thick beard. He narrowed his eyes at Jerrum. 'What you giggling about like a girl?'

Jerrum bit his lip. 'Oh, nothing. Toryn was telling me about exploring and stuff.'

Hamar smiled and nodded at the trees. 'Dreaming again, eh?'

Jerrum shuddered. 'Nightmares more like.'

Toryn took the last post from Jerrum. 'Just making a few journeys in my head.'

Hamar ran his hand along the newly laid fence. 'Dream if you must, but don't let it distract you from your duties. A hard day's work never hurt anyone.'

Toryn eyed the woods. He knew if he even dared to enter without permission, word would soon reach the ears of Marshal Drakelow. Within hours, Toryn would find himself languishing in a cell awaiting trial for trespassing. No, he would have to forget any idea of leaving. The only way out was to join the Archonian Guard, but passing the trial was unlikely. Younger lads in the village, including Jerrum, were stronger and would surely be chosen ahead of him. If he struggled to lift a sledgehammer, how could he swing the heavy blades favored by the guardsmen? They had selected only three in Toryn's lifetime. Of those, one had returned in a box, and no word had been heard of the remaining two for eight years. Of all the men in the village who had seen duty, only Hamar remained. But he had paid a heavy price for his time in service, returning with a crippling injury that had taken years to heal. And as Hamar's memory faded and his stories became confused with the old myths, Toryn's world had shrunk.

He turned away, positioned the post, and stepped back, ready to take a swing, muttering. 'Just what we need, another fence.'

Hamar's attention was on the woods. 'No sign of the wolf, then? Stay wary, lads. There're more hungry creatures about these days. But' — he stroked his beard — 'not all of them are wild animals. And maybe it's not only our crops and livestock that interests them.' He turned to face the darker skies. 'I hear we'll be re-enforcing our border with Noor this summer. Drakelow says they're worried about raiders from the north finding their way down here.'

Jerrum glanced to them both. 'The Archon's soldiers will see us right, won't they?'

Hamar exhaled. 'They can't be everywhere all the time, lad.' The blood drained from Jerrum's cheeks. Toryn nudged Hamar. The old man rolled his eyes. 'You don't need to worry. We can take care of ourselves if needs be, and the guards would come soon enough.' Hamar grunted as he bent down to the soil. 'Anyways, we have other problems to keep us occupied for now. It'll be another poor summer if the early spring's anything to go by.' He groaned as he straightened his back. He held out a gnarled hand cupping a tiny seedling. 'This should be twice the size this time of year.'

'Lucky it's not.' Jerrum laughed. 'You'd struggle to lift it.'

'That's enough of your lip.' Hamar grinned. 'Give me a sword and I could still teach you a lesson.'

Toryn glanced at the plant in Hamar's hand. 'I guess it does look sorry for itself.'

Hamar shivered. 'This ain't right. It's too cold for the

time of year.' He stooped, groaning again as he replaced the shoot. 'We'll need every last one to thrive if we're not to starve next winter.' He spoke softly to the shoot as he patted down the soil. He glanced up. 'This is my seventieth — no, seventy-first spring, and I've never known it like this.' He pushed down on his knees and stood. 'One after the other, no decent sun for... what is it? Three, four years now? If you were to ask me, I would say—' Hamar sighed, shaking his head. 'You've not listened to a word I've said have you, lads.' His brow furrowed as he squinted at the horizon. 'Think we'll call it a day. I've finished repairing the barn door so can give you a hand with the rails tomorrow.'

The three squeezed onto the seat of the cart. Toryn passed the reins to Jerrum. 'You take the old boy in.'

Jerrum chuckled. 'Hamar or Ned?'

Hamar's elbow jabbed into Jerrum's ribs. 'Watch it, next time it won't be my elbow, and it will be sharper.'

Jerrum clicked his tongue. 'Take us home, Ned, before Hamar forgets why he needs his sword.'

He laughed again, but Toryn ignored him, choosing instead to take in the view. The setting sun picked out the furrows in the fields and shed some light between the thick trunks of Midwyche Wood. Ahead, the River Tam still flowed fast with the youth of the mountain springs. Farther to the south, beyond the wood, it slowed and widened as it departed their land and headed for the sea.

The cart jolted as it joined the hard surface of the lane. Hamar mumbled on about the weather, while Jerrum still chuckled at his joke. Toryn stayed silent. The lane climbed gently to meet the bridge that would take them across the river, bringing the first houses of the village into view. The evening sun tinged their thatched roofs red, in stark contrast to the dark cloud above the trees. Wisps of smoke climbed out of chimneys as suppers were cooked for smithies, tanners and those returning from the fields. Toryn guessed Hamar's great—great—grandfather would have seen the same view after his day working on the farm.

2. MORNING MISTS

Elodi strolled out onto the wide terrace high on the south wall of Archonholm. She tipped back her head, opened her arms, and let the warmth ease the bumps and potholes from her aching bones. The long journey south had been challenging for the horses, and her carriage was not built for speed or comfort. Her Chief Advisor, Wendel, had stipulated the new Lady of Harlyn should be seen in the proper ceremonial carriage, and not on horseback. But Elodi had insisted on bringing her horse, Sea Mist. The tall gray had been a gift on her sixteenth birthday from her father. Without a second thought, she had named him after the color of the mists that rolled in from the sea on still, cold days and engulfed her city. She smiled, pleased she had not relented to Wendel's disapproval. The few moments she had spent in the saddle had helped to keep her sanity when the refines of the carriage had felt like a cage.

Elodi pushed the thought of the forthcoming meeting with the Archon to the back of her mind. For the first time since leaving Calerdorn, she was alone. She had given Wendel the morning off on the pretext she could explore the citadel, but the real reason was she wanted a moment without his words of advice buzzing in her ear. She felt guilty. Elodi would need the benefit of his wisdom in the coming months, but for now she would enjoy the blue expanse of sky, and surprisingly, the silence.

Throughout the long winter months, the gray, featureless clouds had shrouded the weak sun and drained her land in the north of both light and hope. She looked up, taking pleasure watching the clouds drift slowly to the east. Elodi turned to gaze up to the Archon's Tower. Standing well over two hundred feet higher than the rest of the citadel, it dwarfed the city's many other towers. Higher still, a fluttering blue banner snapping in the breeze, informed those for many leagues around, the Archon resided within. She wondered who was brave enough to attach the Archon's colors to the post jutting out from the conical roof, and whether the center of the Foranfae Forest was visible from such a vantage point.

Elodi moved closer to the edge of the terrace and glanced down. Close to five-hundred feet below, a narrow bridge spanned the deep gorge separating Archonholm from the Caerwal Mountains. The center of the bridge caught her eye. At the top of its span, her father had fallen to his death almost a year to the day. She pushed down the pain and gazed at the mountains. She had watched the peaks of the Caerwals climb ever higher while still many leagues from Archonholm, but only now could she appreciate their immense size. High above, water seeped through cracks in the mountain wall. Elodi imagined a restless ocean behind, patiently seeking for a weakness in the ancient rock, but thankfully the Caerwals held firm, keeping the real enemy at bay. She focused her attention to the opposite end of the bridge. At the head of the pass, she could just make out the portcullis forming the Lower Gate through the lingering ground mist. Beyond, unseen, stood the great iron and stone of the Caerwal Gate.

The celebration to mark the completion of the latest stage to strengthen the defenses would take place the following week. Her stomach clenched. As a child, she had believed the stories of the Caerwal Gate to be a myth. She could not comprehend a structure standing taller than the highest tower of Calerdorn, but in days, she would stand in its shadow.

The breeze dropped. Far below, the sound of

hammers chipping at the rock, rose to the terrace. Hundreds of men formed chains to carry back the stones to feed the insatiable desire of the Archon to strengthen the city. But how long could they resist if the Golesh hordes broke through with their fabled dark beasts? What devilry had the enemy devised in the centuries since the last battle on the Gormadon Plain? If they had the strength to breach the immense gate, surely Archonholm could not hold out for long?

She shivered and turned back to the mountains.

'One of the best views in the land, they say.'

Elodi spun around. 'Apologies' — she stammered — 'Lord Broon, I was not informed of your arrival.'

'Apologies?' The lord smiled. 'Oh please, there's no need.' He stood back. 'Well, haven't you grown. You couldn't be anyone else but your mother's daughter, tall and with your long, auburn hair. Always said she had the agility and strength to challenge even an Amayan to a duel.'

Elodi turned away. 'Yet not strong enough to survive my birth.'

The lord placed his hand on her shoulder. 'Yet strong enough to keep the fever at bay until she'd brought you into the world.' He leaned against the balustrade. 'It must be... what? You were twelve the last time I visited Calerdorn, so it has to be ten years?'

'Sixteen, and I was only eight.' She grinned. 'I'm certain you had dark hair the last time I saw you.'

Lord Broon laughed and ran his hand across his head. 'Makes me look quite the statesman, don't you think? Also makes my weather-beaten face look even redder.' He frowned. 'Sixteen years. Has it really been that long? Surely not. But would you look at me, forgetting the formalities.' The lord bowed low, groaned as he straightened, and held out his hand. 'Greetings, Lady Harlyn.'

23

'No please, call me Elodi, I don't think I'll ever get used to the title.'

He turned to the mountains across the chasm. 'Oh, you will I'm afraid. Only too soon the responsibility weighs on your shoulders.' He pointed to his hair. 'How do you think I turned gray and got this stoop? And please, you may also drop my title, it's Bardon' — he glanced behind — 'when it's only the two of us.'

Elodi joined him at the edge. 'Thank you. I shall need your support in the coming months. Wendel is immensely knowledgeable and helpful, but a second opinion would be welcome.'

Bardon chuckled. 'Good old Wendel still going strong, eh.' He nodded to the sky. 'Warms my heart to feel the sun on my face again.'

'And comforting to see the defenses at close hand.'

He leaned on the warm stone. 'Your first time, I assume. This must be my fifth, but it still takes my breath away.'

Elodi turned back to the walls of the citadel towering over their heads. She bit her lip. 'I have to admit to being a little anxious about the meeting.'

Bardon raised an eyebrow. 'Just a little?'

She grimaced. 'Well, quite a lot to be honest.'

'So you should, and I as well. I fear he's going to impose new levies. The people of Broon already struggle to meet their obligations. Another rise will not be popular.'

Elodi stepped closer. 'We must make our case for more resources at the Nordruuk border. Not so long ago, the Ruuk clans fought amongst themselves and rarely bothered us, only venturing south in winter when supplies were short. Yet nowadays they're forming alliances. We'll soon require double the numbers to put a stop to the raids.'

Bardon rolled up his sleeve to reveal a scarred

forearm. 'I've had the pleasure of fighting a few in my time, and most have left their mark. Not the easiest fellows to kill.' He pulled a face. 'I dare say I'll be wearing a few more battle scars before long. We too have seen a rise on our side of the mountains. My predecessors did their best to encourage the starving clans to settle in our northernmost reaches, and until recently, it appeared to reduce the raids.' He rubbed his chin. 'I don't think the Archon appreciates our situation.'

Elodi peered up to the tower. 'What's he like? The Archon?'

'Challenging.' He took a deep breath. 'Try not to hold his gaze for long. I'm certain he can read what's on our minds. When you've lived five centuries, I guess intuition plays a major role.'

Elodi felt her pulse rise. 'My father remained wary of him.'

'I was sorry to hear about your father. I always found him to be an honorable man, not to mention a good friend.'

'Thank you. That means a lot. He always spoke highly of you.'

Bardon returned to the ledge. 'I gather it was quite a storm. The wind blows strong along the mountain wall in early spring, and the bridge is difficult at the best of times.'

Elodi's gaze wandered to the mountains. 'What could have possessed him to be crossing on such a night?' A tear formed in her eye. 'There isn't a moment I wish he'd...' She turned away, determined not to cry in front of the lord. Elodi had wept for days in the privacy of her room on receiving the news; but no more. Now she had to be strong.

Bardon broke the silence. 'Allow me to show you the second-best view in the land.' He gently took her arm and guided her from the edge. 'I'll caution you now. It will also

25

take your breath away.' He led her through the archway and down the narrow passageway connecting the north and south terraces.

Elodi shivered as the thick stone shut out the heat of the sun. 'Makes me feel at home.' Her voiced echoed back off the walls.

Bardon spoke over his shoulder. 'I have to say, if offered the chance, I'd live out the rest of my days here. I feel the cold more with every passing year.'

The light grew as they neared the opposite end of the tunnel. Elodi gasped as the world revealed itself. As far as she could see, the green canopy of the Foranfae Forest covered the rolling hills like a thick carpet, coming to within a few hundred paces of Archonholm. The main road passed beneath them, crossing the impressive Menon Bridge, before forking to the east and west to take travelers to the northerly realms.

She turned. 'I hadn't appreciated its size. It took days to travel around the western edge, but it's not until you observe it from here, it sinks in.' She hesitated to ask her question, but already felt at ease in Bardon's company. 'Do you get a... a sort of strange feeling from the forest?'

He nodded. 'I do. There's undoubtedly an eerie nature to the place. The Archon must have the same view. He won't allow a single tree felled, even though it's on his doorstep. The only decent trade we've had in years is down to his demand for timber from our forests in Ormsk. He's had enough wood to build a new gate, a citadel, and have enough left over for a table for his council.'

Elodi shivered. 'Did my father speak to you about Durran Wood?'

'He spoke of a Wyke Wood.'

She shivered. 'The very same. I note the locals' name for the cursed place has traveled.'

He nodded. 'Then yes, he did. Is it still a concern?'

'If I had the resources, I'd have every tree chopped down, burned and the ashes buried.' Elodi sighed. 'If only I could open a door to the past and bring back the Great Dorlan.'

'Ah yes, the noble warrior of Calerdorn. I haven't heard that tale since I was a young lad.'

Elodi managed a smile. 'Every child in our land is brought up with the stories of our heroic son. His deeds at the Draegelan Trench before the ice came, help to chase away a bad dream on a dark night. Our knights still bear his banner.' Her gaze wondered to the north. 'Back in his day they would have numbered in their thousands, but these days we struggle to maintain two hundred.'

'And his legend lives on after eight hundred years? Must have been quite the dashing knight.'

'More like a thousand, or thereabouts. And indeed he was, we still have his likeness hanging in many halls of the city.' She blushed. 'Couldn't take my eyes off him as a young girl.'

Bardon smirked. 'Never hurts to have the odd hero around the place.'

'Oh, what I wouldn't do for one now. In our version of the legend, Dorlan fought and defeated Ormoroth, the scourge of the old northern lands.'

'Dorlan as well, eh? Our legends tell of Gildorul of Keld defeating the old *Scourge of the North* in hand-to-hand combat.' He lunged, jabbed his hands forward and twisted. 'Gored clean through with a single thrust of his great spear.'

Elodi grinned. 'Well, your man may have polished Dorlan's armor. We'll agree to let him have that honor. I dare say every telling embellishes the tale further, but I don't think any are complaining. He'd soon drive out the evil from Durran Wood. I came within a league last year and even from that distance I sensed—'

'The Council demand your attendance in the Great Hall.' They spun around to find a gray-robed, shaven-headed woman standing beside the wall. Without waiting, she turned and walked back inside.

3. OF PAST GLORY

'Sorry there's not more.'

Hamar smiled at Toryn's mother. 'Nonsense, that's plenty, Miram.' Hamar winked at Toryn and scooped a potato over to his plate.

Toryn pulled it back. 'Don't, you'll starve.'

'You eat it, you need it more than me.' He called through to the kitchen. 'Thanks again for having me over, Miram. It's very kind of you. Can't say I care to cook these days.'

'You're always welcome in this house, Hamar. You've had a long day, you deserve it.'

Toryn finished his meal sooner than he would have wished. He pushed away the empty plate. 'Tell me about the gate again, Hammy.'

Hamar sat back, taking the request as a cue to light his pipe. 'Ah, the Caerwal Gate. Only ever caught a glimpse from halfway down the pass. Even from that distance, it looks huge. I tell you, if the Golesh can smash through the Archon's gate, we may as well slit our own throats before they—'

'Hamar!' Miram shot him a glance. 'Do you have to talk about such things over supper?'

Hamar eyed his empty plate. 'Sorry, but the lad did ask.'

Toryn called back. 'Don't worry, it will never happen.' He looked at Hamar. 'Will it?'

Hamar tipped back his head and blew smoke at the ceiling. 'I shouldn't think so, but even if they did, Archonholm will never fall. You should see it.' His eyes wandered around the room. 'If you roamed these lands your whole life, you'd never find another place like it.'

'Doubt I'll get the chance.'

Hamar frowned. 'Sorry? What chance?'

'To leave this place.'

Hamar patted Toryn's hand. 'Maybe you will one day. You should go visit Archonholm. I would say only the highest mountains are taller and sturdier.' He pointed the tip of this pipe at Toryn. 'The Archon's Tower is so tall you can see his blue banner fluttering from ten leagues away. And the defenses grow stronger by the year. I once served on a detail quarrying stone to fortify the west wall. I was a young man back then, so imagine what the Archon has done in all that time.'

Miram bustled over carrying two steaming mugs. 'I should hope he's been busy, seeing as it costs us more and more of our shrinking crop every year.'

Hamar took the mugs. 'Now, Miram. I won't have a word uttered against the Archon. He stood up when no one else could, kept the peace all this time, and we're only safe in our beds at night thanks to him.'

Toryn took a sip of his brew. 'Didn't you say you met him once?'

Hamar frowned. 'Did I? Can't remember. Anyways, why all the questions all of a sudden, Tor? I thought it was only mountains and forests that interested you.'

'Elrik said there's rumors the Archon's knights are coming' — he lowered his voice and leaned forward — 'seeing as it's been twelve years since their last visit to this backwater.'

Hamar glanced to check Miram. 'Them's rumors. Only the Marshal would know for sure, and you won't hear a word from him.'

'It's not just Elrik, others in the village are saying the same.'

'It only takes one spark to start a fire. It's nothing but

a rumor until the horses' hooves clatter over the bridge.'

Toryn put down his mug. 'Well, did you meet him or not?'

'Meet who?'

'The Archon.'

Hamar chuckled. 'Me? Meet the Archon? The likes of you and me wouldn't get anywhere near the man. No, I must have said I saw him once.' He clicked his fingers. 'Ah yes, now I come to think of it, I did, but only from a distance, mind. Tall he is, slender, and has the baldest, shiniest head you'll ever see. He wore a great long, blue cloak, the color of the sky — or, so it would be if only these damned clouds found some other land to smother. I tell you this, even from a bowshot away, you could feel his power. Not that a mere arrow could wound the man — wouldn't touch him.' He grinned. 'Tombold. There's a man who has a few stories to tell.'

Toryn laughed. 'More than you? Surely not.'

Hamar examined his pipe. 'Good old Tom. We shared a few hairy moments together. I wonder what he's up to these days? He's a year or two younger than me, brought up on a vineyard on the plains of Gwelayn. What he didn't know about grapes wasn't worth knowing. And a tough man if ever I saw one. Tough, but the kindest man you'd ever meet.'

Toryn cleared his throat. 'The Archon?'

'Ah yes! Tom once told me a story that from anyone else's lips I wouldn't have believed.' Hamar's eyes widened. 'Tombold was on duty at the Lower Gate when the Archon came to check on the new defenses under construction. Anyways, they were half-way along the pass when a platform collapsed and all these rocks came tumbling down. Tombold jumped clear but several were injured, two really bad.' Hamar jabbed his pipe at Toryn. 'But not our man, oh no. Not one of them rocks landed anywhere near him. Tom reckoned he spied something over the Archon, like a shield — yes, that was the word he used, a glimmering shield conjured up from thin air. The rocks bounced right off the air over his head. Ha! Not one touched him.'

Toryn whistled. 'Some story.'

'The absolute truth. He's a powerful man, and one we're lucky to have on our side.' Hamar sucked on his pipe and let the smoke escape from the side of his mouth, through his whiskers. 'I tell you, lad, iron and stone alone aren't enough to hold back the enemy.' He put down his pipe and folded his arms. 'As long as that man is in Archonholm, we have nothing to fear.'

Hamar nodded to the trees. 'They won't like this one bit. Should be the start of their growing season.'

Toryn's legs grew heavy with the mud clinging to his boots. He stopped and scraped them against a wheel on the cart. 'You're right there, Hammy. Certainly is another chilly morning.'

'There you go, even you've noticed. Spring should have brought out the blossoms by now, yet there're few buds blooming.'

Toryn untied Ned and handed the reins to Jerrum. 'Take him to the bottom field but bring him back here by noon.' Jerrum nodded and led the horse away. Hamar pulled the first rail from the back of the cart, keeping his eye on Jerrum. 'He's a good lad, strong, eager to please, but don't seem able to think for himself. He'll have to buck up if you join the Archonian Guard.'

Toryn took hold of the other end. 'Join? I'd never make it past the trial.'

They hoisted the wood onto their shoulders. Hamar grunted as he took the weight. 'Strength and size aren't everything, you know.'

'So, I'll pass by using my head? Since when did they need clever men?' He held up a hand. 'Sorry, Hamar, I didn't mean no offence.'

'None taken.' He patted the plank. 'Let's nail this into place, eh? It's getting heavy.' He caught Toryn's eye. 'Who knows what they look for these days. They might need you with your—'

'Hammer and nails? I don't think so. I'll be stuck here building fences for the rest of my life.' Toryn gritted his teeth and aimed his blow. He cursed as he missed, bending the head of the nail. He glared at Hamar. 'And I can't even do this right.'

'Never mind. Pull it out and use another.'

He took a nail from his pocket. 'I don't have the right blood in my veins for farming.' He stopped. 'But that's the problem. I haven't. No one knows what trade my folks had, that is, my actual mother and father.' He placed the nail into position, withdrew the hammer and mis-hit it once more. 'Well, I guess they didn't build fences.'

Hamar sighed. 'Don't be so hard on yourself, lad.'

Toryn did not hear him. He muttered. 'Or have a drop of good blood in their veins, leaving a baby in a barn to fend for itself.'

'Don't be judging them too harsh, Tor' — Hamar glanced over his shoulder — 'desperate people do desperate things in desperate times.'

Toryn struck the nail, and this time hit the head. His words struck home in time to the hammer. 'But to... abandon... a baby!' He stepped back. 'How can you know they were desperate? They didn't hang around long enough for anyone to find out.' He pulled two nails from his pocket and placed one in his mouth. He spoke through gritted teeth. 'Perhaps I should try my hand as a tailor, or baker, or even a jester? I have to be good at something.'

Hamar stretched out his back. 'Pass me the flask, lad.

33

Watching you work has given me a thirst.'

Toryn laid down the hammer and handed the water to Hamar. He recognized the expression on the old man's face. 'You going to tell me one of your tales now?'

'Well? Do you need cheering up?'

Toryn nodded and smiled. 'Go on. Tell me that story about the Amayan warriors.' He knew how much Hamar loved the myth.

The old man's eyes wandered to the trees. 'Best fighters who ever lived. Saw one beat four guards in the time it takes to nock and aim an arrow. And not your infantry guards like me. No, these were proper knights, the Knights of the Archon."

'Just the four?' Toryn recalled it was three the last time Hamar told the story.

'Yes, four. Sure, they weren't the First Horse lads of Archonholm, but these knights are still not to be messed with.' He frowned. 'Or was it five? I can't remember.' Hamar took a gulp from the flask and wiped his mouth with his sleeve. 'Anyways, it was more than should have been possible. Witnessed it with my own eyes. We were in Broon, or was it Galabrant? But that bit doesn't matter, the important part is' — he scratched his head — 'remind me, Tor, where do I start with this tale?'

Toryn took the flask from Hamar. 'The captain challenged them to a duel for the best place in the stables.'

Hamar frowned. 'Stables? Don't remember it being about stables, but they do love their horses, mind. But again, that's not the story. The Amayans were deadly. Fight for anyone who pays and pays well. But you need to be wealthy, corrupt, or both to afford them. You have to pay a handsome sum before they'll even consider taking up your cause, I tell you.' Hamar rubbed his lower back and groaned. 'Stables? No, I think it might have been a disputed boundary in the east.'

Toryn passed the water back to Hamar. 'You said they could handle a sword better than any guard.'

'Swords, bows, spears, you name it, nicely balanced, you see. But that's not all.' He winked at Toryn as a smile spread across his lips. 'And...' He beamed.

For a moment, Toryn saw how Hamar must have looked as a young man. 'And... what?'

'I can't recall the duel, but I can remember their faces. Some called them She-Devils, but they were more like goddesses' — he whistled — 'you should see their faces. Beautiful, perhaps descended from the Three Maidens before they fell.' Hamar's eyes glazed.

'No, surely not.'

'Well, of course not, but they could be with their long hair flowing down to the small of their backs. Some as red as a sunset, others flaxen like corn, or black as a night sky. And how they could nock an arrow with' — he cupped his hands in front of his chest and raised an eyebrow — 'like this, I don't know. And their legs. Long legs that go right up to their... saddles.' Hamar smirked as he handed the flask back to Toryn. 'And you should hear the stories other lads tell...' He pulled out the next plank. 'Well, never you mind. We'll have Jerrum back before long, and we won't have emptied the cart.'

Toryn nudged Hamar's shoulder as he took hold of the plank. 'You, old dog.'

Hamar let out a long sigh. 'I wonder what happened to them. Can't be many left these days, they'd be as old as me and would struggle to mount their horses, let alone ride 'em. Shame. If we only had fifty, we could open the gate and give those rascals on the other side a fright.' He chuckled. 'And I'd give my right arm to meet them again.'

Toryn watched his face. He must have told his Amayan stories so often, he believed them to be real. But he said nothing. Many of Hamar's memories were clearly tall tales men told to pass the time. What purpose would it serve to deny them to a man in his last years?

'Hey!'

Hamar looked up. 'What's got him all flustered?' Toryn turned to see his friend, Elrik, run as best he could in the mud towards them. He waved his arms, but they could not hear his words. Elrik scrambled up the ridge and fell panting to his knees.

He gasped as he tried to speak. 'The rumors... they're true. The knights... they're coming. They'll be here this evening!'

Toryn gasped. 'So soon?'

Hamar wiped the mud from his hands. 'Well, this will have to wait now. We'll leave the cart here, save Ned's legs, eh.' He straightened his back and brushed down his shirt. 'Best be making tracks. Can't be late for their arrival.'

Elrik recovered his breath. 'Will there be a feast tonight? I know it's the tradition, but with food being scarce and that.'

Hamar nodded as he invited Toryn to lead them down the slope. 'Of course. And no matter how hard times get, we still need our traditions.'

Elrik shrugged. 'But why? Nothing ever changes.'

'Keeps us on the straight and narrow, lad. Without them, we're as bad as the dark creatures roaming the wilds.' Hamar stopped at the edge of the field. He tried to laugh. 'But there won't be much on our plates. The knights will get the bigger portions. We'll just have to listen to the speeches and chew slowly.'

Preparations for the visit were well underway by the time Toryn had washed, changed into his best clothes, and made his way to the village hall. He glanced up at the tattered bunting crisscrossing the square, guessing the same flags had greeted visiting knights in Hamar's day.

Beneath, dozens of children ferried long trestle tables from the store to the hall, skillfully dodging half a dozen women sweeping the cobbles. At the far end, the mayor lowered the frayed colors of Midwyche while his deputy unfolded the flag reserved for special occasions.

'Toryn! Over here.' His mother pushed through the gathering crowd. 'About time. I was getting worried.' Miram licked her thumb and wiped it across his cheek. 'Still can't trust you to wash your face properly, and yet tomorrow you could be...'

'Don't worry, mother.' He took her hand. '*If* I'm chosen, I'll be fine.' But Toryn could tell she fought to hold back the tears.

She whispered. 'I know it's your duty to go, but' — she stood on tiptoe and whispered in his ear — 'since the day I first held you in my arms, I've dreaded this moment.'

Toryn stiffened as a firm hand slapped his back. He turned as Elrik beamed at Miram. 'Don't he scrub up well?' He grabbed Toryn's shoulders. 'And feel those muscles. Must be from shoveling dung all day.'

Toryn winced as Elrik's hands easily wrapped around his upper arms. But he laughed, twisted out of Elrik's grip and grabbed the blacksmith's wrists. 'And how are these weak arms going to swing a proper weapon when you have to put away your toy hammer?'

'They're here!' The crowd turned to the boy standing on the nearby roof. He pointed. 'I can see the spear tips.'

Toryn searched the crowd. 'Where's father?'

Miram bustled around him, straightening his shirt. 'He's checking the final preparations for the feast.'

'Feast?' Toryn scoffed. 'Shouldn't take long.' The boy scrambled from the roof and joined the end of the line. Toryn's heart pounded against the thin cloth of his shirt. He was eight years old when the knights had last come, but he could remember their glistening helmets and breastplates as if it were yesterday.

Miram tucked at his sleeve. 'Your father's here.' Toryn turned to see his red face as he limped to join them.

Andryn nodded to Toryn and took Miram's hand. 'Everything's ready.' Her relief could be heard by the whole square as the thunder of the heavy horses clattered across the bridge. Six plumes of the riders came into view. Toryn held his breath as the first pair entered the square. But as they drew closer, he could not help noticing they did not seem as grand as he had remembered. The dented armor looked dull, the cloth of their banner faded and ragged, and the riders' faces dirty and unkempt. But their appearance did not appear to bother Hamar. The old guard struggled to hold back his tears as he stood to attention with his chest puffed out and shoulders held back.

'Water!' The captain bellowed at a young boy as he slid from his steaming beast. 'Where's the water for the horses, lad?' The boy twisted away, burying his face in his father's cloak. The rider removed his gloves and ruffled the hair of the youngster. 'My horse may be clever, young fellow, but he can't work the pump with his tired hooves.'

The boy's father rested his hands on the little one's shoulders. 'Apologies, sir. He's a bit over-awed by your arrival.'

The captain grinned at the boy. 'Can't blame you, I was probably the same at your age.'

A knight laughed. 'And that was a very long time ago.'

'Alright, that will do. We have important business at hand.' The captain removed his helmet and ran a scarred hand through his matted, black hair. Grime from the road clung to a face lined by many years of service. For a moment, his gray eyes appeared not to see what lay before them. He blinked and spoke to Toryn. 'Seen any aralaks around these parts, lad?'

Toryn laughed. 'Aralaks?' He glanced to Miram. 'I... I thought they were all trapped in the gorge.'

The captain's half-smile faded. 'Still, never hurts to keep your eyes peeled. We can't keep 'em fenced in forever.' He grimaced. 'Nasty creatures. Keep well away, well out of spitting distance. And be wary of their spindly legs. You don't want all eight of 'em wrapped around you at once.' Again, his eyes glazed. 'Never live to tell the tale. Horrible way to go.'

4. A CAUSE FOR CELEBRATION

Toryn had rarely seen the hall look finer. Bunting hung from the eaves concealing parts of the roof badly in need of repair, and the low light of the flickering lanterns hid much of the neglected woodwork from prying eyes. Yet, despite Toryn's trepidation, his spirit rose as he entered. The smell of the lamps and murmur of the gathering villagers took him back to the mid-winter celebrations of his younger days. But back then, his belly had been smaller and easier to fill — tonight, he suspected his stomach would still be rumbling come the end of the function.

All but the youngest of the villagers sat at six long tables, but only the head table laid out for their guests of honor had a cloth of white linen. At the back, the children sat crossed-legged on a large mat, trying to sit still and silent as they anticipated their supper. Toryn wished he could join them and be blissfully unaware of the importance of the occasion.

Elrik waved from the far table. Toryn turned away from the children and squeezed through the narrow gaps to sit opposite his friend. Elrik beamed and drained his cup. 'Just think, this time next week we could be seven days away from this place.'

Toryn nodded at Elrik's empty cup. 'Might have been wise to have saved some of that wine, I don't think we'll get another.'

Elrik laughed. 'Who cares? Once we're guardsmen' — he nodded at the head table — 'we'll get all the ale and wine we can handle, not to mention—'

'We have to pass the trial first.'

'We'll do it with our eyes shut, although I'm not so sure about the rest of the lads.'

Toryn sloshed the dark wine around the bottom of his cup. 'Hamar says it's not all ale, women and glory, especially if we find ourselves on the Nordruuk border.'

Elrik's shoulders dropped. 'I know, he's told me about the life, but anything has to be better than living in this village.' He lowered his voice as a weaver caught his eye. 'Nothing ever happens, same day every day, except on a rare holiday when nothing happens twice over.'

Toryn tried to laugh. 'But you may find a day when you'd welcome nothing happening.'

All heads turned as Marshall Drakelow entered. He paused at the entrance and peered over his shoulder. He cleared his throat. 'All stand for the Knights of the Archon.' The villagers obliged. Drakelow stepped aside as the captain led in his men. Toryn watched the six stride into the hall. They wore tabards and clothes that had seen better days, but they walked straight-backed and proud as they took their positions at the head table.

The captain held up his hands. 'Please be seated.'

Elrik leaned over. 'Imagine. You and me on the road south, seeing all the places we've only heard about in stories. And Archonholm? As tall and as strong as a mountain, Hamar says.'

'And not forgetting the training. There'll be no ale and maidens before we've finished that.'

'Yes, and the training.' Elrik swished his hand across the table. 'We'll be unbeatable, champions of the Five Realms.'

Toryn studied the men at the head table. Despite the shabby state of their clothes, they appeared strong and battle-hardened. If an Amayan warrior had taken down just one, it would still be an impressive feat. He glanced over to Hamar, who beamed ear-to-ear at the head table.

Marshal Drakelow stood. The room fell silent. He turned to the head table. 'On behalf of the village of Midwyche and the Ward of Darrow, I welcome you to share our humble supper.' He raised his cup to the knights. 'Let's drink a toast to the fine, brave men who keep our lands safe and free.' The room stood and waited for the captain to speak. He said nothing, but they took his nod as a sign to drink. Toryn eyed the wine barely covering the bottom of his cup. He joined the villagers in the toast. 'To the Knights of the Archon.'

The knights drained the wine and banged on the table until the serving girl refilled them. The captain held up his hands. 'Keep it down, lads, you'll scare the young 'uns.' He waited for quiet before turning to Drakelow. 'Thank you, Marshal, for your welcome. Right' — he rubbed his stomach — 'time to eat.' His men cheered as the servers brought plates of pork, potatoes and green beans. Toryn and the villagers had to wait longer for their meagre supper of bread and cheese to arrive. He picked at the contents of his plate, careful not to finish before those at the head table.

When their guests had eaten their fill, and much of next week's ration, the captain stood. In turn, his eyes met each of the young men in the room. He drew a breath as if to speak but paused as a young girl at the back of the hall cried for her mother. The woman excused herself from the table and hurried to the distraught toddler. To the relief of the hall, the girl settled once she laid eyes on her mother. The captain knocked back his drink and winked at the mother. 'If you're finished at the back, I'll start the formal part of the evening.' He straightened. 'As you know, the Archon works day and night to maintain the watch at the Caerwal Gate so you can farm your lands and live in peace. My men devote the best years of their lives to this noble duty. While you sleep in your beds, we remain ever vigilant for the enemy on your behalf. We watch the ports, the rivers, the mountains, and the borders of all lands for signs of intrusion and—' an old man coughed, the captain turned — 'and yes, I'm afraid this means we have to enforce certain restrictions.'

A low murmur rose in the hall. Drakelow held up his hands. 'Now, now, please let the man speak.'

'Thank you, Marshal. I know you would prefer the freedom to travel and trade, but as you're aware, we still have remnants of the dark forces in hiding, no doubt waiting for our resolve to weaken, and of course, we also have to deal with the brigands from the north.' The muttering continued, forcing the captain to raise his voice. 'The restrictions make it somewhat easier for us to track down those still bearing us a grudge. However, these restrictions will need to be stricter from now on.' He took a breath. 'Of late, there has been… let's just say certain events in the east may have been orchestrated from the other side of the Caerwal Mountains. I've—'

Some gasped. All heads turned to their loved ones, three women stood and rushed to their young. Drakelow raised his voice. 'Let's all stay calm. Please, allow the man to finish. I'm sure the Archon has a plan to counter this threat.'

The captain nodded. 'Marshal Drakelow is right. The Archon expected such events. I've advised your Marshal to step up the watch on your borders, and my detachment will continue to patrol this side of the mountains. And besides' — he gestured to the back of the hall — 'while fine men like young Hamar still draw breath, you'll be safe. What do you say, Hammy?'

Toryn turned. Hamar blinked as if waking, surprised to see all eyes upon him. He coughed. 'Sorry, Captain, I was… deep in thought there for a moment. What was the question?' Many laughed, relieved by the distraction.

The captain laughed with them. 'I was saying, while you're still in your prime, these good people have nothing to worry about.'

Hamar's chest expanded until the buttons strained. 'No, of course not. Well that is, as long as the sun comes out and our crops can—'

'See.' The captain tried but failed to prevent the grin spreading across his face. 'As alert and on his guard as ever.' The grin faded. 'But to return to the issue at hand, we must prepare' — he glanced at his men — 'for more unrest.' He bent, picked up his drink and drained the contents as the voices of the villagers rose. The captain held up his hands. 'But! Fear not. The Archon has prepared for this type of thing and has taken necessary steps to counter the threat, and indeed, take action.' He leveled his gaze to Toryn's table. 'All males who've seen eighteen summers but fewer than twenty-eight, please stand.'

Toryn glanced to Elrik as they rose, numbering ten in total. He felt suddenly exposed as all eyes focused on them. The captain pushed back his chair. 'Good. Now, please come to the front.'

Toryn followed Elrik and the others to form a line in front of the head table. He scanned the line; all stood taller and broader than he. The captain moved to the opposite end. He placed his hands behind his back and strolled along the line before turning and returning to his position. 'You.' Toryn's heart pounded as the man pointed a large finger at him. 'You at the end, step forward.' The others shrank back a pace as Toryn obeyed. 'Please, stand to attention.' Toryn pushed out his chest. He approached and stopped opposite. He frowned. 'Aren't you a little small for your age, sonny? Are you sure you're over eighteen?' The men laughed, but the captain ignored them. He rested his hands on Toryn's shoulders. 'I admire your courage, boy, but I can only take those of the right age.' He smiled. 'How old are you? And please, speak the truth."

'Twenty-one, Captain.'

'Twenty-one?' He turned to Elrik at Toryn's side. 'Looks like the big fellow here has been eating this poor lad's ration.' The knights laughed harder. The captain held up his hand. 'Well never you mind, the training and good food will soon build you up.'

'Does this mean—?' Toryn stuttered. 'Sorry, sir... Captain, I didn't mean to speak out of turn.'

His eyebrow raised. 'Speak your thoughts, lad.'

'You said, training. But I haven't' — he glanced down the line — 'none of us have passed the trial, yet.'

'Ah, yes.' He moved to the end of the line. 'This brings me to my next point.' He glanced to the Marshal. Toryn noted the slight nod of Drakelow's head. The captain sucked air through his teeth. 'Due to the extra duties placed upon us in these troubled times, there'll be no trial tomorrow.' Elrik frowned, Hamar stirred and squinted at Toryn. He strolled back in front of the line. 'This year, I will assign all eligible males for training at Archonholm's barracks.' He turned to face Elrik and Toryn. 'Go home, pack your belongings, lads, and be ready to depart at first light.'

Toryn stared into the flames. No trial, no test of strength. They had chosen all the young men, and tomorrow he would leave his home and take the long journey south. For years he had longed to travel, but now he was not so sure.

Miram hurried through. 'Here they are.' She placed a pair of socks on his bed. 'They're thick so will be too warm for the south, but you'll need them for the first part of the journey.' She straightened the pile of clothes, ready for packing in his rucksack. 'Be sure to eat well, and sleep, you'll need plenty of rest if you're—' She spun away.

'Mum.' Toryn took her arm and turned her back to face him. 'I'll be fine. I'll be with Elrik and the others, we'll look after each other.'

She blinked away a tear. 'I know, but it won't stop me worrying and it could be years before—'

'You should take this.' His father stood at the door. Andryn held something wrapped in a cloth under his arm. He placed it on Toryn's bed and removed the cloth. Beneath lay a sword. Andryn picked it up by the blade and held out the hilt to Toryn. 'It's not the finest in the land, but it's not the worst either. Elrik's grandfather made it for my father, he passed it on to me, but as you know' — he winced as he patted his leg — 'I never had the chance to wield it.'

Toryn took it. 'It's heavy.' He raised the blade and thrust it forward as Hamar had taught him.

'Careful.' Miram stepped back.

He lowered the point and glowered at his father. 'Why have you never shown me this before? My wooden sword broke years ago.'

Andryn glanced to Miram. 'I... well... I couldn't be sure you'd ever need it.'

Toryn placed the sword back in the cloth. 'You too, eh? Does no one think I could make it as an Archonian Guard?'

'No, he's not saying that.' Miram covered the weapon. 'He means because you work on the land, we thought you wouldn't be expected to—'

'But Hamar went. He farmed. And you, father, you've got years left before you're too old to work. Jerrum can take my place. Why wouldn't they take me?' He turned his back, grabbed hold of his socks and stuffed them into the rucksack.

'Toryn.' Miram took his hand. 'We have always—'

'He can't go!' All three spun around. Hamar spluttered and coughed as he leaned against the door frame. His eyes fell upon the sword handle poking out from under its cover. He recovered his breath and pleaded with Andryn. 'You can't let him go. You know he can't. They'll find out.'

Toryn turned from Hamar back to his mother. 'Find out what?'

Miram's hand went to her mouth. Andryn raised his hand, but Hamar would not be silenced. 'He has to know. Tell him. Because if you don't, I will.'

5. THE BATTLE ON THE WALL

'Please wait here for the Proctor.' The guide returned the way they had entered. Wendel waited until the guide had shut the door before he spoke, but his words were lost on Elodi. She stared up at the elaborate vaulted ceiling high above their heads.

'Breathe.' Elodi spun as Bardon approached. He smiled. 'It helps if you breathe.'

Elodi took his advice. She whispered. 'Father told me of the Great Hall, but his words don't come close to doing it justice.'

'Err, ma'am.' Wendel stepped in. 'This isn't the hall. This is the waiting area. The Great Hall is on the other side of those doors.'

Elodi's face flushed. 'Yes, well... thank you, Wendel, for putting me right. That will be all.'

'But the meeting?'

'I think I'm as ready as I'll ever be' — she touched his arm — 'thanks to your instruction. But I need to speak with Lord Broon. I will send for you when I'm done.'

Wendel glanced to Bardon. 'As you wish, ma'am. But remember what I said about—'

'I will, thank you.' Her advisor turned and ambled away. Elodi imagined she could see his thoughts whirring above his head.

She stifled a yawn. 'We must have spent the best part of the night preparing for this, but I doubt I can remember half of what he said.'

Bardon grinned. 'Half will be plenty, even if Wendel has done only a quarter of his job. And, if it helps, I thought this was the Great Hall on my first visit.'

Her shoulders dropped. 'Thank you, it does. But these ceilings. Calerdorn is a fine, if aging city, but nothing compares to this place. And those doors… if the gate is as sturdy, surely we have nothing to fear.'

Bardon looked up. 'The Archon takes pleasure from his grand gestures. He's overseen the construction and decoration of all the staterooms, and the quarters allocated to us both.' He leaned closer, lowering his voice. 'I only hope all this grandeur doesn't distract him from attending to the defenses.' But Elodi barely heard his words — she had turned and stood aghast at the huge tapestry covering the entire back wall.

Bardon followed her gaze. 'Depicts quite a scene does it not.'

Elodi could only nod. As a girl she had cowered at the tale of the desperate rear-guard action of the Archon against the full might and fury of the Golesh. The Battle of the Gormadon Plain was both the finest and darkest hour of the Seven Realms before diminished to five. Tens of thousands of the greatest soldiers ever to take up arms had perished in a last-ditch attempt to stop the invasion. Trampled under the hooves of craven beasts surging north, they had laid down their lives to allow time for the completion of the Caerwal Gate. Many more had died in battles to the north as the Archon's armies fought hard to push back the thousands of raiders landing on both the east and west coasts. But all would have been in vain had it not been for the Archon's defiant stand.

Elodi stepped closer. At the center of the scene, three fierce drayloks bore down on the lone, armored figure of the Archon. With a large shield, he fended off tongues of flames spewing from their gaping mouths. In his right hand he held aloft the Sword of the Realms striking at the long, barbed strands of the hags' hair seeking to entwine him. As all fell about him, the Archon stood firm and held up the enemy advance, but at significant cost. As the tale goes, he fought for three days and nights until the signal finally came the gate was ready to close. Rescued by his fearless horse, Arrow, he barely escaped with his life. He had slid from his horse close to death as the gate had swung shut in the face of the raging Golesh and their foul creatures, denied their ultimate prey.

'You can virtually feel the heat of their fire.' Bardon stood at her side. 'Whatever some may think, we do owe the Archon a great debt.'

Elodi studied the black eyes of his assailants. 'They aren't… I am right in thinking drayloks weren't really as terrible as portrayed here.' She turned to Bardon. 'I know we like to scare children by saying a shrieking draylok will drag them from their beds if they misbehave, but' — she pointed to the tapestry — 'they didn't breathe fire, did they?'

Bardon's eyes wandered across the Archon's foes. He blinked. 'Only the Archon knows for sure, and he rarely speaks of the confrontation.' He rubbed his hand across his face. 'I dare say the artist exaggerated their appearance to show our leader at his best.'

'Drayloks or not, he must have immense strength. How could one stand up against such an assault?'

Bardon turned his back on the wall. 'It took the best part of a decade for the Archon to get back on his feet. I trust he's fully regained his strength, as I fear we may have to rely on him once again. The Ruuk to the north are growing stronger and bolder, their incursions are hurting, and yet still the Archon focuses his attention solely on the south.' He dropped back and mimicked drawing a sword from his belt. 'Did you keep up your training, Elodi? You father said you showed great promise as a child.'

Elodi nodded. 'He insisted. When I was eight, he presented me with my mother's sword.' She laughed. 'I could barely lift it, let alone swing it at first. But' — she crouched into a fighting stance — 'as I grew, I soon learned. And, if I may be so bold, I make a formidable opponent in a duel. Never happier than when I have a sword in my hand, or in the saddle.' She swung her arm as if parrying a blow. 'Father instructed my teachers not to go easy on me, and for that I thank him. He made it clear I would lead from the front should it be necessary.' She turned to Bardon. 'But I assume he wouldn't have thought it would be so soon.'

'Let's hope it doesn't come to that.' Bardon replaced his imaginary sword. 'Remind me, what end did your noble warrior, Dorlan, meet? I'm guessing it wasn't old age.'

'Most definitely not, all hero's need an end worthy of a song at the very least.' She hummed the tune but stopped before she attempted to sing. 'It is told he perished as Ormoroth himself fell at the Battle of Talaghir.'

He shrugged. 'Then we can assume he won't be showing up any day soon to save your realm. And our brave Gildorul of Keld must have fallen at his side if the tales be true.'

Elodi looked back to the battle on the wall. 'Then we're on our own. While the songs may raise our spirits, it's disheartening to hear how Harlyn has weakened since those times. Draegnor can hardly be described as a fortress these days, and our forces comprise mainly of part-time farmers and smithies. We have yet to rebuild the ruins of Darrowyche, and all our major ports are in need of repair.' She grimaced at the sight of the embroidered drayloks. 'If Ormoroth lived, he could stroll across the border and take my realm without breaking step.'

'Well, let us at least give thanks to our ancestors for his demise.' Bardon gestured to the doors of the hall. 'But now to more pressing matters. We must prepare ourselves for the meeting with the Archon. We cannot allow them to raise the levies again in such a short time. While we don't have to contend with Ormoroth of old, these raids are hurting us both.'

'Perhaps they'll listen if we make the case for more resources at the old watchtowers.'

'To you and me, that makes perfect sense, but one doesn't negotiate with the Archon in the usual sense, it has to be him who gives, and we have to be grateful. And don't expect to be treated in a manner suited to your status. We may be leaders of our realms, but the Archon and his Council hold all the power. I get the impression the Archon actually sees us as an inconvenience, except when it comes to our levies.'

But Elodi's mind had drifted elsewhere. She stared at the oak doors rising half-way to the ceiling, adorned with golden decorations in the form of branches and leaves. She shook her head. 'Is there nothing ordinary about this place?'

Bardon smiled. 'I must have worn the same face when I first stood here. But don't expect a warm welcome behind those doors. And expect to wait a while longer. I'm sure it's all part of a strategy to make us feel uneasy to the point of questioning our own authority.'

Elodi took her eyes from the doors. 'But in all honesty, what power do we have compared to him? He has the armies, the wealth from the farmlands of Farrand, Archonholm and the palace purse.'

'That may be so, but we must remember you and I represent two of the Five Realms, and if we act together, form a sizeable power.'

'But all the same.' She waved her hand across the room. 'Do you have anything in all of Broon comparable to this?'

'Don't let the architecture, or him, intimidate you. We must stand up to him for the good of our people.' He smiled. 'Your father was a determined man, and you are shot from the same bow. Your people trusted him and therefore they'll trust you. The Archon took a dislike to your father because his loyalty to the people of Harlyn came first.' He turned to her. 'We can't let him have everything his own way. He has to know we will not roll over and bare our bellies every time he demands it.' His eyes wandered across her face. 'You're a clever and determined woman, Elodi, and I predict you'll make a fine leader for your realm in these troubled times.'

She looked away. 'I only hope you're right.'

He took her hand. 'But allow me to do the talking for your first audience. With time you'll learn to handle the Archon as best you can.'

Elodi frowned. 'But won't he expect me to speak?'

He grinned. 'Trust me, he doesn't give anyone the opportunity to speak. But be wary, he's always two steps ahead. He knows what you're going to say before you do. And if he sees any sign of weakness, you'll end up promising far more than your lands can afford.'

Elodi nodded as the knot in her stomach grew tighter. 'Thanks for the advice.'

'And be wary of the Castellan.' He saw her frown. 'The head of the citadel. It's his duty to know everything that goes on in this place, and it's a duty he performs particularly well with relish. He commands the Palace Guard and reports directly to the Archon.'

Elodi turned to the door as it swung open with only the faintest hint of a creak. She whispered. 'How do you deal with all of this?'

'You'll learn.' He nodded to the Proctor standing by the door and raised his eyebrows. 'Otherwise you'll end up like him.'

Elodi turned; she could not recall seeing an older man, or someone with a more crooked spine still able to stand. The Proctor held out a hand resembling the bark of a tree. He croaked. 'The Council will see you now.'

Elodi inhaled deeply, aware what lay beyond the doors would likely take her breath away. Bardon murmured. 'Follow my lead and only speak if he asks you a direct question.'

She followed. The echo of their footsteps would alert the entire palace of their arrival in the hall. And great it was. Elodi could not help glancing up as they passed through the thick doors, aware her mouth gaped wide. Light from the tall, narrow windows sliced through dust trapped in the thick air. Despite the high vaulted ceiling, the hall was hot. Sweat beaded on her forehead and trickled down her spine as she strode beside Bardon, keen to make a confident entrance. At the far end of the hall, a long table covered with a light blue cloth, stood on a low dais. Her heart hammered into her ribs as they drew near. She stumbled as the Proctor halted. The old man tutted and ushered them forward to a spot opposite the center of the dais. The Proctor shuffled back and grumbled as he took his place on a stool to their left. Behind the large table sat the six white-robed members of the Archon's Council, all with stiff backs and shaven-heads. In the middle, the grandest of the chairs sat empty.

'Vice-Archon?' Bardon's voice shook as he addressed a stern, middle-aged woman to the right of the empty seat. 'I thought we had an audience granted with——?'

'Then you thought wrong, Broon. You were granted a meeting with the Council, as you can see. The Archon' — the woman covered her mouth and coughed or chuckled, Elodi could not be sure — 'has far more pressing matters to attend than the everyday affairs of the Five Realms.'

Bardon took a breath and addressed the woman. 'I wouldn't describe raising the levies by fifteen percent as an everyday affair, Vice-Archon.' Elodi shivered despite the cloying heat.

The Vice-Archon's jaw tightened in her gaunt face. 'I disagree. He who keeps our lands safe cannot be troubled with such trifling matters as coin and crop' — her voice rose — 'when he ceaselessly maintains the defenses and keeps a watchful eye on the enemy.' The shiny heads of the Council nodded, catching the sunlight strong enough to pierce through the dust.

But Bardon held his ground. 'Then please inform the Archon if he wishes to raise taxes, he has to allow more trade between the realms, and to do that, the restrictions on those who can travel need revision.'

The Vice-Archon held Bardon's gaze but remained silent. When she spoke, Elodi could barely hear her voice. '*I* will inform the Archon of what I deem fit.' She leaned forward. 'And *I* am quite capable of determining the appropriate trade and travel arrangements. Both Kernlow and Galabrant have no issues with the levy. And I have already—'

'Then can you explain why, for example, the people of Broon cannot easily sell their wool to Galabrant with whom we share a border? And I can't remember the last time I enjoyed a fine wine from the vineyards of Gwelayn.'

The heads of the Council turned to the Vice-Archon. Her chest rose. '*If* you would allow me to finish, I was about to explain.' She picked up a goblet and drank. Elodi's dry mouth would have welcomed a drink of cool water, but noted the aides had set no glasses for them. The Vice-Archon's shoulders dropped as she sat back and held the cup in both hands. 'I have commissioned a review to assess such arrangements. They will report later in the year and then, and only then will I pass judgement.'

'Are you aware…?' Elodi stepped forward and spoke before she realized she had made the decision. At her side, Bardon stiffened. She cleared her dry throat. 'Are you aware, Vice-Archon, the crop yield in the southern wards of Harlyn have diminished over the last five years? We have spent many years rebuilding our farms following the Great Famine so we do not see a return to those dark days.' She took a quick breath as the Vice-Archon moved to speak. Elodi rushed out her words. 'But it is not only our crops suffering with the colder summers. In the north, losses of livestock due to the raids have increased. And, are you also—?'

Elodi jumped as the Vice-Archon's voice rose to the rafters. 'Of course, I am aware! And if you will also allow me a moment to speak, I will inform you of what is currently placing demands on our *limited* resources.' She placed the goblet back on the table and glared at them over the rim. 'Good, I see I have your attention.' The Vice-Archon sighed as if bored with their company. 'Now, as you well know, the Archon has spent the last two years overseeing construction of the tower at the gate. You, as leaders of your realms, will attend its opening shortly. The reason, as I'm sure you will appreciate, is so you can report back to your people how we spend the levies for their protection.' She raised her eyebrows. 'Is that understood?'

Bardon nodded. 'Understood, Vice-Archon. But if the work on the tower is complete, why the need for the increase in the levies?'

The Vice-Archon hissed as she sucked air through her teeth. 'The work is never complete, Broon, the threat is always present. Work on the third stage of the Archon's plan is already well underway.'

Bardon glanced to Elodi. He stammered. 'I... I was not informed of a *third* stage. Why were we not consulted?'

She dismissed his concern with a wave of her hand. 'The Archon cannot risk revealing his hand so freely. As I'm sure you'll know, such information may be valuable to Golesh spies.' She folded her arms. 'I shall raise the levy, and it is your task to justify it to your people.'

Bardon groaned. 'But, Vice-Archon, I fear with lower crop yields in the dismal summers we've experienced of late, means many wards, including mine, will find it difficult to meet the increased levies.'

The Vice-Archon barely concealed a sneer. 'Should we fail, the cost will be immeasurable, Broon, hence the third stage. The Archon is wary the enemy has been silent for many, many years.' She shivered. 'But we cannot become complacent, for all we know they are planning an all-out assault as we speak. We must, at all times, be prepared. But you can reassure your people' — she leveled her gaze — 'the eyes and ears of the Archon are everywhere. Little happens without his knowledge.' Elodi shuffled to ease her aching back; the Vice-Archon seemed to gain pleasure from her discomfort. But Elodi planted her feet and stood tall, determined not to appear weak. The Vice-Archon continued. 'You may also inform your people their levies have paid to install new weapons for the parapets behind the gate. I'm sure that will help ease their minds as they tend to their crops and cattle. And, of course, with the completion of the Caerwal Tower, we have the means to see into the Lost Realms and—'

'Is that wise?' Elodi spoke again before she could stop herself.

The Vice-Archon spluttered. 'Wise? Do you question the wisdom of the Archon' — her lips twisted — '*Lady* Harlyn?' The woman spat out her words. 'He is as wise as you are ignorant. Do you not think his long, extended years have given him the wisdom and knowledge to make these vital decisions?'

Elodi stuttered. 'I... I am concerned about making ourselves known.'

'Oh, they know we are here, and for once we can make them fearful of us. That is why we have built the tower. We want them to know we are watching and are not afraid. Our wise Archon knows what he is doing, Harlyn, it is all part of his grand plan.' The members of the Council nodded in agreement. The Vice-Archon sat back. 'This brings me to the last matter.' She held Bardon's gaze. 'I have signed a decree to re-assign resources from the garrisons in the north to Archonholm for the next stage of the Archon's plan. The process—'

'Vice-Archon!' Bardon gasped. 'Have you not listened to a word I've said?' The backs of the Council stiffened. 'This is not the time to be *weakening* the defenses in the light of increased raids from the north!'

The Vice-Archon's eyes narrowed. 'I listen, Broon. But I have to make decisions, however difficult they may be, for the good of the Five Realms and not just for a few farms.' She straightened. 'You have your own reserves, do you not?'

'Well, yes, but these are—'

'Then train more. Are you telling me you cannot see off a few untrained ruffians armed with wooden sticks?'

Elodi shuddered as Bardon ground his teeth. 'But, Vice-Archon, aside from our small forces of full-time soldiers, our reserves comprise only a few retired, Archonian Guard, the rest are farm-workers and from other trades, they're not experienced fighters by any stretch of the imagination. And, you cannot dismiss the raiding parties of the Ruuk as untrained ruffians. They are better led, better organized, better equipped and—'

'Thank you, Proctor.' The Vice-Archon pushed back her chair and stood. 'This meeting is over.'

6. A CRY FROM THE WOODS

The mug slipped from Toryn's hand and shattered on the floor. 'You met him? You met my father?'

Hamar looked from Miram to Toryn sitting opposite. He took a breath. 'I did... but only briefly, mind.' He scratched his chin. 'It was me who took you both in, you and' — he glanced at Andryn — 'your actual father, that is.'

Toryn slumped back in his chair. 'But I thought... what about the barn?' He stared at the table. 'And my mother? Was she with him?'

Miram whispered. 'No, just you and your father.'

Andryn stood by Miram. He turned to Hamar. 'Perhaps you should tell him what really happened.'

Toryn gaped at them. 'I wasn't left in our barn?'

Andryn wrung his hands. 'No. I'm sorry, son, but we had our reasons for not telling you the truth.' He bowed his head and whispered. 'Hamar? Please?'

Hamar grunted as he pulled in his chair. 'You were barely three, maybe four months old, tiny little thing, with a tuft of dark hair sticking out of the top of your head. It was your screams that woke me. I found you out at the edge of the forest.'

'The forest?'

Hamar nodded. 'You lay by your father's side. He was so badly injured, I thought at first, he was dead. Had you not been crying, I don't think either of you would have survived to see morning. It was the dead of winter and bitterly cold.' Hamar's brow creased as if seeing the events of the night in question. 'I struggled, but I carried you both inside. Nearly dropped the man when he suddenly spoke. I honestly thought he was done for.'

Toryn gripped his sword resting on the table. 'So why isn't he here? Why did he abandon me?'

Hamar held up a hand. 'Oh no, he didn't abandon you, not willingly at any rate. I don't think he had any choice in the matter. He was in a terrible hurry, as if the very shadow demons of the underworld were on his tail.'

Toryn frowned. 'What was he running from?'

'I... we didn't find out for a few days. He could barely talk he was in such a bad way. He grabbed my arm and kept saying *'take my son, please save the boy'*. Then he started speaking another language before passing out. I put him in my bed and could see you were half-starved, so' — he glanced up to Miram — 'I brought you here.'

A tear rolled down Miram's cheek. Andryn rested his hand on her shoulder. 'Hamar was the only one who knew your mother had recently miscarried. That's why we could bring you up as our own and no one would be any the wiser.'

'I don't understand.' Toryn stood and turned his back on the table. 'Why the story about being left in a barn?' He walked to the window and looked out at the clouds streaking across the darkening sky. He spoke to his reflection in the glass. 'And why does it mean I can't go with Elrik and the others?'

Andryn ran his hand down his face. 'This is where it gets a little complicated.'

Toryn spun around. 'Complicated? You mean it's not already? You're telling me I have to abandon my friend, my duty to the Archon, and all because I *wasn't* found in a barn?' He saw Hamar and Andryn exchange a glance. 'Well? Is anyone going to tell me?'

Andryn leaned on the table. 'It's to do with your father.'

Toryn scoffed. 'I'd guessed that much.' He turned

back to the window. 'Who was he? Do you even know?'

Hamar rubbed his neck. 'Sorry, lad. I never found out. He'd gone before I'd risen the next morning.'

'But you said he was badly injured.'

'Oh, he was. Take my word. It amazed me he could get out of bed, let alone walk away. While he still slept, I checked his injuries. I know a fair bit about wounds inflicted by a blade, and he'd suffered many judging by all the scars. But he had others, and not your ordinary wounds. No, these were from dark, poisoned weapons by the look of them. I've treated many in my time but nothing—'

'So why can't I go?' Toryn strode back to the table and snatched up his sword in its scabbard. He swiveled and glared at Hamar. 'You said I can't go. Why?'

Hamar held up a hand. 'Oh, you'll have to go alright, but not with Elrik and the knights.'

Toryn drew the sword. 'You said I can't go because *they'll* find out.' He tilted the blade to catch the reflection of the fire. 'Who? And *what* will they find out?'

Andryn placed his hand on Toryn's, holding the sword. 'Sit down, son. Let me try to explain. But please, put this away.' Toryn's shoulders dropped. He slid the blade into the scabbard and laid it back on the table. Andryn sat beside Miram. 'If you go south, we believe the Archon may see you as a threat.'

Toryn gawped. 'Me? A threat to the Archon? How can the likes of me be a threat to the likes of him?' He slumped into a chair and folded his arms. 'This gets more absurd.'

'Let me try to explain.' Hamar rose. 'When I dressed the man's wounds, I found marks. Back in the day, they trained me to keep my eye open for such signs. I'm afraid your father' — he whispered — 'I believe your father…' Hamar gripped the back of the chair. He glanced at Toryn and sighed. 'You see, I believe your father…' He turned over his hands and spoke to them. 'He had these markings on his palms, they were… the symbols of a wyke.'

Toryn's jaw dropped. 'A wyke! I thought they'd all been… but does that make me—?'

Miram stroked his shoulder. 'Not all sorcerers were bad.'

Toryn stared into the fire, shaking his head. 'My father was a wyke?'

Andryn sat beside him. 'My grandmother told me about wykes. She said some did good deeds. One passed through in her day. In exchange for lodgings, he helped them protect their crop from blight. But others played nasty tricks on unsuspecting folk. Many came to fear wykes and took to hunting them down.'

Toryn turned to his father. 'But you wouldn't know what sort *he* was. And why was he being hunted?' He took his mother's hand. 'Am I a' — his mouth twisted — 'wyke?'

Miram kept her eyes on Toryn's hand in hers. 'We don't know if it's passed on, or a talent you have to learn. No one knows much about them these days. We didn't think any still lived until your father showed up. But if you go south, we fear the Archon may get wise to you.' She placed her hand over his and squeezed. 'The old law still stands. At the very least, you'd be thrown into his dungeons.'

Hamar patted his back. 'But if it helps, I think your father was one of the good 'uns.'

Toryn kept his eyes on the flames. 'How could you know? You never spoke to him.'

'When I first found you, I thought wolves had attacked you. But' — Hamar glanced again to Andryn — 'it turned out not to be wolves, or any creature we'd normally see in these parts.'

Toryn gawped at Hamar. 'What are you trying to say?'

Andryn held up a hand. 'Hold on, Hamar. Let's start with what we know for certain. The day after Hamar rescued you, a company of Archonian Guards turned up asking questions. They were obviously tracking your father and wanted to know if he'd been here. We said nothing, being worried they'd take you away.'

Toryn stared at all three faces. 'And they believed you?'

Hamar nodded. 'Had no reason not to. Word of your father must have reached the ear of the Archon who would have placed a handsome reward on his head. The guards were keen to catch him and left, not wanting the trail to go cold.' He shuddered. 'But they weren't the only ones following you. The dogs and horses sensed it first. You couldn't see it, or hear it, but the air didn't feel right. And at night, it sent a shiver down the spine to be outside. Something watched us from the wood, no doubt about it.'

Toryn thought for a moment. 'But if they pursued my father here, why didn't they go after him?'

Hamar shrugged. 'Maybe some did, I guess that was your father's intention when he left so soon. But whoever or whatever sneaked about in those trees, was also interested in you.'

'Me?' His scalp prickled. 'But I was only a baby.'

'We didn't know for sure, but we weren't going to just sit on our hands. The milk from our cows dried up and then the hens stopped laying. Marshall Stokes rallied the few reserves we had in the village, and we went into the forest to confront them. But if we'd had a dozen men, we'd have struggled. We drove them out, somehow, but at a cost.'

Toryn's fist clenched. 'Why haven't you mentioned this before? Surely, it's a story we should all be told. It's not like anything much happens here to celebrate.'

'Celebrate?' Hamar bit his lip. 'Wasn't much to celebrate. Besides, we didn't want to spread panic. When I say, reserves, we're talking farmers with scythes, clubs and the odd sword. We told the village we'd chased a stray boar away.'

'Oh, the boar story. Then Stokes wasn't gored to death. And the others also?'

Hamar nodded. 'Four in all. But not by a boar' — he whispered — 'a droog. Whoever watched us, had command of a droog and that's no pet dog I can tell you. I can count on the fingers of one hand the men I've known take down one of those vile creatures. And that was five Archonians against the same slippery worm.' His nose wrinkled. 'The poor soul who survived, swore the stench of the foul beast never left him.' He shook his head. 'Such a damn shame. Stokes and the other men didn't stand a chance. And, your dad didn't injure his leg on the farm.'

Toryn gaped at his father. 'You as well? Who were they?'

Andryn's face paled. 'Can't be sure. I can still see them though. A few brawny ruffians showed up. We could have handled them were it not for this other fellow and his droog.' He shuddered. 'A shadowy figure, tall and gangly. Moved all fast and jerky, not natural like. Seen nothing like it in all my days, or since. But it had power, immense power — you need that to handle a droog. But for some reason they didn't seem keen to stay around to fight long. Just as we thought we were all done for, they withdrew and the dread beast went with them. If they hadn't, I doubt any of us would have made it home. But they went all the same, must have gone after your father, we suspect north. And after a few months we assumed—'

They jumped as the door burst open. Elrik and two others collapsed in a tangle on the mat, laughing. Elrik clambered to his feet. 'Sorry, didn't get a chance to knock

64

before these fools fell over.' He brushed down his shirt. 'We're off to the tavern to celebrate our last night.' He glanced at the pieces of the shattered mug on the floor, then to Toryn. 'You coming?'

Andryn answered for him. 'You carry on, lads. He's finishing his packing. He'll join you later.'

'We'll head north.' Hamar stuffed the last of his supplies in a rucksack. He buttoned his coat and threw the strap over his shoulder. 'We'll stay off the roads, stick to the woods for cover where we can. I reckon we'll be a good five leagues away before the Archon's men find out you're missing.'

Toryn snatched his rucksack from the table. 'I should be going south! Where all the able men are going. It's my duty.'

Andryn helped Toryn lift his bag on to his back. 'I know it's hard, son. But trust us, it will be for the best.'

Toryn turned. 'Trust you? After you've kept all this from me until now.'

Andryn placed his hands on Toryn's shoulders. 'Please, for your mother's sake.'

Toryn took a breath. 'Why north?'

'The knights won't want to venture too far out of their way. They'll have other settlements to visit. Once done, they'll be escorting the recruits south.'

Toryn checked his straps. 'I can go by myself. Hamar shouldn't be on the road at his age.'

Andryn patted Hamar's shoulder. 'Nonsense. It's best he goes with you. He knows the way and can show you how to survive in the wilds.' He picked up the sword, wrapped it in cloth and held it out to Toryn. 'Keep this concealed for now.' He stood back. 'I only wish I could go with you, but I'd only slow you down with this leg. Even Hamar can outpace me these days.'

Miram came in from the kitchen. 'I've packed some food for the start. Are you sure you won't need pots and pans?'

Hamar tugged at his beard. 'No, we'll travel as light as we can.'

Miram patted the package. 'Oh, and there's a flask of your father's liquor, but be sure to keep Hamar away from it. It's in case of an emergency...' she turned away.

Toryn stood by the door and looked to his parents. They had taken him in, despite knowing the truth about his father, and brought him up as their own. His jaw softened. 'I'm sure we'll be back before long.' But he caught a look between Andryn and Hamar. He frowned. 'We will, won't we?'

Andryn bit his lip. 'It might be a while yet, son. The Archon's men don't take kindly to deserters.'

'Deserter? But I'd go if I could.'

'I know, Toryn, I know. But they will see you as a deserter all the same. They'd throw you in Archonholm's dungeon for a few years and then put you through the training. But I fear they'd discover your father's... secret before long, and then who knows what they'd do if the Archon thinks you pose a threat.'

Toryn tucked the sword under his arm. 'Still can't think how I could be thought of as dangerous.'

Andryn sighed. 'We can't take that risk. It's not just about you. If the Archon finds out we've been harboring you, we could all suffer. But if you disappear, they'll suspect you wanted to avoid service and took flight. It won't look anything out of the ordinary.'

Hamar turned to the door. 'It'll blow over. We'll be gone a few months and by then they'll be another crisis to keep the guards busy.'

Miram straightened Toryn's coat and brushed down his shoulders. 'Keep him out of harm's way, Hamar. Be sure to bring him back fit and well.'

'As soon as I can, next spring maybe. But don't you worry. I know a settlement about a three-week hike from here. It's well off the beaten track and it'll have been years since any soldiers would have visited. I know a few people there and they'd welcome two men with our skills.' He laughed. 'And don't you worry, Miram. They're fond of their food and ale. He won't go hungry' — he nudged Toryn — 'or thirsty.'

Andryn opened the door. 'You best be making tracks before Elrik comes back.'

Toryn peered outside. 'He won't be able to stand by this time of the evening, let alone find his way here.' His shoulders sagged. 'I'm going to miss him.'

Hamar pulled on the other strap of his rucksack. 'You'll see him again some day. Come on, we'll walk by night and find a spot in woodlands to sleep during the day.' He checked the sky. 'The moon won't be up for a few hours yet, even if it could break through the clouds. It will slow us down, but it'll also mean we can't be seen.'

Andryn grasped Toryn's arms and looked him in the eye. 'I wish it hadn't come to this, son. We wanted to tell you, but—'

'I think I understand.' He embraced Andryn. 'Thanks… for everything. I know I haven't always appreciated your help. But I'll be back, and I'll finally see parts of the land beyond this place.'

He let go as Miram took his hand. 'I won't come outside. I'll only alert the entire village if I start to…'

Toryn hugged her. 'I'll be fine.' He released her, stood back and smiled. 'I'll be back before you know it.' He turned to Hamar. 'Are we ready?'

Hamar winked at Toryn. 'Still have my old map?' Toryn nodded. The old man tried to laugh. 'Then best bring it along. Just in case.'

7. IN THE SHADOW OF THE GATE

The South Gate of Archonholm groaned as it swung inwards. Elodi tugged at her cloak as the morning mist billowed through the archway set in the thick walls of the citadel. Despite the chill of the early hour, she was grateful the day to visit the Archon's new tower had finally arrived. For a week Elodi had had little to do other than consult with Bardon and Wendel on matters concerning their northern realms. She had briefly met the old lords of Kernlow and Galabrant but had been reluctant to spend time in their company. They appreciated little of the pressing matters of the day, preferring instead to tell tales of the daring deeds of their youth, avoiding any conflict that would disrupt their comfortable lives. Elodi had yearned to take out her sword and test her skills against the best of Archonholm, but Wendel advised her it would be frowned upon. Apparently, in this part of the world, women did not challenge the sword masters of the citadel to a duel.

Elodi stood tall with Bardon at the head of two lines, proud to wear the burgundy cloak of Harlyn bearing Dorlan's legendary silver shield. She glanced at Bardon. Despite his stoop and graying hair, he looked a fine sight in his cloak of black, adorned with the white spearhead of Gildorul. He noticed her attention and straightened, managing a slight grin. Behind, the lords of Galabrant and Kernlow, the Steward of Farrand, generals of the army, and heads of the many councils of the city, waited for the Archon's arrival. Lord Kernlow coughed, already out of breath from the short stroll to the courtyard; Elodi wondered how the old lord would manage the long walk down the Caerwal Pass. But that he must. The Archon required all to witness the grand opening of his tower; to be absent would be viewed as a sign of disloyalty.

Elodi turned at the clattering of horses' hooves on the cobbles. At the far end of the courtyard, the fine riders of the First Horse assembled. She wished for her own horse, Sea Mist, but knew this day was all about the show of power by the Archon. While he rode in the comfort of his carriage, the representatives would follow on foot.

Bardon nodded to the rear. The Castellan approached, also on foot. He marched through the lines and stopped at the gate. The plume on his ceremonial helmet drooped under the weight of morning dew. But the dampness could not reduce the impact of his polished armor and bright red cloak of the Palace Guard draped over his slight frame. He turned and raised his arms with his palms together. The Castellan waited until all eyes rested on him. Then, with a flourish, leaving no doubt of the importance of his role in the occasion, he parted his hands until both arms were level with his shoulders. Elodi glanced to Bardon on her right. He turned to face her and took three steps back and motioned she should do the same. She followed Bardon's lead. Murmurs passed along the line as the sound of horses echoed through the courtyard.

'Silence!' The Castellan bellowed. 'The Archon approaches.'

Elodi risked a quick glance along the path. A dozen white horses, with heads nodding, trotted towards them through their lines. The detachment of the First Horse was a grand and re-assuring sight. Sitting ramrod straight with their deep blue cloaks resting on their proud horses' hindquarters, they passed majestically through the lines to the gate, fully aware of the admiring glances drawn their way. Behind, two proud, black horses brought the Archon's carriage into view.

Elodi held her breath. The same design of golden boughs and leaves from the door to the Great Hall covered the sides. She edged back as the carriage passed. Elodi peered inside, keen to see the Archon, but could see nothing but a silhouette. The horses halted under the arch. The Castellan stepped up to the door, spoke in a low voice, before returning to his position at the head of the gathered representatives. Again, with a wave of his hands worthy of a palace entertainer, he motioned for the two lines to reform behind the carriage.

A lone trumpet blew from high on the citadel wall and the procession moved forward. Elodi glanced up at the stones above the gate, admiring their pristine condition. Compared to her city, the citadel was new, dating back a mere three hundred years when the Archon moved to strengthen Archonholm's defenses. Whereas, Calerdorn had endured a thousand years of relentless storms, angered by the walled-city's resistance. Yet still it stood strong, testament to the builders' skill at the height of the Seven Realms' power. Elodi's gaze dropped to the back of the Archon's carriage and wondered what the people of that glorious age would make of today's procession.

They passed out from under the protection of the walls and onto the narrow and southernmost stretch of land in the realms. Elodi's stomach churned as she approached the ravine separating them from the giant wall of the Caerwal Mountains. Ahead, the slender bridge stretched out from the sharp edge of the ravine and disappeared into the mist as if leading to an unknown land. Then, as if commanded by the Archon, the mist rose to reveal the lower reaches of the mountains. Elodi's eyes widened. From her viewpoint at ground level, the dark cliffs appeared to loom twice as high as when she had viewed them from the terrace. She tried to find the top of their peaks amongst the cloud, yet feared she would fall over if she tipped her head back again. But she had no time to take in the view. The front riders of the First Horse reached the bridge. Their powerful beasts trotted confidently in single file up the gentle incline of the narrow pathway. The carriage and the Castellan followed, but Elodi hesitated.

She chanced a glance over the edge to her left. Bardon grasped her sleeve as she wobbled. He whispered. 'Here. Take my arm.'

Elodi stepped onto the bridge. 'I'm fine.' She ran her hand along the rail. 'I appreciate it's a defensive structure, but you'd think they could have made this a little higher. My father didn't stand a chance against the gale that night.' She kept her eyes on the Archon's carriage, determined not to let the thought of her father's untimely death bring more tears; she had to stay strong.

The mist continued to clear as the bridge dipped gently down to meet the opposite side of the ravine. Ahead, the Lower Gate sealed the head of the pass. It stood over fifty feet tall but appeared an insignificant afterthought, as if hastily rammed into the gap between the sheer cliffs.

Bardon followed her gaze. 'That's to keep *us* out. They discourage needless visits to the gate.'

Elodi gawped at the sides of the ominous mountains. 'It must have taken centuries to form the pass.'

Bardon sighed. 'The skills of our ancestors easily surpassed those we possess today.'

She watched as the carriage came to a halt at the portcullis. The Castellan took up a position in front of the horses. He widened his stance, drew his sword, and held it aloft. 'Hark! The Archon approaches.'

A stern face emerged from a small window beside the gate. He turned and yelled. 'The Archon demands entry to the pass. Raise the gate!' Immediately, machinery cranked heavy chains, opening the wooden grill. Elodi peered through the gap, hoping to catch a glimpse of the Caerwal Gate, but a stubborn mist still clung to the floor of the pass.

The Archon's carriage moved forward as soon as the portcullis had risen above its roof. The First Horse, the Castellan, and the two lines of representatives duly followed. Elodi shivered as she walked into the shadow of the short tunnel.

On the other side, it remained cold as the mist refused to release its grip on the night air trapped in the narrow pass. She walked on her toes. 'How far to the gate? I can't see a thing.'

'Just short of half a league, won't take long at this pace. Although' — he checked ahead — 'I'm in no hurry to see what the Archon's been up to. I'd be happier if we kept ourselves to ourselves and didn't poke the enemy.'

Elodi stared harder but could see no more than thirty paces ahead. Yet despite the mists, she sensed the overbearing weight of the mountains towering overhead. They walked in silence, only the echo of the hooves and clatter of wheels filled the pass. Farther down they passed long, shallow ramps rising from the ground on both sides leading to platforms many feet above them. Dark shapes she presumed to be the Archon's new weapons made their presence known in the mist. Beneath, Elodi marveled at the barracks of hundreds of rooms carved out of the rock to house the soldiers, engineers and builders who constantly crewed the gate.

Elodi stopped. A short distance ahead, a shadow hung over them: the Caerwal Gate. They must be close. The carriage slowed, drew to one side and came to a halt. The Castellan repeated the signal, raising his arms to usher them into a line. Elodi noticed a low murmur and the odd chink of metal upon metal. She checked the Castellan's attention lay elsewhere and turned to see row upon straight row of heavily armored knights. So it was true. She knew the number from the tales told to calm frightened children. One thousand elite soldiers stood stiffly guarding the gate as they had done for as long as anyone could remember, always on full alert should the unthinkable happen.

But it was not the sight of their perfectly lined ranks catching Elodi's eye. To the right of the formation, the wide base of a round tower slowly revealed itself as the mist relinquished its hold on the stone. Its windowless, smooth walls tapered as it rose from the ground as if sprouting from the rock. Aware the Archon would step out from his carriage any moment, she risked a glance at the gate, willing the air to clear. But as yet only the ancient runners on which the gate would roll, if ever opened, were visible.

'Pray silence for the Archon.' Elodi jumped as the Castellan bellowed. She jerked back to face the carriage. Two blue-robed men appeared from behind their line. One bent and unfolded a small step below the door. He stood back and nodded to the other who took hold of the handle and opened it. A sandaled foot with long toes stepped out before being covered by the hem of a sky-blue cloak. The tall, thin figure of the Archon descended the two steps and stood a dozen paces from Elodi. His hands rose and removed the large hood. Elodi stifled a gasp. Faint, wavy red markings covered the Archon's clean-shaven head, glowing like hot coals. His harsh gray eyes turned towards the line of his subjects. Elodi shuddered under his gaze and felt this man intuitively knew everything about her — her doubts, fears, hopes and suspicions laid bare.

The Archon said nothing; words were unnecessary. All present could sense the contempt he held for the mere lords, ladies and generals of *his* realms. He gestured to the visibly shaking Castellan to lead him to a dais close to the base of the tower.

Elodi tore her eyes from the back of the Archon to check the gate. Like a lace curtain, the last of the mist drew back to unveil what she had once thought belonged only in fairytales. She cowered in its presence. Towering over four hundred feet tall, the magnificent structure bore down upon them. A lattice of ancient ironwork held great slabs of smooth stone in place, secured by huge bolts Elodi guessed to be three times the thickness of a man's body. At the base, enormous wheels constructed of wood and iron sat upon rails running in an arc to the edges. But the gate was narrower than the pass. On both sides, smooth walls of rock, the same height as the gate, stretched out to the mountains as if raised by the gods to fill the gap.

As the last wisps of vapor streamed over the rim at the top, it suddenly appeared to topple forward. Elodi stumbled for a second time that morning before steadying her feet. She took a breath and gained strength from the giant structure. Surely, if anything could break through this, one thousand knights would serve only to whet the appetite of the hordes for the slaughter to come. But what lay on the other side? Did ranks of Golesh warriors also form ready to attack?

'My subjects.' Elodi's chest vibrated. She turned to the Archon, now standing upon the dais. His voice seemed both loud, yet soft as his words filled the silent space before the gate. He continued. 'You are here this morning to witness the completion of the latest stage of my defenses.' Elodi could not take her eyes from the slender figure of the Archon as even the imposing tower behind appeared to stand in his shadow. 'I shall shortly ascend the stairs' — no one dared to breathe — 'and lift my invocation from the window overlooking the gate.'

A bird cawed. Elodi recognized the call of a mountain

eagle. She looked up. The bird circled close to the top of the tower. It dipped and glided over the gate. Elodi blinked, unsure if she had seen a shimmering blue line above the uppermost iron rail — perhaps another of the Archon's invocations.

The Archon cared not for the bird. He continued his speech. 'And for the first time since securing the pass, I shall look upon the Lost Realms.' He held up his hands as a few gasps escaped the lips of the representatives. 'Fear not. For too long we have hidden from them, cowering behind the gate, afraid of our own shadows.' He clapped his hands. 'But no more. Today, I shall reveal my presence and let them know we are no longer afraid. Today, I shall make them fear us!' The Archon turned to the Castellan and tilted his head. The man jumped as if remembering his duty. He twisted and signaled to the captain at the head of the lines of the soldiers. The captain waved his hand and one thousand spear tips rose, accompanied by a loud cheer. Elodi felt her chest expand at the sound of their praise, but also wondered if it carried to the enemy over the gate.

The Archon allowed them a full minute before speaking. 'I will ascend this tower to let them know *I* am watching *them*. I seek to sow doubt in their foul hearts and set into motion the third phase of my grand plan.' With a swish of his cloak, he whirled about and walked to the small door at the foot of the tower. He withdrew a key from his robes and placed it in the door. The click of the lock echoed across the narrow pass, he opened the door and vanished inside.

Elodi turned to Bardon. She whispered. 'Are we to wait?'

He nodded. 'I expect so. No doubt he'll return shortly to tell us—'

The Castellan bellowed. 'Turn to the right!'

75

Bardon held out a hand. 'But what of the Archon? Are we not to wait for his report?'

The Castellan's eyes briefly wandered to the tower. 'The Archon will be some time. He must prepare before he witnesses the corruption beyond the gate. I am instructed to escort you back to Archonholm.'

Bardon frowned. 'And when do we hear his report?'

He shrugged. 'I have not been told. First, he has to meet with the Council to discuss his findings.' The Castellan turned his back and led the disappointed envoys from the foot of the tower.

8. BORDERS, IVY & TREE ROOTS

Elrik's fine voice rose above the raucous crowd in the tavern as they sang Toryn's favorite song. He stopped. The yellow light from the window laid its path across the square, inviting him back to safety and the world he knew. He resisted the pull and turned away. The song followed them as far as the stables before it faded in the night. Hamar tapped Toryn's shoulder and whispered. 'A knight will be on watch with their horses. We better walk on the grass so as not to disturb him.' They stepped off the path and sneaked past the stables. The man inside whistled a tune unknown to Toryn. He stopped behind a tree.

'What if they come after me? We're no match for their horses on the road.'

Hamar pointed to the gate behind the stables. 'We're not going on the road, remember. They won't find our tracks so easily at night in the woods.' They reached the gate. Toryn winced as it creaked, glancing over his shoulder towards the stables.

Hamar spoke a little louder. 'Don't worry about him. We're out of earshot now. Besides, if they're the same as in my day, he'll have drunk a skin full. You'll likely get more sense from the horses.'

But Toryn remained unconvinced, worried the knight would discover their hasty departure. He kept close to Hamar as they plodded across a muddy field. 'I'll be happier once we're on the other side of the fence.'

'It'll be slower off the road, but we should still cross within an hour, maybe two with having to pick our way around the trees in the dark.'

Toryn stopped. 'What about the Marshal's men?' He

had not given it a thought. 'Won't they be at the fence?'

Hamar stopped to recover his breath. 'I would hope so, it's their job. But they'll be watching outwards, and there're plenty of ways through the woods.'

The time had passed slowly as they had tramped across wet fields, waded through cold, shallow streams, and stumbled around exposed roots in woodland. But eventually Hamar had stopped. He leaned against a tree. 'Here we are.'

Toryn shrugged. 'Here we are... where exactly?'

Hamar pointed past the tree and grinned. 'At the district border fence.'

'Where? I can't see it.'

'Underneath the ivy.' Hamar chuckled. 'It's a disguise, sort of.'

'That?' The rickety fence wound its way precariously around old, gnarled tree trunks. Toryn turned back to Hamar. 'This protects us from the dangers of the big, wide world?'

Hamar patted a post. 'Hardly the Caerwal Gate, I know. But it's sufficed all these years, probably held together by the ivy. The ward's border with Noor is stronger.' Hamar took a few steps along the fence. He nodded over his shoulder. 'The crossing point is on the road a short walk yonder. Drakelow's men know me and would more than likely let me pass with a small bribe, but they'd be wanting to know what you were up to.' He tapped at the fence with his foot. 'Not repaired this section for a while. The roots soon shift the posts. Most districts don't bother these days, seeing as the main fences are stronger and better guarded.' He cleared the ivy and pulled a board to one side. 'After you.'

Toryn peered through the small gap. 'As easy as that?'

Hamar grinned. 'Always been more of a gesture than a

staunch defense. As I said, the sturdier boundaries lie farther to the north and south.' Toryn held his breath, ducked through the gap and stepped out of the land of his youth. He turned to see the large frame of Hamar squeeze through, displacing the planks on either side. He rubbed moss from his coat and turned back to the fence. 'Give us a hand, Toryn. Don't want to make it too obvious.' They replaced the boards as best they could. 'Perfect. So long as they don't look too closely, they'd never know we've been through.'

Toryn squinted through the trees ahead. 'Seems much the same on this side.'

'The scenery won't change for a few days yet.' Hamar adjusted his backpack and strode off, calling back. 'But in another week, you'll soon miss the gentle slopes and woodlands of home.'

Toryn followed. 'I don't get it.'

'What is there to get?'

'Why put the district border in the middle of this wood? Wouldn't it have been better to lay it along the edge? It would be easier to maintain it.'

Hamar nodded. 'You'd have thought so.'

'So why didn't they?'

'Had no choice in the matter. Once the Archon had defeated the threat from the south, it's said he took years to recover. No one knows for sure, but it seems without him around to take charge, the age-old squabbles over the boundaries surfaced again.' He snorted. 'Anyways, once the Archon woke from his slumber he was in no mood for trouble, so he ordered the wards and districts to resolve the disputes fast like, or receive a not-too-friendly visit from his knights who would sort it for them. And seeing as his forces fared slightly better than those of the wards, no one could stand up to him. Everyone needs wood, so it must have made sense to share.' He patted a tree as they passed. 'Best type of tree for building homes and barns.'

Toryn sighed. 'And fences.'

'Well, they're building something down south. More and more of our wood is heading that way these days.'

'Did you ever guard our border? You've never mentioned it.'

'Hardly worth a story. I managed a month once back on my feet. They posted me up north on the crossing at Noor. But I soon grew bored with nothing happening, so I found work where I could use my hands. That's how I ended up on your father's farm.'

Toryn stumbled over a root. 'What was it like on duty?'

'Dull. We drank with Noor's men on the other side, but little else happened. I knew one of them from my days in service.' Hamar grunted as he stubbed his toe. 'Mind you, it came in handy later when….' Hamar slapped his leg.

'When what?'

'Ah, darn it. I didn't mean to mention it, but they turned a blind eye to my comings and goings in the years to come.'

Toryn turned. 'How do you mean?'

Hamar stopped and took the bottle from his backpack and gulped. 'Time for a rest, eh?'

'And… I suspect, a story?'

'Well, if you're going to twist my arm.' Hamar groaned as he sat beside a trunk and leaned back. He reached into his jacket and brought out his pipe. 'Darn. Can't risk showing a light just yet.' He placed it back in his pocket. 'Right. Where was I? Ah yes, I had a bit of trade in the north for a while.'

'How could you trade outside Darrow?'

He chuckled. 'I guess you might as well know, seeing as you're a fugitive now yourself.' He patted the ground.

'Pull up a stool and I'll tell you a tale.'

Toryn took off his pack and crouched next to Hamar. 'I had no idea you'd gone outside once you'd finished your service.'

'And that's how it stays. Not even Andryn knows, and I don't want him to either.'

'Well, he won't hear it from me.'

Hamar patted Toryn's leg. 'Good lad, I don't want to appear ungrateful to the man. He gave me a job when no one else would take a risk on an injured old guard, but farming was never my first choice.'

'But I thought you loved the land.'

'I came to appreciate it, had to, considering it became my life. But why do you think I volunteered for another ten years in the Archonian Guard?' His eyes wandered up to the leaves. 'I wanted to see more of the world' — he winked at Toryn — 'yes, like you. And what made it worse after my first term of service was the thought of living the rest of my life in Midwyche.' His right hand clenched the cloth holding his sword. 'Thankfully, they signed me up for another stretch. But six years later, I took a blade in the hip while brawling with three brigands in Lunn.' He grimaced. 'Cut short my second term, but I wasn't ready to settle. Still not ready.'

'So how did you manage to travel after your service?'

'Well, then.' He scratched his beard. 'It started out doing a bit of trade with the brewers in the Vale of Caran. Their soil is deep and rich, and the surrounding hills protect them from the worst of the weather. Perfect for the hops, makes far better ale than ours, nuttier if you ask me, nothing—'

'Is that where we're heading? To this Vale of Caran?'

'Oh no, not there. Too many soldiers bunk down there, seeing as it's on the Great Northwest Road, and due to the reputation of their ale. No, we wouldn't last long before folk started asking questions. We're heading farther north to Greendell, an old colleague of mine has a place we could stay. It's out of the way and you'll rarely see a guard in those parts.'

'So, what about your travels to the vale? You said it started out as trade, then what?'

Hamar smacked his lips. 'Couldn't you drain a tankard or three right now? Or perhaps a nip of that liquor in your pack?' Toryn pulled his rucksack closer. Hamar sighed. 'Maybe later. Any rate, the owner of our tavern at the time offered to pay me to do the run, seeing as I could look after myself and knew the route. Another old colleague of mine worked the land there, so I readily accepted. But I'd have done it for nothing, it wasn't about the money for me, it gave me the chance to get back on the road.' He laughed. 'And what made it sweeter was the new Marshal, that fool, Drakelow, complimented the barkeeper on his beer, not knowing where it came from. It took him two years to find out and put a stop to my travels.' He snarled. 'The worm. Been stuck in Midwyche ever since.' Hamar clicked his fingers. 'Oh yes, right. Now I remember where this story is going. I heard an interesting tale while on one of my trips.'

Toryn gasped. 'As interesting as this one?'

'Alright, alright, I'm getting to the point. A hop grower told me they'd had problems with some shady characters and a droog.'

'A droog?' Toryn stiffened. 'I didn't want to ask in front of my folks, but I thought the Archonian Guard had wiped them out years ago.'

'Sadly not. I'd say there's still at least half a dozen on this side of the gate. It's said raiders who invaded Caermund and as far north as Saphrir brought scores of the damn things with them. When the Archon drove the remnants of the Golesh into the sea, some fled north and escaped across the ice. But they can't live on frozen water and blubber forever, mark my words. And there's bad folk willing to take the risk and keep them captive for their vile purposes.'

Toryn shivered. 'And is it true? You know… about how they attack and kill their prey.'

Hamar nodded. 'Afraid so. If I had the choice to face either an aralak or a droog, I'd choose the spider every time. An aralak will spit their ghastly poison in your face, wrap their legs around your bloated body, then suck the blood from your veins, all before you can count their legs. Not nice by any measure, but I'd still chance my luck at sticking my blade in its fat, hairy pod than landing a blow on a slimy droog.'

Toryn grimaced. 'Ah, I can't imagine anything worse, so they—?'

'Not now, Tor. I've said enough. I won't talk about them here, at night, in this wood. But listen, I've got carried away. No, it's the fact they saw these characters and the worm only days after our clash with them in our forest back home.'

'My father?' Toryn stood. 'He came this way?'

Hamar nodded. 'Most likely I would say.'

Toryn peered through the trees as if hoping to see him. 'Did the farmer know if he escaped?'

Hamar pushed down on his knees and climbed to his feet. 'Not for sure, but the shadow creatures didn't hang around, so I guess he still led them a merry dance.'

Toryn replaced his backpack. 'I wonder what they wanted with him.'

'You can safely say they don't want to sit down and share an ale together.'

'Could he still be on the run? Can't be easy with those nasty creatures hunting him.'

Hamar shouldered his pack. 'Couldn't say for sure.

But one thing I know, he can handle himself in the wilds. To stay one step ahead of those wily rogues and a droog takes some skill. Once one catches a whiff of you, they don't give up easily.'

Toryn tripped over another exposed tree root. 'How can I be his son? He seems to be clever and resourceful while I'm... well, who I am.'

'Don't be hard on yourself, anyone could have stumbled over that.'

'But it's not that, is it! Do I look like him?'

Hamar nodded. 'You do. You have the same brown eyes and thick, dark hair.'

'But all the same, I could never *be* like him.'

'All in good time. You're still young, plenty of time to build your strength yet.'

Toryn fixed his eyes on the ground, determined not to trip over again. He walked on in silence and let Hamar hum one of his tunes known only to him. Part of Toryn wanted to turn around and head back. If he was considered dangerous or had power, wouldn't the Archon want him in the fight against the enemy? Or... was he the enemy? But what did both the Archon's men and these shadow creatures want with his father? He could not be a foe to both sides.

A sudden breeze brought the chill of the open into the trees. Hamar stopped. 'Must be near the end of the wood. I think we'll rest up here. Dawn's almost upon us and it will be light before we reach the cover of trees again.' He nodded to Toryn's backpack. 'May as well eat breakfast, then we'll sleep and catch something later. I'm sure we'll find a brock or huckle for supper before long. Well, that's if the little folk haven't eaten them all.'

Toryn sighed. 'Little folk?'

Hamar rummaged in his rucksack. 'Now where's that bread?' He looked up. 'You've heard the stories.'

'I have… often, all from you. But little folk? Really?'

'I've said it a hundred times, there's more to this world than we can ever know. It's all there somewhere in the old stories. Ah, here it is.' He pulled out a small loaf. 'You've got the cheese in your pack. But just stories, eh? You don't think they're all made up, do you?'

Toryn found the cheese. 'But the little people? In the woods?'

'Not just little, but old, ancient even. Those that lived in these parts long before we came here. I reckon they hide deep in the forests. We'd scare them, being all big and blundering around like we own the place.' He handed Toryn a chunk of bread and took the cheese. 'My mother saw one once.'

Toryn sniggered. 'A little man?'

'Don't scoff, lad. She may have been young at the time, but she said she could remember it clearly, even in her old age.' Hamar held his hands in front of his face, then stuck his head out and stared wide-eyed at Toryn. 'Peering out from behind a tree it was.'

Toryn could not help but laugh. 'Did she marry the little chap? It would explain a lot.'

Hamar clipped Toryn's ear. 'Whelp. No, of course she didn't. It was only a brief glimpse. Her father had sent her and her brothers out to collect twigs for kindling. She said it was covered with hair and had these great, big eyes.'

Toryn clenched his jaw but could not stop the grin spreading across his face. 'So… was it just your family, or do you know of anyone else who's seen these little, fuzzy fellows?'

Hamar glared. 'We all could have. The tales tell of those who've been among them are changed somehow. If they come back, they have a strange look in their eye and speak of hearing voices in their heads.'

'I've spent a lot of time in the woods and have never

seen one.'

Hamar jabbed a hunk of bread at Toryn. 'How do you know for sure? Do you think they'd let you go home and tell everyone where they live?' He took a bite and spoke with a full mouth. 'They can make you forget. That's how they've survived for so long.'

'But I have no memory of—'

'Ha! Then there you go. Kind of proves my point, don't it.'

'So, not remembering meeting the little folk is proof I've met them.' Toryn's eyes widened in mock disbelief. 'Then perhaps I've seen drayloks and droogs, because I have no memory of them either.'

Hamar clicked his tongue. 'Don't be joking about such things.' He took another mouthful and chewed slowly while glancing around. 'They could be watching us right now.'

Toryn leaned back against a trunk, then bolted upright. 'Did you hear that?'

Hamar looked up. 'No.'

'Thought I heard a twig snap.' He peered around the trunk into the dark.

Hamar stopped chewing. 'See anything?'

'Just a little, hairy man. But wait… no, it was only the trees.' Toryn smirked. 'Would you believe it? I've forgotten already.' He sat back and took a bite of his mother's bread as Hamar sighed. Toryn chewed, not appreciating he was hungry until he tasted Miram's cooking. He also realized he already missed home.

9. THE SINGING STONE

A gleaming silver circle in the puddle caught Toryn's eye. He looked up to see the moon had broken through the clouds as it rose over the horizon. Hamar chuckled. 'Ha! The fairy folk are on our side, see, they've lit the lantern to show us the way.'

Toryn felt the tension in his shoulders ease. His breath blew like wispy clouds as he laughed along with Hamar. 'Good. I'm getting fed up with seeing no more than two paces ahead of my nose.' Toryn stopped at the edge of the trees and peered across a farmed field in the faint light. 'I'd hoped to see a bit more of the world, but this place could be our home.'

'There're more hills and valleys on the way. And the folk of Greendell will cheer you up. They're good people, hard-working and honest. Plus, they enjoy an evening listening to a good tale washed down with a fine ale.'

'That'll make a change. We've been walking for three days and haven't seen a soul.'

Hamar leaned against a crumbled wall. 'Good, that's how we want it. Don't need news of our passing reaching the wrong ears.'

'I know, but I'm starting to think we're the only two left in this world.'

Hamar's head tipped back as he gazed at the moon. 'We're never alone in this world. Trust me, there are greater forces at play we know little about.' He placed his hands on his hips. 'I've seen too many sights on my travels that can have no other explanation.'

Toryn watched the emerging stars as the clouds thinned. 'Do you believe in the Three?'

'Of course, lad. Why wouldn't you? Who do you think created the land, oceans and the sky? Do you think they sprung from nothing?'

'But the Three Maidens? It has to be a fairytale, surely?'

'Until folk can prove otherwise, I'll believe in my *fairytales* thank you. But fairytales have a happy ending, yet the fate of the Three was nothing of the kind. Therefore, it has to be real. Why make up a story with such a tragic end?'

'But an evil force? Greater than your Three Maidens?'

Hamar shrugged. 'Why not? They say the Evil One could not bear to see such beauty of the Three and their creation. Those fair maidens couldn't have imagined something so twisted could exist in a world they'd had a hand in making.' He looked Toryn in the eye. 'When those winter gales blow in from the north, are you telling me you can't hear their wails?' He bowed his head. 'Those poor lasses. Can't imagine the pain they suffered. We used to stuff our socks in our ears when the storms came. Their tormented cries could drive a man mad.'

Toryn laughed. 'Are you sure you stuffed both ears?'

'Oh, you can mock me all you like. You've lived your entire life sheltered in a mostly quiet part of the world.' He wagged his finger. 'But I tell you, you'll see sights soon enough to open your mind.'

'I don't doubt that, I...' Toryn realized Hamar had stopped listening. 'What is it? What have you seen?'

Hamar stroked his whiskers. He squinted at the line of hills. 'I've been here before.' He arched his back and checked ahead. 'Ah, yes.' A smile spread across his lips. 'Yes, I remember.' He turned back to Toryn. 'Fairytales, you say?' He nodded. 'You're in luck. Let me show you something that might change your mind.' Hamar paused for a moment, looking back to the horizon. 'Now then. If my memory still serves me right, it'll be over there, won't take long. A few minutes at most to the rocks.'

Hamar led Toryn along the side of a stream up a gentle slope. He pointed ahead. 'If I recall, we'll come across a thick hedge.'

A dark line crossed their path. 'I see it.' Toryn strode up to find the hedge stood both taller and thicker than it first appeared. He called back to Hamar. 'I can't see a gap, not even over the stream.'

Hamar puffed as he caught up. 'Then we'll get wet.'

Toryn glanced at the water trickling over the rocks. He shivered. 'Can't you just tell me what's behind the hedge?'

Hamar clicked his tongue. 'We'll face worse than this later, boy. And no, I can't tell you, because you wouldn't believe me.' He raised an eyebrow. 'And I don't have the words to do it justice.'

Toryn caught the glint in Hamar's eyes. 'Alright, you've got my interest.' He rolled up his trouser legs, scrambled down the shallow bank and plunged into the water. He gasped. 'It's freezing. This better be worth it.'

Hamar grunted as he dipped his foot in the stream. 'Oh, it will be, mark my words. Keep your head tucked in. These thorns will happily tear the flesh from your cheeks. Perhaps we should take a cutting. Save us the trouble of building fences if we had a hedge like this on our border.'

Toryn shivered as he crawled beneath the thorns. He twisted to check. 'We're through.' He stood and shuddered as his wet skin met with the cold air. He turned to give Hamar a hand. 'I suppose we must come back this way.'

Hamar smirked. 'We do, but you'll thank me later. See.' He pointed over Toryn's shoulder. Toryn turned. The moon peered over the top of a dark, jagged line of rocks sheltering a small wood. The pale light shone through the sparse leaves braving the cool spring air. A narrow path wound its way through the dark trunks. Hamar whispered. 'Just a short way farther, up that path to the rock face.'

Toryn found his feet following the path. The ground rose as they made their way into the wood. Hamar tapped his shoulder. 'Can you hear that?'

Toryn cocked his head. 'Water?'

'Not just water. Keep going, nearly there.'

A short way ahead, the trees thinned out, allowing more moonlight through. Toryn stopped. 'It's a dead end.'

'Is it?' Hamar stepped up to his side. He stooped and peered at the rock face. 'Run your hands along the surface.'

Toryn did as asked. 'I can't see what's... oh, wait. There's a gap.'

'Like a postern gate, see. Those wishing to keep this spot hidden, placed a slab of rock in front of a small gap. Head on, you can't see it, but if you know what you're looking for, you can find your way inside.'

They squeezed through the gap and entered a small clearing to be greeted by the sound of a babbling brook. Toryn's heart stopped. A tall, dark figure stood in the middle. He crouched and motioned to Hamar. 'Someone's here. Could be one of those shadow creatures.'

But Hamar stayed on his feet. He grinned. 'Believe me, if it was, your knees would have given way and your stomach squirming like a huckle in a trap.' Toryn felt his face flush. Hamar took his arm. 'Don't fret, lad, you're not the first to be fooled.' They stepped out into the opening, awash with moonlight. In the center, water bubbled up from a small pile of rocks. Behind stood a slender, black stone, a few feet taller than Toryn. Hamar nudged him. 'Go on. Touch it.'

Toryn approached the stone and placed his hand on the smooth surface. 'It's warm!' He turned back to Hamar. 'How can it be warm in the middle of a chilly night?'

'No idea. We called them Singing Stones. Came across two on my travels.'

Toryn found he could not take his hand away. He turned back to the stone and stroked his palm across its face. 'What are they?'

Hamar scratched his head. 'No one knows for sure, but the Archon gave us strict instructions to report directly to him if we ever found one.'

Toryn peered closer; the rock glimmered in the moonlight. 'So how did you find this one? It's not like you can stumble across it by mistake.'

Hamar nodded. 'Quite so, and by no accident I'm sure.'

'So how did you come across it?'

He thought for a moment. 'A stranger had the locals worried. At first, we thought it was some rogue from the wilds, or a cobtroll from under the mountains.' Hamar held up his hand as Toryn went to speak. 'Oh yes, back then they'd still venture this far out of their caves now and then, usually banished by their own kind. Somehow, they'd evade the watch on the pass, or find a way out through the caverns and tunnels elsewhere. Anyways, this traveler led us a right merry old dance for days, I can tell you. This way and that, no obvious reason for their route, and when we thought we had them cornered, they'd suddenly disappear. No tracks, no sign of a camp or anything.'

'Did you find them? Was it a cobtroll?'

Hamar smiled. 'Oh no, outsmarted us too often, too clever for a cobtroll. No, we soon suspected a lone Amayan warrior was up to no good.' An eyebrow raised. 'That's why we were so keen to stay on their tail. They usually stick together, but it wasn't unknown for the odd one to take on a quest alone.'

Toryn grinned. 'Did you catch up with her?'

Hamar rubbed the back of his neck. 'Almost.' His

eyebrows raised. 'It was a woman, but not an Amayan. We were in for a shock when we eventually got close enough for a brief glimpse. Too old and bent to be a warrior.' He frowned. 'Which made it all the more puzzling as to why we couldn't keep up with her.' He chortled. 'Our captain swore us to secrecy about the whole affair. We were too proud to admit she'd gotten the better of us, so we agreed. We'd never be allowed to hear the end of it. The others would have pulled our legs for years. Ha! We never did apprehend her. The tracks we could follow led us here, but none led away.' He patted the stone. 'Anyways, we found this beauty instead.' He ran his hand down the slab. 'Not sure if we ever reported this one to the Archon, seeing as we'd struck the previous few days from our records.'

Toryn peered at the stone. 'Are there many?'

'I've only heard talk of three in all, usually found by a spring like this fine lady.' He sighed. 'I'd forgotten how good they feel. Another farther north saved a few frostbitten fingers, I can tell you.'

'Why call it a Singing Stone?'

'Ah, well, not sure if it's their proper name. A guard must have found out by accident, but if you tap one with a sword, they make a sound like you've never heard. Stands all the hairs up on the back of your neck it does.' Toryn reached for his sword tied to his pack. Hamar stayed his hand. 'No, not now. You'll alert everyone within a league.'

Again, Toryn felt his face redden. 'What are they for?'

'I can only guess they're part of a watch, maybe a beacon, but easier to maintain with no need for fuel, dry wood and a torch.' He patted the stone. 'All you do is tap it and let your friends know trouble is near.'

Toryn glanced over the surrounding rocks. 'Maybe if it stood on the top of a hill, but what would you see in the middle of this clearing?'

Hamar straightened. 'As I said, only a guess, but you'll

never see a slab of stone such as this anywhere else. You can hit them hard with the strongest blade and it won't scratch, dent, or make a spark. One of my company tried, just to show us how tough he was.' Hamar laughed then covered his mouth. He whispered. 'Sorry, should be more careful. But you'd have laughed if you'd seen his face when his blade shattered like an icicle. Took days for his hands to stop shaking.' He stood back. 'Imagine if we could have used these to build the Caerwal Gate. Wouldn't have to place a watch on it. They'd never break through.'

'But if it's not part of a watch, what could they be for?'

'Got me there. But what I do know is the Archon told us on pain of death not to reveal their whereabouts.'

'But you brought me.'

Hamar shrugged. 'Death will find me soon enough, whatever I do. But be sure you keep it to yourself… just to be safe.'

'Don't worry, I will.' Toryn walked around the stone. 'I wonder who put them here?'

'Not us, for sure. Way beyond the skill of our stoneworkers to create a monument such as this. Must have been folk long before our people came to these lands.' Hamar's eyes glistened. 'I reckon it's the work of the Three.'

The hairs on the back of Toryn's neck stood up. 'Shame we can't make it sing.'

'A shame to be sure. I'd wager it sounds like the very Maidens themselves singing. I would love to hear their song one more time before I'm done with this world.' He patted the stone. 'Perhaps another time.'

Toryn strolled to the far side of the small clearing. He stooped and dipped his hand in the cold water. At first, all he heard was the trickle as it tumbled across the rocks. But then, he could not be sure if it was his imagination, but it seemed a voice sang softly.

Hamar hobbled across the grass. He cocked his head towards the stream. 'My dear mother, bless her, told me if you listen carefully you can hear the echo from the time the Three Maidens first sang their Song of Creation.' He kept his eyes on the stream. 'It's in the water, from the babbling of a brook, to the roaring of the rapids, or in the rustling of the leaves on a tall tree.' He looked up. 'The birds know. You see, the Maidens taught them each a part of the Song, so if the worst happens, they could sing it all over again between them.' Hamar turned to Toryn. 'Still listening? I know you don't believe in magic and myths.'

Only a few days ago, Toryn would have dismissed Hamar's tale as nonsense, but sitting in the moonlight next to the stone, he understood the words of Hamar's mother. He smiled. 'No, honestly, I'm listening. You've not told me this one before.'

Hamar exhaled. 'I seem to remember more of my mother's stories these past few years.' He closed his eyes. 'I must be nearing my time.'

Toryn dipped his hand back in the cold spring. 'Tell me more about the birds.'

Hamar beamed. 'Gladly. Now, let me see. The thrush, ah yes, the song thrush. If I could only hear one bird, it would be them.' He straightened as if reciting a story. 'The thrush will sing and pause' — he tilted his head — 'sing and pause, waiting for the Maidens to answer. But it's all in vain.'

'What about the skylark? They're my favorite. They sing all summer above the fields.'

Hamar held up a finger. 'Whereas the lark will twitter away all day long, hovering high in the sky.' He let out a long sigh. 'I reckon skylarks don't want to stop because they can't bear the silence when there's no reply.' He ran his fingers through his beard. 'Must break their poor little hearts when they're too exhausted to sing and sink back to the ground.'

'And the cuckoo?'

'Can't remember. Most likely come in near the end of the song, seeing as they only know two notes.'

'I never knew you thought about such matters. I mean, you know a lot about farming, but' — he listened again to the soft voice in the water — 'all this. Echoes. Maidens, birds and... and the like.'

A tear formed in Hamar's eye. He smiled. 'You might think I'm an old fool, but—'

'I don't. I can't think of anyone who knows as much as you.'

Hamar blinked. 'I know you and the others have a laugh behind my back, but I don't mind, I really don't. There's little cause for joy these days, so if I can bring a little mirth into your lives, that's fine with me.' Hamar's watery eyes reflected the moonlight as he stared at the stone. He sighed. 'Despite all the darkness and cruelty in the world, if you listen carefully, you can still hear the hope of new life. It's what keeps me going when...' he turned away.

Toryn gave him a moment before asking, 'Should we be going? Can only be a few hours before sunrise.'

Hamar sniffed. 'I think we'll stop here for the day, start again at nightfall.'

Toryn stood. 'But shouldn't we make the most of what's left of the dark?'

Hamar stretched. 'No rush. Greendell has been around for a few hundred years nestling between the hills, it can wait another day for us. Besides' — he yawned — 'I'm tired. We'll sleep by the stone and let the warmth ease our aches away.'

Toryn reached for his backpack. 'Can't say I disagree.'

Hamar laid back on the grass and closed his eyes.

'You won't be needing your blanket. These stones kept us warm on the coldest of winter nights. And you'll feel like a new man in the morning, and then we'll make…' he snored.

Toryn placed his backpack next to the stone. The grass beneath felt softer than his bed, the warmth from the stone made him drowsy and he happily surrendered to the urge to sleep. He lay down his head and closed his eyes.

He pulled the bedclothes closer. Despite the cold, sweat clung to his shivering, fever-wracked body. The wind gleefully shrieked outside, eager to rip the roof from their small house. But it was not the wind keeping him awake. Other voices, dark, fell voices made themselves known amongst the cacophony, rejoicing in the misery the blizzard from the north inflicted upon the land. Shadows danced across the ceiling, and to his innocent eyes, not all looked like shapes made by the trees outside his window.

He shut his eyes and clasped his hands to his ears, trying in vain to think of the last day of summer. His father said you could always tell when autumn was on its way. 'There's something in the air' he would say. He would treasure the last warm day before the chilled air turned the leaves golden. He imagined the sun on his face as he stood at the border of their land and gazed longingly at the winding path leading to the forest.

The scene changed. The skies darkened, and the air grew cool. Yet, he felt no fear. The moon emerged from behind a cloud to show the way. Like the silvery trail of a giant snail, the path invited him to depart his home. A lone voice in the trees called to him. A woman sang. Her words drifted across the meadow and wove her spell. He stepped on the path, took two paces; his body grew light. He tumbled but did not fall. More joined the voice. Their words, unknown to him, held him as he gently rolled head over heels to the trees, away from the monsters of the blizzard, away from the farm, away from the parents who cared for him. Away from his young life to the unknown.

Toryn sat up. At his side, Hamar looked at peace in a deep sleep while the stream flowed on its way as it had done for thousands of years. His face tingled. A voice, like the one from his dream, sang nearby. The high, soft voice of a woman, complementing the music of the stream, so high, and so clear, the woman could be standing by the stone. The moon had risen to a point directly above him, bathing the clearing with a soft, silver light. Another voice joined the first, quickly followed by a third, coming from all directions, weaving their harmonies as effortlessly as the water trickled around the rocks and pebbles.

Toryn's breath caught in his throat. A figure stood at the opening but cast no shadow on the rock behind. The song rose as the figure approached. The visitor spoke a language he did not understand, yet the words brought comfort. He closed his eyes and laid back on the soft grass and let sleep take him once more.

10. A WINDOW ON THE LOST REALMS

'It is as the Archon suspected' — the Vice-Archon's eyes narrowed — 'and feared.' Elodi's stomach knotted as she watched the lines on the woman's face deepen. Elodi had a seat at a long table set out in the Great Hall for the meeting. She sat with the Lords of Broon, Galabrant and Kernlow, opposite the Archon's Council, the Castellan, the generals, and the heads responsible for the day-to-day running of the Five Realms. Elodi had grown impatient waiting to hear what the Archon had seen from his new tower. But after an agonizing two-day wait, Elodi feared the worst, wishing instead not to know.

The Vice-Archon waited for the murmurs to die. She took a deep breath. 'The enemy is gathering. In due time, the Archon believes they will launch an all-out assault through the pass.'

All present drew a breath. The Castellan spoke first. 'And the Archon? May I enquire of his whereabouts?'

The Vice-Archon took a moment to gather her thoughts. 'The Archon is in retreat. He needs to prepare to face the challenges ahead. He has instructed his personal guard about his movements and asked me to deliver his account.'

'Thank you, ma'am. And does he... the Archon, know when we can expect the assault?' The Vice-Archon's eyes stayed fixed on the table. The Castellan cleared his throat. 'Vice-Archon?'

She blinked as if the Castellan took her at unawares. 'The Archon suspects the Golesh will launch the attack before the winter, perhaps as early as autumn.' Her eyes bulged as if seeing the hordes pouring through the pass and across the bridge. She shook her head as if trying to rid the vision from her mind.

The Castellan glanced at the set faces around the table. 'What exactly did the Archon see, ma'am?'

'Machines. He saw machines of a size we've yet to build, being assembled.' Her eyes widened. 'He spoke of a monstrous battering ram capable of tearing our gate clean off its hinges.' Many of the representatives gasped. The Vice-Archon continued her litany of the impending disaster. 'The enemy possesses a dozen trebuchets large enough to hurl boulders the size of a house, and... it turns my insides, but they appear to know what to find on this side of the gate.' More heads turned as if expecting to see spies sitting at their side. The Vice-Archon's face tightened. 'At the rear of the war-machinery, the Archon saw a bridge suspended from a moving platform, of sufficient length to span the gorge' — her voice wavered — 'and wide enough for thirty of those foul creatures to cross shoulder-to-shoulder.'

'What are we to do?' A captain jumped up, pushing back his chair. Others stood and demanded answers. Bardon sitting opposite Elodi remained seated as the color drained from his red face.

The Castellan raised his hands. 'Please, please. We must have calm. Let the Vice-Archon finish the report.'

The Vice-Archon nodded with a stiff neck. 'Thank you, Castellan.' She motioned for all to sit. 'I appreciate this news may come as a shock, but it is vital you know of the magnitude of the threat.' She straightened, re-discovering her authority. 'Of course the activity of the enemy is a concern, but it is not unexpected. We've known for many years this day would eventually come and the Archon has planned accordingly. Yes, they appear to know what they will encounter on this side of the gate, but thanks to the diligence of the Archon, we also have knowledge of their tactics.'

Bardon spoke. 'Vice-Archon, from what the Archon describes, how are we to defend against such an overwhelming and determined attack?'

'I grant it is a large force we face, Lord Broon, but overwhelming?' With a shake of her head, the last of her anxiety fell from her face. 'Have faith in the Archon. He knew this moment would come.' She turned to a man with tufts of gray hair sticking out from the side of his head. 'Brundell, are the modifications to our weapons complete?'

Brundell's eyes widen as if already seeing the possibilities. He nodded. 'Yes, Vice-Archon, we are almost ready.' His mouth curled into a grin as he looked at the confused faces around the table. 'Thanks to the ingenious mind of the Archon, within days our improved weapons stand ready to hurl larger projectiles *over* the gate.'

The Vice-Archon smiled. 'Excellent, the Archon will be pleased to hear of your progress. This will give us the opportunity to disrupt the enemy's preparations.' She frowned. 'You said *almost complete*, what remains outstanding, Brundell?'

'We have a few minor tests to complete, but I am waiting for Barrson to release the required funds.'

The Vice-Archon turned to the oldest woman at the table. 'Privy Barrson. See that Brundell gets all the resources he needs.'

Barrson's fingers twitched. 'But, Vice-Archon, due to spending on the—'

'This is not the time! If the Golesh are victorious, Barrson, I'm sure they will be more than happy to listen to your woes. Then maybe they will re-allocate your funds for a mass grave for our charred corpses.'

The woman shrank back. 'Be assured, Vice-Archon, I will make resources available.'

'Good. And while you're dipping into the purse, be

sure to allocate funds to the builders. Work will start tomorrow to bolster defenses at the gate to slow the enemy's progress.' Barrson opened her mouth. The Vice-Archon leveled her eyes at the Privy. 'Don't fret. Plans to raise the levy will take immediate effect to pay for the war effort.' The Vice-Archon eyed Bardon. 'I take it I have the full support with this measure from the realms?'

Bardon glanced to Elodi. He nodded without a word.

'Excellent. Now back to the defenses. As I announced earlier, the new weapons are in place and the artillery division are being trained in their use. From the parapets we can rain down fire and stone on the advanced forces and aim to incapacitate as many of their weapons as possible. Artillery will hold ammunition in reserve for when they roll out their bridge. We hope to inflict enough damage on it to render it incapable of spanning the gorge.' She took a breath. 'In short, and to put it crudely, our forces will block the pass with Golesh dead and wreckage of their evil machines. Yes, their numbers are great, and the Archon anticipates some will make it to the head of the pass, but they will come to rue the day they thought they could invade with impunity.'

Elodi felt her chest expand. Heads around the table lifted. Could they possibly see off the threat? The Vice-Archon turned her attention to the man at the opposite end of the table. 'General Kragan. What is our current strength?'

Elodi watched Kragan as he shuffled his papers. She guessed the man to be in his late sixties, but his straight back and broad shoulders beneath his dark red cloak belied his age. He lowered his whiskered jaw and flashed his gray eyes as if he relished the task ahead. 'Vice-Archon, our elite forces number close to four thousand swords, half that number are already at the gate, I can mobilize the remainder in under an hour.' Kragan regarded both sides of the table, taking obvious pleasure from the approving nods. 'The Knights of the Archon can assemble six thousand spears at short notice, and of course, the First Horse are always ready. The Archonian Guard exceed fifteen thousand, with another five in reserve housed at garrisons less than two days' from here.' Kragan appeared to gain confidence as he listed his forces. 'I can muster the reserves. Galabrant and Kernlow could be here within ten days, and four weeks for Harlyn and Broon as a precaution.' He referred to a sheet of paper on the table. 'At present, they number just shy of twelve thousand men and women. The artillery regiments are at full strength, but, Vice-Archon, our strategy will require the allocation of more resources to the armory, and therefore I will need extra funding.'

She tapped her finger on the table, motioning to Privy Barrson. 'Granted.'

Kragan nodded. 'Thank you, ma'am. But, if I may ask, what of the eight hundred men transferred to special duties three summers back? I have yet to receive news of their availability.'

The Vice-Archon's lips pursed. 'That will become known once the Archon decides you need to know.' Her eyebrows raised. 'And what of the new recruits?'

The general referred to his papers. 'Three hundred, Vice-Archon. They'll be arriving shortly from Darrow, Perran and Gwelayn.' His mind seemed elsewhere as he fought to remember the question. 'Err... within four months they will be capable of basic defensive duties. But it would help if I knew the readiness of those eight hun—'

'I make that a potential forty-two thousand men and women at arms.' The Vice-Archon held the captain's gaze. 'Am I correct?'

He spluttered. 'Yes, that is correct, Vice-Archon.'

'General?' He looked surprised by Bardon's

interruption. Bardon continued. 'And what of the defenses elsewhere?'

'Broon! This is not the time.' The Vice-Archon glared. 'We have far more—'

'Are we to assume' — Bardon raised his voice, speaking over the Vice-Archon — 'the soldiers posted on the northern border are to remain at full strength? Lack of resources has already forced us to abandon many of our forts and watchtowers in both Lunn and Dorn.'

The Vice-Archon took a breath and lowered her voice. 'Can I remind you—'

Bardon exhaled. 'We in the north do not need to be reminded of the increase in activity on *our* borders. If General Kragan demands our reserves come south, the raids will only worsen.'

Elodi cleared her throat, feeling she should support Bardon. 'Vice-Archon. If we are to provide food for the Archon's forces, we have to protect our farmers. Dorn lost close to three percent of its yield to raids last year alone, and' — she noticed Bardon nodding his approval — 'as Lord Broon stated, the losses will escalate if we weaken our defenses. And we must not forget the mines at Drunsberg provide the bulk of the metals for our armories.'

'Lady Harlyn makes a good point.' All heads at the table turned as the Archon's voice resonated around the hall.

All rose. The Vice-Archon stammered. 'Archon, I was not informed you would be attending this meeting.'

He held up his hand. 'Please, be seated.' Two orderlies brought forward a bigger chair to place at the head. Another moved the Vice-Archon to the side as others shuffled along to make room.

The Archon sat. 'Vice-Archon, I did not originally intend to come this evening. But on reflection, I felt my attendance would be beneficial to all.' Elodi shrank back in her chair as the Archon's eyes passed over her to Bardon. 'I appreciate the concern of our friends in the north.' He held up a finger. 'But, if we should fail against the imminent onslaught from the south, there will be nothing left for these' — he waved his hand and sneered — 'sons of the frozen lands to pilfer. The old foe of the north is long since dead, but I agree with Lady Harlyn. The mines must be secured, and your farmers require protection from these ruffians. They cannot tend their livestock with one hand on a sword and one eye over their shoulders.' He folded his arms. 'General. I have the utmost confidence in your forces and therefore see no need to summon the reserves, even as a precaution. Let them stay in their own lands to see off any threat.'

General Kragan's face flushed. 'Thank you, Archon.' But Elodi could see he was not satisfied.

The Archon turned to Bardon. 'And I am sure, Lord Broon, you can train your own armies in order to take care of these ragtag thieves without the need of my soldiers.' Elodi noted this was not a question. The Archon clasped his hands under his chin. 'I think this vindicates my policy. If anyone present has reservations about allocating more resources in the south' — he glanced to Bardon — 'with the exception of the aforementioned reserves, then please speak and make them known.' He met the gaze of each person sitting at the table. 'Good.' He turned to the soldier standing behind the general. 'Captain! Send word to the north. The remaining guardsmen are to be assigned to Archonholm with immediate effect. As for Drunsberg, they will commit a third of their strength to the defenses here. And send messengers to all parts of the Five Realms informing them of the situation at the gate. We don't want an outright panic, but they will soon notice the movement of soldiers. The Vice-Archon will pen the appropriate words.'

The captain's face gave nothing away of his thoughts. He saluted, pivoted on his heels and marched to the door. But the Proctor's junior assistant failed to notice the approaching officer. The captain skidded to a halt. He spat out his words, not meant for the ears of the hall. 'What are you waiting for, boy?' The assistant stammered an apology and reached for the handle to open the door. The captain scoffed loudly. 'Perhaps I should send you to the gate where you could hold up the enemy.'

The Archon waved his hand at the Proctor. The old man nodded and groaned as he rose from his stool. All at the table watched as the Proctor ushered his paled-faced assistant out of the hall. The Archon turned back to the table. 'General Kragan, Vice-Archon, Castellan, the lords and Lady Harlyn, please stay, the rest may leave.'

The Archon waited until the last of the uninvited had left the room. He turned back to those remaining at the table. 'It has come to my attention some of you are not happy with the rise in the levy paid to Archonholm.' Elodi caught Bardon's eye. The Archon clicked his fingers to the Proctor. 'Have the map brought in.' He watched the frowns and sideways glances of those seated and waited. When all eyes returned to him, he nodded and smiled. 'I think this is the appropriate time to enlighten you on what your taxes have been funding over these last few years.' The Archon's eyes shone. 'And something the Golesh will not be expecting.'

11. Moonrise over Caranach

Hamar stroked his beard. 'Good. The skies are clear. Won't be long now, see, it's getting lighter over yonder.' He swigged from the flask and passed it to Toryn. 'Will be quite a view from the top of this ridge.'

Toryn welcomed the break and took a long drink. 'How do you do it? You're three times my age yet you keep walking.'

Hamar patted his thigh. 'Training and experience. Spent my life on my feet. Didn't prance about on a horse like a knight. And even my injury couldn't keep me off 'em for long.' He gripped Toryn's shoulder. 'You'll soon get the hang of it.'

Toryn peered to the horizon. 'How far is the range from here?'

'Barely a league I reckon, or thereabouts.'

'A league?' Toryn's heart raced.

'Oh yes, we're that close.' Hamar stretched his back. 'We've been traveling north and a little way east. Our going might be slow in the dark, but we've easily covered thirty leagues, twenty-four as the crow flies, and at least six have been eastwards.'

Toryn stood on his toes. 'Can't see a thing yet.'

'Be patient.' Hamar put the flask back in his rucksack. 'We'll be better off on the other side of this ridge. Don't want to be standing like two statues with the moon rising. Other folk mad enough to be up at this hour would soon spy us up here.' He paced a short distance. 'That boulder over there will do.'

They crossed the top of the ridge and walked the short distance to a large rock. Hamar sat at the foot. 'Good to get out of that chilly breeze, eh.'

Toryn eased his tired legs and sat beside him. 'Did you…?'

'Did I what?' Hamar rummaged inside his rucksack and pulled out a bundle of cloth. 'Ham? It's keeping well with it being cooler up here.'

Toryn nodded. 'I'll take a slice, thanks.'

'Bread? Best finish it before it goes too hard and breaks our teeth.' He tore off a chunk and handed it to Toryn. 'So? Did I what?'

'Did you dream? Last night, at the stone.'

Hamar smiled. 'I wondered when you'd ask.' He nodded. 'Oh yes, we all had them at the stones.' He took a bite of ham. 'Did you see a woman?'

Toryn's face tingled as it had the previous night. 'I saw someone, couldn't tell if it was a woman.'

Hamar finished chewing. 'She's a woman alright.' He pointed his bread at Toryn as he spoke. 'To some in my company, she appeared as their mother, others said their wives, and' — he chuckled — 'a few young ones swore she was an Amayan rider who was only too happy to… well, you know what I mean. Strange what being away from home so long can do to your head.'

'It didn't feel like a dream, though. I'm sure I'd woken from one, an odd one at that.'

'It's the stone. There's a magical power in them. Can change a man.' His eyes wandered to the rock behind them. 'How did she appear to you? Like your mother?' He grinned. 'Or an Amayan?'

Toryn tried to recall. 'Neither, but I can't say for sure, I saw only a dark figure. She spoke. Could have been talking to me, or herself, I couldn't tell because I didn't know the tongue.'

Hamar sighed. 'Shame, I can still remember mine clearly.' The creases on his brow faded as he smirked.

'Always the Amayan for me back in the day. But last night it was my dear mother.'

'But the voices. Did you hear singing?'

Hamar scratched his head. 'No, can't say I heard a song.' He smirked. 'Mind you, in my younger days I'd have been so distracted I doubt I'd notice, even if serenaded by the Maidens accompanied by a choir of faeries.'

'It sounded beautiful, like one of my mother's. If I was unwell, she'd sing and help me sleep.'

Hamar laughed. 'Miram? Sing? Begging your pardon, I know she's your... mother, and I have the deepest respect and all, but help you off to sleep? You'd more likely have to leave the room if she sang.'

Toryn glowered at Hamar. 'Well, you're wrong, she has a wonderful voice.'

'Then she must've saved the best for you.' He turned. 'Here it comes.' Toryn stood. The rim of the moon peered over the top of a jagged, dark ridge cutting right across the horizon as if a giant plow had pushed up the land. Hamar joined him and nudged his shoulder. 'Just you wait.'

Toryn held his breath as the moon climbed higher, etching out the sharp line of the mountains against the lighter sky. Three ominous peaks dominated the range, with the tallest overshadowing her two sisters. From this distance, Toryn had to tilt his head right back to see the lofty pinnacle of Caranach. His eyes grew wider as moonlight kissed the snow-clad upper reaches on the south facing slopes. Like the noble blade of a warrior of old, Caranach's silver peak thrust impossibly high, threatening to tear the delicate fabric of the night sky, stretched thin as it spanned the world. Toryn stared, convinced he could see the stars bunching where the mighty blade's tip snagged the sparkling sheet.

Hamar whispered. 'Hard to believe Caranach is the furthest away of the three.' He glanced at Toryn. 'And satisfying to know, the vaults holding the demons are as deep as the mountain is high.'

But Toryn was in no mood to debate the myths. He peered at the darker smears on the mountain. 'One day I'm going to stand on the top and touch the sky.'

'Then you'll be the first. Many have tried, but most don't make it to the lower reaches. Brutal place, the Kolossos Mountains, with many strange beings who won't tolerate you tramping all over their territory.'

'They wouldn't stop me.'

Hamar smiled to himself. 'You'll be needing an army then.'

'Or my father.' A flickering light in the valley caught Toryn's eye, quickly joined by another. He instinctively crouched. 'What's going on?'

Hamar squinted. 'That'll be the farmers of Caran starting their day early... and a sign for us to move off this ridge.' He clicked his tongue. 'Shame I can't pop down and see old Bonnar.'

'Older than you?' Toryn smirked.

'I'll ignore that. But I guess there'll be another time.' Hamar pointed to the path. 'On we go.'

Toryn bent to pick up his pack and took one more look at Caranach. He felt suddenly drawn towards it, as if the ground did indeed sag under its immense weight. The mountain demanded his attention, his awe, and his loyalty. It was as if it held a secret from the dawn of time, a secret he had to discover. And once revealed, he would—

'Come on, lad. Take your eyes off it, we have to be making tracks.'

Toryn turned away. He nodded to the lights in the valley. 'When did you last visit?'

'The Vale?' Hamar headed off down the slope. 'Must be a couple of years back. Good soil. Gets plenty of rain as the clouds shed their load to make it over the mountains.

And, of course, those peaks shelter it from the worst of those bitter north easterlies.'

Toryn counted four more lights. 'Be nice to speak to them. I wonder if any have been to the mountains.'

'They'll be like us. Folk don't change a great deal until much farther north.' He rubbed his hands together. 'It's the harsh winters, not to mention the unwanted attention from the clans of Nordruuk.' He patted Toryn on the back. 'That way, lad. Step lively now. This track will take us down to the woodlands and on into Noor. Then you'll get your wish. The landscape changes dramatically from there on.'

'How far is Greendell from the edge of the realms?'

Hamar rubbed his chin. 'Must be at least sixty, maybe even seventy leagues, I'd say.' He nodded. 'Yes, about an eight-day brisk hike, depending on the weather. That and the terrain don't make for easy going.'

'Shush!' Toryn grabbed Hamar's arm. 'There's someone behind.' They crouched in the long grass. Toryn whispered. 'I heard the grass swish.' He squinted. 'Can't see anything in this light.'

'Look out the sides of your eyes. You'll see better.'

Toryn held his breath. 'No, still nothing.'

Hamar crawled up beside him. 'Could be a brock on his way back to his hole. They can grow to quite a size.'

Toryn rose to his heels. 'You're probably right. I doubt any other fool would be up at this hour.'

Toryn groaned. He missed home and would give anything to stretch out on his bed for one night. He rolled on to his side and rubbed his lower back. He had been so tired he had not noticed the tree root jutting out from the undergrowth where they had rested — but he could feel it now. Hamar still slept, curled into a ball between two twisted roots. Above, the leaden sky bore down on the treetops, bending the branches until they creaked under the weight.

Toryn climbed to his feet. It was a short walk to the edge of the wood, and a safe distance from the small settlement below in the Vale. Hamar snored. Toryn guessed it would be a while longer before he would wake. He tiptoed away and headed for the open ground. It felt good to be walking in daylight again, and he soon found what he longed to see. Rising unchallenged by the lesser mountains in the range, Caranach climbed high, capturing passing clouds on its peak. If anything, the westerly slopes appeared steeper and more treacherous than those visible from his home. It would be harder going than he had imagined, but he knew he could find a way to its summit.

Toryn risked stepping out of the trees. The ground dipped gently down to the Vale. In the distance, a lone horse pulled a cart across a bridge towards the tiny village. Hamar was right: this could be his home. Back in Midwyche, Andryn and Jerrum would be riding the cart back home after a day laying the new fence; Miram would be in the kitchen preparing a meagre dinner; and what of Elrik? How far had he and the others traveled south?

Toryn glanced back to the ridge behind the trees. Were the Archonian Guard searching for him? Surely, he was not worth the effort. He sat on the damp grass and looked back to the village. Hamar had told him of the countless settlements left to rot, abandoned following the so-called victory over the invaders from the south. Toryn could not begin to imagine the suffering of his unsuspecting people as they endured the bitter legacy of their triumph. First came the deadly plague. Too late did they discover their defeated foe had infected livestock with some foul concoction that spread rapidly through the weakened population. But if the survivors thought they could recover come spring, they were cruelly deceived. The green shoots that should have signaled the rebirth of the realms, emerged gray and withered, corrupted by poisoned soil that took a generation to cleanse.

Toryn shook the image from his head, grateful he had not lived in such times. The village below flourished. Wisps of smoke rose from dozens of houses clustered around a square in the middle, and he swore he could smell freshly-baked bread. But the mountain drew his attention. Did a young man from the village below share the same dream of climbing Caranach?

The sun broke through the clouds, spilling its light along a narrow strip close to the edge of the mountains. Toryn stood to get a better view. A white tower glistened at the foot of a sheer cliff as it thrust up from the green slopes of the foothills. It had to be the Darrow Watchtower at the mouth of the Kolossos Pass. Long before anyone could remember, their ancestors had constructed the route through the mountains to allow faster trade between the east and west. Hamar had spoken at length about the achievements of the engineers and builders of old. Unimaginable today, they had built both the passes of the Caerwal and Kolossos ranges. Toryn laughed as he remembered Hamar's jibe that the only thing the engineers at Archonholm could pass these days, was wind.

He followed the hard line of the shadow. Without the pass, the journey south to skirt the range would take a full month longer, thus preventing trade in food at the time. But as Hamar had told him, the inhabitants of the mountains had resented the intrusion and regularly attacked the convoys. They had built garrisons at both sides and several smaller forts along the route, thus enabling the pass to function. But following the restrictions on movement after the war, only the Archon's forces were allowed access, and even they preferred to avoid the passage fraught with danger. The pass was all but sealed with watchtowers posted at the east and west garrisons.

He jumped. A flash briefly bathed the middle slopes of Caranach with an unnatural light. He took a few steps forward. Was that smoke? A dark smudge climbed the north face, fading as it dispersed the higher it floated.

'Thought I'd find you here.' Toryn turned. Hamar grinned. 'Knew you wouldn't be able to resist the view.'

Toryn blinked away the after image. 'Did you see that flash?'

'Lightning. Had to be.'

'No, not lightning, it was green.' He pointed. 'Over there. In the pass.'

Hamar peered at the mountains. 'It's a long way off. Could be your eyes were tricked.'

'I don't think so. I'm sure it was green.'

'Most likely cobs then. The pass has been all but closed for decades.' He mumbled. 'Likely up to no good again.' He turned back to the trees. 'We'll mention it to the guards when… oh wait, we can't, we're not supposed to be here.'

Toryn followed Hamar back to their campsite. 'Did you ever see one?'

'A cobtroll? No, but that doesn't mean they don't venture out. A guard in my company saw one. Stooped little chap, but with strong arms and legs. Very pale, apparently. Had enormous eyes and a large head too heavy for its scrawny neck to hold. Mind you, he said it could move quick when it had too. We used to hear stories of them kidnapping young children from settlements in the Vale.'

'Children?' Toryn shuddered. 'What did they do with them?'

'Can't be sure if the stories were true, or just used to

scare the little blighters to come in at night and go to bed.'

'Still, not a nice one to tell your children.'

They reached the tree where they had slept. Hamar shrugged. 'Well, they shouldn't bother us here, I doubt they'll come this far from the mountains without cover.' He checked the sky between the treetops. 'Hope the weather is kind to us for a few days longer. If we push on, we'll cross into Noor this evening where the hills won't be so gentle. We can't use the main bridge so you'll get your feet wet. The Great Elda widens out after the fence.'

'So how are we going to cross?'

'There's a ruin of an old bridge farther down river we can reach by wading out. Shouldn't come higher than your belly before we reach it.' Hamar crouched, pulled a knife from his pack, and licked his lips. 'Now let's see if my trap has caught us a tasty breakfast.'

12. TO SING NO MORE

Toryn pulled his blanket tighter. 'It's definitely growing colder. My clothes still feel wet from the Elda, and that was two days ago. Shame we can't light a fire.'

Hamar nodded. 'Once we reach them hills yonder, we might risk a small one. Pity, I could do with a smoke right now.' He shuddered. 'I don't think spring will show her face around these parts for a while longer.'

Toryn rubbed his hand. 'You were right about Noor's fence being sturdier.' He held up his finger. 'Got a nasty splinter squeezing through that one.'

Hamar tried to laugh but only shivered. 'The going will become a little hairy before long. We'll be heading up that valley across from this lake. Nice and easy to start but turns into a ravine farther up.' He winced. 'Lost a man there once. Poor lad. First month of his service. Slipped, went over the edge onto the rocks below, and turned the rapids red. Very narrow path, more of a ledge really. We'll have to travel by day, too dangerous in the dark.'

Toryn reached into his rucksack and pulled out the map. 'Isn't there another way?' He flattened out the tattered cloth. 'I seem to remember a road running through to the mines.' He peered at the faint lines, but the clouds dulled the light of the moon.

Hamar squinted at the map. 'There are two. We can't risk the Great Northwest Road.' He pointed. 'It's that way. While it would be longer, it's certainly easier, but it's the major route for deliveries from Drunsberg, escorted by the Archon's men. They'll be on the lookout for suspicious folk. And I should know, did the same journey a dozen times taking silver and ore to the jewelers and smithies at

Archonholm.'

'And the other route? You said two.'

'Worse than the first.'

Toryn sighed. 'Thought you'd say that.'

'Sorry, lad, not my fault. I didn't make the world the way it is.'

'What's wrong with the second route?'

Hamar ran his fingers through his tangled hair. 'It would take us well out of our way and onto the road to Calerdorn. Shame, such a beautiful city, centuries old with more spires than a huckle has spikes. I'd love to see it again before my days are done, but anyways, there'll be even more guards on those crossings.' He stretched out his back. 'Sorry. The ravine it is.'

Toryn delved in his backpack. 'I suppose it would be good practice for when I climb the mountains.' He pulled out the cheese and unwrapped it. He passed it to Hamar. 'That's the last piece.'

Hamar handed it back. 'You have it, you'll need your strength for the road ahead.'

'Thanks.' Toryn took a bite and chewed slowly, wanting to make it last. How long would he have to wait to taste his mother's food again? 'But what about you? You need to eat.'

'I've got some dried meat.' He glanced over this shoulder. 'If the moon comes out full, we could catch ourselves a fish or two.' On cue, the moon peered around the edge of a cloud as if gazing upon its reflection in the still waters.

Toryn laughed. 'I see your fairy folk have lit the lantern again.' He looked to the lake. 'Not a breath of wind. Makes it look like glass.'

'See, still on our side. A couple of fish would see us right until we get to Greendell, and they'll taste far better than the tough, small creatures we'd catch around these parts.' Hamar stood and scanned the low line of hills on the opposite side of the lake. He walked to the shore.

Toryn called over. 'Something wrong?'

Hamar smiled. 'Not wrong, not wrong at all.' He pointed to the hills. 'It may be dangerous, but I reckon we should find another one of those stones.' He nodded. 'Yes, I'm sure of it. The Archon rewarded us handsomely for reporting its location. Brought myself a decent sword and a comfortable pair of boots.' He turned and scratched his head. 'Now, just need to remember how it was hidden. But I'm pretty sure it will come back to me as we get close.'

Hamar waded into the water and bent. 'Ah yes, we've enough light to see the little silvery fellows.' He motioned to Toryn. 'Come on, lad. The fish will be close to the surface now, coming up to the warmer water.' He shivered. 'Not that it feels too warm to me.' Toryn strolled to the edge. Hamar held up a hand. 'Nice and slow please, don't want to frighten our supper away.'

Toryn stood on the riverbank. The fast-flowing water glistened despite the clouds obscuring the moon. He turned to face the south. Elrik would be in the warmer climes of the realms by now. He wished he could be with his friend, and not only because of the weather. Come winter, Elrik would be ready to join the Archonian Guard, whereas he would be... what? Still hiding in Greendell tending livestock? He thought of Elrik wearing his guard's armor with a heavy sword on his belt, ready to serve the Archon. Toryn could only picture himself standing in a damp field, wrapped in a cowherd's smock smeared with mud and dung.

Toryn bent and dipped his hand in the water and felt its force. In no time, his fingers numbed, and the cold seeped up to his elbow. He withdrew his hand — it stung. Toryn turned as Hamar made his way down the bank. 'The water feels strange, it's—' Hamar stumbled towards him. Toryn caught his arm and pulled him back. 'Steady, you don't want to be falling in the river and getting all wet and cold again.' The old man tried to stand straight, but Toryn felt the strength leave Hamar's body. He slumped against Toryn as he helped him up the bank and lowered him onto the grass.

Hamar groaned, bringing his hands to his face. He mumbled. 'Sorry, Tor. Give me a moment.'

'Was it the fish?' Hamar shook his head. Toryn crouched opposite. 'No, of course not, couldn't be. We ate the same one.' He lifted Hamar's chin and checked his face. 'Could be a chill from standing in that icy lake.'

Hamar shivered. 'I can feel it in my bones. It's not right. Shouldn't be this cold in spring, even up here.'

Toryn stood and searched the valley ahead. 'How far to the stone?'

Hamar straightened. Toryn could see it took a great effort. He pointed a shaky finger. 'Around the bend ahead. Halfway up the hill there's a rocky outcrop, and a narrow entrance into a cave. The stone's inside.'

'Narrow?' Toryn laughed, trying to cheer his friend. 'Will you get in? You must have been a lot slimmer back then.'

Hamar chuckled. 'Don't worry about me. I'll squeeze through.'

Toryn held out his hand. 'Ready to walk?'

Hamar waved it away. 'No need. I'll be fine.' He pushed on his knees and Toryn was sure he heard his joints creak, but Hamar managed to stand. He swayed, took a step, lurched forward and grabbed hold of Toryn's arm. 'Get me to the stone, that'll see me right.'

Toryn took the full weight of Hamar but held firm. 'Come on, old boy. I'll get you there.' He peered along the path and hoped Hamar could find it, or even make it that far. He had not considered what he would do if Hamar became ill and unable to walk.

They made slow progress as Hamar needed to stop often to steady his head. The moon had long since set before they finally rounded the bend in the valley. Toryn clutched his stomach and nearly dropped Hamar.

'You now? Got a chill?'

'It's my guts.' Toryn grimaced. 'They're all churned up, and I've got the strangest taste in my mouth.'

Hamar tried to laugh. 'Look at us. We're a right couple of crocks. Can't find that stone quick enough, eh.' He took some of his weight from Toryn. 'Not far. I can manage.'

Toryn grunted as he tried to straighten against what felt like a knife twisting in his stomach. They staggered along the path, but every step drained Toryn's strength. He dropped his gaze to the floor as his eyes ached, and his skin prickled.

Hamar mumbled at his side. 'Something don't feel right. It's the air, it ain't right, ain't right at all.'

Toryn too sensed a change. 'What is that? Smells like something died.'

Hamar failed to hear him. He slurred his words. 'Get to the stone, make it sing, that'll make it right.' He sprawled forward, bent double. 'It ain't natural, not right.'

Toryn yanked Hamar back to his feet. 'Can you remember how to find it? You said it was in a cave.'

'Make it sing, yes, we'll make it sing, make everything right again.'

'Hamar! Hamar?'

'It's wrong, all wrong... wrong, I tell you.'

Toryn stopped. A pile of rubble lay strewn across their path. His eyes followed the line of stones up the slope. He need not have worried about finding the concealed entrance to the cave. A short way up to his right, he could make out a dark opening in the hillside. He muttered to Hamar. 'Don't think you'll have any problem squeezing through that gap. Looks like half the hillside has collapsed.'

Toryn swallowed hard as a low squeal issued from the exposed cavern. He forced his legs up the hill with Hamar at his side, but soon stopped to gain his breath. He turned to Hamar. 'Can you feel that? The ground, it's throbbing. And the noise. It's setting my teeth on edge.' But Hamar's head stayed bowed as he continued to mutter to himself. First Toryn's toes, then his shins and knees grew numb until he could barely feel the ground beneath his feet. Hamar lurched. Toryn could not hold him a moment longer. He helped him to the ground. 'You rest here. I'll come back for you when I've found a way to the stone.'

Toryn forced his heavy legs up the hillside, but each step became harder, as if wading against a fast-flowing river. His head swirled and his vision blurred, but he finally reached the cave. He scrambled over the rubble and stumbled inside. Toryn stopped. It should have been darker, but he could clearly see a tall shadow on the rear wall of the cave. The Singing Stone rose defiantly from the debris of the collapsed roof. But this stone did not sing — it wailed.

Toryn took a step and entered another world. The wail became a shriek, bursting his ears and almost cleaving his skull in two. He clasped his eyes shut against a harsh green light saturating the rocks. Toryn reeled, choking on the foul-tasting air clogging his nose and throat, before pitching forward to vomit. He cried out, snatching back his hands as his palms stung at the touch of the cave floor. Toryn clutched his pained hands to his ears, but nothing could shut out the cry from the stone. He kneeled back and dared to open his eyes. His heart sank. Three small rocks surrounded the tormented stone. They pulsed with the sickly green light, violating the cave. Jagged fingers of steaming fluid seeped from the rocks and groped at the base of the Singing Stone. Toryn gritted his teeth, pained by its anguish, and forced himself to his feet. Bowing his head as if laboring against a gale, he took a step towards it, convinced he could somehow end the torture. But with every agonizing step, the pulsating ground sapped his strength, filling his bones with the same poison he knew corrupted the ancient stone.

The three encircling rocks grew brighter, as if welcoming Toryn to their world. His resolve deserted him. He collapsed. The skin of his cheek burned against the floor, but he had no strength to pull himself free. With every pulse of the rock he felt his body weaken, knowing any moment his bones would crack and share the fate of the stone.

Two hands grasped his frail ankles and dragged him back, scraping his skin across the rough cavern floor. The screaming stopped. His bones welcomed the solid ground beneath, before his world turned black.

Toryn brought his hands to his throbbing temples. He opened his eyes and stared at the flickering embers of a campfire. He turned to find he lay close to the cave, sheltered by the rubble from a stiff breeze whistling through the valley. He swallowed and groaned as the sides of his parched throat scraped together. 'Ah, you're awake.' Hamar put down his pipe and held out his hand. 'Here, thought you'd need a drink.'

Toryn sat and waited for his head to stop spinning. He croaked his thanks and drained the mug with three gulps. He checked Hamar. 'You look a little better.'

Hamar nodded. 'And in better shape than you, it seems.'

Toryn rolled out his stiff shoulders. 'Thanks, Hamar.'

Hamar frowned. 'It was just a cup of water.'

'No, I meant for pulling me out of that place.'

The lines on Hamar's forehead deepened. 'Pulling you out…? I didn't pull you out of no cave.' He nodded to a spot down the hill. 'I woke up over there about an hour ago. And judging by the moon, we've slept through an entire day and half the night.'

Toryn followed his gaze. 'Something inside that cave brought me to my knees. I thought I was done for, but then someone dragged me out.'

'Nah, lad, you must have dreamed it. We were both in a bit of a state. Could have been the fish, or a chill we caught in the lake. I had strange ones too.' He hooked his thumb to the cave. 'And I was wrong about the stone. Had a quick look, but there's no sign of one.'

Toryn took a deep breath, trying to clear his head. 'No, you were right. The stone *was* there, last night, I'm sure I saw it.' The anguished wail echoed in his head. Toryn climbed carefully to his feet. 'It was under attack. Didn't you hear the screams? Thought my ears would burst.'

'Attack? Screams?' Hamar grinned. 'Have to say your dreams sound more dramatic than mine.'

'Wait.' Toryn held up his hands. 'See. Scratches. And I have burns on my hands and face.' He clenched his fists. 'I can feel them.' He held out a hand to Hamar. 'Come, you need to see this.'

Hamar grumbled. 'Alright, if it makes you happy, but then we eat.'

Toryn took a flaming stick from the fire. 'This should do.' He picked his way through the crumbled rocks and led Hamar into the cave. 'The stone is over—' He held the torch higher but could see no sign of it.

Hamar sighed. 'See, empty. You must have dreamed it.'

Toryn kneeled by the small rock close to the entrance. 'Look at this. It glowed last night, and don't ask me how, but it damaged the stone.' He raised the torch. 'There's two more over there.'

'Them's rocks. Must have fallen from the ceiling when half of it collapsed.'

'But they're placed in a triangle, all the same distance from each other, and from where the stone stood in the middle.' He grabbed Hamar's arm. 'Careful, the ground burns inside those rocks.'

Hamar shrugged it off and took a step. 'Feels fine to me.' He stooped to examine one of the smaller stones. 'Bring the light, lad.' He ran his hand along the top. 'You might have a point. Feels icy cold, and' — he bent forward — 'they're not natural. Someone has hewn these rocks.' Hamar directed Toryn's hand with the torch. 'And see here, there's letters of sorts.'

Toryn squinted. 'Don't look like any words I know.'

Hamar groaned. 'They won't.' He held his hand to his brow. 'I've seen this writing before.' He shuddered. 'I won't talk about it here, but you can be sure these aren't kind words.' He backed away from the rock. 'We should leave.'

Toryn turned to the center. 'Wait, I don't understand. Everything seems the same as I remember from last night except for the—' He took a step. 'Oh no, it can't be.' At the center, a trickle of water gurgled up from where the stone had stood. But it had disintegrated, reduced to a small mound of black dust, slowly turning into sludge at the edges as the water oozed across the floor.

Toryn crouched and scooped a handful. He held it up and let the powder slide through his numb fingers. Hamar stared at the falling dust. 'Such a shame. What could have done this?' His jaw dropped; his gaunt face carried every one of his seventy-one years. His voice trembled. 'It's a shame, a damn shame. I don't know what they're for, but I know the land will be worse off for its loss.'

'Here, look at this.' Toryn held out a piece of cloth. 'Torn from my trousers. Must have been when you dragged me out.'

'Then I guess it must have been me.' Hamar glanced to the entrance. 'We need to leave, Tor. The words on these rocks have power, the wrong sort of power.' He rubbed his chin. 'That's how we got all mixed up in our heads.'

Toryn crouched by the rock. 'Any idea what these words mean?'

'Don't get too close' — Hamar took Toryn's arm — 'this place isn't safe. We should go. And no, I don't know and don't want to know what they mean.'

Toryn shuddered. An icy chill crawled up his spine as the rock seemed to whisper the words etched on its face. He stood. 'I agree.' He followed Hamar out of the cave.

Hamar grimaced at the fingers of sludge trickling from the cave, down the hill towards the river. 'Word of this should be sent to the Archon, but I don't know how.' His legs buckled and he slid to the bank.

Toryn placed the dying torch on the cold rock and sat beside him. 'How you feeling?'

He spoke through his fingers. 'Tired, hungry and ancient.' He dropped his hands. 'Let's move farther up the valley, eat, then get as far away from this place as we can.'

13. AN AUDACIOUS PLAN

The lines of wisdom and experience on General Kragan's face deepened to a level of doubt and disbelief. He gaped at the Archon as he struggled to form his question. The Archon did not allow him time. 'Good. If the general of my armies did not know of my plan, I am encouraged.' He placed his chin in his hand and observed the old map sitting on an easel at the head of the table. 'I have long suspected the Golesh would launch an attack, and therefore have planned a riposte before they can gain a foothold north of the mountains. This has been kept secret until now, because, if this reaches the wrong ears, I will lose the element of surprise.' He turned to the table. 'And therefore not a word of this is to be spoken outside of this hall until the fleet has sailed.'

Elodi breathed out. She could not take her eyes off the map revealing the world beyond the Caerwal Mountains. Bardon stammered. 'How is this possible? We've not built ships since you changed the seas.'

The Archon slid his hand across the map. 'You are wrong, Broon. Six years ago, I decreed the old port of Caermund to be re-built.' His hand came to rest on an inlet on the east coast of Farrand. 'Yes, you all know the stories. When I bent the waters, unpleasant creatures from the depths washed up on the shores at Caermund, which unfortunately led to a number of... incidents.' He tapped his finger on the old parchment. 'But once I'd sealed the area, I soon drove them back into the sea. And now, I am pleased to report, the finest fleet to sail in many a year awaits, eager to depart.' He looked to the general. 'And yes, that is where I assigned your men for special duties.'

General Kragan found his voice. 'But, Archon, to send the bulk of our elite forces out to sea is' — he stammered as he glanced around the table — 'is surely—'

'A bold stroke of genius the enemy will not suspect.' The Archon ran his finger in a curve from Caermund, out to sea, and back to a bay in the south. 'A fleet of forty-four ships will carry our finest soldiers, fastest horses, and light artillery to Umnavarek. From there they will strike forth into the Lost Realms ready to—'

'But' — Kragan held up his hand — 'please forgive my interruption, Archon, but how can we possibly know what awaits us far to the south?'

The Archon took a breath. 'Do you question my judgement, General?' Kragan opened his mouth, but the Archon continued. 'Because if you do, I'm sure I can appoint another who will be happy to take your place.'

Kragan stammered. 'No, of course not, Archon, I am not questioning your judgement, I… need to know what I'd expect to encounter, so I can assemble an effective force for the task.'

The Archon held the general's gaze for a moment longer. 'Good, I shall proceed to explain my strategy, then you can decide on your *appropriate* force.' He scanned the faces at the table. 'Yes, I admit this is an audacious plan, but if we are to pre-empt the Golesh's strike which, no doubt, will be fearsome, extreme and could ultimately result in our demise, we have to be bold.' He held up his hand as Kragan moved to speak. 'At this moment, I can predict with certainty, every foul creature with a weapon in its clawed hand, and hatred consuming its heart, will shortly be swarming to the gate. The enemy concentrates its malice purely on the pass and not on the coast. They desire our fertile lands, our riches, and are hungry for slaves. Trust me, Kragan, they will not be watching the ports for which they have no use.' He turned to the Vice-

Archon and nodded.

'Thank you, Archon.' She rose and stood at the other side of the map. 'When the time is right, the Archon will lift his invocation and allow the ocean currents to flow naturally again. The fleet will take no more than two days to reach Umnavarek.' She fixed her gaze on Kragan. 'General, once the force has landed, the objective is to head west and strike onto Elmarand. As you know' — she raised an eyebrow at Elodi — 'or may not, Elmarand was *our* principal city before the Golesh drove our ancestors out of the Second Realm. We've no reason to believe that has changed and can therefore assume Elmarand will still be of strategic importance to them. We cannot know exactly what to expect as the maps are centuries old, but I doubt the backward, war-mongering hordes have built anything superior to that of our elders. I think we'll find the walls of the once great city will be in a state of disrepair and provide little-to-no obstacle for our elite forces.' She stood back. 'General, that is the strategy, I will, of course, charge you with determining the tactics.'

Kragan pushed back his chair and cleared his throat. 'It will be an honor, Archon, this is an audacious plan, but may I ask, what is to happen if… once we retake Elmarand?'

The Archon stood. 'As stated, the enemy's resources are converging on the gate. Your aim, Kragan, is to cause disruption, and cast fear in their hearts for once. Upon securing Elmarand, you shall proceed to take the surrounding primitive farms and livestock, after all, they also must eat. Take what you need to sustain your forces, then burn the rest. The Golesh will have no choice but to divert resources from the gate to regain control of their city and farmlands.' The Archon folded his arms. 'And when they're finally defeated, we can free our people from the southern realms who, for too long, have suffered at the hands of this vile race.'

Kragan glanced at the Castellan. 'And how long will our expeditionary force be expected to hold out against their greater numbers?'

The Archon's mouth curled into a rare grin. 'Rest assured, it won't be for long.' He pointed to the pass on the map. 'Using my gift of *farsight*, I shall observe events from the tower. When I see the smoke of your endeavors billowing in the southern skies, I shall focus my energy and sow seeds of doubt in the hearts of the Golesh. It will take a great deal of effort on my behalf, so the Vice-Archon will manage day-to-day events here at the citadel. But once news of the incursion reaches their ranks, they will have to dispatch a sizeable force to deal with it.' He rubbed his hands. 'At that moment, my trebuchets shall rain destruction over the gate onto their war machines before they can be deployed against us.' The Archon raised an eyebrow as Kragan drew breath. 'Yes, General' — he turned to the others at the table — 'then my counter-strike will, in time, reclaim the Lost Realms. I will catch them unawares.' His eyes flashed. 'When I open the Caerwal Gate.'

14. A DARK, REMEMBERED TALE

Toryn looked anxiously at his feet as he tried not to stumble from the narrow ledge down into the ravine. To his left, the river surged through the narrow gap as if agitated by the rocks' attempt to delay its journey. At each twist, water splashed up, groping for their feet as if trying to snatch them from the cliff in its frustration. Toryn shouted to make himself heard above the gushing water. 'It might have been better in the dark. Then I couldn't see what's waiting for me down below.' He braced as another wall of water slammed into an outcrop at his feet. 'Would have been better if the builders had made it wider.'

Hamar laughed and called back. 'It has been. It's easier going than when I last came this way.'

'Just how narrow was it?'

Hamar stopped and turned. 'It wasn't made for big folk. I reckon it was built by the dwarfs who used to live in these parts, or perhaps even cobtrolls.'

'This far out?'

'We're not far from the Kolossos range. And way back then there were settlements under the hills to the west. We found evidence of one near to where that stone used to be.' Hamar shuffled a few more paces. 'Ah, this will do nicely. We'll rest here.' He disappeared into a cove carved out of the rock. Toryn followed, happy to be off the ledge and away from the angry river. He took off his rucksack and rubbed his aching shoulders under his damp clothes.

Toryn looked behind Hamar. 'It's bigger than I thought, room for ten at least.'

Hamar rolled his blanket onto the floor. 'Would have

been a busy route before our kind came this far north.' He banged his head on the low ceiling and cursed. 'Definitely smaller than us, whoever built it.' Hamar peered to the back of the cave. 'Must have been cobtrolls. See, there's a bend at the back to shelter them from sunlight. They shun the big, fiery ball in the sky.'

Toryn grinned. 'Why? Do they burst into flames?'

'Course not. No, it's their eyes. Can see well in the dark, far better than you or I, but they'd be practically blind in sunlight.'

Toryn unwrapped the last fish and held it to his nose. 'Smells alright. I'll light a fire.'

'I suppose that's one advantage of it being colder. The food lasts longer. But never you mind, this time tomorrow we'll be feasting by a roaring fireside in Greendell.'

'And then what?' Toryn snapped the twigs. 'Six months of doing what I've been doing for years back home?'

Hamar sighed. 'Let's get there first, eh. This gorge forks farther up, we turn right and it's only a few hours before we reach the small plain nestling between the hills. Greendell sits right in the middle.'

Toryn made a small pile of sticks and struck the flint. He turned to Hamar. 'Back at the Singing Stone, you said you'd seen the words on those rocks before. Can you remember where?'

'Thought you'd ask.' Hamar sat. 'A place called Durran Wood.' Toryn pushed a stick through the mouth of the fish. Hamar pointed to the fire. 'Careful, not too close. You don't want to scorch the flesh.' He took a smoldering twig from the fire and lit his pipe. 'The locals call it Wyke Wood.'

Toryn looked up from the flames. 'Wyke Wood? I guess they didn't name it after a *good 'un* then.'

'The fish, lad. Keep your eyes on the fish.' Hamar

shuddered. 'It most certainly wasn't. And I reckon it wasn't one of the mischievous sods who'd cause an outbreak of boils on your backside if you didn't pay them. No, the fiend in that wood was far worse. And still causing problems from what I hear.'

The shelter darkened. Toryn blew on the fire. 'Is it far from here?'

'Far enough. Stands to the south of Mawlgrim Mire. In fact, they make good neighbors. You wouldn't want to pass the time of day in either. The wood's a dark place, sturdy fir trees, only ones capable of growing that far north. Tall with thick growth that turns the middle of the day to night. Very dark.' The flames flickered in Hamar's wide eyes.

Toryn waited for him to continue, but this was a story the old man seemed reluctant to share. He pressed. 'How did you come to be there?'

Hamar drew on his pipe. 'It happened in my second year of service. We were following up reports of the usual suspects up to no good in the area. Anyways, we found their tracks soon enough and came across a deserted campsite, right on the edge of that damned wood. But the strange thing was what the tracks told us. These rascals are easy to follow as they blunder about without a care, but' — he frowned as if trying to work out the mystery — 'they left their camp in one line with an equal gap between them. We counted sixteen tracks. Just lined up facing the trees and walked right in. Very unlike them. They took nothing, no weapons, supplies or equipment. We found all their provisions left behind.'

Hamar gazed at the shadows dancing on the wall. He let out a long sigh. 'We weren't keen about going in after them, not after what the locals had told us. Strange goings on, noises at night, livestock dying of fright, even people disappearing. They'd abandoned the settlement of Durran ten years earlier, said it was too close for comfort.'

Toryn remembered their supper. He took it from the fire, broke off a piece and handed it to Hamar. 'How come you've not mentioned this before?'

Hamar placed his pipe on a rock and accepted the fish. He took a bite and watched the entrance as he chewed. 'There are certain things you don't want to remember. I must've pushed the events of that day deep down, or most of it at least. But seeing the letters on those rocks dragged it all back up. The funny thing is, I can't say for sure what happened, we were all... changed, altered afterwards.'

'You went into the wood? I thought you said you—'

'We had this new captain, keen to impress his seniors, so he insisted we go in and either capture them or find their dead bodies and take evidence back with us.' He pointed to the rucksack. 'Pass me the flask, my mouth's gone dry.' Toryn realized he had a morsel of uneaten fish in his mouth. He chewed as he passed the water to Hamar. 'Thanks.' He took a long drink and wiped his beard. 'We convinced our captain to wait until morning, making sure we camped a fair distance away. The following day, twelve of us go into the wood.' He shivered. 'Straight away it didn't feel right. The sun shone that morning, but it grew dark once under those trees, and a chill soon crept into your bones. If there'd once been paths, the scrub had long since smothered them. Despite it being a small wood, a mere thicket compared to Foranfae down south, we feared losing our way in its shadows. So, we set markers using fallen branches to guide us back out.' His eyes widened. 'Then we heard the screams. I thought I'd long forgotten them. Heard nothing like it before, and never want to hear the likes of it again. At first, we thought it were children, but they'd never be in that place alone.' His hand clenched the flask and his face paled. 'They had to be the cries of the poor fellows we pursued. These were tough Ruuk, used to terrible hardships, living with violence, but I couldn't imagine the suffering and pain causing them to shriek as they did.'

Hamar took another gulp from the flask; Toryn noticed his hand trembled. 'Well, we'd heard enough. We pleaded with the captain to leave as there'd be none of them left to capture. Thankfully he agreed, vowing to come back in greater numbers later. But if we'd had a hundred men, I still wouldn't want to face what's lurking in them trees.' He placed the fish bones on the floor. 'Then the screaming stopped, but that made it worse.'

'How?'

'It was the silence. And we suspected whatever tormented those poor souls now came for us.'

Toryn shuddered. 'What about the writing?'

'I was getting to that. You see, we didn't find our way out as intended. We followed our markers, but some mischievous imps must have moved them, leading us in circles. We wandered about for hours, becoming more uneasy and confused. Then we noticed markings scratched into the tree bark. Ruffians pass messages between themselves in such a way, but these were the same as those on the rocks at the cave. Just to see them made you feel unwell.'

'How did you get out?'

Hamar snapped the twig in his hand. 'Not all of us did. And I don't rightly know how I escaped. I can remember feeling dizzy, stumbling about, and hearing whispers all around us.'

Toryn's face tingled. 'Whispers? I heard voices back at that cave.'

'Told you they were the same.' Hamar held his gaze. 'I have no memory of how, but I found myself alone among those dark trees.' He took a deep breath. 'Then the

screaming started up again, but this time it had to be my
fellow guards. I'm not proud to say….' He swallowed. 'I'm
not proud to say I ran.' He stroked his chin. 'We'd trained
together, fought, laughed and survived many a scrape
together, but under no circumstances would I go back to
help them. I ran, bumping into tree trunks, tripping over
roots, but I kept going. I don't know how long I ran, but
when I eventually got out, it was already night.'

Toryn could barely speak. 'How many escaped?'

Hamar's lips held tight. It was a full minute before he
spoke. 'Just me, my old friends, Jacken, and Tombold, the
one who told me the story of the Archon.' His head
dropped. 'We lost nine, including the captain.' He ran his
hands down his face. 'That explains why we felt funny the
other night. Those markings are an incantation, I'm sure of
it, casting its devilry on that poor Singing Stone.'

Toryn added more wood to the fire. Hamar's shadow
loomed large on the back wall of the shelter. 'Did you ever
find out what was in those trees?'

'No, and I don't care to know.'

'The guards sent no one to find out?'

'Didn't have the men to spare. The locals don't go
near it, and the new maps mark Durran and the wood as
unsafe. The Caerwal Gate takes priority, always has, and if
whatever is in those trees, stays in those trees, the
Archonian Guard won't waste any more men.'

The hair on the back of Toryn's neck prickled. 'But
the words on those rocks? Don't that prove whatever is in
those trees now ventures outside its borders?'

15. IN THE ARCHON'S WISDOM

Elodi rested her hand on the cool stone, drawing comfort from the thickness of the wall. She tried to ease the tension in her shoulders, but the Archon's confidence troubled her. Not more than a league from where she stood, an immense force mustered with the sole aim to enslave the good people of the Five Realms. Could the Archon and his armies break through and defeat them? Or would opening the gate hasten their doom? She looked out of her window to the forest. The moon brushed the treetops with a silver coating, but if sunlight failed to penetrate the thick canopy, the mere light of the moon would not persuade Foranfae to give up her secrets.

Elodi sat on the ledge and leaned back against the cool wall. If an ancient power existed amongst the trees of Foranfae, they needed it now. Surely, all their lands would fall in a matter of months, if not weeks, should the enemy overwhelm Archonholm. The lucky would die in the onslaught, leaving the unfortunate survivors to suffer a life of thralldom at the cruel hands of the Golesh. Her stomach knotted. And what of her? She forced down the panic rising in her throat and stroked the stone of the ledge. She had to be strong for the people of Harlyn. The magnificent, yet aging walls of Calerdorn would buy them little time to flee against a determined attack. Even if they could set sail, would they find shores unknown on an unpredictable and unforgiving sea? Elodi closed her eyes and imagined the sound of the waves crashing against the rocks far beneath her room in the walls of Calerdorn. She shuddered. As the ruler of Harlyn, Elodi's foes would have devised an unpleasant, drawn-out end for her. The seas may be treacherous, but she would sooner take her chances and risk the currents dragging her to their depths, than allow the enemy to take her alive.

The tap at the door woke Elodi. She had not been aware she had dozed, but it had been a long day and she must have curled up on the stone sill and let sleep take her. She rose and went to the door. 'Who is it?'

Her aide spoke. 'Lord Broon is here to see you, ma'am.'

She buttoned her gown and opened the door. The man stood by Bardon. 'Ma'am. The lord assured me you would see him at this hour.'

'Yes, by all means.' Elodi stepped aside. 'Please, do come in, Lord Broon.' She turned to her aide. 'Thank you, and, please can you ensure we are not disturbed.' He bowed and closed the door.

Bardon's eyebrows rose. 'I see the Archon gave you one of the finer rooms. Perhaps he is keen to impress.'

'It is somewhat luxurious compared to home, but I can't think why the Archon would want to impress me.'

'Oh, he has his ways. He never won your father over fully, so I suspect he's keen to gain your support.'

Elodi ushered him to a chair by the window. 'Would you care for a bite to eat, or something to drink? I could have my maid prepare us a late supper.'

'Wine will suffice, thank you. I've eaten too much today.' He patted his stomach. 'Not used to the portions here, I've become accustomed to the rations of Keld.'

'I noticed there appears to be no shortage of food and drink in the south.' She poured two glasses of red wine and sat opposite. 'Have you had time to consider the Archon's strategy?'

Bardon gazed into the dark liquid in his glass. 'I agree with him on one matter.' He took a sip and rolled it around his mouth before swallowing. 'I doubt the Golesh will expect to see our ships sailing up the bay at Umnavarek, but whether it will work is entirely a different matter.' He met Elodi's gaze. 'How about you?'

She swirled the wine in her glass. 'Father taught me about tactics and strategy, and of course I have Wendel and Captain Aldorman to assist with the daily skirmishes involving Harlyn's reserves, but an invasion fleet is way beyond my experience, and Wendel's for that matter. But my primary concern is the opening of the gate. For centuries it has kept them out, and despite what the Archon says of their weapons, I'd rather we placed our faith in its strength and keep it shut fast.'

Bardon drained his glass. 'It does seem a high-risk strategy with too many critical components. Should the ships fail to reach their destination, or the expeditionary force not win through to Elmarand, or even if they succeed, can they capture and then hold the city?' He stood and walked to the window. 'And, as you say, is the Archon wise to open the gate? What if these seeds of doubt he promises to sow, cannot find fertile soil amongst the Golesh?'

Elodi nodded. 'And what if they choose not to send numbers south to retake Elmarand? Do they value the old capital? It could be a burned-out ruin for all we know.'

Bardon's shoulders dropped. 'Too many assumptions for my liking. If the Archon opens the gate and is confronted by a full-strength enemy, what chances do we have of keeping them out if a third of our force, the elites at that, are stranded in the south?' He rested his hand against the wall and turned back to Elodi. 'What strength do you command in Harlyn?'

Elodi stood and went to his side. 'Just shy of two thousand, but barely five hundred of those could be described as soldiers. The rest are mostly farmers or from the trades.'

'And how long to muster the full reserve?'

'About a week. The beacons can send the call in an hour, but those in the south of the realm can take days on foot. But' — her hand went to her mouth — 'the command brings them to Calerdorn to be allocated to the borders. That's where the threat traditionally manifests. But if we have to defend the south, we'll need a new signal.'

'It's the same for Broon. We may have a larger army, but again, they're ready to head north. If the Archon can't hold the assault at the gate, and then loses the bridge, the enemy will simply split its force, strike up either side of the Kolossos, then conquer each of us at will. Alone we are not strong enough to defend, but if we join forces with Kernlow and Galabrant and send our forces south to confront the Golesh, we leave the north open.' He leaned back against the wall and closed his eyes. 'We find ourselves in a difficult position.'

Elodi took a deep breath. 'One matter still puzzles me, something the Archon has failed to mention.'

Bardon opened his eyes. 'Yes, I too noticed. Am I to assume you refer to who leads the Golesh?'

She nodded. 'He talks of the hordes and their unruly nature, but if he believes they pose such a threat, surely they have a leader to devise and command the invasion.'

'And I would stake all the riches of Broon, granted, that's no fortune these days, it's the same leader responsible for splitting the Seven Realms, and' — his face paled — 'had the power to summon the drayloks.'

Elodi froze. She recalled the embroidered gold and red braids depicting the flames spurting from their cavernous mouths. 'I... I thought the tapestry was a work of art, and the hags more of a symbol than for real.'

Bardon slumped. 'I'm afraid I wasn't entirely honest with you. And for that, I offer my apologies. I used to think the same as you. Then it became a hope, then a desperate wish they were from the weaver's imagination.' He sighed. 'But now…?'

She stared at him. 'You're saying the tapestry is accurate? These creatures are—?'

'The *Draedalak.*'

Elodi's scalp tingled. 'I don't know that word.' But as she spoke, deep down, part of her recoiled at the name.

Bardon's eyes widened. 'Few do, and nor should they. It's the old name for drayloks which I will not readily repeat.' He turned back to the forest. 'My father spoke of such matters shortly before he passed on. I must admit at the time I took it to be the ramblings of a dying man beset with fever, but a dread has taken hold of my heart these last few months, and with the news of activity beyond the gate, his last mutterings now seem all too real.'

Elodi placed her hand on his shoulder. 'Of what did he speak?'

Bardon returned to the table and refilled his glass. He offered more to Elodi; she understood from his gesture she would be wise to accept. He sat and leaned back in his chair. 'There are records in the Hall of Scrolls, rescued from the fires of Elmarand, that speak of such manifestations. My father was a scholar researching the history of the first two realms. He claimed he read four recovered scrolls from Elmarand here in the archives, but I've since tried and failed to locate them. However, on my last visit I discovered a room under lock and key, I suspect what he read may well be secured behind that door.'

Elodi felt the chill seeping into her bones. 'And you believe him?'

'Unfortunately, yes I do. My father had kept it to himself, hoping these drayloks had long since disappeared from this world, and that he fretted over nothing. Back then I guess it was the least of his worries with other

139

pressing troubles of the day and no sign of the enemy for centuries. But now the Archon speaks of an invasion… it feels all too real again.'

Elodi collapsed back into her chair. 'What do we know of them?'

'Little, especially about their origin. But on one issue, the tales make clear — they cannot cross into this realm unless summoned by a great power, and then only for a short time. And those who offer that invitation must have the strength to firstly control, then resist their fury if not satiated. And, if all three fought at the last battle against the Archon, the summoner would have commanded immense power to bring them at their bidding.'

Elodi set her glass on the table. 'Yet, the Archon defeated them. We must take encouragement from his success.'

Bardon nodded. 'Yes, but defeat may be too strong a word. He held them at bay and barely escaped with his sanity, and he didn't, ultimately, face the one who summoned them.'

Elodi frowned. 'But why didn't their leader challenge the Archon? The beasts would have severely weakened him, all but guaranteeing the enemy a victory.'

'I can only assume they would have been occupied dealing with the drayloks, and therefore unable take part in the battle in person. The act of the summons alone must have taken its toll.' He tried to raise a smile. 'Perhaps, if we're lucky, the beasts slayed their summoner when they were denied their prey.'

'Then why does the Archon not mention this person, being or whatever they are? Even if to dismiss the myths and give us less to fret over.'

Bardon looked to the window. 'My father believed the Archon has little recollection of what happened on the Gormadon Plain. The few who prevailed on the battlefield long enough to witness the horror have long since passed away. Whether they contributed to the archives or the making of the tapestry, we don't know. Only the Archon survives those dark days.'

'And if these… what did you call them?'

'Drayloks will suffice.'

'If these drayloks survive to this day, can they be called upon again?'

'That is my concern.' Bardon stood. 'We must seek an audience with the Archon, hopefully alone. After all these years, I remain wary of Kernlow and Galabrant. They're old and stuck in their ways and, unfortunately, will believe without question anything the Archon chooses to tell them.' He turned to leave. 'I shall speak to the Proctor, or if that comes to nothing, the Castellan.'

Elodi hooked her arm under his and walked him to the door. 'Will he listen?'

He exhaled. 'I take encouragement from the Archon making his invasion plan known, be it at this late stage. Let us hope he is open to our concerns.' Bardon's hand paused on the handle. He looked back to Elodi. The lines on his face softened. 'Not the easiest time for you to take the title of Lady Harlyn, but, if we can work together it will make it easier for us both.'

Elodi took his hand. 'Thank you, and yes, you have my full support.' She blushed. 'For what it's worth.'

Bardon patted her hand. 'More than you think.' He turned, and she watched him leave, seeming more stooped than when he had entered.

Elodi closed the door and rested her back against the ancient carvings. She yawned and stretched. 'To bed, I think.' She jumped at the knock at the door. She opened it. 'Did you forget—?'

'Sorry to trouble you at this late hour, ma'am.' An old man stood fidgeting at her door with his eyes fixed on the floor. He wore the uniform of the Castellan's men.

She straightened. 'Well? What is so important at this late hour?'

He glanced both ways. 'Begging your pardon, ma'am but… but I have news, ma'am… about your father.'

16. A CHANGE OF PLAN

Toryn had woken during the night, convinced he had heard footsteps outside their shelter. He had left Hamar to sleep and ventured out onto the ledge alone, but the impatient waters below had drowned out any other sounds of the night. The moon had gone and no matter how hard he peered out of the corners of his eyes, he could see nothing. A whole nest of droogs could have slithered along the ledge and he would have been none the wiser.

'Not too far to go now.' Toryn looked up to see Hamar pointing ahead. 'See.' They had reached the fork in the ravine in good time that morning, despite the heavy rain drenching the path. The ledge had finally widened as the slopes had retreated and opened up the sky. Hamar turned. 'This will take us down to the bridge where we can cross the river.'

'Be good to get out of this rain.' Toryn shivered as another trickle ran down his back. 'I'm soaked through.'

'We'll soon dry off in front of a roaring fire.' Hamar winced as he rubbed his back. 'Looking forward to sleeping on a bed again.' He groaned. 'If there's one thing I miss when I'm on the road, it's a comfortable bed, and it seems more desirable as the years pass.' Hamar tightened the straps on his backpack and set off.

'Will we find a bed?'

'My old friend, Jacken will put us up at his place.'

Toryn laughed. 'You have a lot of *old* friends.'

'Comes from being an Archonian, never forget your fellow guards who've stood by your side and had your back in sticky situations. Mind you, it's been a good few years since I last saw him, but once a brother-in-arms,

143

always a brother-in-arms.'

Toryn's stomach rumbled. 'It's been a while since we've had a decent meal.'

'Now there we're in luck. The pasture is good in the valley. Explains why it's the best tasting meat in the land.' He licked his lips. 'Could murder a nice bit of roast beef.'

With a spring in their step, they soon reached the lane leading to the bridge. Toryn tapped his foot. 'Good to be on a proper road. Feels like we're back in the land of the living again.'

Hamar laughed. 'We've not been gone two weeks yet. You should try living in the wilds for six months at a stretch.'

Toryn sniffed the air. 'I can smell the roasting beef on the spit.'

Hamar frowned. 'I can smell something, but that ain't my dinner cooking.' They hurried on and rounded the bend. Toryn's heart sank; the pall of thick, black smoke billowing high into the air, and the anguished mooing of cattle, dashed any hope of sleeping in a comfortable bed. Hamar's shoulders sagged. 'Oh no, not here, not this place.' They hastened across the bridge and passed a small fenced field. Hamar glanced at the cows. 'That's odd. The raiders have left them alone.' He squinted at the gate. 'Come on, there must be survivors in need of help.'

Toryn felt for his sword as they passed beneath the shadow of the smoke. 'Is it safe?'

Hamar tilted his head. 'It's quiet. If the raiders were still here, they'd be singing their rotten throats raw, and taunting the poor souls chosen for their games.'

'But we're many leagues from the border. Do they usually come this far?'

Hamar stared back down the road. 'Not to a settlement of this size. No, this is troubling. I hear they're bolder of late, but I can't think how they came to be this far south and, in such numbers to do this.' He stopped and kneeled to examine the road. 'I don't get it.'

Toryn spat out the acrid taste of the smoke and wiped his mouth. 'Get what?'

'There's no sign of a struggle. This is the only way into the place, but all I can see is tracks from wagons.' He held out a hand. 'Help me up, lad.'

Toryn took Hamar's arm and pulled him to his feet. 'Could they have hidden in the wagons?'

'They would've searched wagons coming through the gate, and if they'd found any brigands, there'd have been a skirmish.' He scratched his head. 'If only a dozen Ruuk came through, you'd see signs of their rough-shod boots in the dirt. But they'd need more than that. This place may be a backwater, but the old guards living here could easily handle raiders. Unless...' Hamar turned back to the entrance. 'We need to find Jacken. Perhaps he can shed light on what happened here.'

Toryn could not take his eyes from the smoldering buildings. The thatched roofs had gone, leaving open shells with blackened struts jutting up to the sky. He gawped at the senseless destruction — this could have been his own village. And what had happened to the people?

Hamar coughed. 'I'd say this took place late yesterday judging by the embers.' He pointed to the pall of smoke hanging over the village. 'But something still burns.'

Toryn searched the gaps between the buildings. 'Where is everyone?'

Hamar shook his head. 'This is strange. You'd expect to find the dead and injured from both sides lying where they fell. They wouldn't have had time to bury them yet.' He took a deep breath and stuck his head inside the door of the nearest house, then walked to the next, returning while shaking his head. 'Both empty.' He pointed down

145

the street and strode with a purpose. 'We'll try the square. If there was a last-ditch attempt to save the place, that's where they would've rallied to stand any—' He stopped. 'What the…?'

A few paces ahead, a blackened hole several feet deep obliterated the path. Toryn walked to the edge. His stomach churned as he peered at the bottom. 'It's like a giant rock landed on this spot.' He turned to Hamar. 'Have you seen anything like this before?'

Hamar stared over the rim. 'Never. Can't think what could have done this. We have trebuchets at the gate, but they couldn't hurl a shot as large' — he turned back towards the stockade — 'or as far. Besides, I doubt you'd drag an enormous war machine to this place. It's hardly a fortress.'

Toryn paced around the perimeter of the hole. He steadied himself as his head spun. 'It's still hot. And look at the ground, it's like glass.'

Hamar staggered across the earth, thrown up at the edges. 'Let's check the square. It seems to be where the smoke is coming from.' They found their way to the opposite lip of the hole and walked the short distance to the center of Greendell. The square was twice the size of Toryn's village, but no bunting brought color to the scene. Long gouges lined the charred ground as if torn up by huge clawed hands. At the center, a smoking mound marked where the flagpole would have flown the colors of the village.

Hamar put his hand on Toryn's shoulder. 'You wait here.'

'But—?'

He clenched Toryn's arm. 'Stay put.' He watched as Hamar's hunched figure made its way to the mound. He stopped at the edge; his hand went to his mouth. Hamar moved to the other side and kneeled. He reached forward and took a small object from the smoldering heap. He held it up to the light, then staggered forward. Toryn took a step to help him. Hamar's voice croaked. 'Stay there! Don't come over.' He stood and shuffled back to Toryn. As he neared, Toryn could hear Hamar muttering to himself. 'This is evil, they didn't deserve this...' He stopped a few paces away — his eyes wide; his head shaking. 'Get me to the other side of the bridge please, Tor.'

Toryn looked over his shoulder to the square. 'What is it, Hamar? What did you see?'

'Please, get me away from this place.'

Toryn took his arm and felt Hamar shake. He helped him out of the settlement, over the bridge, and lowered him to the soft, grassy bank. Hamar stared at the ground. Toryn lit a small fire and heated a mug of water from the river, while Hamar sat muttering to himself. Toryn added a shot of their emergency liquor from his flask. 'Here, drink this.'

Hamar gladly accepted the mug and gulped it down. He wiped his lips. 'Sorry about that, lad. It's been many years since I've seen anything so grim.'

'What was on the bonfire?'

Hamar choked. 'They didn't deserve that.' Tears brimmed. He opened his hand. The object from the ashes glinted in the pale sunlight.

Toryn took it. 'You have one of these.' The old man's hands went to his face as he sobbed. Toryn sat beside him and rested his hand on Hamar's shoulder and said nothing. He watched as a light wind picked up and lifted the smoke, sending it down the valley as if washing the evil away.

Hamar cleared his throat. 'It's a long service medal.' He held out his hand and Toryn placed it back in his palm. Hamar turned it over to reveal a name. 'We joined at the same time and went through training together.' He wiped his face. 'Jacken survived many skirmishes, including Wyke

Wood. He was injured a dozen times but always fought back, only' — his jaw clenched — 'only for some coward to throw him onto a bonfire when he deserved a quiet end to his life. My old friend didn't even get to die with his sword in his hand.' Hamar turned to Toryn. 'That's no way for a man like him to go, or the others. These were good, hard-working, honest folk.'

Toryn's mouth soured with the taste of the dead. He spat. 'Was every poor soul from the village on the mound?'

'No' — Hamar took a deep breath — 'mainly the older folk from what I could tell. I hope the rest fled, otherwise the scoundrels would've snatched them for some foul purpose.'

Toryn stood. 'The Ruuk do this?'

Hamar raised his hand to the village. His arm dropped. 'This isn't the work of the usual brigands.' He struggled to his feet. 'Yes, the Ruuk burn and pillage, but they wouldn't destroy the place, they'd leave it so they could come back the following year when their bellies are empty. And they wouldn't murder the elderly.' He held his chin. 'It don't make sense. The livestock are still in the field. You'd need a small army to overwhelm the place and cause this much havoc. There must be sixty head of cattle in the meadow, but they haven't touched them. The gate is still secured. An army would have taken them for the road, or at least slaughtered and roasted a few after their victory.'

Toryn looked back to the charred village. 'Do you have an idea who might—?'

'Norgog.' Hamar's lips curled. 'From the far north. The Ruuk differ from one clan to the next. Those close to the border are much like us, except they don't have a decent bone in their body. Farther north, on the other side of the Trench, the clans become more troll-like, perhaps related in ways to cobtrolls but bigger. While many of the Ruuk clans can be a handful, they're nothing like the

Norgog. They're from the places well beyond the boundaries of our maps. We had another name for them: Hammerskulls.'

Toryn's shoulders bunched. 'Wouldn't want to meet them on a dark night.'

'You're not wrong, lad. The hammer is their weapon of choice, and their heads sort of look like one.' He winced. 'Flat faces, elongated skulls, and they have a tough, gray skin that requires a keen blade to pierce. But you need a thick skin to survive in the frozen lands.' His hand gripped the hilt of his sword. 'They're shorter than other Ruuk, but broader, stronger, and aggressive. It takes a lot more force to bring down one of those beasts. But I've only ever seen them across the border, and never this far from their lands. Too warm for them, you see.'

Toryn shivered. 'Too warm? Here?'

Hamar nodded. 'And lucky for us it is. And hopefully, if it was them, they've gone back whence they came.' He reached into his jacket and took out his pipe. He pointed the tip to the north. 'But if this is the work of the Norgog, who's commanding them? What's driving them this far south?' He scratched his head. 'But there'd still be footprints.' Hamar took out his tobacco, grimaced, and replaced it in his pocket. 'Had enough smoke for one day.' He waved his empty pipe across the valley. 'We must report this. The Archon needs to hear of this right away. Greendell has always kept to itself, only trading with a few places in the autumn. If we don't tell anyone, it could be months before anyone discovers the atrocity.'

'I thought we had to keep out of sight.'

Hamar exhaled. 'Not after this. Change of plan. This is serious. Hand me the map, lad.' Toryn unpacked the map and laid it on the grass. Hamar stooped and ran a blackened finger across the cloth. 'Drunsberg, yes, the mines at Drunsberg. It's about four days from here, maybe three if we stride out. We can take the proper road now, seeing as there's no need for stealth. They have messenger birds at the mines. They'll get word to Archonholm in under two days. If we see guards before then on the road, that will be all the better. Whoever did this will do it again. They have to be stopped.'

17. THE HORN OF ARCHONHOLM

'Tombold, ma'am.'

Elodi held out her hand to the chair. 'Please, take a seat, Tombold.'

'Thank you, ma'am.' He groaned as he lowered himself into the chair Bardon had not long vacated.

Elodi remained standing. 'What news of my late father?'

Tombold kept his eyes to the floor. 'I... I...' He moved to stand. 'I shouldn't be here, ma'am. It's wrong of me, I shouldn't have—'

'Nonsense!' Tombold froze. Elodi lowered her voice. 'Sorry, what I meant to say was, if you have news of my father you have every right to be here, regardless of the hour.' He settled back in his chair. Elodi sat opposite. 'Now please, take your time.'

Tombold took a breath and met Elodi's eyes for the first time since entering the room. 'I... pardon me, ma'am, but you have the exact same eyes as your father, kind and knowing.' He looked away. 'Begging your pardon again, ma'am.'

She edged forward and patted his hand. 'There is no need to keep *begging my pardon,* but thank you for asking.'

Tombold managed a smile. 'My pleasure, ma'am.'

Elodi sat back. 'Now, please, what of my father?'

'I shouldn't be telling you this, the Castellan will have my guts for bowstrings. Oh, begging your... I mean, sorry to bring the language of the barracks to your fair ears, ma'am.'

'Again, no need. I've heard worse.' She cleared her throat. 'My father?'

'Terrible, such a tragedy. I was fond of Lord Harlyn and feel you have a right to know.'

'Thank you, I appreciate you have taken a risk to visit, but as you say, the hour is late. Shall we start by how you knew Lord Harlyn?'

'Of course, ma'am. I was the aide assigned to him by the Castellan on his last visit. I'm way too old for most duties in the citadel. Twenty years on the road with the Archonians, and another thirty working for the Castellan has taken its toll. These days I'm not so fast with my sword, so I'm a mere aide for visiting dignitaries.'

'But surely, still an important duty.'

'Thank you for saying so, ma'am, but most of the important folk rarely speak to me, but your father was different. We spent many an hour talking well into the night. He showed an interest in my life in the citadel, and my family and children, well I say children, my sons are fine men now, both assigned to the Caerwal Gate.'

Elodi's stomach knotted. 'The Gate? General Kragan must value them highly.'

Tombold beamed. 'Oh yes, ma'am. Always ready to put their lives on the line for the Archon.'

'Well, let's hope it never has to come to that.' But in her mind, she saw iron and stone crashing down as the Golesh poured through the gap, crushing its gallant defenders with impunity. She straightened. 'We must place our faith in the Archon to protect us all.'

Tombold nodded. 'Oh, I do, ma'am, trust him with my life, and my family's.' He suddenly remembered the reason for his visit. 'Oh yes, Lord Harlyn. He had this long, private meeting with the Archon. Following that, he requested I take him to the Hall of Scrolls.'

Elodi stiffened. 'Did he say why?'

'Why? To me?' He chuckled. 'We spoke of many things but not of affairs relating to governing the realms, ma'am.'

'Of course not, and I apologize for interrupting. Please, go on.'

'Unnecessary, ma'am.' He took a breath. 'Well, I did as he asked, took him to the archives and waited outside. He had been gone a good few hours when suddenly he returned. I have to say, he didn't seem his usual self, looked a little pale even. I enquired about his health, seeing as it's part of my duty, but he insisted he was fine and dismissed me for the night.'

Elodi held his gaze. 'And this was the night he…?'

Tombold's head dipped as he whispered. 'Yes, ma'am. I'm afraid so.'

'What happened?' Elodi fought to slow her breathing. 'Do you know of his actions after you left him?'

He rubbed his hands together. 'Please, ma'am, know that I didn't abandon your father. I was simply carrying out his instructions. Had I thought he was in danger, I would have stayed with him.'

'No, of course I understand. I can see you're a man of honor, a man who keeps his word.'

Tombold bowed his head. 'Again, thank you, ma'am.' He ran his hand down his face. 'It was a day or two after he… fell, Arawold, a guard from the Lower Gate, came to see me.'

'The Lower Gate?' Her grip on the arms of the chair tightened. 'Then this guard would've had a perfect view of the bridge.'

'Err… yes, ma'am, but I'm afraid his captain relieved him from duty before… what happened to your father. No, he came to tell me Lord Harlyn had requested entry to the pass in the early hours of the morning, shortly after he'd dismissed me for the night.'

'How? I thought only the Castellan's men had access to the pass.'

Tombold chuckled. 'Goes to show the benefit of taking an interest in people's affairs. You know your father. Few could say no, and I guess Arawold was the same.'

Elodi sighed. 'That is certainly true.'

'But I'm afraid on this occasion I believe it's what led to his death.'

'I guess he would not have been on the bridge during the gale.'

Tombold frowned. 'Gale?'

Elodi's stomach tightened. 'I'm led to believe there was a storm.'

His brow furrowed. 'Storm, ma'am? The night was still with a full moon like tonight. I'd seen Lord Harlyn walk across the bridge many times. He enjoyed watching the sunset from the middle, and he was as sure-footed as a mountain goat.'

Elodi stood. Her hand went to her mouth. 'Then it can't have been an accident.'

'That's why I'm here, ma'am. I would have come sooner, but the Castellan had put me on duties outside the citadel. I'm convinced your father's death was no accident. How could it be on such a still and clear night?'

Her heart raced. 'This changes everything.' Elodi stood and walked to the window. 'We live in dangerous times if we're not safe in Archonholm.' She turned to Tombold. 'How could a visit to the gate result in his death?'

Tombold shrugged. 'Now that I can't rightly say. The Castellan does not tolerate visits by unauthorized people, especially as the Caerwal Tower was close to completion at the time, but it's not punishable by death. Besides, there would have been a trial had he done wrong. Something's not right. Arawold said your father had been gone two hours before he himself was relieved of his duty. He was reluctant to report his entry, seeing as it would have got him into trouble, but he did all the same. Had to, really. I guess he thought Lord Harlyn would have been back before the morning when his duty would normally end.'

Elodi turned back to the room. 'Is that unusual? To be replaced before the end of the watch?'

Tombold nodded. 'Yes, ma'am, most unusual, and more so seeing it was a Castellan man replacing Arawold. It would normally be a man from the garrison. But it could be word reached the citadel Arawold had broken with correct procedure and had to be relieved, but nothing else was ever said about it. Not even called before his captain to explain his actions.'

A distant rumble caught her attention. She quizzed Tombold. 'Is that thunder? There's not a cloud in the sky.'

'It happens this time of year, but more often in late summer. Must be coming from over the mountains.'

Elodi peered through the window. As a child, she loved to watch the storms roll in from the sea. While other children cowered under their blankets, she had stood on the balcony to feel the full force of the wind and watch the towering waves glisten in the flashes of lightning. She stepped onto the window ledge as another thunderclap, this time louder, rolled over the city. She gazed up at the sky. 'No sign of lightning, must still be some distance away.'

Tombold cocked his head. He stood. 'Begging your pardon, ma'am, but I'm not so sure that is thunder.'

Elodi turned her back on the window. 'Then what could it be? It sounds like it's coming from the south.'

He stammered. 'Probably nothing to worry about, ma'am, I'm sure it's—'

Her breath caught in her throat as the rising call of a horn echoed through the corridors outside. The door knocked. 'What do you think it could be?'

155

The blood drained from Tombold's face. His mouth gaped. 'Well, I never... I never thought I'd live to see the day, ma'am. I never' — he straightened — 'we must go, we must go to the Great Hall. It's the safest place in the citadel.' He turned as the door burst open. A Palace Guard staggered to a halt. For a moment, he looked confused by Tombold's presence, but waved his hands. 'Quickly, ma'am, the Archon has decreed an emergency. You are to make your way to the Great Hall.'

Elodi turned to Tombold. 'What is it? What does that horn mean?'

Tombold took her gently by the arm but forcefully led her to the door. 'Ma'am, it's the Horn of Archonholm.' His voice broke. 'The Caerwal Gate, ma'am, it's... it's under attack.'

'Your sons!'

'They know their duty, ma'am. Mine is to ensure everyone gets to the hall.'

Elodi released her arm. 'Thank you. I too have my duty. Let us make haste.'

Outside, a palace aide tried to calm and organize the people rushing from their rooms, but his pale face and wide eyes fooled no one. Elodi followed the lead of Tombold and climbed the stairs leading to the Great Hall. Ahead, a large man stood panting. Elodi drew level. 'Lord Kernlow, do you need help?'

He struggled to breathe as he leaned against the wall. 'You... you go on.' Kernlow coughed and spat out his words. 'I'll hold those savages here for a while.'

Elodi almost laughed before she could see he was serious. 'We'll be in safe hands then.' She motioned to an approaching aide to assist the lord. Elodi turned and reached the top of the stairs with Tombold, along with many inhabitants of the citadel bustling about in shock. She scanned the throng but failed to locate Bardon. On the wall, the eyes of the tapestry demons burned with renewed fury as if sensing their time had come. Her heart pounded. Had someone summoned the *Draedalak*? Could these monstrosities be raging at the defenders of the gate at this very moment?

She spun away. Wendel arrived. He struggled to regain his breath and for the first time in Elodi's life, had no words of advice to offer. Tombold tugged at her arm as she realized she had stopped. 'Quickly, ma'am.'

The crowd swelled through the doors into the hall. Close to a hundred had already gathered beneath the cavernous ceiling. Elodi stood on her toes but still could not find Bardon. A cry went up from a window. She rushed to see what had caused the commotion and peered over the heads of those with the same idea. The moon picked out the thin silvery line of the bridge spanning the black gash of the chasm. A single figure ran across the bridge towards them, bearing a torch above their head. The runner stumbled. Elodi held her breath, fearing he would fall and share the same fate as her father. Thankfully, the runner regained their feet and made it to the north side.

Some left, satisfied the runner would come to the hall to report events. Elodi and Tombold edged forward into the gaps left behind. Elodi took eight paces into the recess before reaching the window, noting it was twice the depth of the wall on the north side. She pressed her face against the glass. From the height of their position, she could see over the top of the Lower Gate and a fair distance down the pass. She gasped. The mountain walls of the pass flickered. Fire! She turned to Tombold. He caught her eye. His jaw clenched as his shoulders bunched. Elodi squinted to see the Caerwal Gate, but the sides diverged and only the faint orange sky could hint of the horror Tombold's sons faced.

The clattering of hooves brought her attention to the foot of the bridge. Tombold swallowed. 'That'll be the First Horse, ma'am.' Elodi craned her neck to see them forming into lines. He continued. 'Take comfort, they're two hundred and forty of the finest horses and fighters in the land, ma'am.'

She watched as a few horses resisted their riders' efforts to get them into position. Her hands pressed to the window. What would be on their minds? Since their early childhood, they would have been told the stories of the evil beyond the gate. Now they sat in their glistening armor on jittery horses, about to ride into the domain of their nightmares. She turned to Tombold. 'But what can they do against the machines the Archon has seen?' She saw a flicker of doubt pass across his face.

Tombold pushed out his chest and pulled back his shoulders. 'They're well-trained, ma'am. Their speed and agility will disrupt an advance long enough to ready our weapons on this side. I'm sure we can rely on the Archon.' But Elodi watched the skies glow brighter as the fires spread at the gate and hoped Tombold had not misplaced his faith.

The anxious voices of the hall faded. The door at the opposite end opened. Without looking, Elodi guessed the Archon had entered. In silence, he took his place on the dais and stood by his seat behind the long table. The Proctor appeared by his side. He raised his hands. 'Please settle, the Archon assures me you are not in immediate danger.'

'Thank you, Proctor.' The people in the room stood taller as the Archon's voice eased their anxiety. 'I can tell you the Caerwal Gate is *not* breached or damaged.' The murmur rose before the Archon raised a hand. 'What you see is the result of two speculative projectiles hurled over the gate, nothing more. Yes, there are casualties, but the defenses remain intact, and the mustering of the First Horse is purely a precaution, a drill, if you please.'

General Kragan entered. The crowd parted as he marched to the Archon's side. The general spoke in a low voice as the Archon nodded. He waved his general away and turned to the hall. 'Ladies and Gentlemen, if you would proceed to the terrace, General Kragan informs me our new weapons are moving into position and will retaliate within minutes.' He clapped his hands. 'I'm sure it will be quite a spectacle as we rain fire and destruction down on their vile war machines.' He turned to the general and raised an eyebrow. 'It will be an impressive show of strength, and, one I'm sure will set back the Golesh's preparations and make them think twice about repeating such an act.' With that, he turned and left the hall.

A dozen aides lined up and ushered the people out onto the terrace overlooking the Caerwal Mountains. Elodi shivered as she strode into the night, but not from the chill in the air. She jumped as Lord Kernlow took her hand, raised and kissed it. 'A pleasure to finally meet you, Lady Harlyn.'

Elodi removed her hand from his. 'But we've already... Yes, Lord Kernlow, and you as well. And thankfully, you appear to have no need to defend the stairs.'

Kernlow shook a big, hairy fist at the mountains. 'Shame, I stood ready for them. They'd have got a bloody nose if they'd tried to pass me.'

Elodi fought the urge to grin. 'Yes, I'm sure they would.'

Kernlow clicked his fingers at Tombold. 'You there, would you be a good man and fetch the good lady and myself a warm drink?'

Elodi held up her hand. 'He's here at my behest. His sons are at the gate, he's not on duty as such.'

Kernlow blustered. 'Not... not on duty? When is an aide not on duty?'

Elodi insisted, 'When he is here at my bidding.' She turned. 'Lord Kernlow, I trust you know my Chief Advisor, Wendel. I'm sure you two have issues to discuss considering what's unfolding at the gate.'

A shout went up from the terrace. Elodi spun around as two white arcs streaked through the night. The sky flashed as the projectiles erupted, then silence, followed by a muffled roar seconds later. Kernlow cheered as two more streaks raced south and exploded. But Elodi could only think about the poor souls stuck in the middle of the destruction.

'Ha!' Kernlow's substantial frame nudged her, almost knocking her from her feet. 'That'll teach the brutes to attack us, eh?'

'Yes, I suppose it will.' Elodi felt for Tombold; his face a mixture of elation and dread. She turned to Kernlow. 'I only hope it doesn't encourage them to accelerate their plans to attack.'

His gray eyebrows knotted. 'Nonsense, my dear. We'll have set them back weeks, possibly even months. And if they try it again, we'll let them have a few more volleys.' He splayed his fingers. 'Boom! Ha, I bet they didn't expect that.' Kernlow chuckled. 'Boom! Never saw it coming.'

Elodi caught Tombold's eye. 'Well, I hope you're right for all our sakes. Now if you will excuse me, I will retire, it's been a long day.'

Kernlow attempted a bow. 'Of course, my Lady.' He straightened as best he could and beamed. 'But what a day' — he pumped his fists — 'an historic day at that. And if I may be so bold, I would—'

'Wendel?' Elodi turned away, pretending not to hear what Kernlow was about to be so bold about. 'Seeing as you're both here, would you be so kind to speak to Lord

Kernlow about plans to strengthen our shared border fences?'

Wendel stuttered. 'I... I thought it might be worthwhile to discuss—'

'Later. For now, in the light of what has just occurred, I think it's wise to speed up work on the border defenses.'

He nodded. 'Of course, ma'am'

'Thank you.' She turned. 'Tombold, would you be so kind to escort me back to my room?' She allowed him to lead the way through those remaining on the terrace and back into the Great Hall. Once inside, she placed a hand on his shoulder. 'I can make my way from here. You must go to your wife and find out about your sons.'

Tombold rubbed the back of his neck. 'That's very kind of you.' He held out his palm. 'I will walk with you, if it's alright with you, ma'am? I shall be going the same way.'

'Of course, it will be a pleasure to have your company. As Lord Kernlow stated, it's been an historic day.' She stopped. 'Have you seen Lord Broon this evening?'

'I passed him on the way to your room, ma'am.'

Again, Elodi scanned the many faces in the corridor. 'I can't think where he'd be. I need to speak to him. If you see him on your travels, could you be so kind to ask him to come to my room?'

'Yes, ma'am, I'll—'

'Tom!' A guard with a blackened face rushed over to them.

'Arawold.' Tombold hugged the man. He stood back. 'Were you at the gate?'

Arawold struggled to catch his breath. 'I'd arrived minutes before. It all happened so fast, no one saw them coming. The first exploded at the foot of the gate, must be at least fifty dead and twice that injured.' Tombold's head dropped. Arawold grabbed his arm. 'But not your lads, Tom, not yours. Bryok escaped without a scratch, Edwald took a knock but he'll recover.'

Tombold tilted back his head, briefly closing his eyes. 'Thank you, Woldie, you don't know how good that is to hear.' He placed his hand on Arawold's shoulder. 'And your lads?'

'Off duty and in the shelter, thankfully. But it doesn't look good for Dravo's boy. He's in a bad way, don't think he'll make it to morning.'

Tombold winced. 'Poor lad, so young.' He glanced back to Elodi. 'You said two strikes, what of the second?'

'Hit the tower. The roof collapsed crushing dozens more below.'

Elodi touched his arm. 'And the gate? Is it damaged?'

Arawold noticed Elodi for the first time. He took off his cap. 'No, ma'am, I don't think the enemy targeted the gate, just slung their shots over the top. I guess to let us know they mean business.'

Elodi noticed Tombold glance over his shoulder. 'It's late, please go to your wife and find your sons, thank you for your' — she checked Arawold — 'candor earlier, I look forward to speaking again.'

'My pleasure, ma'am.' He turned and called back. 'And if I see Lord Broon, I'll be sure to pass on your request.'

Elodi pushed back the blankets, kicked out her legs and gave up trying to sleep. Her exhausted body pleaded to rest, but her mind refused to relinquish its hold. Every time she closed her eyes, her head filled with images of the Caerwal Gate cracking asunder and fell creatures swarming through the gap. And then, Tombold's account of her father troubled her. What had he discovered that led to his death? And what of Bardon? What if he had met with the same fate as her father? Had not Bardon also visited the Hall of Scrolls?

Elodi swung her legs off the bed and stood. She threw on her gown and walked to the window. Outside, the sky to the east glowed pink as the sun prepared to bring in the new day. Elodi took the hint and walked over to her wardrobe. She ran her fingers along the dozen outfits her maid had deemed fitting for a state visit, but her hand stopped at the most practical, and one suitable for riding. Today, she first had to find Bardon, then make arrangements with Wendel to return to Calerdorn. Whatever the Archon had planned for the months prior to his *audacious* plan came second to her people. And she needed to oversee recruiting more numbers into Harlyn's small reserve army now they had sole responsibility for defending their borders and re-enforcing the Drunsberg Mine. If the mine fell into the hands of the Ruuk, and the supply of metals lost, it could severely disrupt the Archon's plans. Bardon had been right; she had held the position for just a few months and already Elodi felt the weight of her title bearing down on her aching shoulders.

18. A KEY, A SCROLL & A MASTER

The Castellan disrupted Elodi's plans before she had finished her breakfast. He had sent a messenger at first light to request she attend a private meeting. She had hoped to find Bardon beforehand, but all her efforts to locate him had come to naught. She decided against changing, preferring to remain in her everyday clothing rather than letting the Castellan think she had dressed specifically for the meeting.

As the morning bell struck, she pulled up a chair in front of the Castellan's table. His eyes wandered around the books stacked high on his desk before coming to rest on Elodi. The Castellan attempted to smile but failed, appearing embarrassed by his effort. He brushed away a strand of hair from his cloak. 'Lady Harlyn, I trust you slept peacefully after last night's events.'

Elodi lied. 'Yes, thank you, Castellan.'

'General Kragan informs me our counter-strike silenced the Golesh and will have forced them to withdraw from the gate. I doubt they'll be repeating the same error of judgement any day soon.'

'That is good news.'

'Encouraging to know our defenses can withstand such an assault.' He leaned forward; Elodi guessed the small talk was over. 'And I hope your late night visitor didn't cause you distress. I must apologize for my aide's behavior.'

Elodi stiffened. 'An apology is unnecessary. Tombold proved to be most helpful during last night's attack.'

His fingers drummed the desk. 'All the same, Tombold was wrong to visit at such a late hour. I have assigned him elsewhere. He won't bother you again.'

'I object. He was not *bothering* me, he—'

'I would advise you against entertaining men in your quarters after nightfall. Some may regard it as inappropriate.'

Elodi stood. 'I will *entertain* whoever I please, Castellan, and I would thank you for keeping your nose out of my business.'

The Castellan waved his hand. 'Lady Harlyn, please sit. I meant no offence.' Elodi sat slowly. He continued. 'But everything that goes on in this citadel *is* my business. And because I make it my business, I can assure you, you are perfectly safe—'

'More than can be said for my father.' It slipped out. Elodi had not intended to bring the subject up at this stage, but the Castellan's attitude irritated her. And she could see her statement caused obvious discomfort.

'But… by all accounts he—'

'He did *not* fall, and I can assure you he would not have taken his own life.' She took a breath. 'I am informed no storm struck on the night in question.'

'Lady Harlyn.' He placed his hands on the table. 'I am responsible for the safety of the Archon, the Council, and all who live, breathe and serve in this place. I'm sure you can appreciate the challenges that come with the post, especially with the news of activity in the south.'

'Then you have neglected your duty, otherwise my father would still be alive.'

His face reddened. 'Lady Harlyn, as you are aware, the threat is always present, there are many spies in our midst and as vigilant as I and my men can be, I cannot guarantee absolute safety at all times.'

Elodi held her nerve. 'Do you think Lord Harlyn fell' — she narrowed her eyes — 'or took his own life?' He blinked. 'Or was my father pushed off the bridge?'

'As I said, there are spies who wish to sow discord. We don't know how many agents working for the Golesh are among us.'

'Here? In Archonholm?'

The Castellan sighed. 'Yes, even in Archonholm. But I cannot let it become common knowledge. Far better don't you think for people to believe one story than to create panic. What would it do for morale if the people knew the Golesh were active within our stronghold?'

Elodi tried to read his expression. Could it have been a spy? Had her father discovered a secret in the archives forcing the enemy to have him silenced? She sensed the Castellan saw her doubt. He straightened. 'As someone who holds high office, ma'am, I'm sure you can appreciate the challenges I face every day. I must keep order and maintain the people's faith in the Archon for the good of all the realms. How am I to achieve that if people are suspicious of the person working next to them? And this leads me to the purpose of this meeting.' He picked up a sheet of paper from his desk, closing the matter of her father's death. 'Do you know of Lord Broon's activities last night?'

'No.' The Castellan held her gaze. She stuttered. 'You surely don't think he had anything to do with the attack on the gate?'

'No, of course not. But last night came as a shock, and as of now, I know the actions of all those in the citadel, all that is, except Lord Broon.' He lowered his voice. 'Therefore, I cannot be certain of his well-being.' He scratched at a knot in the wood of his desk. 'Have you seen the lord since the incident at the gate?'

Elodi glanced at the gray mountains outside the window behind the Castellan. 'No, I have not.'

'Then I have further investigations to carry out.' He looked back to Elodi. 'I hope we don't have another crisis on our hands.'

She tried to smile. 'I'm sure he will show up soon, he is a resourceful man.' Her jaw tightened. 'As was my father.'

Elodi stood at her window watching the last of the stubborn morning mist rise from the Foranfae Forest. Back in Calerdorn, she would stroll the ramparts high on the inner wall at dawn, but rarely saw the sun. She raised her eyes to the horizon. Many leagues to the north, her people suffered while her loyalties lay divided. Elodi had to prepare Harlyn for the coming storm, but she had to know how her father had met his end.

Without a second thought, she crossed the room and opened her door, desiring fresh air. Elodi assured the guard she did not require his attendance and strode away before he could question her judgement. Deep in thought, she rounded a corner and bumped straight into Bardon, coming the other way at speed. Without breaking step, he hooked his arm in hers, swung her around and whispered. 'To the North Terrace. We have little time.' She struggled to match his long strides, but kept pace for the sake of his urgency.

She went to speak. 'Where have you—?'

'Not here. Wait until we're alone.'

The sun had yet to reach the North Terrace, and as yet, people had stayed away. Elodi shivered in the citadel's shadow. 'Here, wear this.' Bardon removed his cloak and placed it around her shoulders.

'Thank you, it's' — she looked at his clothes — 'have you been up all night?'

He nodded as they walked to the north wall. 'I made the most of the commotion and paid a visit to the Hall of Scrolls.'

Elodi gasped. 'Were you not worried? I thought the

Golesh had breached the gate.'

'Of course, but what could I have done to make any difference? I'm surprised you didn't also make the most of the disruption.'

She leaned on the cold stone. 'I was otherwise engaged. I had another visitor after you left. He had news of my father's last moments.'

Bardon spun around. 'Who?'

'One of the Castellan's men, an aide assigned to my father.' She touched his arm. 'You must be careful. On his last night, my father visited the Hall of Scrolls, and' — her hands clenched — 'it was no accident.'

'Can you be sure?'

'The Castellan's man said there was no storm. He could not have fallen. But what did he read in the archives that sent him straight to the gate?' Elodi glanced over her shoulder. 'Please, you must be cautious.'

Bardon winced. 'It may already be too late for that. I suspect the Castellan's men are looking for me.'

'I've just come from a meeting with that odious man, and yes, he seems keen to know of your whereabouts.'

'Meeting? All because of me? I apologize for creating an awkward situation.'

She waved her hand. 'Not at all, I took the opportunity to question him about my father. But listen, this can wait, what of your evening?'

'When the alarm sounded, the guard rushed to his post and left the old Master of the Scrolls and a few young fellows in charge.' Bardon turned to face the citadel. 'Did you know the Master has to be blind?'

'That doesn't surprise me.'

Bardon sighed. 'I'm afraid I abused my position and brow-beat one of the boys to give me access to that locked room.'

'They left the key with a boy?'

'They had no choice. Apparently, the Archon has it in his possession day and night, but in the event of an imminent attack, his chief aide brings the key to the hall. The aide would prepare the most valuable, and as I suspect, sensitive archives for an evacuation. Should the horn have sounded the signal for a withdrawal, the scrolls would have gone to the Menon Gate and transported up country, but to where I can't be certain.' He laughed. 'To my good fortune the Master took ill. Must have been the shock of the alarm.'

Elodi's hands clenched. 'What did you find?'

'More than I could have hoped, and not where I'd have thought to find it. First, there's little in the manner of scrolls kept behind lock and key. Everything up to the last dozen years before the closing of the gate, and then for several decades after, are kept in the public area. But as for the fifty or so years in between' — he frowned — 'there appears to be little written history.'

'Ah yes, in Harlyn we refer to that time as the Lost Years.' Elodi fastened Bardon's cloak around her neck. 'My father said they lost much during the war, then later as the Archon recovered and the land suffered. We lost our way, our leadership, and of course, we'd lost countless thousands in the struggle in our realm alone.'

'And the same appears to be true with the archives.' Bardon nodded. 'Yes, I'm familiar with the term, but in Broon we call it the Age of Shadows.' He cocked his head. 'Have to say I prefer our name. More dramatic, don't you think?'

Elodi smiled. 'Maybe, but ours is a more accurate description.'

'I'll grant you that. But regardless of what we call it, I did not think it was as far-reaching. But with so little to show for nigh on fifty years, I must have been wrong.' He held up his finger. 'However, in a way it made my task easier. It took only an hour to check the few scrolls in the locked room. But one caught my eye, written many years *before* the gate was closed.'

Elodi could barely contain herself. 'So why would they keep them under lock and key when all other records of that time are available?'

Bardon snapped his fingers. 'Exactly! And it made for an interesting read, leading me to believe we're right in suspecting there's more to the aimless masses beyond the mountains.' He drew Elodi closer. 'From what I can make out, they had a leader, and a powerful one. But what came as a shock is—'

'Lord Broon.' They turned. A young Palace Guard strode across the terrace and came to an abrupt halt. He saluted. 'Lord Broon, the Archon requests your attendance.'

Bardon winked at Elodi. 'The Archon, no less?' He turned to the young man. 'Requests? I take it I have a choice?'

The young man stammered. 'Err, no, Lord. I believe the Archon is keen to see you this minute, sir... Lord.'

Bardon smiled. 'I understand, in fact, I would' — he glanced to Elodi — 'we would both be very *keen* to see the Archon. Please lead the way.'

19. THE ARCHON'S LAST STAND

'I see Broon and Harlyn are, as usual, thick as thieves.' Elodi felt the stone floor vibrate as the Archon spoke. He leveled his gaze and raised what would have been an eyebrow had he had a single hair on his head. He continued. 'Just like the old days before the building of the gate, I would wager. The man stood as straight as a watchtower in the center of a circular room at the top of the Archon's Tower. Elodi tried not to stare but she could not take her eyes from the markings on his skull. She had not been mistaken at the gate; they did in fact glow in the sunshine pouring through the narrow doorway behind him.

The Archon relaxed and almost managed a smile. 'I rarely allow entry to my private quarters, but these are unusual times which call for unusual deeds and, unfortunately, I cannot guarantee whose ears may overhear our conversation anywhere but here.' He fixed his eyes on Elodi; she wondered if her words with the Castellan had already reached his ears. The Archon's voice rose. 'Lady Harlyn, I trust you slept well last night despite the rash act of those brutes?'

Elodi nodded. 'Yes, thank you, Archon, it is a fine room worthy of a palace.'

'I am pleased to hear it.' The Archon stepped aside and held out a hand to the narrow door leading outside. 'Please, be my guests. We can spare a few moments before the formal part of our meeting.' Elodi stiffened. The Archon read her mind. 'It's quite safe, if a little daunting at first, but I think you'll find the view will make it worth conquering your fears.' He smiled. 'Ah yes. Perhaps, keep your eyes closed for a moment. Think of it as a test of your trust in me as I lead you outside.'

Elodi's pulse hammered in her ears as the sunlight turned her eyelids red as she shuffled out through the doorway. She slid the back of her hand along the smooth wall to her left as she followed the Archon's voice. 'You may open your eyes now, Lady Harlyn.'

Elodi blinked, unable to see anything apart from the wooden boards beneath her feet. Bardon drew a sharp breath and slipped his arm through Elodi's. 'Just a precaution.' She raised her head and grasped the rail. A bird swerved, surprised by their sudden appearance in her domain. But Elodi forgot her fear as her eyes were drawn to the sky. So much sky. Like a vast, blue dome it spanned the world, protecting the Five Realms from the unknown above its roof; only a few wispy clouds speckled the otherwise pristine ceiling. Beneath the dome, the green canopy of the mighty Foranfae Forest stretched out to the horizon, vying to draw her attention from the sky.

Bardon swayed. 'Whatever you do, don't look down.'

Elodi edged back to the solid wall behind while keeping one hand on the rail. 'I have no intention.' She gazed at the horizon beyond the forest where a faint gray smudge emerged from the far reaches of the trees. She pointed. 'Would that be the southern peaks of the Kolossos, Archon?'

'You are lucky, Lady Harlyn.' The Archon beamed, appearing to take pleasure from their awe of the view. 'It's a rare day when it's clear enough to see them, they are many, many leagues yonder.' Elodi felt the air thicken as the Archon stepped closer, as if it repelled her. 'But unless you have the power of *farsight*, you are most likely looking at a cloud.'

Elodi glanced to Bardon. 'Then it is an impressive cloud.'

The Archon placed his hands on the railing. 'I come out here every day regardless of the weather.' He took a deep breath. 'It reminds me of what I am fighting for. And' — he turned and walked around the tower — 'if you look to the south, of what I seek to resist.'

Elodi edged her way to the south side of the tower. Her jaw dropped. The view to the north inspired; the view to the south threatened. Even from the top of the tower, the mountains still dominated. Seeing them from the high vantage point gave Elodi the impression they stood even taller and steeper. Inevitably, she could not help but seek the narrow pass dissecting the Caerwals. Deep within the pass, the light from the midday sun picked out the gray stones and rusted iron of the great gate. From her elevated position, it seemed the very gods themselves had brought a slab to the world and wedged it between the steep slopes. But she could not help thinking, it appeared too small to hold back the menace in the south.

Elodi allowed herself one step away from the wall at her back to take a closer look. Were those flickers of light beyond the gate? Could they be reflections from war machines moving to their border? She swallowed as the pressure in her ears grew.

'Yes, I believe we are seeing the movements of the enemy.' She jumped; the Archon stood at her side. In the bright light, his eyes looked different. At the gate she would have described them gray as a dull blade, but now they comprised many colors that changed as his eyes moved.

She stammered, speaking before she could think. 'Are we prepared to face the challenge, Archon?'

A flicker passed across his eyes. 'Of course, Lady Harlyn.' But Elodi could see the veins in his temple bulge. He sensed her attention. 'I won't deny we face a determined, well-armed foe, but I believe my superior mind and the skill of our forces will win the day.' The pressure in her ears subsided as he turned and strode past Bardon. 'Please, follow me.'

She stopped and placed her hand on Bardon's resting on the rail. 'Can you see movement? Over the gate?'

'I'm afraid these aging eyes of mine can barely make out the gate. What do you—?'

'Lord Broon, Lady Harlyn. Here, if you please.'

Bardon spoke into Elodi's ear. 'Is it me, or is he different?'

She checked the Archon couldn't see them. 'He seems more… like us?'

He nodded. 'Maybe he doesn't feel the need to put on his airs and graces away from his subjects.'

Elodi took his arm. 'But I'd still prefer not to keep him waiting.'

The Archon stood opposite the doorway. He raised his hand to the rail. 'Please, come and see.' Bardon edged closer and peered over the edge. Elodi shuffled forward and looked down onto a courtyard surrounded by stables. A dozen knights on horseback rode slowly across the cobbled yard. As one, they leveled their lances and rode at speed towards a line of targets hanging from a beam spanning the opposite end. The Archon described the scene. 'Behold, the First Horse as you witnessed late yesterday. Two-hundred and forty of our finest knights are ready to ride to the pass at a moment's notice. They have taken an oath to lay down their lives should the Golesh break through.' He lowered his voice. 'I have their absolute loyalty. Do I have yours?'

The hairs on the back of Elodi's neck prickled. She turned, feeling suddenly vulnerable. 'You have my absolute loyalty, Archon.' He held her gaze. Elodi felt as if he searched her thoughts. 'The people of Harlyn will stand with you, whatever the danger.'

'I hope that is a vow you can keep, Lady Harlyn.' He turned. 'And you, Broon. Can I trust you in these troubled times? And before you answer, be aware the Castellan informed me of your nocturnal activities.'

Bardon moved back from the rail. 'Of course, Archon. But that does not mean I cannot follow up on my own hunches.'

'Hunches?' The Archon tilted his head. 'Perhaps you can enlighten me on these *hunches* of yours. That conveniently brings us to the formal part of our meeting.' He turned his back and entered the tower. Elodi caught Bardon's eye; the sightseeing had concluded.

The two entered the room to find the Archon already sitting on a smaller version of his chair in the Great Hall. 'Do make yourselves comfortable.' He motioned to two seats placed before him.

'Thank you.' Bardon waited for Elodi to sit before taking the seat on the left.

The Archon's eyes darted to Bardon. 'While Lady Harlyn slept peacefully in her bed last night, I am informed you chose not to avail yourself of my hospitality, preferring instead to roam the corridors.' His mouth curled at the corners. 'Would it, perchance, relate to your *hunch*?'

Bardon straightened. 'I shall get straight to the point, Archon. Please, can you clarify an issue that concerns us both?'

The Archon's jaw tightened. 'That depends on the nature of your concern.'

Bardon took a deep breath. 'Naturally, the welfare of our people is a responsibility we take seriously.'

'Of course, I would expect nothing less.'

Bardon cleared his throat. 'You speak of the Golesh as a primitive horde, but surely, Archon, they could not possibly trouble us if that were so.' He caught Elodi's eye. 'Archon, do you know who commands the force beyond

175

the gate? And would that be the same leader you faced in the last battle?'

The Archon's eyes flashed. 'I defeated…' he adjusted his robe. 'The head of the enemy forces perished on the plains of Gormadon.' Elodi held her breath. Few had heard the Archon speak of the battle.

Bardon held his gaze. 'How? Surely, a leader with the power to summon the drayloks could not be defeated by a mortal, even one such as yourself?'

'Nonsense.' The Archon waved his hand. 'And I'm surprised, no shocked, disappointed even, that a man of your standing should believe such fairytales.'

'But what of the demons? Someone wielding significant power summoned and commanded them.'

'Simply the babblings of fools.'

Elodi stuttered. 'But the drayloks were real.'

The Archon spat his reply. "Of course they were real, woman! Do you think I fought for three days against men in costume? Drayloks were a great evil, a blight on the old world, but no longer.' He lowered his voice. 'I fought them to a standstill and thus weakened them to the point they could not recover. No word has been heard of them since.'

Elodi asked, 'But why the gate? If you defeated the drayloks, why the need to retreat?'

The Archon leveled his gaze. 'May I remind you, Lady Harlyn, behind the drayloks, over eighty-thousand rabid creatures, including wykes, droogs, aralaks and other corrupt beings, howled for my head on a spike. I was exhausted, our forces all but destroyed, our armory spent. What do you suggest I should have done? Ask them politely to come back once we'd had time to recover?'

Elodi blushed. 'No, of course not, Archon. I apologize if I've caused you offence.'

Bardon stepped in. 'But what of their leader?'

The Archon edged back and waved their concern

away. 'The Golesh are leaderless, it's the sheer weight of their numbers that is a concern. Even the smallest creatures can take down one many times their size should the numbers be in their favor.'

Bardon stiffened. 'Archon. Who is Uluriel?' The hairs on the back of Elodi's neck prickled as the room chilled. The Archon sat perfectly still, but Elodi noticed his face tighten as if trying to prevent his mouth opening.

After what seemed like a full minute, the Archon blinked twice and finally spoke. 'The name means nothing to me.'

Bardon pressed. 'I found her referenced in only one scroll, but one kept under lock and key.' He leaned forward. 'The archive names her as the head of the *Order of Echoes*.'

The Archon swallowed. 'That is true.'

Elodi's stomach fluttered. 'Archon? What is... was, this Order of Echoes?'

The Archon scoffed. 'Nothing of importance.' He spoke through tight lips. 'A faction claiming to possess knowledge from the ancient days. They once had influence, but the wise leaders of the day exposed the primitive nature of their beliefs prior to the division of the Seven Realms.'

Bardon glanced to Elodi. 'But Archon, if Uluriel held a position of power before the Seven Realms failed, I would have thought you'd have knowledge of her?'

His voice recovered. 'I did not say I had no knowledge of the woman. I stated the name means nothing to me, and I will not honor it by speaking it aloud.'

Bardon caught Elodi's eye. 'So you know the name?'

'Know? Yes, of course, I know her name! But she is no more and therefore irrelevant.'

Bardon pulled a face. 'Irrelevant?' He turned and

spoke to Elodi. 'According to the archive, Uluriel rallied and led the mass armies of the Golesh.' Bardon's voice rose. 'Did she split the Seven Realms?' The Archon's jaw clenched so tight, Elodi feared his teeth would shatter. But Bardon was not prepared to let the matter go. 'Archon, did she summon the *Draedalak*?' The Archon's face reddened as his eyes faded to gray. Bardon continued. 'Did you face Uluriel on Gormadon Plain?'

'Enough!' The Archon thrust out his arm. Elodi shrank back at the force of his command. But his hand trembled. His eyes flickered, then closed. His head dropped forward.

Elodi's voice wavered. 'Archon? Are you… unwell?' But he failed to respond. The Archon sat upright with his head bowed, his lips moved but the words held no meaning. Elodi went to his side. She crouched and touched the back of his hand. 'Arc—' She jumped back as the Archon leaped to his feet. His right hand shot out as if clenching a sword; he drew his left arm across to shield his body. His gray eyes bulged.

The Archon threw back his head and bellowed. 'Begone! Begone, craven beasts.' Elodi and Bardon staggered back as his voice thundered, shaking the tower. The room darkened. The Archon's face contorted until he no longer resembled their leader. Elodi stood aghast, certain she could see the Archon in his last stand at Gormadon. He thrust the Sword of the Realms to his right and yelled. 'Rise! Rise up.' His body shook as if ready to break; his wide eyes stared, pleading for an ally to ride to his aid. But none came. The Archon flinched, ducked, crossing his arms in front of his face. His voice broke as he sobbed. 'Help me… I'm finished.' Lifeless arms dropped to his sides as tears streamed down his face. He mumbled. 'I beg you. Rise and send these demons back to the darkness.' The Archon slumped, standing as if held up by a staff.

The room lightened. The Archon's eyes opened. Elodi gasped. He appeared frightened, unsure of where he stood. Gone was his power, his authority, he stood as a hollow shell, bereft of its owner. He groaned, ran a hand down his face, turned and strode through the door. Without a pause, he climbed onto the balcony railing.

Bardon rushed to his side. 'Elodi!' He dived and caught hold of the Archon's legs as the man strove to jump. Elodi ran. She skidded to a halt, crashing into the iron railings and nearly toppled over the edge. She grabbed the Archon's robe and yanked. All three fell back, but the Archon had not given up. With surprising strength for a frail body, he twisted and pulled, trying to break free of their hold. But Bardon was strong. He held firm, and with Elodi's help they dragged him back inside. Elodi slammed the door shut, and with that, the fight left the Archon. He lay panting and sobbing on the floor. Bardon stared at Elodi. 'What...? What just happened?'

'I really don't know. Let's sit him down. It's unbecoming for him to be on the floor.' The Archon flinched, but otherwise seemed oblivious to their handling. They eased him into his chair and stood back. A trickle of saliva ran from the corner of his mouth, down his chin and onto his robe. Elodi examined his face. 'Should we fetch a healer?'

'I think it wise if we keep this to ourselves for the moment.'

'Can he recover from this?'

He shrugged. 'The Archon has the power to heal, but whether he can heal himself is another matter.'

Elodi stood and let her head settle. She sat on the chair next to the Archon. 'The mention of Ulu... that woman must have triggered the memory. I would say he was re-living the battle on the plain.'

Bardon shook his head in amazement. 'I can't begin to imagine what he must have endured in those three days he held the enemy at bay.'

Elodi stood and blocked the door to the balcony. 'Just in case he tries that again when he wakes.' She nodded to the Archon. 'I wonder if he has buried the memory deep to stop this happening.'

Bardon peered into the Archon's face. 'He must have been successful until our visit.' He carefully turned their leader's head. 'I can't see any sign of injury.'

The Archon's eyelids flickered. His lips moved, but he made no sound. Bardon stepped back as his eyes opened. The Archon looked about the room, appearing as if lost.

Elodi stayed by the door. 'Are you well, Archon?' He blinked. She glanced to Bardon. 'You... passed out. Lord Broon and I were troubled by your distress.'

The Archon sat upright and straightened his robe. 'You need not concern yourselves.'

Bardon frowned. 'But Archon, I think it would be wise to see a healer. You just tried to throw—'

'No need, Broon.' His voice recovered. He held up his hand. 'This...' the Archon regarded Bardon and Elodi as if trying to recall the reason for their presence. He carefully climbed to his feet and walked to the back of the room, running his hand along the wall to steady his wavering stance. He pulled a braided cord and turned to Elodi. 'This matter is closed. My man will escort you back to your quarters.'

Elodi stopped at the tapestry of the battle. 'Thank you. I will spend a few moments here with Lord Broon instead of returning to my room.'

The tall Palace Guard hesitated. 'The Archon instructed me to escort you back to your quarters, ma'am.' He turned to Bardon. 'My Lord.'

She looked to the wall. 'It's but a short walk from here, and I wish to take courage from the Archon's glorious victory.'

'As you wish, ma'am.' He turned as if to leave but changed his mind; suddenly he did not seem so assured in his palace finery. 'I... I'm not sure if it's my place to ask, but as my sole duty is to ensure the Archon's safety, I would value your judgment.' He checked no one else listened. 'I could not help but overhear the Archon's distress in your meeting.' He glanced to the tapestry. 'Is the Archon... is... our leader unwell?'

Elodi read Bardon's thoughts. She spoke quietly to the guard. 'The Archon is under great strain at present, but I'm sure we can rely on him to lead us through the next few difficult months.'

'Pardon me, ma'am, but this isn't the first time this has happened.'

Elodi's chest tightened. 'When? How often?'

'It's the nights, ma'am.' He leaned closer. 'A guard stands outside the Archon's quarters whenever he is inside. Only three share this duty, myself included. I've done this for nigh on twenty-five years, but lately we've noticed his discomfort when he sleeps.'

Bardon held the man's gaze. 'Discomfort? Does he have nightmares?'

'When I say sleep, the Archon doesn't sleep like you or I, Lord. He does not have a bed. He sits in his chair and goes into a trance. Most nights I can hear him talking the entire time' — he blushed — 'but please note, I make no attempt to listen in on his thoughts. The door is thick, and we're instructed only to enter at the Archon's request.'

Bardon raised his hand. 'I would expect no less from a Palace Guard of your standing.'

The man relaxed. 'Thank you, Lord.'

Elodi placed her hand on his arm. 'We appreciate your

loyalty to the Archon, but we too share your concern. Could you elaborate on what you referred to as the Archon's discomfort?'

'He's always talked, but these last few months it's become nothing short of what I can only describe as panic in his voice.'

Elodi's skin prickled. 'Panic?'

'He shouts, ma'am, and often I detect two voices. It sounds as if another is in the room.'

Elodi frowned. 'Yet there's only one entrance.'

'Two, actually.' Bardon explained. 'There's the door to the balcony. But I guess you could hardly call that an entrance.'

The guard stiffened. 'I may have misled you, Lord. It sounds like he's arguing with himself, but in two distinct voices.'

Bardon glanced at Elodi before asking his question. 'And can you hear what is being said?'

'Only the odd words, Lord. *Begone, arise,* and lately I've heard him yell, *imposter.* But scream would be a better description.' He glanced to the tapestry. 'I hope that helps.'

Bardon kept his voice low. 'Thank you, and again, we appreciate your loyalty and concern for the Archon's well-being. And please, do inform either myself or Lady Harlyn if you witness other such episodes.'

Elodi watched the guard leave. 'In a selfish way, his account makes me feel a little relieved. At least we know the mention of Uluriel alone didn't cause his distress.'

Bardon took her hand. 'I have to agree. And we've learned the enemy were not a leaderless rabble.'

Elodi looked back to the tapestry. 'I wonder if he relives the battle every night.'

'I'm amazed he can still function if that is the case.' Bardon's eyes moved across the scene of the battle. 'Does Uluriel yet survive to lead them to this day?'

Elodi shuddered. 'The weavers may not have done those beasts justice judging by the Archon's reaction.' She examined the tapestry. 'But I imagine it would be difficult to capture their likeness with mere thread.'

Bardon sighed. 'I wonder how much he remembers of those days. From what we witnessed, I'd say he came close to losing his mind.'

'And close to losing the battle.' Elodi studied the woven shadows at the Archon's side. 'Who was he calling upon to *rise and send the demons back to the darkness?*'

'If the accounts are correct, he had no one left to call upon. His forces were all but spent, and he had no standing reserves in the field.'

She raised her finger. 'The guard mentioned, *imposter*, I don't recall the Archon saying that during his… episode.'

Bardon examined the Archon standing defiant in his armor. 'Poor man must have been hallucinating, but perhaps, it helped to preserve his sanity in those desperate moments.'

Elodi turned her back on the scene. 'But is he in any shape to do it again?'

20. THE END OF THE ROAD

The Great Northwest Road narrowed as it climbed on its last leg to the mines of Drunsberg. For centuries, the road had served as a vital artery in the prosperity of the Seven Realms, delivering people, produce and peace-keeping forces to their destinations fast. But since the loss of the lands south of the Caerwals, and the imposing of the Archon's restrictions, seldom few trod its weather-beaten track. Now only the Archonian Guard and the large wagons transporting the metals from the mines to Archonholm used the road.

Toryn stepped across a deep trough left by the heavy wagons to peer over the edge. His head spun as he gazed down the sheer walls of the ravine until they merged into a dark line far below. Hamar took his arm. 'Careful, lad. They say it takes a week to reach the bottom.' He chuckled. 'Not that it matters, you'd be dead long before that, bouncing off the sides, or if that don't finish you, you'd die of thirst before your body smashes to pieces at the bottom.'

Toryn scrambled back. 'A week? You're pulling my leg. Nothing is that deep.'

'There's only one way to prove it, but I'm sure you don't want to try. Come on.' Hamar turned back to the road. 'We didn't march up here in record time to admire the view. Besides, I think you'll also find Drunsberg town quite a sight.' Toryn opened his mouth, but Hamar turned his back and strode up the road. He called back. 'You'll have to wait and see.'

Toryn did not have to wait long. He stopped and gawped. Thick tree trunks jutted out from the sides of the ravine like braces supporting a barn roof. But this was no roof. The trunks held up a huge platform housing the town over the chasm. Toryn stared in disbelief at the buildings tilting towards the edge, wondering how they did not topple over into the ravine. Smoke rose from dozens of chimneys sticking out at all angles from rickety rooftops. He called to Hamar a short distance ahead. 'Is it safe?'

Hamar stopped and grinned. 'Said you'd be impressed. But don't you fret, lad. It might look precarious straddling the gap, but the town has withstood decades of the bitter gales howling in from the north.' He shivered. 'And believe me, the wind gathers strength as it funnels down the gap. If it was going to fall, it would have done so years ago.'

Toryn counted the rooftops. 'It has to be three times the size of our village.'

'Strange place, I'll give you that.' Hamar took a gulp of water from his flask. 'As the mines grew, so did the need for more homes, not to mention taverns, but there's no land to be had in the mountains. On that platform sits the New Town, or so it was called when built many years back.' Hamar handed his flask to Toryn. 'But the oldest part is in the mountain. Inside is like a brock's sett with passageways, halls and rooms hewn out of the rock. Lower down, the tunnels lead to the mines.'

Toryn stared at the dark beams. 'When were you last here?'

'Must be forty, no wait, forty-five years back. I was on a duty escorting the precious metals south to the smithies at Archonholm.'

'What are the folk like?'

'Tough. Have to be. Most work the mines for iron ore, but the real riches are found in the seams deep under the mountains. That's where you find the metals to make

the fine swords for the ladies, lords and knights.' He
clicked his fingers. 'Would snap ours in two with the
lightest touch.'

Toryn winced. 'Can't say I'd want to work below
ground.'

Hamar set off. 'We'll leave that to the miners, eh? Our
job is to get word to the Archon about the attack on
Greendell.'

'What happens then? Where do we go?'

Hamar scratched his head. 'Can't say I've given it
much thought. They're bound to ask why we were there in
the first place, but hopefully the seriousness of our news
will concern them more than two harmless travelers.'

'What if they don't believe us?'

Hamar frowned. 'They'll have to. Never crossed my
mind they wouldn't. What the——?' They pulled up in front
of a barricade with a narrow gate. Hamar scratched his
head. 'Don't remember this being here.' Hinges creaked as
it swung open. Two guards emerged. The taller of the two
leveled his spear at Toryn's chest.

'State your purpose at Drunsberg!'

Hamar murmured. 'Leave this to me, lad.' He held up
his hand and addressed the guard. 'We're unarmed, well
what I mean is I don't have my sword in my hand right
now, it's in——'

'State your purpose, or turnabout and return the way
you came.'

Hamar retreated. 'Let's all stay calm. We have news
the Archon must hear.'

The first man laughed. 'The Archon? I'm afraid you're
several hundred leagues too far north.' He grinned at his
colleague. 'What do you think these two scruffs could
possibly know that the Archon would find so important?'

The second man shrugged. 'I doubt it's where to get a
hot bath.'

Toryn raised his voice above the mirth of the guards. 'There was an attack at Greendell, they killed—'

'Then what's the problem, sonny? It would be news if there *wasn't* a raid these days.'

Hamar disagreed. 'This is different. These were not Ruuk. A dark power destroyed the place.'

'And what would you know, Granddad?'

Hamar straightened and held up his arm as if challenging the man to an arm-wrestling bout. 'I'll have you know I served sixteen years in the Archonian Guard, back in the day when we earned respect. The name is Hamar.'

The guards withdrew their spears. 'Hamar? Not *the* Hamar of Darrow?'

Toryn gawped. 'They know you? After all this time?'

Hamar beamed at the guards. 'The very same.'

'Then why didn't you say so? Sorry about the… banter, but you know what it's like to spend twelve hours on watch.' He tapped his forehead and grimaced. 'Especially on an early morning after a heavy night.' He stepped forward and gripped Hamar's hand as they held their forearms together. 'Good to meet a veteran, and one of such standing. Stories of your escapades are still doing the rounds.' Toryn stood astonished as both the guards bowed. 'Please, accept our apology, Hamar.'

'Accepted. Never enjoyed the long watches myself. Now can you please take us to your captain?'

The second nodded over Hamar's shoulder. 'Sorry, but I have to ask. Who's your companion? And where you from?'

'This lad? Oh, he's… my grandson. We had business with a veteran from Greendell. We saw the smoke, went to see what had happened, and came here to report it. Trust me, this isn't your usual raid, it's far more serious. And a number of veterans met with a ghastly, undeserved end.'

The guard nodded. 'We're seeing more attacks in the area, but we can't be everywhere. Best get you two inside.' He turned and called over the gate. 'Open up, Gregor. You'll never guess who's come to join us?'

A face peered over the top. 'Unless it's a dozen Amayan warriors, or at the very least, six, I'm not interested.'

'Ha! You wish. No, you fool, it's Hamar, Hamar of Darrow.'

Gregor tugged the gate open. 'You're kidding.' He extended his arm like the first guard. 'By the Three. I look forward to hearing the stories later.'

His colleague called through. 'Take them to Ox, but keep it to yourself. There'll be a stampede once word gets out old Hamar is here. It's vital the captain hears what they have to say first.' He saluted and led them through. As they passed, the first guard patted Hamar's shoulder. 'It'll be good to have you with us.' He pointed to his backpack. 'Hope your sword is sharp, your eyes still good, and your arm strong. You may need your skills before long.'

Gregor led them up the final approach to the South Gate. Ahead, the barricade spanned the ravine, standing three times the height of a man. Gregor saw Toryn's eyes widen. 'The northern fence is twice the height. Can't be too cautious these days.'

Beneath the platform, a small trapdoor opened. Filthy water spewed from the beast. A breeze blew the waste towards Toryn. Gregor took his arm. 'Careful, sonny, you might be dirty from the road, but you don't want to be taking a shower in that muck.' As they drew close, another door opened; this time Toryn made sure he stood well clear of the edge.

Gregor stopped at the gate and called up to the barricade. The gate swung open and a waft of stale air washed over them. Toryn held his nose. The guard laughed. 'You get used to it after a while. You'll have to if you want to breathe.'

Once inside, the scale of the settlement took Toryn's mind off the stench settling at the back of his throat. The road ran uphill along the side of the gray mountain towards large slabs of stone about a hundred paces ahead. Gregor informed him. 'That's the entrance to the mines, and where we're heading.' Beyond, the fortifications on the north side of the town, rose between the buildings like a black wave gushing down the ravine.

A trumpet blared. Gregor ushered Toryn and Hamar off the track. 'Stand aside, there's wagons off to Archonholm coming through. We'll clear the way and take the scenic route.' He led them down a narrow alley hemmed in by wooden buildings four floors high. The air thickened in the gloom as the old structures leaned so far over, their eaves shut out the sky. Gregor spoke as they squeezed passed the inhabitants going about their morning duties; most involved sloshing buckets of water along the alleys strewn with debris from the night before. One yelled. 'Stand clear!' He knocked back a bolt and a trapdoor burst open. Three men brushed the swill towards the gaping hole, then stood back, leaning on their brooms as the waste evacuated the town.

Gregor grinned. 'A recent addition to the place. Very useful, but watch your step. We've had the odd accident.' He chuckled. 'It may be the quickest way out of Drunsberg, but I still recommend the road.' Gregor waited for the men to secure the door before guiding them around the edge and farther up the alley. He called over his shoulder. 'The captain's quarters are close to the entrance to the mine. You'll be pleased to hear the air is a little fresher up there.'

Toryn whispered to Hamar. 'How can they live like this?'

The old man shrugged. 'As I said, there's riches to be made here. Not so for the guardsmen, but they rotate on escorting the wagons, so get two months at a time away from here.'

They reached the end of the alley and stepped out into the small square in front of the mountain wall. Two-dozen steps led up to a wide opening fashioned into the rock like an entrance to a grand hall. Toryn marveled at the intricate carvings of trees surrounding the entrance. Hamar nodded to the decoration. 'Obviously they had more time on their hands in quieter times. And you can see what they missed living so far north.'

Gregor led them up the steps. At the top, Toryn turned back to the town. He marveled at the haphazard roofs sloping at all angles. Newer houses appeared to be built on top of older structures, or slotted into spaces once considered too small. He hoped the struts below could still bear the town's weight.

'This way, lad.' Gregor ushered them through the entrance to the mines. Inside, Toryn shivered in the cool air, but as Gregor promised, it smelled a little better. A long tunnel lined with doorways, stretched out before them. Toryn counted twenty-two flaming torches jutting out of the smooth walls before the tunnel dipped steeply down.

Gregor pointed to a wooden door under a low arch. 'You wait here. I'll go find Ox, I mean, Captain Bulstrow.'

'This is grave news.' The captain thumped his mug down, sloshing the dark liquid onto the table. Bulstrow lived up to his nickname. Toryn pictured the man bearing a yoke on his broad shoulders and hauling a plow with ease. Bulstrow drummed his fat fingers on the smooth wood. 'I've received no reports of raids that far south before yours. I can't understand how a sizeable force could have crossed over our border without detection.'

Toryn dared to speak. 'Could they have killed all the guards at a post? Then they couldn't send word.'

The captain exchanged a glance with Hamar. 'It's possible, but they would have released the birds immediately on sighting such a force, meaning we would have word of it.'

'Oh, I see.' Toryn's faced grew hot.

Hamar came to his defense. 'He has a point. We saw no sign of a response from the folk of Greendell. Whatever attacked them came in fast. And the damage suggests they had a weapon or some devilry to hand, the likes I've never seen. It's possible they could have taken an outpost by surprise, thus not giving them time to release the birds.'

Bulstrow sighed. 'That could be so. Our numbers are down. Archonholm recalled my most experienced men only two days ago.'

'Numbers down!' Hamar stiffened. 'How many do you have?'

The captain picked up his pipe. 'I have one-hundred and twenty able men at arms.' He shuffled in his seat. 'Well, most of the time, depending on the night before.'

Hamar whistled. 'Not nearly enough. Must have been nearly twice that in my day, and we only had to cope with a few rebels. Nothing like the raids I hear about these days. How are you expected to hold on to the place with so few?'

'We survive. We've added more defenses since your day, and there's close to two hundred miners, many who can handle a weapon.'

Hamar drained his cup. 'Even so, it makes little sense to put the mines at risk.'

The captain reached into his jacket. 'You'll only be too aware, Hamar, common-sense rarely features in command's decisions, but the Archon himself issued the order. Something about activity he'd seen over the gate.'

'The Caerwal Gate? How?'

Bulstrow found his tobacco and offered it to Hamar. 'He's built a tower by all accounts.'

Hamar took a pinch of tobacco. 'Activity in the south… we could do without that.'

Toryn's stomach knotted. 'But surely the Golesh can't break through the gate?' He looked to Hamar. 'You said it could never happen. Or even if they did, the defenders of Archonholm would drive them back.'

Hamar's face grew pale. 'And yet the Archon sees fit to withdraw resources from the mine.' He rubbed his chin and stared at the table. 'Perhaps he saw something that poses a greater threat to the gate than we've always assumed.' He slumped back in his chair. 'This is grave news. We're threatened from the north, and now the south? I only hope the Archon's control over the sea still holds.'

A guard burst through the door. He stood gasping. 'Apologies, Ox' — he glanced at Hamar — 'err… Captain, but we've just received news the Ruuk have broken through Drunshead.'

Bulstrow groaned. 'Not again. Yet another repair job. I've been telling command for years we need to bolster *that* gate.'

The man cleared his throat. 'The survivors reckon the swine will be here within the hour.' He fidgeted with the handle on his sword. 'And, Captain, the Ruuk number at least three, maybe as much as four-hundred.'

Bulstrow stood. 'Four?' He straightened. 'Not seen those numbers before. Hopefully, they won't be able to resist plundering the store at the gate, or the top mine. That'll delay them. Sound the alarm, make it three blasts. Best fetch the miners out for reserves as a precaution.' The guard saluted and left.

Hamar pushed back his chair. 'Happy to help, Captain.' Toryn stood with him and drew his sword.

Bulstrow held up his big hand. 'Please, there's no need. They might have the numbers, but they won't trouble us. You've done your stint, Hamar, I couldn't ask you and the young lad to put your lives on the line. My men may seem ragged, but they're well-drilled and experienced. Two outsiders on the barricade may only hinder them, even an old guard of your standing. Trust me, Hamar, when word gets around, it will be enough for the men to know you're here.'

Hamar unwrapped his sword. 'I can still handle myself. You don't have to worry about me, Captain.'

Bulstrow stayed Hamar's hand. 'Thank you, but I cannot accept your swords'. He strode to the doorway and peered out as the horn blasted its three notes repeatedly. He turned back. 'We'll hurl a few rocks down on their heads as they draw near. That should see them off, but you could assist with the fire buckets. This place is one big tinderbox. It only takes one clumsy archer to kick over a brazier to leave nothing for the robbers to pilfer.'

'But...?'

'Please, Hamar, do I have to issue an order?'

Hamar backed down. 'No, Captain. Toryn and I will be happy to assist at the rear.'

The captain nodded. 'Good. You'll do me a great service if you can prevent my backside getting scorched.' He opened the door and yelled. 'Elwold! Two new volunteers for fire duty. Show them the drill.' Bulstrow turned and steered Toryn and Hamar through the door. 'Bring your swords, keep them handy.' He glanced at Toryn. 'Just in case, lad.'

Toryn's fingers gripped the hilt on his sword as tight as the knot in his belly. He knew many stories of gallant soldiers in battle and always imagined himself at the front, killing the enemy with sweeping blows, but at this moment, his stiff neck and shoulders felt incapable of such feats.

Toryn filed out after Hamar to be met by a plump, red-faced man. The man held out a hand. 'Elwold's the name, retired from the guard twenty-five years past, now the best cook in Drunsberg, not that it's saying much in this place. Anyway, it means nothing, because today, gentlemen, we're all firefighters on this watch.'

Hamar held out his forearm. 'Hamar, retired more years than I care to remember.'

Elwold grasped Hamar's arm in the same way as the guard at the gate. '*The* Hamar? Get away. Always a pleasure to meet a brother. Perhaps when this is over, you can amuse the men and let us know which of the tales are actually true.'

Hamar laughed. 'Easy. All of them!'

Elwold's belly wobbled. 'Ha! I think you'll find every teller has embellished them a little over the years.' He turned to Toryn. 'Who's the boy, Hamar? Looks too young to have taken the Oath.'

Hamar wrapped his arm around Toryn's shoulders. 'This is my grandson, Toryn. And we'll both be honored to join you for a drink when this nonsense is over.'

'Excellent.' Elwold clasped his enormous hands together. 'Right! Time for duty.' He turned and led them to the side of the mountain where three pumps jutted out from the rock. 'The water comes up from the river beneath the mountain, so plenty to go around. The problem is getting the buckets to where they're needed.'

More overweight men stumbled to the pumps, red-faced and gasping for air. Toryn guessed they were the cooks, barkeepers and smiths of Drunsberg. Elwold addressed the unlikely fire crew. 'The rest of you know the drill, but for the sake of our new recruits.' He nodded to Toryn and Hamar. 'Let's remind ourselves, shall we? And judging by the disaster of the last drill, I suggest you all listen up.' He pointed to the foot of the wall. 'Buckets over there are already filled for such an emergency, so you stand by them if the blighters break through, or one of our own clumsy oafs starts a blaze. Wherever we're needed, form a chain two-deep. Pass the full buckets down the right, the empties come back on the left.' He strolled down the line and patted Toryn's head. 'You boy, you can work the third pump. Seen one of these before?'

Toryn nodded. 'Yes, sir, we have a similar one on the farm.' Three of the men laughed.

Elwold winked at Toryn. 'Elwold will suffice, lad.' He pointed to the end of the line. 'You two work the others. The buckets will come back fast, so be ready.' Elwold groaned as he pushed out his belly to stretch his back. He sat on a stool by the pumps. 'I'll direct the operation from here.' He grinned at Toryn. 'Don't look so worried. We suffer at least one raid a week these days, but they rarely make it within bow shot.'

Hamar grunted. 'But with four-hundred?'

Elwold frowned. 'That many?' He waved his hand. 'The lads on the murder holes will thin them out, doesn't matter how many there are, they can only advance six abreast at most. A few rocks raining down on their thick, scabby heads will make them regret coming this way. And what the rocks don't take down, the archers will finish off.'

Another horn blast caught their attention. Elwold beamed. 'Our lads have sighted the bleeders.' He clapped his hands. 'Tell you what, ladies. We'll head up to the balcony on the barracks where we can watch the start of the show. If the odd one or two make it past the welcome party, we'll still have time to man the stations.' He rubbed his hands together. 'Make a change for us to see action.

The Drunny Gate usually has all the fun.' He grinned. 'Like the old days, eh, Hamar?'

Toryn's heart hammered into his ribs as they made their way through the narrow alleys to the barracks. He caught Hamar's eye. Hamar patted a joist as they ducked beneath. 'Plenty of firewood around. I hope for our sakes they don't get too close.'

Elwold showed them inside and up two flights of rickety stairs. Toryn stepped out onto the balcony. A row of rooftops stood between them and the barricade. Archers lined the battlements to their left. At the main gate, Captain Bulstrow's red plume stood out from the fifty guards rushing to take their positions. The knot in Toryn's stomach loosened. Bulstrow's men did indeed appear a little ragged, but he would not want to square up to them in a fight.

Elwold nudged Toryn. 'See up there? They'll stop them.' Jutting out from the side of the ravine, thirty men stood ready on a high platform. 'And see those rocks? Let's just say, our guests will get a traditional guards' welcome.' Elwold slapped Toryn on the back, almost knocking him from the balcony. 'Here they come! When will they learn, eh? Their arrows won't leave a scratch on the platform, and they'll have to weather the storm to get anywhere near our gate.'

Toryn peered at the dark line slowly making its way along the road. He clenched the rail as he spotted squat Ruuk warriors waving hammers, halberds, and maces above their heads, taunting the soldiers on the platform. The blood left his face. Elwold placed his hand on his shoulder. 'It might look grim, but they won't get the chance to use those weapons.' He pointed to the platform. 'Wait and see.'

'They've got wagons, three of them.' Hamar squinted at the line. 'You'd think that would slow them down.'

Elwold mocked. 'Well! What a cheek. If they think they'll be taking plunder back in their carts, they must think again.'

The man standing next to Toryn leaned on the balcony rail. He gasped. 'They're big wagons. Seen none like that before.'

Elwold laughed. 'Makes them easier to hit.' The first dozen ranks had passed beneath the platform. A score of trap doors slung open. 'Here we go, lads!' The invaders beneath raised their shields. Elwold shook his fist. 'Not enough, you blighters.' A hail of rocks of all sizes scattered the front rows, sending many tumbling over the side. Toryn shuddered as they fell silently as if accepting their death. But Elwold bellowed. 'That's just for starters. They may have thick skulls, but they won't stop—'

'Those aren't wagons!' Toryn turned to see the covers open. A ballista emerged with a large bolt protruding from behind a protective shield. He stared wide-eyed as it slowly raised its glistening, metal head.

Elwold tried to cheer the men. 'Even if it reaches, it will only make a bigger hole for our lads to drop more rocks on—' The large arrowhead burst into flames. Elwold roared. 'By the Three! To the station.' Toryn froze. But as the guards on the top platform surged forward to destroy the weapon, a blazing bolt shot forth, smashing through the floor under their feet. The wood shattered with a painful crack, sending large splinters in all directions, impaling the light-armored men, rushing to escape. At least six fell. The bolt exploded, spewing fire down the platform, trapping more unfortunate victims. Toryn twisted away as the first burning men toppled off the edge with their arms flapping as they plunged to a horrible death. But the men on the platform had yet to accept defeat. They renewed their efforts and rained down rocks, destroying the first ballista. Toryn held his breath as the remaining two rolled into position, raising their metal noses with disdain to the platform.

'Toryn!' Hamar held out his hand. 'You need to man the pump.' Toryn stumbled forward. 'Quick, lad, they need us.'

The horn's urgent call filled the air as Toryn dodged between the emerging miners collecting weapons from the armory. His eyes darted from one determined face to another, encouraged he found no sign of panic. They reached the pumps. Elwold grabbed the nearest bucket and thrust it to Hamar. 'No chain, too far to the platform. Here, take this and follow the others, they'll lead you to the stairs.' Toryn ran to the pump, but Elwold handed him a bucket. 'You too, lad. We need as many as we can to douse the platform, and fast. We'll have to fill on return.' Toryn took the bucket with the sight of the burning men falling from the ledge still in his mind. He gripped the handle and turned to follow Hamar.

Shouts from the barricade drew his attention as the archers released their first volley at the invaders. His spirit lifted, but plummeted as he spied the stairs. The open steps led over the top of the barricade and climbed steeply up to the platform. As he took the first step, the structure groaned and buckled under his feet. The men on the stairs above cried out. Hamar yelled back. 'Another bolt has hit.' Toryn hesitated as the stairway shook. 'And a third!' Toryn fumbled with his bucket as he grabbed the rope to his left. He glanced up as another man tumbled to his doom. Thick, black smoke billowed into Toryn's face, stinging his eyes and filling his nose and throat. He blinked away hot tears and tried to spit. But his dry mouth failed to rid him of the bitter taste of burning wood... and flesh.

Hamar called back. 'Keep your eyes down. Be sure of your step, keep going.' The first of their fire duty crossed them on the stairs. With wide, white eyes glistening from their grim and blackened faces, they hurried back to refill their buckets. Toryn took another step. He knew his duty, and right now, the water in his bucket was worth more to the defense of the mines than the sword in his belt.

He reached the top. A guard engulfed in violent flames, stumbled towards them thrashing his arms in pain. Toryn pulled back his bucket, ready to drench the poor soul, but the man behind stayed his arm. He yelled. 'He's done for. Water's for the wood.' The burning soldier staggered to the edge and threw himself over. Toryn turned back to the front and into the heat, scorching his eyeballs.

The platform tilted and crackled. Hamar cried out. 'Back! It's going to collapse.' Toryn slung the water towards the nearest flames and spun around. He lurched forward, away from the weight of the blaze bearing down on his neck and shoulders. He squinted through his streaming eyes, desperate to find the steps. Choking, he called out. 'Hamar?'

'Behind you, lad. But I can't see.'

'Take my arm.' He felt Hamar's firm grip. 'First step coming up.' Men tumbled and reeled along the swaying stairway, but thankfully kept their footing. Shouts from the barricade rose as the wood splintered along its length, hurtling towards them, threatening to throw them clear. Toryn jumped onto the barricade, dragging Hamar with him as the stairway twisted from beneath him. He turned. The invaders had slung chains around two flaming struts. One had splintered; the second looked ready to break. The section above the first strut lost the battle and collapsed, sending flaming planks flipping and spinning like sycamore seeds falling from a tree. With horrifying speed, the rest of the platform succumbed, ending the agony of the few unfortunate men fighting the fury of the fire.

Throaty cheers from the victors below drowned out

the dying screams of their victims. Toryn collapsed, gasping for clean air in the cloying smoke. He coughed hard as men stumbled over him to safety. Hamar grabbed his shoulder and pulled him up. 'We have to get off the barricade. They'll be here in minutes.' Toryn nodded and together they hobbled down the last part of the steps still standing. At the bottom, rows of stern-faced miners clutching swords, axes and hammers greeted them. One nodded to Toryn. 'Nice try, lad. Now leave them to us.'

Hamar mumbled in Toryn's ear. 'I hope they can fight as mean as they look.' They passed the reserves to find Elwold slumping on the stool by the pumps.

He stood, gasping for breath. 'Form a line, lads.' Elwold's face paled as he counted the returning duty. 'Six lost. That's not good.' He lifted his head and tried to raise his voice. 'Quench your thirst, wash the grime from your eyes, then same as before. This could get a tad perilous from now on, so stay on your toes.'

Toryn took his place at the pump and filled a calf skin to be passed down the line. Elwold patted his shoulder. 'Don't forget yourself, young man.' Toryn stuck his head under the pump and ran the cold water over it and down his back. He cupped his hands and splashed his face and drank as a horn sounded on the barricade.

'To your posts!' Elwold slapped the first man on his back. 'Buckets to the pumps. They must've cleared the road and are advancing.'

Toryn's shoulders burned as he worked the handle, but he clenched his jaw and refused to rest. Each man placed their bucket on the floor, nodding grimly to Toryn as they picked them up. He made a note of their dogged faces and wondered how many would return. If the marauders could destroy the platform so quickly, what chance did they have? And how would it end? Toryn's throat tightened at the dread of dying in a ball of flames, but having his skull caved in by a mace appealed even less. He clenched the handle of his sword. Toryn could hold his own against most of the boys of Midwyche, but they sparred with wooden weapons, and he had never got the better of Elrik. He thought of his friend. Elrik would have passed into Kernlow over a week ago and be strolling in the sunshine through the vineyards of Gwelayn; he dearly wished he could be at his side. Toryn hoped Elrik did not think worse of him for absconding. He managed a wry smile. If Elrik could see him now, standing in line waiting to defend the vital mines of Drunsberg.

'Loose!' Toryn looked up to the barricade. A volley of arrows flew from the wall, but surely too few to halt the enemy advance.

Shouts at the gate. 'Ram!' Captain Bulstrow waved frantically. 'Back to the gate!' Guardsmen left their posts on the wall to rush to their captain's side as they lifted large struts to bolster the wood. The miners edged forward, but their leader held them firm.

Toryn called to Elwold. 'Why don't they sling their fire at the barricade?'

Elwold pointed. 'Take a guess. One strike and the whole town would go up. No, they don't want to destroy the place, they want it for themselves. This isn't a raid. It's a full-blown attack and they intend to wipe us out and keep the town.' More men ran to the gate carrying thick planks. But they were too late. With a crack like breaking bone, the gate shattered as the head of the ram burst through, throwing many of the defenders clear. The miners in reserve braced. Elwold put his bucket down. 'We won't be needing these now. Draw your swords, lads, and may the Three be with you.'

21. A Shattered Sword

Toryn tightened his grip on his sword. But what could he possibly do against the battle-hardened marauders of the north? He had grown up tending the land and repairing fences, while the Ruuk had been fighting since big enough to hold a weapon. The weak died first, leaving the best fighters to lead the raids. Toryn had suffered only the odd bruise and splinter in combat practice with their crudely made wooden swords; the warriors about to burst through the barricade would have recovered from far worse.

'Stick close to me, lad.' Hamar's eyes widened as the first raider through the gate fell with an arrow in his eye. 'Keep your stance wide and aim for the gaps in whatever stolen armor they're wearing.' Hamar seemed to coach himself as much as Toryn. 'Don't swing, there won't be space. Thrust, twist and pull back. They're brutes; strong, with thick, tough skin, but nothing you can't handle.' Toryn watched in horror as more squat and sturdy raiders smashed their way through the gate. Another volley of arrows found targets, but not enough to thin the numbers pouring through the gap.

Hamar spoke fast. 'Necks, armpits or groin. You don't have to kill them, just bring them down, make it harder for those behind to join in. Remember, thrust, twist, pull back.' He mimicked the move. 'Thrust, twist, pull back.' Hamar clicked his fingers as if remembering. 'And be wary if there are Norgog among them, the short ones. Can't say I saw any in their ranks earlier, but be wary all the same. Armpits only for them, softest part. They barely have a neck, and you'd have to stoop to strike the groin.' He paced on the spot, repeating his advice. 'Short and wide, target the armpits.'

The last remnants of the gate shattered and collapsed. Dozens of jubilant raiders cried out as they burst forth like water through a breached dam. The Drunsberg guards surged forward to stem the flow, but they numbered too few to hold fast. Toryn's insides churned. The guttural roar of the attackers rose as they forced the defenders back, step by step. Men and Ruuk died. Toryn's throat closed against the rising bile. Halberds slammed down onto old helmets and armor, cracking skulls and severing limbs. It looked nothing like the great battles of the legends. No heroes, no acts of bravery, no masterful one-to-one combat, just a mass brawl of jabbing, slashing and gouging of anything within reach. This was chaotic slaughter, but a slaughter the driven raiders were prepared to wage regardless of losses. Men fell, to be trampled under the feet of friend and foe. No dying in the arms of comrades with last words of comfort and forgiveness: you died where you fell; you died alone.

Toryn kept his eyes fixed on the red plume of Captain Bulstrow, pinning his hopes on a victory while the Ox still fought. The captain held his ground in the center of the melee. His bloodied sword rose and fell with a ferocity that shocked Toryn. The big man bellowed his challenge to any who came near, quickly dispatching those who dared to accept. But the enemy's heavy weapons and superior numbers matched whatever the defenders could muster. Toryn struggled to breathe as the attackers bludgeoned their way through thinning ranks to surround the captain. But if Drunsberg's best fighters fell, how could the miners and bucket carriers survive?

'Ox is down!' Elwold yelled. 'Stand ready, lads.' Toryn searched for the red plume, but it had gone. He stared aghast as a dozen raiders leaped forward and rained down blows on the spot their injured leader had fallen. His fellow guards fought hard to reach him, but they fought in vain. A cry went up. A large raider raised the trophy of the cleaved helmet of the captain high. Toryn twisted away in disgust as he could see Ox still wore it upon his head.

The commander of the reserves thrust his hammer into the air. 'Forward miners!' Close to a hundred miners rushed the enemy. Toryn's spirit lifted as their impact pushed back the onslaught. Their picks and hammers slammed down onto their targets, crushing the Ruuk front ranks under blows with the strength to splinter solid rock. But the momentum faltered as the masses flooding through the gate forced their dead into the reserves. More surged up the steps to the barricade, taking down the remaining archers and tossing them into the ravine. The miners fell back.

Hamar grabbed Toryn's shoulder and pulled him close. He yelled into Toryn's ear. 'I'm sorry it's come to this. I should never have brought you this far.' Toryn turned, but he had no words. Hamar was right. What was he doing in the middle of this battle many leagues from home? He thought of his mother. Would she hear of how he died? Or would she still be watching the roads for his return next spring.

'Stand fast!' Elwold planted his feet as three raiders burst through the miners' line. Toryn gripped his sword as one hurtled straight at him. The Ruuk's wide eyes burned with rage from his broad, flat face. Elwold drove forward, swinging his heavy blade down onto the creature's crude helmet. The attacker stumbled. Hamar sprang to Toryn's aid, driving his sword straight into the eye of the stunned Ruuk. The Ruuk recoiled, staggered back and fell under the boots of the next wave crashing through the sparse line of defense. A second Ruuk thundered into the miner at Toryn's side. A third raised his spiked mace, ready to smash it down on Toryn's skull. Hamar recovered his balance and crashed into the attacker's side, yet failed to deflect the force of the blow. Toryn thrust up his sword to parry. His blade shattered. But it had done its job. The head of the mace narrowly missed his shoulder. His attacker planted his feet, preparing to strike. He raised his weapon, but Hamar finished him with a thrust deep into his exposed armpit before he could strike. Yet Toryn could not evade the Ruuk's glare as he died, full of hate for a man he had never met.

'To the mines!' The reserve had lost the surprise of their impact. They turned and ran towards Toryn and the firefighters, but many took only a few paces before falling under the raiders' blades and axes. But it slowed the advance.

Elwold turned. 'Back, lads, back to the mines. We'll hold them there.'

Toryn froze as the line of defense disappeared. Nothing now stood between him and the mass ranks of the jubilant marauders. Hamar took his arm. 'Move!' He had time to meet the wild eyes of the Ruuk warrior still clutching the captain's helmet. Toryn dropped his broken sword, turned and dashed up the steps to the entrance of the mine.

'Here!' Elwold grabbed hold of the shaft of a wagon. 'Give me a hand.' Toryn ducked under the shaft and took hold. Three more joined them. Elwold heaved. 'We can block the entrance. There's two more behind.' The man beside Toryn cried out. He fell to his knees with a spear sticking out of his gut. Elwold bellowed. 'Come on ladies, heave!' More rushed to fill his space, and with great effort, they wheeled the fully laden wagon into place. The rest of the guards held the foot of the steps as the miners positioned the next wagon. Elwold climbed onto the toe board. 'Get the last into position but leave a gap.'

Toryn found himself beside Hamar with their

shoulders to the wheel. He nodded to the guards desperately trying to hold their line on the steps. 'Why don't they retreat? They're getting slaughtered.'

Hamar grunted as he pushed. 'We never run away from a skirmish. Not a step back! They'll wait until they have ground to defend, then they'll regroup.' An arrow whistled close to Toryn's ear. The man at the rear was not so lucky. He fell — his cry cut short as a second arrow pierced his throat.

Elwold yelled to the defenders on the steps. 'We're ready!' He turned to the wagon. 'Get set, lads, hold firm.' Toryn watched in anguish as the first of the guards scurried through the gap in the wagons. Elwold peered down the steps. 'Almost... wait... three more... two more... now!' Toryn's lungs felt close to bursting as they strained to roll the cart across the gap. Three raiders made it through, but quickly fell under blows from the miners' hammers.

Toryn collapsed against the wheel. Hamar puffed and panted by his side. 'I see you remembered the drills from the village square.'

Toryn's heart still pounded against his ribs. 'I barely managed one parry.'

He grinned. 'But good enough to save your life, eh.'

Elwold patted Toryn's head. 'You did well, young man. Not easy, your first battle. Good job on blocking that hammer blow. Would have split your skull clean in two. Shame about your sword. We must find you another.'

Hamar pushed against the wagon and stood. Elwold held out his hand to Toryn. 'Come on, it's not safe. These crates may be full, but they won't hold them back for long.'

Toryn took his hand. He rose and peered beneath the cart. 'They've stopped. Have they had enough?'

Elwold sighed. 'Afraid not. They have us where they

want us… trapped, there's not a lot we can do from here. They've had their sport, but won't want to get injured or killed just to bleed a stuck pig.' He climbed up on the wheel and stuck his head over the top of the canopy. A hoarse shout went up from the Ruuk raiders to greet him. Toryn could not understand their words, but mocking sounded the same in any language. Elwold clambered off the wheel as an arrow flew overhead. 'They'll be planning their next move. I only hope they're all out of flaming bolts.'

Toryn picked a splinter from his palm. 'You said they wouldn't risk using them now they've captured the place.'

'Not out there, but look around you. The only things to burn in this cave are us. Flames won't damage the entrance, and I doubt they have our welfare uppermost in their minds.'

Toryn closed his eyes and saw the poor souls plunging into the ravine as they burned; the halberd no longer seemed such a painful way to go after all.

'Outstanding work, Elwold.' A bloodied guard slapped Elwold on the back. Toryn recognized the man who had first alerted the captain. He nodded to the gate. 'Great shame about Ox. At least he made them pay dearly.'

Elwold turned to Toryn. 'This is Dorek, a fine guard if there ever was. And a man you want by your side when your back is to the wall.'

Dorek sighed. 'Then let's be thankful it's a ruddy great, thick mountain wall.'

Elwold glanced over the barricade. 'What about Blander?' Dorek shook his head. Elwold groaned. 'Fendy? Woolber? Grobble?'

'Not one, all bought it at the gate, though Grobble wouldn't have felt a thing. Bolt went straight through his belly.'

Elwold's jaw clenched. 'Quicker than one of my

week-old meat pies.' He bit his lip as his eyes glistened. 'Tragic, just tragic. Poor Grobble. One of my best customers.' Elwold's chest heaved. 'You'll be in charge now, Dorek.'

He blew out a long breath. 'I am indeed, but it's not what I had in mind when anticipating my first command.' Dorek turned to the entrance. 'Never seen them fight like that. Something has driven them into a state of frenzy. And yet so organized.'

Hamar saluted Dorek. 'What now, Captain?'

The new captain smiled. 'It feels strange to have Hamar of Darrow call me *captain*. I'll have to stay on my toes with you under my command.' His smile faded. 'I've yet to assess the situation fully, but of one thing I can be sure. That baying mob outside hold all the best cards. But at least their superior numbers count for little now we've less to defend.' He pointed up. 'And I suspect they know nothing of our defenses on the cliff face.' He saw the creases on Hamar's brow. 'Ah yes, a recent addition. Took a year, but am I glad we made the effort.' He peered over the wagons. 'However, I think we'll keep that one up our sleeves a while longer to let them bring more men into range.'

'But what about the town?' Hamar glanced over his shoulder. 'Won't a counterattack cause a lot of damage?'

'We can always rebuild. Those brigands don't have the skills we do.' Toryn watched how the captain held himself. Despite their dire situation, he stood tall with his shoulders back and kept whatever doubts he harbored to himself. Dorek strode along the makeshift barricade. He turned to the men and raised his voice. 'Listen up! We're not finished yet. Elwold? Please organize your men and twenty of the reserve to move rocks and rubble up to the rampart. We might make a few more *trapdoors* on the platform, but if it means more of those scum fall to their deaths, it's a price I'm willing to pay.'

'Sir.' A young boy rolled from under the wagon behind them. He stood, brushed himself down and saluted Hamar. 'Sir, I did it.'

Hamar pointed to Dorek. 'I think you need to be addressing him, boy.'

The boy wiped dust from his eyes. He blushed. 'Sorry, sir.' He blinked and turned to Dorek. 'Sir... Captain. I did it.'

Dorek frowned. 'Did what, sonny?'

He caught his breath. 'What Ox commanded.'

'That's Captain Bulstrow to you, lad, but I guess it doesn't matter now. And what did he command?'

'He said' — the boy closed his eyes and recited the captain's order — '*Release the birds if they break through the gate,* sir.' He beamed. 'And I did, I sent the birds, and all with the right messages.'

Dorek placed his hands on the boy's shoulders. 'As soon as the gate fell?'

'Yes, sir. Just as Ox... the captain said.'

Dorek ruffled the boy's hair. 'Well done, lad. You might have saved everyone's skin.' He turned back to the cave. 'More good news, men. This little hero sent out the birds. Word will soon reach Calerdorn.' The men cheered. Dorek smiled. 'We can now expect reinforcements here within three days. We can hold out 'til then, no problem.' The captain peered out of the entrance. 'Did you come up the steps, boy?'

'Yes, sir... captain.'

'And they didn't see you?' Dorek smiled at Elwold. 'Huh. How about that, eh? Could be useful.' He crouched and looked into the boy's grimy face. 'You're a kitchen hand, aren't you, lad? What's your name?'

Elwold squinted at the child. 'Name escapes me, but he scrubs them pots and pans so clean you can see your face in 'em.'

The boy blinked. 'My name?' His face paled. 'My name?'

Dorek caught the boy as he staggered forward. 'Steady on, young fellow. Maybe you need to—'

Toryn jumped back as the boy threw back his head and screamed. He twisted in Dorek's arms and snatched the sword from the captain's belt. He wriggled free, turned, thrusting the blade into Dorek's throat. The captain's eyes bulged as he stared down at the blood spurting from the fatal wound. He choked, clutched his neck and collapsed, dying as he fell.

Toryn no longer recognized the boy as his face contorted in rage. The boy held out the blooded-blade and jabbed it at them. He yelled with a voice that could not be his own. 'My name? You ask *my* name?' Toryn's blood stopped in his veins. The boy spat out his answer as if the words scorched his throat. 'You'll come to dread the day you first heard *my* name!' The boy's mouth closed — the sword clattered to the floor. His eyes rolled up so only the whites showed. He swayed and fell beside Dorek.

Elwold gasped. 'What the—? By the Three.' He poked the boy with his foot. 'I reckon he's dead.' Toryn kneeled at Dorek's side, appalled by the captain's face, frozen in a state of shock. Elwold grunted as he crouched by him. 'Tragic, just tragic, such a good man, and such a bad way to go.' He looked back to Toryn. 'And with his own sword. Have you ever...? Well, I never... And the poor lad. Shame, what a waste. What got into—?'

A cheer went up outside. A foul taste rose in Toryn's throat as the defenders rushed to the barricade, anticipating an attack. He joined Hamar as he climbed up to prepare for their last stand. But the raiders remained at the foot of the steps, raising their voices and weapons as they parted down the middle. At the rear, a lone hooded figure emerged from their ranks.

The figure strolled through the widening gap and climbed the steps with a grace belying its scrawny stature. It stopped a dozen paces from the barricade, but its face remained hidden by the hood. It spoke in a whispered croak that set the teeth on edge of all who heard. 'I see my messenger completed his task.' The creature raised its hand. The boy's body jerked, then went limp. It cackled. 'Fast and strong for one so young.'

Hamar groaned. He grabbed Toryn's sleeve and pulled him down. 'It's one of them, Tor. It's one of them.'

Toryn's mouth filled with bile. 'A wyke?'

Hamar nodded. He whispered. 'It has to be. And not a good 'un. There's something very dark about this one. I can feel it from here. May the Three save us.'

Toryn shivered as the creature made its demand. 'Who speaks for the condemned?' Its bony finger gestured. 'Come forward.'

The men cowered behind their shelter. They exchanged glances until all eyes fell upon one; the unfortunate man could only be Dorek's brother. The blood drained from his face, but he straightened and assumed his new duty without question. He climbed onto the top of the middle wagon. The raiders jeered until cut from their throats by a snap of the dark figure's fingers. 'Ah! And by what name to you answer to?'

'Por...' his voice shook. 'Porek. And your messenger murdered my brother.' Voices of support bolstered Porek. He raised his voice. 'You stand on sovereign land of the Five Realms. You kill and murder men of the Archonian Guard and miners of Drunsberg. Tell me your name. I won't rest until you're brought before the Archon to answer for your crimes. And—'

'Cease!' Porek froze. 'I will tell you my name, but know this, you will die with it on your lips before you can

211

utter it beyond this place.' Hamar cursed under his breath. Toryn peered through the gap and fought to calm his shaking body. The creature raised its arms. The sleeves of its robe slid back to reveal arms with gray skin stretched thin, barely able to cover the bones. 'My name is Uldrak. I claim Drunsberg as my own and order you to yield to my command.'

Toryn caught Hamar's eye. The old man's jaw clenched as his grip tightened on his sword. He whispered, 'Never.'

Porek cleared his throat. 'And what if we choose to dispute your claim?'

Uldrak laughed. 'Choose? You think you have a choice?' The Ruuk laughed and taunted the guards. Uldrak raised his arm. 'If it's a choice you want, a choice I will give. Surrender to me, or die slowly. But know this, your capitulation will cause great hardship, I do not deny. I will put you to work and it will end in your death, but a death you will welcome. However,' — it scanned the faces peering between the gaps in the barricade — 'I would prefer to grant you the torturous death I have planned for every one of you, should you be foolish and elect to fight.' It pointed to the sky. 'You have until the sun sets to decide your fate.' A faint, white grin appeared under its hood. 'But it would be remiss of me not to forewarn you. I prefer to kill after dark.'

22. A JOURNEY UNFORESEEN

Elodi stopped at the spot her father must have stood in his last moments, but could not bring herself to look down. A small group of the Castellan's men watched from the Lower Gate, forming a line to let her know she could not venture any closer. But she had no intention. She had come out to clear her head in the cool, evening air and determine her next move. But part of her had always wanted to see the famed mountain wall change color in the sunset. And she was not disappointed. To her right, the sinking sun exposed thousands of shallow undulations in the wall, casting jagged shadows across the face of the reddening rock.

But her head refused to let her enjoy the spectacle. A short distance to the south, an immense dark force gathered; to the north, more raids threatened her own realm, and in the middle, the Archon fought his own demons, leading Elodi to fear it compromised his judgment.

Shouts from the bottom of the ravine drew her to the rail. Far below, men loaded the last of the rocks from their days' work into large buckets to be hauled to the surface. A gray line of bent-backed quarrymen started the long climb up the stairs, cleaved out of the side of the chasm.

'A fine sunset if I ever saw one.' Elodi turned to see Bardon striding across the bridge.

'And perhaps the only thing I shall miss when back in Calerdorn.' Elodi smiled. 'Apart from your good self, of course.' She noticed the shadows beneath his eyes. 'How was your meeting with General Kragan?'

'Long. And one that' — his shoulders dropped —

'I'm afraid leaves me in a bit of a predicament.'

'Oh?'

He looked to the mountains. 'Actually, predicament is the wrong word. I don't have any choice in the matter, not unless I want to defy the Archon and start a revolution.' Bardon gripped the rail. 'Which, by the way, is not my intention.'

Elodi placed her hand over his. 'Well? Are you going to tell me? Or do I have to resort to interrogation.'

'I'm sorry.' He turned to face her. 'You were right. The Archon is keen to get us out of the way since we've seen a weakness, he'd prefer kept hidden.' Bardon exhaled. 'He has requested I accompany General Kragan on his *audacious* mission to the south.'

'What?' Elodi took his arm. 'But you can't. What purpose would it serve?'

Bardon watched the quarrymen. 'And of course, when I say *requested*, we both know what that means.'

'What's his official reason?'

His brow creased. 'The Archon insists a ruler of a realm be present in order to lay claim to Elmarand. You know how keen he is on proper procedure. Obviously Kernlow and Galabrant are either too old, too fat, too stupid, or all three of them. Kragan could not expect them to handle the sea voyage, and, I suppose, the hardships to come. They're decent, loyal men, but their finest days are well behind them. But *we* know that doesn't figure in the Archon's thinking.' He rubbed the back of his neck. 'Which leads me to wonder, what has he planned for you?'

Elodi turned back to the mountains. 'I don't suppose we could refuse.'

'Not if it's sanctioned by the Council, which of course, it will be tomorrow.' The sun touched the horizon.

Elodi drew her cloak around her shoulders. 'We should go inside. I assume I will receive my summons shortly. When are you leaving?'

'Two days.'

She groaned. 'So soon?'

'I will oversee the final preparations of the fleet at Caermund.'

Elodi's shoulders slumped. 'And how long before you'll be ready to set sail?'

He shrugged. 'Just a matter of weeks. The Archon is keen to move fast, following events at the gate.' They turned their backs on the mountains and strolled towards the city.

Elodi stopped at the foot of the bridge. She looked up to Bardon. 'What if…? What happens if you don't… return?' Her eyes dropped.

Bardon took her hand. 'Please don't worry about me. I'll make it back, somehow.'

'But there are so many things that could go wrong. If you survive the sea voyage, what's waiting for you at Umnavarek, then Elmarand?

'No need to fret. We Broon folk are a tough breed, you have to be to survive childhood, especially in Keld.' He chuckled. 'Mind you, in the typical manner of my people, preparations will already be underway for the tournament to find my successor. And if it's as tough as my trials, the realm will be in safe hands.'

'I wish we had the same tradition in Harlyn.' She spoke to herself. 'Then I wouldn't find myself in this dreadful position.'

Bardon patted her hand. 'You have the right blood running through your veins. You're made of sterner stuff than you think.' He looked her in the eye. 'And remember, I volunteered to undertake the trial to become Lord of Broon, it's what I desired. Whereas you had no such choice. Harlyn's Charter thrust the title upon you, but you accepted all the same. I admire that, and when the time

215

comes, I think you may surprise yourself.'

She tried to smile. 'I hope you're right. But I'd feel happier if I knew you were safe. If you manage to make landfall, what next? No one, not even the Archon, can know what you may encounter.'

'Elodi, please. I'll be with our elite forces, and I can still handle a sword.' He squeezed her hand. 'I'll be fine.' But his eyes did not carry the same conviction as his words.

23. FIRE AND ARROWS

The years had fallen from Hamar as the resolute face of the legendary guard replaced that of an old man. Hamar sat cross-legged with his chin resting on the pommel of his sword as they waited for Captain Porek to enter the hall. The surviving guards, miners and tradesmen of Drunsberg totaled little more than a hundred and forty, with another twenty at the barricade. They could not know for sure the size of the force outside, or if more had arrived since the pause in the battle, but all suspected the enemy outnumbered them many times over.

Toryn searched the faces in the torchlight. All wore the same expression as Hamar, and he did not look like a man about to surrender. They sat in a hall with rough-hewn walls blackened by years of burning torches. Hamar had not exaggerated when he described the old parts of the mine as a brock's sett. They had passed through a labyrinth of tunnels to reach the main hall deep within the mountain, leading Toryn to believe they could hold their position until help arrived.

Toryn turned to Hamar. 'You never mentioned you were known throughout the land. You tell many stories, yet don't speak of the deeds that earned your fame.'

Hamar chuckled. 'Hardly throughout the land, just the odd quarter of the guard. Nothing to tell of, really.'

Toryn shook his head. 'You're too humble. It's an honor to be at your side.'

'Now you're pulling my leg.'

'No. Honestly, it is. And to think we made fun of you behind your back… sometimes. But don't you worry. When I get home, I'll put the lads right. That is, if I make it home.'

Hamar patted his arm. 'We're not finished yet. Look at all these fine men around you. Them scoundrels outside will suffer when we get our act together.'

'Shame about Dorek.' Toryn winced. 'What a way to go. And Ox.' He watched as more men came bearing torches to light the hall. 'Why Ox?'

Hamar shrugged. 'He was captain. He had to lead from the front.'

'No, not that. Why did his men call him Ox? You'd think with a name like Bulstrow they'd have called him, Bull, judging by his size.'

Hamar chuckled. 'Oh that's Archonian humor.'

'Then it's lost on me.'

Hamar nudged him. 'What do bulls have, that oxen don't?' He grinned. 'Get it?'

Toryn laughed as Captain Porek entered. He strode to the long table at the center and climbed onto its ancient top. Porek's hushed tone carried to all in the hall. 'I won't try to make our situation sound better than it is.'

'We've been in worse.' A few of the old soldiers chuckled.

Porek forced a smile. 'I wouldn't be so sure, Walda. But we've had one piece of good fortune. When the attack platform collapsed, it sent the second ballista over the edge into the ravine. This means as far as we can tell, they have only one left, but of course we don't know how many bolts remain, or if they've since brought in more battle toys.' He put his hand on his chest. 'But let's not worry about them. Let them be fearful of us. We're not a foe to be treated with disrespect.' His chest expanded. 'Remember.' He turned to face each man as he spoke. 'We are the Archonian Guard. We never take a step back. And we have miners who are the bravest, hardiest fools I've ever met.' He continued to circle the table. 'And who here would want to come between Elwold and his next meat pie?' More laughed. 'And let's not forget our new arrivals.' He held out his hand to Hamar. 'We have amongst us young Hamar of Darrow who's won more fights than old Walda has had women.'

'But that makes it only two!' Elwold beamed at Walda as the room erupted.

Porek held up his hand. 'Settle down, lads. Our time for deciding is running out. The skinny runt offered us an ultimatum, but I for one don't trust a single word coming out of that crooked rake's mouth. How can any of us believe the likes of him... it, whatever you call a wyke. I can't trust a devil who takes the life of a young boy and my dear brother to deliver a message he could have delivered in person. We know little about these creatures, but I think we can assume he's not a man of honor. And it goes without saying, you can't trust a Ruuk farther than you could throw his ugly mother.' All heads nodded in agreement with the captain. 'Hence, for that reason, I for one will not surrender to *his* command. But I will offer you the choice.' He held out the palm of his left hand. 'If you so wish, you are free to walk out of here and take your chances with those outside. Or' — he raised his other hand — 'you stand with me and we hold our ground and show these brigands they can't take us lightly.' He folded his arms. 'What is your choice? Leave or fight?'

All stood, raised their weapons and yelled. 'Fight!'

'Good. But, if there's one promise from Skin 'n Bones I do believe, it's his threat of a sticky end for survivors. So, let's vow to deliver a swift and honorable soldier's end for each and every one of us left standing, should the worse outcome become inevitable.'

Toryn turned to Hamar. The old man's jaw tightened. 'No need to worry, Tor. I've got your back.' Toryn did not need to ask what he meant.

Porek clapped his hands. 'Whatever awaits us outside will learn a tough lesson tonight. You do not take the Archonian Guard and the miners of Drunsberg lightly.' He lowered his voice. 'And, we still have a few surprises of our own.' He rubbed his hands together. 'I've sent three miners to bring up a barrel of Shreek's Rage.' The hall filled with a murmur. Porek raised his voice. 'Only as a last resort, mind. We all know that black powder is not fussy about who it blows to pieces. But let's see the smirks torn from their Ruuk faces if they gain the main entrance and we ignite it, eh!'

The men cheered. Porek drew his sword, holding it high to catch the flames in its blade. 'We'll make them pay dearly for every foot of the mines they try to take from the Archon. And I promise a year's supply of ale to the man who separates the wyke's maggot-riddled head from his scrawny neck.' Porek jumped from the table. 'To your positions.' He cried out over the cheers. 'For Ox, for Dorek, and for the Archon!'

Hamar put his arm around Toryn as they marched tall from the hall. 'You'll do fine, Tor. We'll be well out of harm's way on the parapet.'

Toryn still had thoughts of the promised honorable death. 'But should they break through, we'll have little time to fall back and reach the second line of defense.'

'Trust me, lad. You'll soon find the speed in your legs with those rogues on your heels.' Hamar grumbled. 'Now I'll have to stop talking if I'm to make it up all these steps.'

After two short stairways and a few tight bends in the tunnels, they reached the stone spiral stairs leading up to the parapet. Ahead, Hamar puffed as they climbed the steep steps. He chuckled. 'Should the worst happen, at least it will be easier coming down.'

The stairwell opened out onto a narrow parapet cut out of the mountainside with a rampart coming up to

Toryn's waist. He shuddered in the icy breeze blowing down the gully. A red-faced Elwold met them, waving them along to their positions. He put his finger to his lips. 'Keep the noise down. We don't want to give the game away just yet.' Toryn ran his hand along the steep wall to his right. Above, heavy clouds bore down on their heads, resting on the mountain ridges and sagging into the gorge as the sky strived to support their weight.

Elwold pointed to the end of the ledge. 'Your rocks are in that pile. That'll get you started. There's more in this bunker should you need them. Your job is to drop them on the scum reaching the steps.'

Toryn picked up a large stone from their stockpile. He passed it from hand to hand, prepared to take the lives of the raiders below who would never know what had hit them.

Hamar read his mind. 'It ain't pretty, but remember, every skull you crack is a Ruuk who'd slit your throat, or worse, without a second thought.'

Elwold tapped Toryn's shoulder. 'You'll have the least creaky knees among us, lad.' He pointed to the rampart. 'Can you take a peek and let me know what you see.' He took Toryn's arm. 'But, I'll warn you now, it's a decent drop.'

Toryn's stomach remembered staring down into the abyss on their way to Drunsberg, but he gritted his teeth, crouched, and peered over. Flickering torches lined the road running along the side of the ravine. He turned back to Elwold. 'They're formed along the road. There's only a small group in front of the entrance.'

Elwold nodded. 'They're not so daft. They'll fear we could set fire to the town as a last resort.'

'But wouldn't that destroy it?'

'Porek won't care. Towns can be rebuilt, even something as complicated as this, but men can't.' He chuckled. 'Besides, Porek will blame the raiders for the damage.' He swore under his breath. 'Ah. I bet the swine have our buckets lined up just in case. Take another look. How many torches can you see? To the nearest dozen will do.'

Hamar tried to joke. 'Easier than counting sheep. Your dad would want to know the exact number.' But counting sheep in a green field was preferable to hanging over the hard edge of a parapet slicing into your gut. He peered over. The enemy ranks stretched far back, both up and down the road clinging to the side of the mountains. He tried to count in tens, but it became harder as the torches merged into one farther along the road.

He pushed back. 'Must be at least two hundred, possibly two-fifty.'

Elwold gulped. 'Torches! Oh dear, not good. If four or five share a torch, that's' — his lips moved as he counted — 'that's a lot.' He turned. 'Podge, go tell the captain we reckon there's around—'

'A thousand... at least.' Toryn completed the sum.

'So many?' Elwold lowered his voice. 'Yeah, tell him, but let him know we'll try to half their numbers from up here.' Podge turned, obviously relieved for the chance to leave the parapet. Elwold picked up a rock and patted its smooth surface. 'They'll have to come into range sooner or later to attack, and they'll be closer together. Can't miss. And it won't matter if they've shields. From this height, our rocks will crush anything. Even the thick heads of those squat fellows.' He laid the rock on the ledge and glanced below. 'Stay ready, lads. Won't be long now.'

Toryn leaned on the wall. Despite the cool air, his shirt stuck to his clammy skin. He gazed at the clouds and wondered if he would ever see blue sky again. Would this be his last day? Thirty men in total lined the parapet. Older miners and the men from the fire patrol stood ready. But what devilry did the shadowy leader below have up his baggy sleeves?

Hamar put his arm around his shivering shoulders. 'The waiting is the worst part. You'll be fine when it starts. Once the blood's up, you'll be surprised at what the body can endure.' He pulled up the sleeve on his cloak and ran his finger along a scar running from his hand to his elbow. 'I got this defending a village in Lunn. A blade opened my whole arm. Didn't feel a thing until I passed out from the loss of blood.'

Toryn laughed. 'Thanks, that makes me feel better.'

'That's the spirit. Tell you what, when this is over, we'll share a beef supper, washed down with—'

'The sun must be down.' Elwold waddled back along the narrow pathway towards Toryn and Hamar. He glanced over the edge. 'Sure enough, here comes the bony fellow.' Elwold crouched back down. 'Here, Toryn. Take another peek, lad, and keep an eye open for the signal.'

Toryn's legs trembled as he stepped up to the rampart. 'Couldn't we aim a few rocks at their leader? If we take him down, it would give us the advantage.'

Elwold shook his head. 'No, lad. He's come to deliver his message, so he's not a target. We don't play dirty like them. Which is unfortunate, because on this occasion I'd have no qualms splattering that creature's innards all over the steps, even if it did mean breaking the rules.' He turned to the others and whispered. 'Ready, lads. Remember, keep the large stuff for their heavy weapons.'

Uldrak stopped halfway up the steps. Toryn strained his ears to hear Porek's pronouncement. But Uldrak's answer carried to every reluctant ear within Drunsberg. 'That brings joy to my heart. I shall take great pleasure in relieving your thick heads from your shoulders, after you've begged me to end your miserable lives.' Uldrak raised his arms. A cheer went up from the Ruuk as they surged from both directions of the road toward the barricade.

Toryn searched for the signal. Elwold sensed his unease. 'Not yet, Porek will wait until there're more heads to split. We won't want to give our position away too soon.' Toryn's leg jiggled as more Ruuk came into range. 'Patience, lad. The man knows what he's doing.'

Toryn yelled. 'There!' The flaming arrow shot from the entrance. Its yellow path streaked through the dusk towards Uldrak, but struck a Ruuk behind.

Elwold bellowed. 'Let 'em have it!' They leaped up as one and hurled the first volley of stones. Toryn watched his rock crush one and scatter more. But he had no time to think of the life he had taken. He reached for the next and heaved it over with the same result. But as soon as a gap opened, it quickly filled as more raiders rushed to be the first to storm the barricade. The clash of swords rang out below. Elwold yelled. 'Keep going, lads! We're hurting the blighters.' An arrow struck the rampart beneath Toryn and split in two, failing to trouble them. Sweat poured from his brow, but he stuck to the task and shoveled rocks over the edge as fast as his burning muscles could manage. After the eighth, he paused to catch his breath. Below, their efforts appeared to be working. Rubble from shattered rocks, and bodies of the dead and dying, hampered the advance of the attack.

Hamar shouted. 'Ballista!' A gap opened as the large wagon rolled out from between the buildings. Hamar swore. 'It's twice the size of the others.'

Toryn's eyes widened. 'Could that be the weapon that struck at Greendell?'

Hamar groaned. 'We're in trouble if it is.' He stared wide-eyed at the weapon. 'It's out of range, we can't sling the heavy stuff that far.'

'Well, they can't reach us up here.' Elwold hung over

the edge. 'But they can hit our wagons.' He turned. 'Archers! Bring down the crew.' But the miners were no bowmen. Despite their best efforts, they could do nothing to slow its advance.

'Toryn! You have a go.' Hamar took a bow from a miner and thrust it at Toryn. 'I've seen you on the square, you've a keen eye and a steady hand.'

Toryn took the weapon. 'I'll try.' He nocked an arrow and aimed at a dark figure pushing the heavy weapon into place. He slowed his breathing, trying not to think about the consequences if he missed. Leveling his eye on the target, he let his fingers open. His arrow shot forth, flew true, and struck home. The creature stumbled and fell; the miners on the ledge cheered. But another soon took his place at the ballista.

'Try using fire.' Elwold wheeled a pot forward, full to the brim with a flaming liquid. Toryn held the arrowhead long enough for the flames to take. Quickly, he repeated his preparation, aimed and let fly. It hit the intended target, but in seconds the ballista crew dowsed the fire. But Porek's archers below noted Toryn's attempt. More flaming shafts streaked from the entrance with many striking home. 'It's working.' Elwold slung another rock. 'Look, the flames are taking hold.'

In a race against the counterattack, the Ruuk hoisted a large bolt onto the machine. Elwold bellowed. 'Take them down! If they hit the barricade, we're done for.'

Toryn chose his victim and let loose. The raider stumbled, but the arrow sticking from his leg did not stop him securing the bolt into position. 'What they got there?' Hamar pointed to three men behind the weapon. All wore masks and long leather tunics. Two carried a large barrel, the other held a long stick with a wad of cloth at the end.

Elwold roared. 'It's their fuel. Can you hit it?'

Toryn checked his supply. 'I have one arrow left.'

Elwold nodded to Toryn. 'Then make it count.'

Toryn's hand trembled as he held the arrow to the fire. He turned back to face the weapon edging ever closer. He fought against his heaving chest, gulping for air while blinking away sweat stinging his eyes. But he dared not let them down — he knew what he had to do. Toryn wiped his brow, took a deep breath, and nocked his flaming arrow. He relaxed his knees, stood tall and let the solid rock steady his stance. He raised his bow, aimed, imagined the flight of his arrow striking the target, then let fly.

Toryn willed the arrow forward, following its yellow path as it streaked home. It hit! The carriers leaped back, dropping the barrel as the flames eagerly licked around the old wood. Toryn jumped back as the cask exploded, spurting burning globules over the weapon and surrounding Ruuk. Elwold slapped him on the back. 'Good shot! That'll show them.' Below, the raiders ran forward, desperate to put out the flames. But the water only fueled the blaze. Toryn clasped his hands to his ears as the fire burst and burned with a ferocity he never thought possible.

Elwold bawled over the din. 'Keep the rocks raining on their scabby heads. We're winning, don't let up. They can't take this for much longer.' The attackers withdrew, rushing to evacuate the platform should the town burn. But one lone figure remained. Uldrak strode to the ballista, now blazing out of control. Dozens of burning bodies lay about the weapon, many caught as they had hurled water onto the flames. Uldrak stopped, folded his arms and bowed his head. Elwold laughed. 'What's the fool doing? Praying for the—' Uldrak flung open his arms and sent a blast of rippling air across the platform. The flames hissed and died. Elwold gawped. 'What the? Well, I never.'

Uldrak spun around and strode back to the foot of the steps as the Ruuk surged back into the attack. Elwold grabbed another stone. 'He's in range! Crack his vile head open. One hit should bring the skinny bastard down.' Toryn took hold of a rock and lifted it above his head. He lunged and hurled it at Uldrak. His fingers grasped the rampart as it flew straight. But the rock shattered before it could find its target. More stones and rubble broke and bounced away as if an invisible shield protected Uldrak.

The fighting ceased. An eerie silence descended. Uldrak raised his head to face the parapet. Toryn's guts turned to water as unseen eyes bored into him. Suddenly, he did not feel safe so high above the battle.

Hamar clutched Toryn's arm. 'It's what Tombold saw. Remember? His story about the Archon at the gate.'

Toryn stumbled back. 'If he's as powerful as the Archon, what chance do we have?'

Hamar's legs gave way. He collapsed against the mountain wall and covered his mouth. 'This is worse than I thought. The Archon has to know.'

Uldrak's rasping voice echoed through the ravine. 'I salute your efforts, men of the Five Realms.' Toryn found he could not resist looking over the ledge. Uldrak had ascended to the top of the stairs and stood directly in front of the entrance. 'You are indeed worthy of the Archon's name, but your time is over, and my patience grows thin.' He threw back his cloak and pulled out a shard of stone. 'I had wanted to do this the conventional way, but your futile resistance leaves me no choice.' He thrust his arms out wide and bowed his head as he had at the ballista. He raised the shard higher, chanting ancient words, numbing the skulls of all unfortunate to hear.

Hamar cursed. 'By the Three! Don't ask me how I know, but that's... that's the language scrawled on the trees in Wyke Wood.' He clasped his hands to his ears. 'Don't listen, don't let them foul words get inside your head.'

Toryn did as he was told, but it made little difference. Uldrak's fell voice grew louder and higher, rising to a shriek beyond the range of a mere wyke's throat. More voices joined the cacophony, shaking the very walls of the mountain. Toryn cried out, pressing harder against his ears, but failed to shut out the screams. His eyes ached, but he could not look away from the wyke. The shard in Uldrak's hand throbbed green. He grasped the stone with both hands, raised it above his head, lunged and thrust it into the steps. The ground shuddered in horror, throwing Toryn from his feet. A hoarse cry went up from the Ruuk. He stumbled back to the ledge. Below, the steps had splintered as the shard blazed, burning Toryn's eyes. Uldrak lurched from the stairs, gasping for breath, but the damage had been done.

The wyke turned and staggered away with the help of two Ruuk, who reeled as if hurt by Uldrak's touch. The crack hissed. Fingers of a sickly green hue seeped from the rock, groping for the entrance to the mine. A foul taste spread through Toryn's mouth, and a stench like Elrik's forge hit the back of his throat.

Toryn grasped Hamar's wrist. 'It's what I saw in the cave.'

Elwold lurched to their side. 'You've seen this before?'

Hamar nodded. 'A few days back. The lad saw the same devilry destroy a Singing Stone. We're in trouble, no doubt about it. We can't fight this evil.'

Elwold groaned. 'A Singing Stone? Destroyed, you say? I've seen only the one, but it had to be the most beautiful thing I'd laid eyes on.' He shook his head. 'A sad day, it is a sad day to be sure.'

Two arrows shot from the entrance towards Uldrak's back, but they broke and clattered harmlessly to the ground before they could reach their target. Uldrak turned as if to admire his work. The poison from the green stone had reached the entrance, dividing and bulging like angry veins. Toryn leaned as far as he could over the edge. Five streaks slithered under the wheels of the wagons, two either side climbed the rock wall, sprouting fronds akin to ivy as they rose faster. Screams from below echoed across the ravine to be greeted by cheers from the raiders rushing the barricade.

But Elwold was not beaten yet. He stumbled but steadied his feet to hoist another rock. 'Fight, lads, fight for your lives!' Toryn helped Hamar pick up a large stone. They struggled to the edge and heaved it over the rampart. But it was futile. They were too few to make a difference to the hundreds rushing the entrance. He stopped, panting in the dank air. Toryn stared down at the rock face. The green veins had risen halfway to the parapet. His legs numbed. He glanced down between his feet; the rock flickered as if a green light shone up from the bottom of a pond. The cold spread from his legs to his groin and stomach. Men clutched their bellies and fell to their knees. Toryn caught his temple against the rock as he collapsed. His head pounded, but he raised it to listen, desperate for the men to ignite the Shreek's Rage to greet the invaders. But the men below failed to light the barrel, most likely brought to their knees like Toryn.

Drunsberg had fallen.

Elwold stumbled passed him. He spluttered. 'Fly. Fly, damn you.' The large man wobbled, throwing up his hands. A bird cawed an angry retort as it opened its wings and beat at the thick air, but Toryn's vision blurred and he failed to see if the bird escaped. Green turned black, bringing relief to the deep ache in his bones.

24. TO PLOW THE PLAINS

'Leave some for her. She won't be happy if you butcher the lot of 'em for fun.'

'Hang on, Grebb. Uldrak promised them a long, painful death. I'm only carrying out his order and I have a few tricks I want to try on these scum.'

Grebb scoffed. 'Nah, he's out cold after using that stone, he won't stir for a day or two. But some of these fellows look useful. She'll thank us for bringing 'em in. I don't mind angering him, but not her, no, not the lady. Even Uldrak is wary of *her*.'

The harsh tongue butchered the language, but Toryn recognized enough to stoke the dread in his gut. From the echo of the voices, he guessed the Ruuk had brought him to the main hall. And judging by his bruised face and the cuts to his knees and elbows, they had dragged him by his ankles down the stone steps from the parapet. Toryn risked opening a swollen eye. In the torchlight he saw the table where Captain Porek had delivered his speech to raise their spirits; but how hollow those words now seemed.

Toryn lay among forty or so men, all in a similar state, but he could not see Hamar. The two raiders stood close by. To his relief, they did not resemble the Norgog clans Hamar had feared. These must have been Ruuk from close to the Draegalen Trench as only their flat, wide faces and shorter stature set them apart from men of the Five Realms.

Toryn shut his eyes as Grebb called out. 'You take this one's legs. We'll chain 'em and load 'em on the carts before they wake.'

The other cackled. 'They won't know what hit 'em, eh, or where they are when they wake. Here, grab this one.' The body next to Toryn slid back, leaving a streak of dark blood across the floor.

'We'll take as much as the carts will carry. That should be enough to please her. These brutes make good fighters, but you should see what they can do once she's got inside their heads.' He laughed. 'We had a dozen of these boys at the border. Been with the lady for only a short while. We sent them in first and let them go wild.' He spat. 'Shame though, nothing left for us to do once they'd finished.' He called over to the entrance. 'Here, lads, give us a hand.'

More trampled into the hall. The body next to Toryn moved. Grebb yelled. 'Not him, far too fat. He'll take up room for two and I don't reckon he'll ever fight again. We can send him to work down the mine, or to the mountain.' He cackled. 'They can wedge him into the cracks to keep out the draft.'

Toryn squinted and saw a raider release Elwold's leg. He groaned inside as another bent over the large man. 'No, he's mine.' Toryn heard a chink of metal. 'See. He wears the medal.' He called out. 'Hey, lads. This one will be good sport.' Toryn clenched his fists, ready to spring to Elwold's defense. But his shoulders sagged. In his battered and bruised state, he was not sure he could stand. Even if he got to his feet, what could he do against hundreds of hardened-fighters? He gasped as a kick landed on his ribs. 'Grab this young 'un, may last a few months longer than most if he's trained right.' Rough hands took hold of his ankles and yanked him across the floor. Toryn clenched his jaw. 'Not much of this one, eh. Be quicker to carry him.' A foul-smelling Ruuk slung him over his shoulder. Despite the pain, Toryn let his body go limp, desperate not to be considered good sport.

'Put him down!' Toryn knew that voice. He twisted

around to see Hamar with his sword leveled at the throat of his carrier.

The Ruuk grumbled. 'Let's not make this difficult, old man.' He called over this shoulder. 'Hey, Grebb, I thought you'd disarmed them all. This one still wants to fight.' He flung Toryn to the floor.

Toryn scrambled to his feet. 'I'm with you, Hamar.'

He held up a hand. 'This isn't your fight, Tor. Stay back.'

'How about me?' Elwold swayed as he stood beside Hamar. 'I'll take out the ugly one.'

Hamar beamed and patted his back. 'Then you'll have plenty to choose from!' Elwold clenched his fists and squared up for the fight.

The raider laughed. 'Fists, fat boy? You're going to do this with—?' Elwold lunged with surprising speed and landed a blow. Toryn winced as the crack echoed back from the cave walls. The raider staggered, cursing and spitting blood as he glared at Elwold.

Elwold chuckled. 'If it's to be a fair fight, then yes, I'll do it with me fists.' He winked at Hamar. 'Or how about I use just one hand?'

The raider regained his balance and straightened. He struggled to speak as his jaw swelled. 'You're going to regret that, fatty.' He reached to his belt.

'Looking for this?' Elwold held out the crude sword. 'Fast for a fat one, eh? Thought I'd use a blade after all. We haven't got all day.' He grinned at Hamar. 'Some moves you don't forget from the good old days.'

The dis-armed raider edged back. He called to the entrance to the hall. 'Hey, you out there! Get your dirty carcasses in here. We have a couple of old guards who don't know the fight's over.' Four Ruuk rushed in, swords and axes drawn.

'Hamar?' Toryn pleaded. 'You can't escape, there's

232

too many.'

Hamar turned. 'I don't intend to escape, Tor. But I don't intend to die as *sport* for these bastards.' Two more raiders blundered into the hall. Hamar nodded to Elwold. 'An honorable death? Sword in hand?'

Elwold grinned. 'An honor to be with you at the end, Hamar. No better way.' With an unspoken command, they launched at the six Ruuk. Hamar moved with a speed Toryn thought was beyond the old man. The raiders did not expect the move. The first fell clutching his gut, the second lost a hand from Hamar's swift strike, clasping the bloody stump to his neck as Hamar's blade opened his throat. Toryn jumped up and tried to grab the sword from the fallen raider's hand.

A thick arm wrapped around his neck and yanked him back. 'Not you, boy. You're to be fodder for the lady's ranks.' Toryn wriggled and tried to stamp and use his elbows against the raider, but he was too strong. He dragged Toryn towards the entrance.

More Ruuk joined the fight. Elwold roared, blocking a blow from an axe and cracking his attacker's nose with a head butt. He lunged at the next, but his strength faded as his advanced years began to tell. But before the next attacker could raise his weapon against Elwold, Hamar drove his sword deep into the Ruuk's chest.

Toryn's captor yelled. 'Come on, ladies, work together. You're making these old codgers look good.'

The attackers paused. They exchanged glances, and the five placed themselves in a semi-circle. One growled. 'The fat one first. Krull, you keep the other one out of it.' Toryn closed his eyes and four charged Elwold. The big man bellowed. 'For the Three!' Metal clashed against metal, but other blades found softer targets. A sword clattered to the floor.

Toryn cried out as the Ruuk jerked his head back by

his hair. 'Watch and learn, boy.' He reluctantly opened his eyes, feeling he should give Hamar and Elwold the honor of witnessing their last moments. Elwold had sunk to his haunches, clutching his side and coughing up blood.

Grebb kicked Elwold's sword aside. 'This one's mine.' He held the point of his blade to Elwold's throat. 'But don't worry, we've got all night.'

'Ready for the plains, Elwold?' Hamar felled Krull with one strike as he glanced behind to watch Grebb. Hamar parried another blow, knocked Grebb's blade aside and saved Elwold from a miserable end with a thrust to his chest. Elwold's eyes bulged. Then, with a nod to Hamar, he managed a grin as he collapsed on his front and died a guard's death.

Grebb yelled. 'No! Leave him, he's mine.' But the remaining raider leaped forward and plunged his sword into Hamar's stomach. He scowled into Hamar's face as he forced the blade deeper. But Hamar returned his foe's stare, refusing to show pain. His attacker stumbled back, alarmed by the old guard's defiance. Hamar grabbed the blade and pulled it free from his gut with a grunt. He straightened, turned to Toryn and winked. Hamar dropped to his knees. His head and shoulders slumped. And there he remained, looking as if he kneeled by a newly planted tree in his small garden, giving thanks to the beauty created by the Three Maidens.

Grebb and the raider argued, but Toryn only had ears for Hamar's last breaths. He stared through burning eyes as the rise and fall of Hamar's chest slowed, then finally stopped. He cried out Hamar's name, wrenching at his captor's arm, desperate to rush to his side. But he could not break free. Toryn could only stare as his old friend's long and eventful life ended with a sword still in his hand, and his foes slain by his side.

Toryn slumped, bowing his head as the tears streamed

down his face. Hamar's killer kicked the old man's body to the ground. The Ruuk restraining Toryn, shoved him against the wall. 'Go on, cry like a snotty runt. Your tears won't bring him back.' He strolled forward and nudged Hamar with his foot. 'Not a bad fighter for an old boy.' He sneered at the bloodied raiders standing over the body. 'Shouldn't have killed him just yet. He could have taught you dumb lugs a few useful moves.'

One sneered. 'Nah, these wasters were too slow. Maldy got what he deserved, letting the fat one take his sword.'

Toryn twisted away. His eyes stung and his jaw ached as he fought to drive down his grief, determined not to let the Ruuk take pleasure in his agony. He glared at their flat, expressionless faces. One day he would exact his revenge for taking his lifelong friend from him. This was the man who had rescued him from the woods; the man who had taught him most of what he knew; amused him with his stories, but most of all, the man who had been there for him when he had felt like an outsider in his own village.

Toryn forced himself to look back to Hamar. The raiders had rolled him onto his back and searched his pockets. One snatched the chain from his neck, took Hamar's medal, and stuffed it in his pocket before the others saw it. Toryn took a deep breath. Hamar looked at peace, content even. Given the choice, perhaps Hamar would have chosen this way to die. Better to go down fighting than to slowly fade away on his sickbed, or worse still, as sport for the raiders. Toryn calmed down and made a vow to the Three. He would find a way to honor the man in the way he deserved. But he would have to be patient and wait for the right moment.

A blow to the back of his head brought an end to the tragic day.

25. THE WINGED MESSENGER

Elodi ran, ignoring the disapproving glances. She rounded the corner to see Bardon's door open. Was she too late? She skidded through the door and caught her breath. 'Oh, thank the Three I haven't missed you.'

Bardon stood next to a large trunk. He turned, putting on a smile. 'What concerns you on such a fine day?'

She fought to recover. 'A message... from Drunsberg, it's... it's under siege. A bird came in this morning.'

A shirt slipped from his hand. 'Under siege? This is bad news. If taken, it could disrupt the Archon's campaign.' He slammed his hand on the box. 'We knew it was madness to reduce the defenses. Now he has to send more men north to relieve it.'

Elodi picked up the shirt, folded it, and placed it in the open trunk. 'But will it change his plans for the fleet?'

'I doubt it, he seems determined to send the elites south.' He closed the lid. 'I guess we know your *mission* to get you out of Archonholm.' Bardon fastened the strap. 'Could your forces resolve the situation at the mines?'

'A detachment left Calerdorn yesterday. But if these raiders pushed the Archonian Guard into a siege, I'd question whether my forces could do anything to help.'

Bardon turned to the window. 'Those coming south can only be as far as Noor at most. The Archon could send them back, but would they be enough?'

Elodi sat on the trunk. 'Have you been to Drunsberg?' Bardon had not. She continued. 'It's not about numbers. The road is narrow and exposed, approaching from both directions. That's why I'm struggling to think how the raiders could have reached the barricade, let alone take the town.'

'They've taken the town? I thought you said it was a siege?'

'It is. According to the message, the raiders broke through the barricade and now occupy the town. I assume the guards have retreated to the mines. The raiders must hold the ravine and the platform.'

Bardon exhaled, shaking his head. 'Then it's far worse. I thought it was a matter of clearing the road to bring in fresh soldiers.'

Elodi gazed at the forest outside. 'This is more than a group of raiders from the north. They must have had help to breach the defenses. And will the Ruuk be satisfied with just holding the mines?'

Bardon sat beside her on the trunk. 'Are you concerned for Calerdorn?'

'We can easily hold back the usual rabble, but if more come such as those who took Drunsberg...'

Bardon stood. 'I will send word to Keld for reinforcements to march to Calerdorn's aid, if, of course, that is your wish.'

She touched his arm. 'Thank you. Your offer is most welcome.'

'For defensive purposes, may I suggest a detachment of spearmen? I'm afraid it wouldn't be more than four hundred, but they're tough and a match for anything the north could throw at them. I'll request a division led by Captain Ruan. He's a very capable soldier, experienced in the ways of the Nordruuk rogues. Trust me, I wouldn't want to square up to him myself.'

Elodi smiled. 'I can believe that. I will ask my staff to speak to your people to arrange safe passage.' She stood and took his hand. 'Thank you, I hope I'm in a position when I can return the favor one day.'

The Castellan's man entered. 'They're ready to leave,

Lord.'

Bardon released Elodi's hand. 'This is the last, Fernald. Please take it down and let them know I'll be with them shortly.' The man turned to the door and clicked his fingers. Two large orderlies entered the room, hoisted the trunk onto their shoulders as if empty, turned and left.

Fernald cleared his throat. 'Will there be anything else, my Lord?'

'No, thank you, that will be all. And I appreciate your assistance during my stay, brief as it was.' Fernald bowed and left the room. Bardon held out his arm. 'Would you be so kind to accompany me to the Menon Gate, Lady Harlyn?'

Elodi wrapped her arm in his and felt her heart sink. A hundred thoughts passed through her mind, but not one made it to her lips. She sighed. 'How long will it take to reach Caermund?'

'An arduous seven days, I am informed. A detachment from the First Horse are to escort me. I hope I can stay on the back of their beasts. It's been a few years since I last rode at speed.' He stretched his back. 'I trust my belongings won't be too far behind in the wagons, I've gotten used to life's small luxuries.' They reached the top of the stairs leading from the citadel.

Elodi stopped. She turned to Bardon and clutched his hands. 'This is madness. You know it, I know it.'

He smiled as best he could. 'Duty calls. If the Archon wishes it, it will be done. My steward is capable enough, he will have received the messages. The people of Broon are stronger than most. And as our constitution stipulates, if he receives no word from me for one month, the trials to find my successor will commence.' He held up his hand as Elodi went to speak. 'But let's hope it doesn't come to that.' He laughed. 'Who knows? I could be Lord of both Broon and Elmarand before the summer is done.' He turned and led Elodi down the steps.

She reluctantly followed. 'I wish for all our sakes that turns out to be true.'

Elodi found their parting harder than she had anticipated. In the short time of her visit, Elodi had come to cherish Bardon's friendship. She stood at the Menon Gate along with a large crowd to watch the departure. If the Archon had craved secrecy only days before, he now seemed keen to make a show of Bardon's departure. But she could see why. The one hundred and twenty knights of the First Horse accompanying Bardon raised everyone's spirits. Elodi took hope from the powerful horses and fine men in their glistening armor, riding with confidence under their fluttering banners. If the rest of the elite forces allocated to the fleet were half as imposing, perhaps it was possible to take Elmarand and win the impending war. But much depended on what lay in wait beyond the mountains. And, despite the Archon's assurances, the fleet would still be sailing into the unknown.

A black speck in the sky caught her eye. High above, a messenger bird glided the last part of its long journey. With its wings stretched wide, it circled with ease, slowly descending as it made its way to the North Tower. Elodi watched with awe, standing among the bustling crowd returning to their duties. How she longed to soar above the city, forget her worries, and bathe in the warm air. How she envied the bird, majestic in flight, oblivious and untroubled by the gravity of the note carried in its pouch. But she had her own duty to perform, just as the bird above. Elodi turned to follow the messenger as it dropped towards the tower, open its wings and reach out its claws to land on the ledge. Without knowing how she knew, Elodi suspected the bird came from Drunsberg to bring news that would change the course of her life. She did not have to wait long for confirmation.

'You may enter.' The Proctor opened the door to the Vice-Archon's room. The woman sat as she had in the Great Hall, impossibly straight with a stern, if pale face. The Vice-Archon's hand rested on her desk. Beneath, a piece of paper, curling up at the edges, carried news Elodi would not want to hear.

26. Brothers in Chains

Toryn's throbbing head lolled on his aching neck and cracked onto a hard surface behind. He blinked away stars to find he lay in a wagon used as part of the make-shift barricade back at the mine. A shaft of moonlight streaked through one of the many rips in the canopy. The light fell on a dozen guards and a miner he recognized from the parapet. Most slept, or grumbled as their battered bodies rolled about on the hard floor. Toryn winced as the wagon hit a rut and the rusty bands securing his wrists and ankles dug into swollen, bruised flesh. He tried to swallow, but the foul taste in his dry mouth would not shift. Visions of the sickly green hue of Uldrak's poison creeping up the rock face, came flooding back. But what of—?

Hamar! Toryn groaned. His head dropped back and the remaining tears he had stemmed in the hall, flowed. Hamar had always seemed ancient, so the boy in him had clung to the belief the old man would always be at his side. But now he was alone, truly alone. It was Hamar who had put up with his youthful antics, spawned from the frustration of being confined to his tiny village. It was Hamar who understood his need to discover the realms beyond the fences. Toryn now appreciated Hamar's stories were as much for his benefit as they were for Hamar to preserve his memories. The tales had served to soothe his restless soul, and satisfy his curious mind. They allowed Toryn to experience the outside world, and thus prevent him doing anything that would get him into trouble. He knew in a way Hamar would always be at his side. For every situation, Hamar had a story to offer advice, cheer him up, or to calm him. Wherever he would find himself,

Toryn knew he could rely on the old man's words to come to mind. And, in an odd way, it was an honor to have been with him at the end, no matter how brutal it had turned out. He had glimpsed how Hamar must have fought in his prime. Toryn managed a smile. Hamar and Elwold may have been long-retired and out of practice, but Toryn took pleasure in the shock on the raiders' faces as the old guards had taken them by surprise.

The wagon lurched, stirring more men awake. Toryn studied his fellow captives strewn about the boards. Were all of them like Hamar? But that had not helped against the devilry Uldrak unleashed. His stomach recalled the burning eyes beneath the creature's hood. If more like Uldrak led the Ruuk, how could they repel such a force?

The wagon rode over another bump in the road. Toryn needed to know what lay outside. He shuffled around, bearing the pain between gritted teeth to look out of a gap in the canvas. The mountains had gone. A plain covered in a blanket of snow stretched as far as he could see in the moonlight. He wondered if it stayed this flat until it eventually reached the Draegelan Trench. He imagined determined ranks of his ancestors defending their lands with their spear tips and armor glinting in the light of the moon. But what dark force had threatened them to justify constructing the deep trench? Hamar had said no matter how impressive the Caerwal Gate, it paled compared to the feat of digging the trench. Toryn had listened in awed silence as Hamar told of the near-impossible task of transporting the quarried stone south to build Calerdorn and Keld. He had sat wide-eyed, trying but failing to envisage the sight of the huge wagons, made from whole tree trunks, hauled by giant beasts across the rough terrain. He smiled as he wondered how much of the tale was Hamar's invention.

Toryn gazed up at the sky. The light of a thousand

stars spilled through a wide gap in the clouds. He risked sticking his head out farther to find the bear and wolf. It took a few moments but he found them; here they fought their endless duel for supremacy of the north, a little higher in the sky.

A horse approached. He ducked back inside and bit his tongue against the sharp pain cracking his skull. The miner opposite stirred. Toryn wiped the tears from his face with a tattered sleeve. The miner nodded over Toryn's shoulder. 'They're taking us north. That's us and another wagon behind. Hope you've brought your coat.' He shivered. 'We passed through the Drunny Gate yesterday morning. I don't think they'll be closing it for a while, not much left.' He grinned, pointing to his mouth. 'Just like my teeth. But I didn't have too many to lose *before* the fight.'

Toryn frowned. 'Wait, did you say yesterday?'

'They must have drugged us. That'll account for your muzzy head.' The miner pointed to his temple. 'Didn't work on me for some reason. Ha! Must be down to the poison passing for ale in the tavern I spend most of my time. But I'm forgetting myself. The name's Jedrul, from Lunn. But I prefer Jed. I'd shake your hand if I could.' He pulled on the chain. 'It seems our hosts aren't so keen to let us enjoy the ride and make new friends.'

'Toryn, from Midwyche, that's in—'

'Darrow.' Jedrul chuckled. 'I used to dream about living on the west side of the peaks to escape the bitter easterlies.' He struggled to sit up. 'I passed through Darrow, let me see, must be twenty years ago, to come to Drunny, been here ever since, well, until today.'

Toryn tried to return the smile. 'I guess it's warmer this side.'

'And far prettier. Lunn is as grim as it sounds, grim even for Broon. Mostly flat from the ocean as far as the eye can see. The only features are bogs and lakes, but they offer no shelter. The wind comes howling in from the sea and meets no resistance until the mountains.'

'Hamar, my err… grandfather, told me about the place. But he wouldn't be in a hurry to return. Sorry, no offence.'

Jedrul grinned. 'None taken. You won't find any in Lunn who'd disagree. They say the wise leave, and only the fools return.' He looked up. 'Now I come to think about it, that doesn't make any sense. Funny. It's taken me twenty years to figure that out.' He pointed to his cheek. 'Anyway, you can also spot folk from the east coast. Doesn't matter how long it's been since we left, we still wear our Lunn Leather faces.'

'Leather?'

'Skin as tough as a cow's hide. All down to the never-ending salty breeze.' He winked. 'You folks this side of the mountains would call it a gale. They say if it ever stopped blowing, we'd all fall over seeing as we're so used to leaning into it. My grandma called it a lazy wind.' He grinned. 'Couldn't be bothered to go around, so it just went straight through you.'

Toryn laughed despite the pain. 'What part are you from?'

'Flint, by the sea.'

'North of Keld, isn't it?'

Jedrul flinched as he slapped his thigh. 'You've heard of it? And know where it is!'

'The map! I've got Hamar's map, oh wait.' Toryn patted his leg. 'Ah yes, still have it. Surprised they didn't search me and take it.' At least he had more than the memories of Hamar to keep — but for how much longer?

Jedrul snorted. 'I bet it only has the name of the place on your map. Nothing else is worth a mention, apart from the cliffs. The headland juts out to sea like a bony wyke's finger.'

Toryn welcomed the distraction to talk to someone from the other side of the mountains. He cheered. 'You've been down the mines for twenty years?'

'Better than spending my time in Lunn. It was the mines, or a lifetime of the wind stripping the skin from my bones. Not for me, much happier under the ground. The wind don't blow down there, and it's not so bad with the heat from the torches.' Jedrul glanced around the wagon. 'Others may moan about the harsh conditions at Drunsberg, but it was a big improvement compared to my home, and I was better fed. But I suppose I'll be getting a change of scenery now.'

Toryn looked at his fellow captives. 'What do you think will happen to us?'

Jedrul shrugged. 'We'll survive somehow. Whatever they have planned for us can't be more dangerous than mining the deep seams.'

Toryn remembered the words from the cave. 'I heard a raider say they're to train us for the ranks of the lady. Any idea who she is?'

Jedrul chuckled. 'I doubt they mean the good Lady Harlyn. I saw her once.' He tried to whistle through his broken teeth. 'What a beauty. She visited Drunny with the Lord a while back. A fine woman if ever I saw one.' He sighed. 'Hair the color of a sunset. Not that I've seen one for a while. Ha! Make that a sunset *and* a young woman.' He nudged the leg of the guard next to him. 'You awake, Roold?'

The man groaned. 'Let me sleep. Wake me when we arrive, or my breakfast is ready.'

Jedrul chuckled. 'Might be a while before you eat bacon again. But listen. The lad here says they're taking us to the lady. Do you know who she might be?'

Roold wiped his hand down his face. 'Nope, ask Nander. He claims to know every woman from the mountains to the sea. Now let me sleep.'

Jedrul rolled his eyes. 'Can't be too many in these parts.' The wagon jolted, sending the men tumbling into each other. Jedrul pushed himself up and stuck his head through the canvas. He dropped back inside. 'We've changed direction, my guess is we're heading west, there's little to the east, or the north for that matter. We can only be a few leagues from the trench, and then it's all ice beyond, so they say.'

Toryn turned away from the cold air. 'Are we still in Dorn?'

'Oh no. We're well out of the realms by now. Bet you never thought you'd ever see the day you'd be outside the Five.'

Toryn slumped. 'Can't say I did.'

'Oi!' The rail behind Toryn shook. 'Keep it down or we'll make you pull it, and the one behind.'

Another laughed. 'You'll be needing all the sleep you can get, so make the most of the ride, boys.'

'You awake?' Jedrul nudged Toryn's foot. He opened his eyes and groaned to see it was still night, but at least they had stopped moving. Outside the wagon, torches flickered as their captors sang and laughed. Jedrul sat back. 'We stopped a while back. They're cooking a hog on a spit, one stolen from our stores, but I don't suppose they'll leave any for us.'

Toryn's stomach rumbled as the rich smell of roasting meat wafted in. 'I can't remember the last time I ate a full meal.' His breath vaporized in the bitter air.

'I wouldn't waste time looking forward to the next one.' Jedrul nodded to the opening. 'Be lucky to feed off the leftovers.' More men in the wagon woke at the smell of supper.

Roold sat. 'Any clue where we are, Jed?'

'Judging by the racket they're making and all their blazing torches, I can safely say we're still north of the border. They don't seem to care who sees or hears them.'

Roold shuffled, trying to find a better position. 'How many escort us?'

Again, Jedrul answered. 'No more than thirty I'd say.'

'We must number at least twenty. Charming. If they think they have enough to prevent our escape, they should think again.'

Nander raised his hand and jangled the chain. 'But they're not wearing the jewelry.' He pulled his arm back. 'And we appear to be fastened to the floor.'

Roold lifted the chain to the light. 'These are ancient, must be a weak link somewhere. Come on, ladies, wakey, wakey and check your chains. I doubt those scum took much care securing these to the wagon. If we can break it up, we can throttle the swine in their sleep. That'll teach them to fill their stomachs with our meat and ale.'

Nander groaned. 'Who made you captain, Roold?'

'I did. I'm the senior in this wagon at least, and Porek is in no state to lead.'

'Why not?' Nander narrowed his eyes at Roold.

'He's dead. I was at his side when the green stuff took him down. Poor sod had no chance. Both him and his brother so close together.' He rattled his chain. 'Like it or not, I'm your new captain, so make a start on these links. The closer we get to where these swine want to take us, the less I rate our chances.'

'What if that wyke creature is with them?' Jedrul peered at the shadows of their captors looming on the wagon's canvas. 'Don't think I could strangle him before he conjured up something horrible.'

Toryn spoke. 'I heard he'd be out cold for a couple of days after his trick with that stone. Mind you, the same raider said Uldrak was wary of this lady we're being taken to.'

Jedrul chuckled. 'Now that makes me feel so much better.'

Nander scowled at Toryn. 'And what do you know of the world? You don't look old enough to shave.'

Jedrul stiffened. 'Don't you talk to young Toryn like that. He took down that ballista with a single arrow. Saw it from the parapet.'

Nander sneered. 'A fat lot of good that did. Might have been better to take a bolt through the chest and end it quick.'

Roold hushed Nander. 'He managed more than you, Nandy.' He beamed at Toryn. 'A fine shot from a fair distance, young man. I think we can make you an honorary Archonian considering our predicament.' He turned to the other men. 'Any objections?'

Toryn felt his chest expand as the men, apart from Nander, signaled their approval. It was only a shame Hamar could not be with him. He nodded to Roold. 'Thank you, Captain.'

'Roold will do.'

Toryn had to ask. 'When Hamar and Elwold fought the raiders at the end, Hamar asked Elwold if he was *ready for the plains*. Hamar never spoke of any plains to me. What does that mean?' The men in the wagon bowed their heads.

Roold nodded. 'And quite right he didn't. He'd have sworn the Oath. It's known only to those taking it, but seeing as you're one of us now, I don't think—'

Nander cleared his throat. 'He's not yet. We've not done the initiation, and he hasn't sworn no Oath.'

Roold held up his hand. 'Never known you to be bothered about proper ceremony. But you're right. Once we're out of this mess we'll do it the proper way. But we'll take it as read it will be done, but seeing as we don't know what lies ahead, I think it's only right and proper to inform the lad. We don't want him waking up not knowing where he is, should the worst happen.' Roold straightened as best he could. 'Did your friend, Hamar, put Elwold out of his misery?'

Toryn whispered. 'Yes. Elwold was on his knees. A Ruuk said he had plans for him. Hamar fought off two and... finished Elwold with one blow.'

Roold beamed. 'Hamar was a good Archonian, one of the finest. I'm sure we'd all have been honored to have fought by his side and let him hasten our way to the Plains.'

Toryn bit his lip. 'He was, and not a bad farmer either.'

'Then he'll be at home on the Plains of Evermore. It's where we go if we die with a sword in our hand, or at the hand of a brother when our honor is at stake. It's said the rich soils of the plains grow the finest wheat for bread, and, of course, hops for ale, and—'

'Must be over-crowded after yesterday.' Nander sneered. 'Come on, we all know it's just a tale to make us fight.' He looked around. 'You can't honestly believe we'll all get a farm in Evermore, can you? There can't be enough to hand out to all those who've died in battle. Knowing our luck, we'll wake up in a pigsty.'

Jedrul laughed. 'Then you'll feel at home.'

Roold glowered. 'Come on, lads, don't mock the Promise. It's written we all get a farm, by the Archon no less, and that's good enough for me.'

But Nander refused to be silenced. 'Then I'll make you this promise. If I wake up after taking a sword in my gut, only to find I'm farming a field next to you, Roold, you're welcome to all the ale I can brew.'

Roold tutted. 'If they put me next to you, I'd happily drink the lot if it means I stay too drunk to listen to you rambling on.' The men laughed. Toryn joined in, already understanding why Hamar called them his brothers.

'Got one!' Jedrul held up his chain. 'Here, look. I've prized this link open with a spike I pulled out of the wood.'

'Outstanding work.' Roold patted Jedrul on the shoulder. 'Now the rest of you get to it, there has to be more links we can break.' The raucous laughter outside grew louder. 'They're well on their way. I reckon in a few hours we'll have our chance. I doubt this disorderly bunch will think to leave anyone sober enough to watch over us.'

Nander licked his lips. 'I hope they don't eat all the meat. My stomach thinks my throat's been slit.'

'Well, let's hope your belly doesn't turn out to be right.' Roold winced. 'Any of you come across that green poison before? My head still hurts.'

'I...' Toryn stopped as all eyes fixed on him. 'I have. Me and Hamar saw rocks ooze that stuff and destroy a Singing Stone.'

'A Singing Stone?' Roold gasped. 'That can't be good, oh no, not good at all. I've never had the luck to find one, but Elwold, rest his soul, spoke of them. Where was this?'

Toryn's stomach churned at the memory. 'About a few leagues south of Greendell.'

Roold nodded. 'That'll be the Wend Gap.'

'Wait.' Nander frowned. 'I heard you came from Greendell to report the attack. What were you doing in the Gap? Why not take the road?'

Toryn felt his face flush. 'We... Hamar...'

'Give it a rest, Nandy, stuff's happening that's well out of the ordinary. I think we can ignore a minor misdemeanor.' He laughed. 'Come on, think about it. What would a veteran with Hamar's reputation and his grandson be going to Greendell for?' He winked at Toryn. 'I would say Hamar had a bit of business there, eh?'

But Nander was not convinced. 'How do we know he's not a spy? Funny how the attack came shortly after they arrived.'

Roold reprimanded Nander. 'Leave it, you can't go accusing a veteran, a veteran who's shown his loyalty to a fellow brother only hours ago and made the ultimate sacrifice. You should… shush.' He cocked an ear and whispered. 'It's gone quiet. Surely, they can't be asleep already.' The wagon lurched. Roold groaned. 'No, we can't be on our way? So soon?'

Jedrul sighed. 'Seems these fellows aren't the ragtag bunch we had them down to be.'

Roold tried to sit but fell back as the wagon dipped into a trough. 'Or they fear Uldrak's boss more than they desire the taste of a fine ale. This isn't good news.'

'We're turning again.' Jedrul stuck his head out of the canopy leading to shouts of protests from their captors. He dropped back. 'We're going south. Must have passed the worst of the marshes.' He grabbed a rail. 'Better hold on tight, lads, we're in for a bumpy ride through Mawlgrim Mire. Let's hope the bog grims are tucked in deep for the night. Wouldn't fancy one of them digging its long, grimy fingers into my throat.'

Toryn took hold of the bar behind. 'Bog grims?'

'It ain't all flies and mud, lad. I've heard there's creatures living under the sludge, and they're quite partial to human flesh when they can get it.'

Roold laughed. 'Don't listen to him. It's all nonsense. You should know better, Jed, than to listen to those tales.'

Jedrul shook his head. 'I know plenty who've seen them. But if you don't believe me about the bog grims, at least hold your noses if you have a hand to spare. I've heard the mire don't smell too good.' He rubbed his chin. 'Must be taking us back into Dorn. But that don't make sense.'

Roold groaned. 'There's only one place south from here where they'll be taking us.' He pulled up his chains. 'I know where this mystery lady of theirs dwells. Back on those links, lads. I don't care if I have to chew my own hands and feet off to get out of this wagon, I ain't letting them take me to Wyke Wood.'

27. THE OLD LADY OF THE SEAS

Elodi took a deep breath of salty air, hoping to settle her stomach. She stood at the helm of an ancient, but proud ship as it sailed out into the choppier waters, away from the protection of West Haven's bay. The messenger bird had delivered but a few words, but those few words had sent a shudder through Archonholm.

Sorcerer. Large force. Bulstrow dead. Mines lost.

Elodi had dropped the hastily scrawled note on the Vice-Archon's desk as if it had burned her fingers. The mines of Drunsberg had fallen into the hands of the Ruuk. Taken by a force that, according to the Archon, should never have made it past the watchtowers on the border. But to have the strength to take what should have been an impregnable position held by his own men, was a hammer blow. Only a year ago, she had accompanied her father to inspect the new fortifications. She could remember the look of relief on his face, satisfied he had done enough to secure the supply of resources so vital to the defense of the Five Realms. Sadly, the modifications had obviously not been up to the task.

Sorcerer. The word had twisted an icy blade in her gut. There had to be a wyke in the north. And not just a sorcerer who could sour milk and stunt crop growth; this one must wield significant power to have taken the mines. The Vice-Archon had dismissed the mention of a sorcerer as the panic of a desperate man, or one trying to make an excuse for failing to hold their line. But Elodi knew the men of Drunsberg would only yield to a far superior force. This confirmed her worse fear. She knew exactly where the creature leading the raid must have originated: Durran

Wood had not lost its centuries-old name for nothing.

The Vice-Archon had brushed aside her request for a meeting with the Archon. Wendel had insisted the Vice-Archon did not have the authority to refuse without consulting the man himself. But the Vice-Archon had invoked emergency wartime powers and informed Elodi the Archon was at rest, preparing for the tough months ahead, and could not be disturbed. But Elodi and Bardon knew otherwise.

Wendel had referred to the emergency laws and demanded Archonholm send a sizeable force north to march on Drunsberg. But while the Council eventually agreed they should retake the mines, events in the south took priority, thus few resources could be spared. Just how few shocked Elodi. The Council allocated a miserly one hundred Archonian Guard for the task, and most of them recently trained, meaning Harlyn's army of part-timers would have to be deployed. Yet, even if Elodi re-assigned the bulk of her army, the force would still number less than six-hundred. But if a wyke held Drunsberg, she feared six-hundred casualties and no mine would be the only foreseeable outcome.

But to Elodi's surprise, the Council gave her a ship moored at West Haven to hasten her return to Calerdorn. Other news had also encouraged her at a time of otherwise grim events. In a rare move, the Council had granted Bardon's men from Keld, permission to take the Kolossos Pass. If they could negotiate the treacherous route, they would arrive in Dorn in around ten days, but Elodi was reluctant to use them for anything other than the defense of her city. The relief company, sent from Calerdorn at Captain Bulstrow's request, had turned back on discovering a siege underway by a large force. She did not blame them. They had numbered only fifty and would have achieved nothing more than adding to the high toll, paid in vain.

The ship swayed. Elodi looked up to see they had cleared the headland. To the south, the steep slopes of the Caerwal Mountains dropped and sliced into the sea. On a rocky outcrop, the West Watchtower, dwarfed but not overawed by the mountains, kept an unerring eye on the open waters. But the sight did little to ease Elodi's stomach. Beyond the watchtower, gigantic waves surged, swirled and collapsed as if a monster of the deep stirred up the seas to rise against the land.

Elodi looked away, thankful for the Archon's invocation to keep the way north closed to Golesh ships. Her vision blurred as her head sought to come to terms with the swelling sea. But the guards on the main deck fared worse than Elodi. Most of her fresh-faced soldiers hung over the side, struggling to keep their meagre breakfast rations from the fish. What chance had she of retaking Drunsberg? These soldiers were barely out of training. Only the captain, Gundrul, an aging ruddy-faced man from Lunn, and a handful of the others appeared to be older than Elodi. And to her dismay, Gundrul looked only a few years younger than Tombold.

She turned her back on the carnage below and fixed her eyes on the coast. The green hills of Tamarand would watch over them until nightfall before giving way to the estuaries and flat lands of Gwelayn, the southern ward of Kernlow. But while part of Elodi longed to see the jagged cliffs of Dorn, she knew as they sailed into the cooler climes, the seas would not be so tolerant of their presence. The ship's captain believed they could make the port of Calerdorn within six to seven days, but much depended on the will of the prevailing wind.

The ship rolled and dipped. Elodi tried to ignore her unsettled stomach. She recalled the three days it took to reach the port of West Haven. Elodi had welcomed the chance to gallop the open road on Sea Mist. She had no love for the ceremonial carriage and was thankful it would make its empty way back to Calerdorn by land. But while she rode west, Bardon, the man she now regarded as her closest ally, headed east.

The deck rose. Elodi pulled her hand from the taffrail as yet another splinter dug into her palm. She turned and stumbled towards the helmsman. He thrust out a thick arm. 'Steady, ma'am. Don't want to be falling overboard, do we now.'

'Thank you. And... sorry.'

'No need, ma'am. First time at sea?'

She swallowed. 'Yes, and for my horse.'

'The horses will be fine below deck, ma'am. They soon get used to it.' He cursed as he lost his grip on the wheel. 'As I was about to say, it'll be best for you also. The sea breeze ain't too kind to a lady's soft skin, ma'am. You can see what it's done to me over the years.' He laughed. 'And I'm sure you don't want to end up with a face like mine.' He rubbed his cheek. 'Just need the barnacles, and I'd be mistaken for a rotting hull.'

Elodi recalled the old fishing boats in Calerdorn harbor. He made a good point, but she did not want to hurt his feelings by agreeing. She looked up to the sky. 'I prefer to be in the fresh air, and... where I can see land.'

'Then may I be so bold to suggest, ma'am, you keep your eyes on the horizon out to sea. Helped me my first time out of port. Staring at land that doesn't move can make it worse in my view.'

Elodi turned away from the coast. 'Thank you, I shall try it.' But the sight of endless water added another knot to her stomach. As a child she had dreamed of sailing into the unknown beyond the horizon, but that had been from the safety and stability of solid rock beneath her feet. She tried to take her mind from the voyage. 'I didn't catch your name earlier, helmsman.'

He smiled. 'I'm rarely asked, ma'am, and helmsman sounds a tad grand for what I do.' He stepped out from behind the wheel and took a bow. 'Helmsman Horace at your service, ma'am.' He grinned. 'And may I say what a pleasure it is to have the good Lady of Harlyn onboard.'

Elodi nodded, instantly regretting the move. She swayed, keeping one eye on the nearest rail as she swallowed. 'So… tell me, Horace, how long have you been at sea?'

He eyed the sail billowing overhead. 'Since the tender age of ten, so getting on for forty years.'

Elodi could not prevent her eyebrows from rising — his face suggested it had been longer. She smiled. 'And have you sailed to Calerdorn before?'

Horace chuckled. 'I don't think you understand, ma'am. I may have been at sea many years, but only the few miles up and down this stretch, and then mainly hugging the coast. I'm a fisherman by trade and we catch all the fish we can handle in the warmer waters, and rarely have to go out of sight of land.' Horace wrapped his strong arm around the top spoke and wrestled back control. 'Not sailed the open seas much, and rarely beyond Traitor's Isle. But don't you worry, ma'am. I've had a few years learning how to handle a proper lady of the sea like this old beauty.'

She eyed the coast. 'Can we stay this close for the entire journey?'

Horace scratched his chin. 'Not with a draft this deep. The old maps show too many rocks ready to rip us apart. We'll have to head out when we reach Noor, farther still at Dorn before we can turn in and sail for Calerdorn.'

Elodi turned back to focus on the hills. 'And Captain Blunden? Does he have knowledge of these waters?'

'Old Blowers?' Horace bit his lip. 'Not really. He's the

skipper of our fishing boat. It's all new to him as well, but don't you fret, ma'am. He knows the ways of the sea. Blowers has navigated these waters for many a year, even went as far as the port of Rhydor in his youth, or so he says.' He patted the wheel. 'But it don't matter, ma'am. This old bird knows the way. She would have sailed this route hundreds of times back in her day before the wars ended.' He nodded to her hand. 'That'll explain the splinters, ma'am. The *Celestra* is older than the Caerwal Gate itself.'

Elodi's stomach tightened a little more. 'Thanks, just what I needed to hear.'

'Pardon, ma'am? My hearing ain't what it used to be.'

'I said, I'd be interested to hear more about this old ship, the *Celestra* you called it?'

He beamed. 'Her. It's a *she*, ma'am. And yes, her name is *Celestra*. A fine old name for a fine old lady.'

Elodi repeated the name and found it eased her mind. 'What would *she* have been used for back then?'

Horace grunted as he heaved the wheel against the current. 'She may have carried soldiers in the worst of times. But otherwise it would have been cargo, most likely wine, flour, livestock and cotton.'

Elodi jumped as the deck creaked. 'How did the *Celestra* survive this long?'

'We can thank the shipwrights of old, ma'am. They reasoned it would be wise to keep the odd ship sea-worthy. But of course, they also fought for their trade. No shipwright worth his salt wants to waste his skills building carts, huts and barns.'

'I should imagine not.'

'Besides, they couldn't bear to see them slowly rot. But over the years as they died and with fewer wrights replacing them, they only had the numbers to save this old girl.'

'Lucky for us they did.'

'Lucky to be sure, ma'am, and thankfully the Archon had the wit to keep at least one ship on the west coast seaworthy, giving us permission to take her out when we had time.' He lowered his voice and nodded to the main deck. 'And I hope your soldiers are better on dry land, then they might have a chance of taking back Drunsberg.'

Elodi gasped. 'You know about the siege? And the purpose of this mission?'

'Oh yes, ma'am. It's all the talk on the docks. Not good at all if we lose the mines. Especially, with things being as they are these days.'

She groaned inside. The Vice-Archon had said they would not release the news, fearing it would lower morale. How had a fisherman come across the news so soon? And what of the invasion fleet? It would be difficult for the elite forces to go unnoticed as they traveled to Caermund. If news of their movements reached the wrong ears, they would struggle to make the landing at Umnavarek. She turned to Horace. 'How did you find out?'

Horace shrugged. 'Everyone knows, ma'am. Maybe one of your young guardsman spoke to a local in West Haven, but it's common knowledge all the same.'

'I see. Thank you, Horace, I think I will take your advice and head below deck. I have a few matters to deliberate.'

Elodi soon came to enjoy life onboard the *Celestra*. Sea Mist and the draft horses seemed comfortable. The weather had been kind, allowing them to make excellent progress to reach the coast of Darrow sooner than Captain Blunden had expected. The *Celestra* creaked and groaned, but had remained true to Horace's word, seeming to know the way. Elodi's young guards had become accustomed to the waves, and their spirits had risen as their rations had stayed down. For her part, Elodi enjoyed imagining how the *Celestra* must have looked in her prime. She had run her fingers along the carvings on the cabinets in the grandly named stateroom, imagining the lives of those who had sailed with her in the past.

But this was no time to linger on a bygone era. The immediate objective of re-taking the mines with a small, inexperienced force had to be addressed. With her limited resources, Elodi believed a blockade to be the most obvious course of action in order to starve the raiders into taking rash action. She could not stomach the thought of sending young men to what would surely result in certain death, if they tried to storm the town. But as Wendel pointed out, they had no idea when the last delivery of supplies had been made. Not to mention the dangerous task to move men north of the Drunshead Gate through territory held by the enemy. And the captain of the Archonians, Gundrul, could not rule out reinforcements arriving from the north, while they had little hope of the Archon allocating more guards. Elodi began to question whether the Archon wanted the mines back, or if the mission was indeed a ploy to remove her from Archonholm, as Bardon suspected.

Elodi studied the stern-faced men around the table in the stateroom. At her side sat Wendel, appearing to relish the challenge. They faced Gundrul and his four sergeants. Of these, only Gundrul and one other had served in Drunsberg. Gundrul had the look of a man who had seen and done much in a long and eventful life. Thick, gray hair covered what she took to be a wise head sitting on his broad shoulders. Despite his age, his bronzed, thick arms suggested strength and an ability to handle a sword. But Elodi took hope from the deep furrows on his brow. Gundrul was a thinking warrior, one she trusted would not rush in with a reckless show of bravado — his age bore testament to that.

Re-assured, Elodi took a breath. 'Thank you, gentlemen. We've had enough time to think about a strategy, now it's time to bring them to the table.' She read the first lines of her notes. 'The initial report from Drunsberg stated the raiders had three ballistae firing bolts of fire. Unfortunately, there's no mention of any being destroyed.' Her eyes recalled the panicked scribbles of the last message. 'As you are aware, the most recent communication revealed something none of us wanted to hear. We don't know who wrote it, but one thing is obvious — they were in a state of despair. If a wyke leads the raiders, who knows what we could be up against.'

Gundrul placed his hands on the table. 'With all due respect, ma'am, I don't think a mere wyke could cause *despair* amongst the guards at Drunsberg. What did he do? Make it rain? Give them a nasty cold? In all my years of serving the Archon, I've come across only one, and I have to say, the tales make them out to be far worse than the pathetic creature I met.' He folded his arms. 'My men may be fresh out of the barracks, but I'm confident they can take care of a *wyke*. All the dangerous sorcerers are long dead, ma'am. It had to be down to the heavy weapons and their sheer numbers.'

Elodi's pulse quickened. Why should these world-weary men take any notice of what she had to say? But the Archon had entrusted her with the task, regardless of his motive, therefore the responsibility lay on her shoulders. Elodi held up a hand. 'Please, Captain, we cannot ignore the fact these raiders overwhelmed a force thrice the size of ours on this ship.' She held his gaze. 'And the soldiers at Drunsberg were more experienced, and in possession of the mine, not to mention a hundred or more miners in reserve.' She clasped her hands and looked at the other faces around the table. 'I have to assume the raiders had something new, something our men did not expect, or had not encountered before. And I suggest' — she glanced back to Gundrul — 'something of which we have no knowledge. Was it only the use of the ballistae? I think not. Surely, these weapons were of limited use once they'd taken the town. Yes, they could storm the entrance to the mines with them, but, as you know, once inside they would be useless in the labyrinth of halls and tunnels. Yet, the last message tells us the mines have fallen into the hands of the Ruuk.'

Elodi waited for a response from the men around the table. They listened! And still they sat, as if waiting for her to continue. Heartened by their response, she obliged. 'Gentlemen, from recent events I have had the misfortune to witness, and new knowledge coming to light, I am certain the unknown we're up against *is* a powerful wyke of old, and one worthy of the dark tales you will have heard.'

Gundrul leaned back. His eyes wandered across the knotted wood of the tabletop as if searching for a hidden message. Elodi waited. After a full minute, he nodded to himself and raised his eyebrows. 'Then, if this wyke of yours is as you say, ma'am, stealth is our only course of action.' Elodi heaved a silent sigh. Gundrul turned to each of his men in turn. 'But powerful or not, these creatures still have to rest sometime. We can be sure the scoundrels under his command will help themselves to the ample stocks of ale, so I would act at dawn, ma'am. We send two men over the barricade when his forces will be out cold. They open the gates, let us in, and we dispatch most of the swine before they can find their swords.'

His sergeants nodded their approval. But the plan was not enough to convince Elodi. 'Can we be sure the raiders are as ill-disciplined as you believe? They did, after all, take the mine.'

Wendel spoke before Gundrul could answer. 'Ma'am, we have another option.'

Elodi turned. 'And what would that be?'

He straightened. 'I've read all the documents relating to the mine.' Wendel glanced to Elodi. 'Now you can appreciate why I insisted on bringing my records.'

Elodi smiled. 'I do, Wendel. Please, go on.'

'It's not known to many, for obvious reasons, but there's an old tunnel we could exploit. I suspect cobtrolls dug it long before the mines came about.'

Elodi's hopes rose. 'And where does this tunnel surface?'

'There's a small, concealed entrance half a league south. We could gain access to the older parts of the mine long abandoned. But bear in mind the cobtrolls were smaller than us, and while we have widened parts, it would be difficult for someone even of your height, ma'am.' He nodded to Gundrul. 'And nigh on impossible for the captain and for half his men.'

'But the other half?' Elodi sensed an opportunity. 'Could we gain an advantage by deploying a force behind the raiders?'

Wendel stroked his chin. 'I would defer to the captain, ma'am.'

Gundrul sat back. 'If I had a company of men experienced in fighting in such conditions, then I'd say yes, but with these young lads, I can make no promises. They can handle a sword and give a good account of themselves in a one-on-one fight. But this is different. You need an old head on your shoulders for a mission such as this. At best they might free hostages, that is, if the raiders spared any of the defense force, but—'

'I could lead them, Gunny.' Gundrul turned to the sergeant on his left. The captain cleared his throat. The sergeant followed Gundrul's gaze to Elodi. 'Oh yes, sorry.'

He straightened. 'I could lead them, Captain.' Elodi tried unsuccessfully to prevent the grin spreading across her lips.

Gundrul clasped his hands. 'Ma'am, this is Cubric, but if he insists on being informal, then everyone calls him Cub' — he narrowed his eyes — 'including the men under his command.'

Elodi smiled. 'I have no issue with being informal, Captain, so long as it means we get the job done.'

Gundrul relaxed. 'Well, as you can probably guess.' He nodded to Cubric. 'This skinny fellow could easily sneak through a cob's tunnel with room to spare.'

Cubric grinned. 'We have a saying in Kernlow, ma'am, if it ain't nailed down, the big man will eat it. That'll account for my wiry frame. And by big man, I'm talking about our dear old, Lord Kernlow.'

Elodi laughed for the first time in a long time. 'I guessed as much. I've had the honor of meeting him. He's quite the—'

Wendel stiffened. 'Ma'am.'

Elodi turned; she knew that face. 'Thank you, Wendel.' She leaned forward and placed her hands on the table. '*If* a small company of men make it through this tunnel, what course of action could give us the advantage?'

Cubric raised his hand. 'If I could make a suggestion, ma'am, Captain.' Gundrul nodded. Cubric continued. 'As you know, I've done service at Drunny... Drunsberg, three times in fact, and I heard some interesting stories from the miners.'

Gundrul groaned. 'Do we have time for this?'

'I'll be brief, but if I may, ma'am, this could be important.'

She nodded. 'Please, do carry on.'

'There's a detachment of miners who carry out exploration beyond the deep seams. It's unpleasant work owing to the cramped conditions, and the fear the tunnels could collapse at any moment. Many of these men are from my region, owing to our size, so I got to know them well.' He lowered his voice. 'And here's the thing. One told me how they used to open new seams. They used a black powder, that when exposed to a flame would explode like a dropped oil lamp, but with such a blast it would crack open the rock. The miners call it Shreek's Rage on account of the noise and destructive power. Think what we could do with that.'

Elodi frowned. 'Do you know of this powder, Wendel?'

He kept his eyes on Cubric. 'It's not been used in decades. The powder's too volatile, caused many accidents and, sadly, casualties. Hence, it was banned, and all stocks dumped at the bottom of the ravine.'

'Ah, but not all of it.' All heads turned back to Cubric. 'One cache was stored so deep, no one was willing to risk bringing it back to the surface. I'd say at least a dozen barrels are still in a cave down there, if we could find—'

'What would we do with it?' Wendel rubbed his brow. 'Ma'am, this is an extremely dangerous substance, even if we could locate this cave, would it still be useable after all this time, and if it is, can we deploy it without killing all those brave enough to have made it through the tunnel?'

Cubric shuffled in his seat and rubbed the back of his neck. 'Well… now you mention it, I once saw a chap light the stuff.'

Wendel choked. 'The realm prohibited its use long before you served at the mines.'

'Err… yes, that it was, sir, but a man has to relieve the boredom of the long, dark hours below somehow. You could still find small amounts of the powder in places, and they'd set it off, just for fun like. It's easy, and judging by the small pile that nearly blew out my ears and brought down the ceiling, I'd say a few handfuls would be more than enough to take out a good number of those damn raiders, and possibly even this wyke fellow.' He clasped his hands and pulled them apart. 'Boom! Those we don't blow to pieces will be scared half to death, perhaps long enough for the rest of our force to storm the town. And if we could set it off close to the wyke, if we don't kill him, we could trap him under rubble.'

Gundrul smiled. 'You may have said something useful for the first time in your life, Cub.'

Cubric beamed. 'And it's only taken fifty-odd years, eh, Gunny... Captain.'

Elodi patted the table. 'It's a start, gentlemen. I'll send a bird to Calerdorn to have a map of the mines ready for when we arrive.' She turned to Wendel. 'Unless...'

'No need, ma'am.' Wendel pulled a sheet from his files and handed it to Elodi. 'I can't vouch for its accuracy, but it's the most up-to-date chart in my possession.'

Elodi examined the network of dotted lines delving deep under the mountains. She passed it to the captain. 'If you and Cubric can locate the cave with this powder, we may fashion a workable plan.' Her stomach surged towards her throat as the ship climbed an enormous wave, then sank as they plunged down the other side. A bell rang on the deck. Elodi clutched the table. 'I think that concludes our meeting for now. We shall convene this evening for further deliberation.' She glanced at the blank faces opposite. The bell continued.

Wendel addressed the men. 'Lady Harlyn wants another meeting this evening to discuss the plan.'

Elodi went to rise. 'Yes... thank you, Wendel. And could one of you please find out why that bell—'

A young crewman burst through the door. 'Excuse me, ma'am, gentlemen. Blowers... Captain Blunden says we should prepare for a storm.' He pointed back through the door. 'The sky to the north has turned black.'

Elodi ignored Wendel's request to stay. She had to see for herself and rushed out of the stateroom. Up on deck, the sun still shone. A light rain fell, but one look north revealed this was just the vanguard for the storm to come. Her jaw dropped along with the *Celestra* as she dipped into a shallow trough.

Night reared up ahead of its time. The northern horizon had gone, as the black sea merged with storm clouds, ready to vent their fury at the fools beneath them. The ship rose, then plunged as the first waves fleeing the squall slammed into the bow. Men scrambled up the main and mizzen masts, frantically taking down the billowing sails. Elodi stumbled and staggered her way to the helm. Horace and Blunden had already lashed themselves to the rigging with thick rope. They fixed their eyes on the clouds and failed to notice her presence until she spoke. 'Can we ride this out?'

Blunden's mouth gaped before he could answer. 'We'll… have to, ma'am. We've no chance of outrunning it.' His face passed into shadow as the clouds shut out the sun. He yelled to the men on the mast above. 'Get them mainsails down or they'll drag us to the bottom as soon as the storm strikes.'

The wind strengthened, hurling icy rain at Elodi's back. She searched for the coast. 'Could we make it to land in time?'

Horace shook his head. 'Be worse off, ma'am.' He jabbed his finger. 'We need to head out to sea. We've reached the coast of Noor.'

Elodi pointed to the shore. 'What about Eldamouth? Or Seransea? Could we make port?'

'Wouldn't want to risk it, ma'am. If we get it wrong, the rocks will tear the old girl's hull to shreds and throw us to the mercy of the sea. And if we're not smashed to pieces on the rocks, we'll meet our doom trying to clamber up the cliffs.'

Elodi turned and wished she had listened to Wendel. The towering wall of clouds climbed to the very ceiling of the world, seeming too heavy for the sky to constrain. Below them, terrified white horses, whipped into a frenzy by the tempest, dashed towards them on violent waters. Elodi grabbed Horace's shoulder as the ship climbed a wave. She yelled into his ear. 'What do we do?'

His eyes stayed fixed on the threat ahead. 'Keep up our speed and head straight at it. That way we hopefully won't capsize.' Horace grappled the wheel. 'But we do have one thing in our favor, ma'am.'

Elodi stumbled as the *Celestra* rode the next wave. 'We do?'

'Yes, ma'am.' Horace grunted. 'Our weight. We have, let me see, with your men and our crew, one-hundred and twenty men, plus your horses and supplies. Might just stop us capsizing.' Horace stared down the deck. 'But it's all down to the foremast. If it don't hold fast, we're done for.' He chewed his lip. 'It ain't going to be an easy ride, but that's our best chance.'

Blunden yelled above the rising wind. 'Ma'am! Get down below! That's an order. Disperse your men across the decks and get them tied down. Secure everything that means anything to you, so it don't wash overboard. Then fasten yourself to a stout pillar. Windows will get smashed and there'll be plenty of water crashing through. This is going to get a lot worse before it gets better.'

Elodi needed no order. She grabbed Horace's arm. 'May the Three be with you both. Good luck.' The men nodded grimly and checked their ropes. Elodi staggered across the deck as a towering wave struck the *Celestra*. She grabbed the railing as the stinging spray sought to snatch her from the deck. She gawped into the dark waters below;

an enormous creature moved beneath, gliding as if undisturbed by the commotion on the surface. Elodi watched it head towards the coastline — she wondered whether she would see Calerdorn again.

28. Firelight & Demons

'I'm out.' Jedrul lifted an arm with the chain hanging free. He grabbed the other end and pulled it taut. 'Who's for throttling a Ruuk neck or two?'

'Hand me that spike.' Roold wrestled with his ankle. 'One more to go and I'm with you, brother. Take a peek outside while we finish.' Toryn gritted his teeth as he pried open the clasp wide enough to pull his red-raw ankle free. Roold nodded at him. 'Nice going, lad. Nander? You lot? How's it going?'

'Almost done.' Others around the wagon broke their links and clutched improvised weapons ready for an attempted escape.

'See anything, Jed?'

Jedrul ducked back inside. 'Be daylight in an hour, but thick cloud's heading this way, I can't see a single star over yonder. Must be a perilous storm brewing in the north out at sea. Swear I can smell it in the air. But thankfully it's a lot sweeter than the stench of the mire.'

Roold clutched a bar and steadied himself. 'That'll suit us, the darker the better. Right, listen up, brothers. The numbers are against us, but they'll have a belly full of ale so will be slow.' He turned to Jedrul and Toryn. 'I can't ask you to fight without the promise of a piece of land on the plain, for that you must take the Oath now.'

Jedrul stood tall. 'Then we'll take it.' He beamed to Toryn. 'You up for this?' Toryn nodded.

Roold turned to the others. 'Any objections?' None spoke, not even Nander. 'Then raise your right hand.' Roold cleared his throat. 'Better make this the short ceremony, and quieter than usual, eh, lads? We'll also forgo the initiation for now. Repeat after me.' He took a breath. 'I swear my allegiance to the Archon.' They duly repeated his words. Roold looked around him. 'Hold on. Where's that spike? We don't have a sword.' Nander pulled it from behind his back and handed it to the captain. Roold spat on the rusty tool and rubbed it on his shirtsleeve. 'This will have to do.' He held it towards Toryn. 'Place your right hand on the... blade. Best make it the sharp end, at least. Now repeat.' He pushed out his chest. 'I promise to lay down my life for the Archon, in service for the Five Realms, and in defense and the honor of my brothers.' Toryn, then Jedrul completed the Oath. Roold spoke to the others in the wagon. 'Not a step back, brothers.' The men echoed the words. The captain smiled at their new recruits. 'Then may you plow the plains in peace or die an old man—'

'Knackered in a plump wench's bed.' The men laughed at Nander's jest.

Roold turned. 'Let's stick with the formal words please, this isn't the time.' He nodded to Toryn and Jedrul. 'Well, you get the idea.' He held out his forearm to Toryn. His heart pounded as he clasped Roold's arm in the fashion of a guardsman. Roold smiled. 'Welcome to the Archonian Guard.'

'Shut up in there!' The wagon rattled as a club struck the frame.

Roold pointed to the canopy. He whispered. 'That one will be the first to feel my chain around his throat.' He squatted and gestured to the men to huddle around. 'Right lads, there's another wagon in this convoy. We don't know if they're alive, dead, still in chains or free, but the more the merrier as they say. Toryn, you take the spike and head for it once the fun begins, and free as many as you can.' Toryn nodded, proud to accept his first order. Roold tightened his grip on his chain. 'We're up against swords

271

but I reckon we can take out a few before they know
what's hit 'em. They'll be a few on horseback, but a chain
around their necks will soon bring them down to our level.
Whip or throttle the blighters, I'll leave that to you.' He
turned to Jedrul. 'Best take one last look.'

Toryn's heart hammered so hard, he feared their
captors would suspect something was afoot. Jedrul dipped
back inside the wagon. 'From what I can make out, there's
three on horseback this side, must be more with the other
wagon and more at the front. I can see torches at the head
and rear, but they're not shedding much light on us.'

'And the ground? Do we need to worry about the
bog, Jed?'

'Not a problem. I reckon we've passed through the
worse part of the mire. Looks frozen on both sides.'

Roold staggered to the rear of the rolling wagon.
'Good. We're going now. We'll split both ways. Keep it
down, we don't want to alert them too soon. But before I
give the command' — he lowered his voice — 'brothers,
whatever happens, I want to say what an honor it's—'

Jedrul laughed. 'Give it a rest, cappy. Just give the
damn command.' Toryn fought for air as his lungs
struggled to find room in his tight chest. He watched
Roold, half-hoping he would change his mind.

He did not. Roold held up his hand. 'Okay, ready,
lads? Now!' He tore open the canvas and leaped out.
Toryn stumbled forward from the back, armed with a
short chain and the spike. Ahead, the others tumbled out
after Roold. The canopy of the wagon behind opened,
three men jumped clear. They must be free. Toryn reached
the step. More men poured out from the other wagon, and
he guessed they would not need him. He jumped, landing
heavily on his ankle on a frozen ridge of mud. He rounded
the side of the wagon as the cry went up. Roold whipped
his chain around a Ruuk on horseback and yanked him to

the ground. Two more went down before the escorts on foot at the head of the convoy could rush back. Roold finished off his victim and snatched up his sword. The first of the troops clashed with the guards, but Roold was too skilled with a blade to be troubled. The horses whinnied, two reared up, throwing their riders to the mercy of Roold and his men.

A shadow ran at Toryn, his blade glinting in the torchlight as he raised it above his head. He remembered Hamar's advice and planted his feet. Toryn pulled the chain taut, keeping the spike clasped in his right hand. The sword slashed down. He thrust up his hands. Sparks flew from the rusty chain. He dipped to one side and shoved, deflecting the force of the attack down. Toryn lunged and thrust the spike into his assailant's exposed neck. The big Ruuk grunted and fell dead.

'Get his blade!' Jedrul lashed out with his chain and caught another across the face.

'You take it, I'll use the spike.'

Jedrul grabbed the weapon. 'Stick with me, lad.' They reached the front of the wagon. At least twenty of their captors remained on foot and hurriedly formed a line. Roold, Nander and five other guards now wielded swords. They smashed into their confused foe. Four fell in an instant as Roold wheeled, ducked, and drove on to the next. More captured weapons were passed back to the rear as they gathered pace. Only a dozen of their foe survived the onslaught. They edged back, retreating into a circle. One from the middle launched his torch over the heads of his comrades. It arced through the dark, landing on a wagon at the head of the convoy. The flames soon took, engulfing the canvas, illuminating the field of battle.

'Surrender!' Roold held up his hand to halt the attack. The Ruuk in the circle laughed. Roold leveled his sword at the chest of the commander. 'Surrender or you'll all die.'

The Ruuk laughed harder. 'All die? Not a chance. It is you that should surrender.'

Roold held his nerve. 'But you're surrounded, outnumbered and outclassed.'

The commander tilted his head. 'Outnumbered? Do you think we don't have the wit to count?' He pointed his axe at the flaming wagon. 'You better watch your backs. Our beacon over there is bringing forty more here as we speak.'

Nander stepped up to Roold. 'Do we believe him? He could be bluffing.'

Roold shrugged. 'Makes no difference. If he is, we'll finish them off and we're free. If he ain't and more are coming, I'd sooner die here than let them take me to this lady of theirs. Then we're still free. I'm not about to give up my farm for the promise of a visit to Wyke Wood.' He turned to the others. 'What say you?' Fists clenching swords and chains thrust into the air. Roold bellowed. 'Then we fight!' He raised his sword. 'Take 'em, lads.' But before he could move, Toryn's legs buckled. The ground shook. He slumped to his knees, falling onto his face as if he had taken a blow to his gut. He recoiled as the burning wagon spat and hissed. His brothers cried out. Toryn forced himself onto all fours. Around him, the men stood with their arms hanging limp by their sides, bathed in the green hue of the newly ignited wagon fire.

The guards gaped at the crackling flames. A black form took shape with a long, pointed head bowed forward, and arms folded across its body. The figure grew. Warriors on both sides flung themselves to the ground, burying faces in hands should the sight of the foul beast scorch their eyes. But Toryn could not tear his eyes away. The quivering creature reached its full height, three times the size of a man. It lifted its distorted head and opened its arms. To Toryn's horror, the arms extended into jagged, bat-like wings. It tipped back its head, screeched and launched into the air. Toryn gagged in the warm stench of death as its beating wings fanned its corruption over the cowering men. He dared to look up, instantly regretting the move. Black, glistening eyes glowered back.

The demon entered his head.

It shrieked a hideous and gleeful song, threatening to split his skull in two. Toryn writhed, clasping his hands to his ears, ready to tear them free to end the agony. But at the point of surrendering his soul, another voice, a woman's voice, soothed his pain. The words of her song wove around the harsh timbre of his tormentor, expelling it back to the void. As quickly as it came, the voice faded, leaving only an echo of her song. Toryn lay back on the grass and felt his body sink as if on a soft bed. He closed his eyes, ready for the sweet dreams he knew would follow.

'Wake up! What you grinning about, fool.' Toryn flinched as a foot struck his ribs. He opened his eyes to freezing rain lashing into his face. The wind howled overhead, driving dark clouds towards the mountains far to the east. Two hands grabbed under his arms and hoisted him to his feet. His head spun as he turned.

Jedrul tried to smile. 'Morning, brother.' He rubbed the back of his head. 'I have to say, being an Archonian isn't as grand as I'd hoped.'

Toryn watched Roold and the others being woken in the same brutal manner. He whispered to Jedrul. 'What happened?' He stretched out his neck. 'What was that thing?'

Jedrul yawned. 'What thing?'

'The creature… in the flames?'

Jedrul scratched his head. 'Didn't see no creature, just the fire turning green as that skinny fellow showed his face. Some trick, I have to say.'

'Don't you remember? You all stopped and stared.' Toryn turned away. 'Never mind. I must have been mistaken.'

Jedrul peered at the top of Toryn's head. 'Must have taken a knock in the fight.' He turned. 'Here, Roold, young Toryn says he saw—'

'Shut it! No talking.' The large Ruuk who had goaded them earlier strode towards them. His thick tongue struggled with the strange words, but he had no trouble making himself understood. 'Get in line and stand still.' He jabbed his sword at Jedrul's stomach. 'I'll gut the first man to move, and I'll make the rest of you carry his steaming innards. If I had my way, I'd finish the lot of you right here.' He chuckled. 'But someone is keen to meet you.' He turned and clicked his fingers. Two shorter Ruuk brought chains and straps. 'You can walk the rest of the way. But don't you worry your pretty little heads, it ain't far, two days at a brisk pace.' He laughed. 'And don't be expecting any comforts when you arrive.'

29. GODS OF THE DEEP

The *Celestra* had weathered many storms during her long life at sea. In her youth, guided by an experienced helmsman, she would have met the squall's challenge with relish. But now, in her dotage, and with long years idling in calmer coastal waters, every joint creaked, groaned, and strained in the storm. The gods of the deep waters both coveted and loathed the *Celestra*. For too long, she had defied their lust to drag her down to adorn their graveyard of wrecks. But the old lady's unexpected voyage had stirred their greed. The small fishing boats interested them not, and over the centuries their resentment had grown, now discontent and bored with the rotting, barnacled carcasses of their prey. With glee, they had rushed north to rouse the cold air and hurl it down the coast at the *Celestra*. With the wind whipping up the waters from above, and the monsters beneath the seabed stirring the depths, the gods provoked a storm, the likes not seen for many a century. Yet, the shipwrights of old had excelled with the *Celestra*, and despite her age, she would resist with every knot and fiber not to become a trophy for the gods.

Elodi screamed at the wind. The windows had long since gone. Icy fingers of the sea groped inside, eager to snatch a victim to haul into the water. The rope cut deep into her sides as she gasped for air in the salty spray. How much longer could she last? The wailing wind rose. Below, the horses squealed, and men cried out. Elodi's throat burned as she screamed uncontrollably, fearing the storm would tear the sky asunder, freeing the void to suck the world into its maw. Her stomach twisted as the valiant

Celestra climbed a gigantic wave, followed by a brief respite from the gale as she plummeted into the trough. But if Elodi thought the worse was over, she was mistaken. A gust slammed into her side, sending the *Celestra* reeling. She clasped her numb hands to her ears, clenched her jaw, and screwed her sore eyes shut, but nothing could keep the cacophony at bay. She yelled, pleading to the deities of all the stories she had ever heard, frantic for one to answer. But no answer came. They were alone, helpless against the might of the sea and force of the wind as the elements conspired to banish them from the world of the living.

Elodi knew madness waited to take her. She clung in desperation to the retreating part of her sanity, but had to accept she was losing the battle for her mind.

A fresh voice entered the fray. No, not a voice, a shriek! A primeval scream of pure hatred joined the storm, an ancient, unbridled evil, resentful of all living beings. And it came for her soul. Her bleeding fingers grappled with the knot. She had to break free. She had to surrender to the sea before the beast riding the tempest claimed her. It craved her. It had a place for the Lady of Harlyn within its vaults beneath the mountains. But the knot held firm. Elodi collapsed, the fight had gone. Her limbs flapped like those of a corn doll shaken by an excitable child. She had nothing left; she awaited her fate.

Silence. Calm. Elodi opened her stinging eyes and blinked in the bright sunlight. She looked about the stateroom. This was no subterranean vault, nor the seabed. She wriggled her fingers. She had survived! Elodi had been close to the edge of her world and returned. The *Celestra* had ridden the storm. She untied the rope. Wendel lay nearby. A trickle of blood ran from the corner of his mouth down his pale skin. She clambered to his side and shook his shoulder. 'Wendel? Don't you leave me now.'

He rolled on his side and opened his eyes. She gasped. 'Oh, thank The Three. For a moment... I...'

Wendel brought his hand to his face and murmured. 'I have a mild headache' — he winced — 'and a few bruises, but I shall survive, ma'am.' He tried to sit.

'Take your time. I'll see if I can find help.' Wendel obliged and lay back. Carefully, Elodi rose to her feet. How long had the storm raged? She must have blacked out as the *Celestra* had bravely navigated the waves.

Horace? Blunden? She rushed to the door or what remained. It hung limply from one hinge as the wood of the frame had split. Elodi climbed over the door and found a similar scene of destruction in the galley. A pale-faced Gundrul emerged from his cabin, but Elodi was in a hurry to check the crew before she could worry about her men. She grasped his shoulder. 'Please, see what can be done for Wendel, and then check the horses.' She turned and headed for the steps.

Once up on deck, the full force of the storm became apparent. The foremast had gone, taking part of the deck with it. But it must have lasted long enough for Horace to steer them clear. She turned to the stern and climbed the broken stairs. The young lad who had brought the warning of the storm, crouched over Horace as the helmsman struggled to sit. Elodi froze. Horace held the end of a frayed rope. Tears streamed down his red cheeks. He looked up as Elodi approached. 'The waves took old Blowers.' He held out the rope. 'Tore him clean off the deck. Didn't have time to grab him. One minute he stood by my side, the next...' he dropped his head into his hands.

Elodi kneeled at his side. 'I'm sure you did everything you could. It's a miracle any of us survived, and that's all down to you and your crew.'

His shoulders shook. 'Never thought it could be so

rough. I've been at sea in storms before, but nothing… nothing ever as ferocious. We lost six good men along with Blowers.' Horace straightened and opened his eyes. He groaned. 'My poor lady. See what it's done to her.'

'But she's ridden it through and kept us' — she stared at the sea — 'most of us safe.' Her throat tightened at the thought of Captain Blunden and his men beneath the calm waters, having sacrificed their lives to save the ship.

Horace's eyes widened as he surveyed the damage. 'Must have passed out. Don't remember seeing the mast go.'

She helped Horace to his feet. 'What now? Can we make it to shore?' Elodi turned. Her heart stopped. 'Which way? I can't see land.'

Horace wiped his face and pointed. 'That way, ma'am. But I can't say how far as I've no idea how long we've been drifting, and whether the sun is rising or sinking just yet. I'll have a better idea when the stars come out, so long as there's not too many clouds.'

Elodi fought down the panic; she could not stomach facing another storm. 'Can we make it without the front mast?'

'We still have two, and the sails we saved. But if another storm hits, even one half as bad as the last, I can't make any promises.'

'Then let us hope the wind has blown itself out.' She searched the horizon, yearning to see the thin, dark line of the coast. More men stumbled out onto the deck, many nursing cuts and bruises, but thankfully few had suffered worse injuries. Gundrul climbed the steps to the helm; Elodi noticed the color had returned to his cheeks. He nodded to her. 'Ma'am, Sea Mist is fine if a bit shaken, but I'm afraid three of the drafts didn't make it. I've offered my men to the crew to help with repairs.' He turned to Horace. 'I heard about Captain Blunden. On behalf of the

Archonian Guard, I offer my condolences. May he go peacefully to the… sail the calm, warm seas of the next world, or wherever you sailors end your days.'

Horace bit his lip, glancing at Elodi. 'Thank you, Captain, and yes, may he find peace wherever he finds himself.'

Gundrul extended his hand and grasped Horace's forearm. 'And a hearty thanks from all of us for your truly heroic deeds.'

Elodi thought it impossible, but she was sure Horace blushed. He stammered. 'Again, thank you, but it will all be in vain if I can't get you safely back to shore.' Gundrul searched the horizon. Horace sought to reassure. 'As I told Lady Harlyn, while I know which direction to head, I can't yet say how long it will take.' He turned. 'Now, if you will allow me, I will ask you to clear the helm, I have plenty to do if we're to reach Calerdorn.'

Elodi suddenly felt in the way. 'Of course.' She turned to Gundrul. 'We'll see if anyone needs attention below and let you proceed with the tasks at hand.' She nodded to Horace. 'And again, thank you. I will ensure the Archon gets to hear the tale of the *Celestra* and her crew's heroism.'

His eyes widened. 'The Archon? Much obliged, ma'am, but let's hope it has a happy ending.'

Elodi and Gundrul left the deck. She touched his arm. 'How are the men, Captain?'

'The men are fine, ma'am, a bit battered and bruised, but they'll survive. They're trained well and their loyalty to the Archon will keep them going where others would fail.' But Elodi wondered for how long. Had Horace saved them only to meet with a more unfortunate end on dry land?

The rising sun on the second day since the storm, revealed a sight they had all longed to see. Eight slender towers rose into the narrow strip of pink-tinged sky, peering over the cliffs of Dorn. Horace had kept his word. On consulting the star map, he had predicted correctly the time it would take to reach their destination.

'So that's Calerdorn, ma'am.' Horace squinted at the towers.

Elodi shivered in the cool morning air. 'And a finer sight I couldn't wish to see.' She clasped his shoulder. 'I never thought I'd see it again during the storm.'

Horace sighed. 'I only wish Blowers could have seen your city. I've heard tales about it for as long as I can remember, but I never thought I'd walk its cobbled streets.' He turned. 'Is it true you can see beyond the Draegelan Trench from the highest tower?'

Elodi laughed. 'Not quite. We look out onto the Dornan Mountains, but it's still quite a spectacular view.'

'Oh, that's a shame. Always wanted to see the land outside the realms.'

'I'd rather not know. Judging by the folk raiding our lands, I can't conceive there's much to offer. My father tried countless times to agree terms of peace, but they seemed reluctant to negotiate.' Elodi checked they were alone. 'Horace? Before the storm struck, I thought I saw a large creature pass under the ship. Did I imagine that? It was easily larger than the *Celestra*. Do such beasts exist?'

The helmsman beamed. 'You must have heard the sorry tale of Behemora.'

Elodi stammered. 'Well yes, but I always thought it was just... a myth.'

'You're one of the lucky ones. Few have seen her. She rarely comes close to shore.'

Elodi stared into the deep waters. 'Have you?'

'Once... maybe. We were out for the night, well out to sea, waiting for a shoal to come in on a warm current. The moon shone bright, so I'm certain I saw her, if only briefly. An enormous beast with a jagged spine broke the surface like a glistening blade. So big, I thought a lost island had emerged from the depths. Then I heard a swoosh and she was gone; the boat rose in her wake. She must be as big as they say. And I'm pretty certain I've heard her sing.'

Elodi's eyes widened. 'Is that part also true?'

'On the quietest of nights, you can hear her calling for her mate. Such a sorrowful sound , but seeing she's been separated from her beloved since the changing of the world, I guess it ain't going to be a merry song.'

Elodi watched the *Celestra's* wake. 'Well, I never.'

'Makes you wonder don't it, ma'am. How many creatures roam this world we don't know about. And why we have to worry about being strangled in our beds by those we do know about.' He leaned on the wheel. 'Sometimes when I'm out at sea, especially when it's all calm and quiet, I wonder why I choose to go back to shore.'

Elodi nodded. 'I must admit, it has been a pleasure to be away from the troubles of the realms. Perhaps, I could get used to life at sea. Just as long I never have to endure another storm.'

Horace smiled. 'Only if you're very lucky. Now if you would please excuse me, ma'am, I must be about my duty.'

'Of course, Helmsman, but I wish to talk again about your experience at sea.' He beamed and returned to the helm.

Wendel's gray head appeared above the deck. He staggered on the last few steps, stopped and grabbed the rail. 'Ma'am, if I may be so bold, I order you to put an arrow in my back if you ever see me step near another ship.'

'You do look a little peaky again this morning.' Elodi patted him on the back. 'Then I will obey your order if I see you approach Calerdorn's dock.' She checked no one stood within earshot. 'Talking of orders. I was pleased how the meeting went with the captains before the storm.'

Wendel nodded. 'Indeed it did. We now have a number of feasible options to consider.'

'Well... yes, but I meant I was pleased they actually listened to my views.'

He shrugged. 'It is their duty, ma'am. You lead this mission.'

Elodi turned to him. 'But I want them to listen because they value my opinion, and have faith in my judgement, not because it's their duty.'

'Ah, I see. It will come with time, ma'am. And I suspect you'll have plenty of opportunity to earn their respect in the coming weeks. We'll have—'

'Ma'am!' Gundrul ran from the bow. He turned and pointed farther up the coast. 'Smoke, a lot of it. See that smudge? I don't think it's a cloud.'

She looked to the coast. 'It's drifting in from the border.' Elodi groaned. 'The fort at Draegnor must be under attack, and a successful one judging by the amount of smoke.' Her eyes stayed fixed on the telltale smudge. 'Wendel. Send a bird at once. If word of the raid hasn't yet reached Calerdorn, they must keep watch and prepare for an attack on the city. And also inform them I'll be landing in a matter of hours.'

'This will be the last bird, ma'am. Let us trust there'll be no more delays.'

'We have to have hope, Wendel. Drunsberg, now this? What do we do with such limited resources? It will be a challenge to trouble the raiders at the mines, let alone take them back, and then offer any real help to Draegnor. And I'm certain the Archon will ignore my requests for more resources.'

Wendel stepped to her side. 'Remember, ma'am, you

have four hundred of Broon's men arriving any day soon.'

'Well, there's some good news at least.' Her fingers dug into the damp wood of the old ship. 'We can't get back a moment too soon.'

30. A WARM WELCOME

At first, the heat from the flames had been welcome. Toryn had not realized how deep the cold had penetrated until the feeling returned to his limbs. But now they ached, a deep, agonizing ache, refusing to let go despite the heat. They stood in a line, chained together at the ankles, with a roaring fire crackling at their backs. He and his fellow guardsmen had endured the brutal two-day march with little rest, the odd scrap of food, and an occasional drop of foul-tasting water. Toryn had suffered the most. His colleagues were tough, used to hardship and strenuous work. Whereas Toryn's life on the farm, and even the trek with Hamar, had not prepared him for such treatment. He had marched in a trance, watching his feet as they trudged in silence, hour after hour to the relentless rhythm of the line. He had not noticed the dark, spikey treetops of Wyke Wood peering over the hill until his stomach had knotted.

'Get back in line!' A fist struck Jedrul's midriff. He stiffened, determined not to bend, and stepped back. Toryn recognized the Ruuk who delivered the blow. Grebb, the raider who had fought Hamar and Elwold, stood opposite. Grebb sneered. 'Stay there until I tell you to turn.' Toryn arched his back as the cloth of his shirt felt ready to burst into flame. He glanced out the side of his eye to Grebb. The Ruuk's lips moved as if counting.

'Alright, you lot. Turn!' Toryn winced as the clasp rubbed against the raw skin on his ankle. But that was soon forgotten as he faced the fire. He shut his eyes, but still they smarted against the heat. Grebb laughed. 'You'll soon be warm.' He mocked Toryn. 'Need to have you ready for your training, eh.' Toryn turned his head, but

Grebb strode forward and grabbed his hair, forcing it back to face the front. 'Too hot for you, sonny? Would you be happier north of the Trench?' He pushed Toryn's head. 'Nah, too weak. You ain't going to last long in the wood.'

Toryn stiffened, determined to show Grebb he was not finished yet. His fist clenched as he imagined smashing it into Grebb's flat, gray face. He blinked away the heat of the fire and looked towards the wood. Behind the hot, shimmering air of the fire, the black tree-tops quivered like dark grasping fingers, clawing at the air, groping for lost souls to lure into its lair. Toryn's fist unclenched; Hamar had described this place well. The tall firs stood defiant against the cold, challenging the daylight to pierce its murky shield.

'Right, where's the sorry leader of you filthy lot?' Grebb strolled down the back of the line. Toryn caught sight of Roold out of the corner of his eye. Grebb pushed him in the back, sending him closer to the bonfire. 'There you go, cappy. That'll dry you off.' Grebb stepped up to his side. 'Need you looking your best to meet the lady.'

An injured guard at Roold's side wavered and fell. Roold stooped to help him stand, but Grebb shoved him aside and grabbed the ailing man by the throat. He hoisted him to his feet and yelled in his face. 'Stand or you'll be on the fire!' The poor man groaned as Roold and Nander hooked their arms in his and held him upright.

Grebb seized the man's hair, yanked his head back and peered at his face. 'Don't you waste my time. I didn't bring you here to die.' He let go and chuckled. 'Well, not just yet.'

An old Ruuk behind the column croaked. 'Watch out, Grebb, *he's* coming.'

'Enough!' Uldrak's rasp set Toryn's teeth on edge. 'Stand them down, fool. I want them ready to fight, not ready to eat.' He flicked his hand — the flames died. The relief was immediate, but short-lived. Uldrak stood before the smoldering ashes. His hooded head turned, prompting a shudder to pass down the line. Toryn could not see the wyke's eyes beneath the shadow of his hood, but he recoiled as an icy chill scraped across his face. Uldrak rubbed his gray hands together. 'Let's take a closer look at you.' His thin lips curled. 'Archonian Guard? More like withered, old maids.'

Grebb stood at Uldrak's side, but Toryn noticed he kept a few paces between them. He pointed a trembling hand towards Roold and stammered. 'That... that one's the captain.'

Uldrak stopped opposite Roold. 'In all but name, but he'll do.' He moved to the man propped up by Roold and Nander. The wyke spat. 'This one's no use. He'll be dead in two days from those wounds.' He clicked his bony fingers in the guard's face. The sick man choked and collapsed. Uldrak's nose wrinkled as he regarded the fallen guard. 'Unchain him and dump the carcass on the heap. That'll keep the wolves off our backs.' Roold went to move. Uldrak snapped. 'Don't!' Roold froze. The wyke jabbed a finger at Roold's chest. 'Unless you also want your bones tossed to the wolves, I suggest you stay in line.' Two of Grebb's crew hurried forward and removed the fallen guard.

Jedrul whispered between clenched teeth. 'Poor sod. Won't get his farm on the plain.'

Uldrak passed Nander. Every muscle in Toryn's body clenched as he drew near. Uldrak stopped. He twisted to face Toryn. Toryn's head spun. His heart raced, his stomach turned, but he stood firm. Uldrak took a step closer. Beneath his hood, faint features of a gray, lined face came into view. Toryn fought back the bile rising in his throat as dull, yellow eyes met his, freezing his insides under the wyke's glare. He felt his body sag as Uldrak stepped back. He raised his arm. A finger extended from his sleeve, pointing at Toryn's head. 'Keep an eye on this one.'

Grebb scoffed. 'What? The boy?'

Uldrak spun to face Grebb. 'Yes, the boy! Fool.' Grebb shrank back as Uldrak hissed. 'This one has a half a brain which makes him twice as dangerous as you.' The wyke twisted back to Toryn. The wrinkles at the side of Uldrak's thin mouth deepened. Toryn breathed out as he moved on and strolled to the end of the row. Uldrak turned and rasped. 'They'll do. Take them into the wood.'

Grebb staggered back. 'Me? But I thought...?'

'You don't think. I don't need you to think. Just do as I say. I have business on the border.' Uldrak swung his cloak to leave, then stopped. He jabbed a finger back at Toryn. 'And make sure you take *that* one to see the lady.'

The tall firs shut out what little light the thick clouds allowed to pass. But it wasn't the gloom that troubled Toryn; it was the whispers. They began the moment he entered the outskirts of the wood. The voices spoke another tongue, one he knew to be that of the scrawls on the rocks that had destroyed the Singing Stone. At first, they goaded him, then taunted until the remnants of his confidence lay in tatters. Now the voices made a promise, a cruel promise of a slow, painful demise. But not one ending with the merciful release of death. They would break him, crush his spirit until he became as them, a slave to all that is evil. But part of him would remain true. Not out of kindness, but in a cruel act of spite. The good in him would witness the depraved deeds his masters demanded of him, but without the chance to redeem the evil meted out by his own hands. And Toryn believed them.

He stumbled on, no longer feeling the ground under

his feet, or the clothes on his skin. Not that he cared, for his mind numbed as it emptied. Toryn could not remember a time when he had not tramped beneath the canopy of leaden branches, bending under the weight of the damp air. The face of an old man with a gray beard; fields of swaying barley bathed in the orange light of a late sun; a distant mountain top. They flashed briefly before his eyes, then faded. He walked alone, struggling to remember his name, his home and the faces of his friends. But the voices in his head persisted, and with every whisper they took a little more.

Toryn spluttered and gasped. Icy water ran down his face. He jerked upright. 'Mother!' He choked as a clasp around his neck yanked him back.

'Ha! Always call for their mother. No, not your mother, boy.' A voice. Not a whisper, more of a croak. 'But I'm the closest you'll get to a mother around here.' The dank air smelled of plowed fields on a wet autumn morning. Toryn shuffled back. His hands groped in the dark, finding tree roots jutting from an earthen wall.

He squinted, peering into the gloom. A shadow moved in what he assumed to be a small cell. 'Where am I? Where are the others?'

The figure limped closer. An old man bent and placed something at Toryn's side. He grunted. 'Always the same question. Where am I? *Where am I?* Isn't it obvious?' He groaned as he forced his back to straighten. 'But no, never, how are you today, Dohl? Did you sleep well, Dohl?' The man turned, dragging his feet as he made his way to a slither of light. 'Nobody worries about poor old Dohl, poor old, knackered Dohl who's been on his feet all day.' Toryn blinked as the door creaked open. The silhouette of the crooked man stood briefly in the light. Toryn guessed he would have been a tall man in his prime, but the years had obviously weighed heavily upon him. His spine was so curved, he had to pull his head painfully back to look ahead.

The man muttered, 'He'll do as he's told, no need to ask Dohl what's on his mind. Always clearing up the mess.' He pulled hard against the door, scraping it across the ground as it shut. The man talked to himself as he secured the bolt. 'I remember a time when...' he scuttled out of earshot.

Toryn slumped against the wall at his back. His hand went to the object Dohl had left him and found a chunk of bread. He bit into the hard, stale bread. It tasted foul, but his hunger got the better of him. As he chewed, he peered about the room illuminated by slivers of yellow light spilling through cracks in the ancient wooden door. Dohl was right. He sat in an underground cell in the middle of Wyke Wood. It could not be worse, yet thankfully the whispers had stopped. But what about Roold, Jedrul and the others? Toryn finished his bread, certain his stomach would suffer before long, and slumped against the wall. He had no memory of how he had arrived at the cells, or being separated from the guards. Perhaps, if he found a way out, he could locate Roold, and together they would escape this cursed place. Grebb was reluctant to enter the wood, so they could be few in number, or equally reluctant to fight. And if others were in the same, poor condition as Dohl, they would meet little resistance. The wood of the door was old and rotten in many places. If he could reach, it would not take much force to break.

Toryn edged onto his side and slowly rose onto all fours. He tugged at the chain attached to the ring around his neck: it was short, too short, and he could only rise to a crouch. He examined the wall. The chain attached to a hook buried in the earth. He pulled. It shifted a little. His spirits rose. If he could free the hook, he would have a sturdy chain to choke Grebb.

Toryn leaned back and wrapped a few links around his hands. He tightened his grip, drew a breath, ready to yank the hook free.

A cry. More joined. Cries of pain and terror came from outside. His hands dropped, he slumped to his knees and fell onto his face. The whispers told him to let go; the whispers told him to listen to the anguish of his comrades; they promised him he would soon meet their mistress; they boasted of changing times when nothing would ever be the same again.

31. Not a Moment to Lose

Elodi could have sworn she felt *Celestra's* bow swell with pride as the crowds cheered the ship's arrival. Losing her foremast could not diminish her grandeur as she glided effortlessly through the gateway into Calerdorn's dock. None in the city had ever laid eyes on a ship as fine as the *Celestra*. Not since the glory days of old, had the big ships graced the wharf.

Elodi watched the eager faces of those lining the quayside as the crew threw the ropes to secure to the harbor pilings. She saw joy tinged with hope but feared the *Celestra* flattered to deceive. Elodi smiled and waved, not wanting to deny her people a moment of relief from the dark days, no matter how brief. If her Council had released the news of the attack on Draegnor, it did not show.

Elodi strode to the gangplank and joined Wendel and Gundrul at the front of the guards lining the *Celestra's* deck. She glanced at the narrow plank. Not long ago, she would have balked at crossing it, but she had survived the worst the sea could throw at her, crossed the narrow Caerwal Bridge, and stood atop of the tallest tower in the Five Realms. Without hesitation, she linked arms with Wendel and Gundrul, and walked tall, back into her realm. The voices of the crowd rose as they parted to allow Elodi and her company through. But she could not help notice their faces change as they watched the guards disembark — many just a year or two older than their young sons.

Elodi's Council had received no word from the fort at Draegnor. This could only mean one thing: the attack had been sudden and successful, allowing no time to send a message, or worse, all had died, or had been captured for purposes she dare not contemplate. Elodi and her council had debated long into the night on what action they should take. Her commanders argued for a swift counterattack, but Elodi had sided with Wendel. Even if they sent a sizable force, could they retake their fort against an unknown number? Yet, the uncomfortable question remained unanswered. Could the incursion be the first sign of a full invasion? Could an army comprising the clans of Nordruuk be preparing to march on Calerdorn? If Elodi sent half her forces north, they would likely be overwhelmed in open country, leaving the rest of her realm vulnerable. After much deliberation, Elodi had come to the conclusion the defense of the city had to be her top priority.

As the first of the morning light shone through the hall's windows, her scouts had returned, and to Elodi's relief, they had found no evidence of an enemy advance on Calerdorn. With that news, the Council agreed to Elodi's request to take a quarter of the garrison to support the guardsmen to retake Drunsberg, but on the agreement they would return the moment the Ruuk made a move south.

Elodi watched the last of her councilors depart the hall. She eased herself back into her chair and covered her yawning mouth. 'I deeply desire a long, undisturbed sleep in a soft bed that doesn't sway.' She turned to Wendel. 'And you too, I need you to be sharp and alert over the coming days.' She closed her eyes 'Will we ever have peace, Wendel?'

He let out a long sigh. 'Peace? Was there ever a time there wasn't a struggle somewhere in the Five Realms?'

Elodi rose from her chair and stretched. 'But this has the look of an all-out war in the making.'

'I agree, ma'am. Recent events do seem to signal

difficult times lie ahead.'

'At least we can be thankful Lord Broon's men made it through the pass unscathed. I don't know what I would have done had they suffered an ambush.'

'Ma'am!' Gundrul entered. 'Excuse the intrusion, ma'am, but I have news.'

Elodi's head dropped. 'Dare I ask if it is good news?'

He thought for a moment. 'Err... possibly both good and bad.'

Wendel wrestled with his chair to stand. 'Well, spit it out, man. We don't have all day.'

Gundrul turned to Elodi. 'We have sightings of enemy wagons heading south towards Wyke Wood, ma'am.'

Elodi clicked her tongue. 'It's Durran, Captain. I will not have it called that name here.'

'Apologies, ma'am.' He cleared his throat. 'We have sightings of enemy wagons heading south towards Durran Wood.'

'Thank you, Captain. I hope that turns out to be the bad news. And the good?'

He smiled. 'They're escorting prisoners, both guards and miners from Drunsberg, and possibly more from other captured outposts. We can thank the Three they're alive.'

Elodi gripped the back of her chair. 'How many?'

'The scouts reckon around a hundred so far, and I suspect they're in good shape. They're traveling in small bands, which makes me think their captors are still wary of them, even in chains and weaponless.'

Elodi walked around the table, thinking out loud. 'Why are they taking them to the wood? If they wanted them dead, they would have done so already. What do they want with those... no, we can't let that happen.' She turned to Gundrul. 'We cannot allow those poor men to be taken under its boughs. If we could apprehend the wagons, are your men capable of freeing the prisoners? They would prove a most useful addition to our forces.'

Gundrul grunted. 'I'm certain they're up to the task, but I'm afraid, the sighting was early yesterday. They will gain the woods before we could reach them, ma'am. That makes it a little more complicated.'

Elodi groaned. 'It does indeed.' She walked to the map behind the Council's table. Her eyes wandered from Calerdorn to Durran Wood and farther south to the Kolossos Pass. She stroked her chin. 'Yes, it could work.' She spun about. 'Gentlemen, I believe we have a new objective.' She turned back to the map. 'There's no time to waste. We must rescue those men from the wood before they come to harm. But I believe we might turn events to our advantage.' She strode back to the table. 'Wendel, give the order to assemble our knights.' She stopped. 'No, too much of a risk. Let's say half their strength, but do it immediately. Then recall the Council, I don't care if they're fast asleep in their beds, bring them back!' Wendel turned to leave. 'Oh, and Wendel? Please arrange for my armor to be made ready.'

'Your armor, ma'am?'

'Yes, Wendel, my armor!' He opened his mouth, but Elodi waved him away. She turned to Gundrul. 'Captain, I want you to accompany me and the Knights of Calerdorn.'

'Ride with you, ma'am?'

'I believe you're acquainted with the leader of Broon's regiment, Captain Ruan.'

Gundrul straightened. 'That I am, ma'am. We go back a long way. He retired from the Archonian Guard to take a command in Lord Broon's ranks. I can't say we've always seen eye to eye, but I wouldn't want anyone else at my side in a tight spot.'

'Good. Then I want you by my side when I meet them on the road.'

'And the guards, ma'am?'

'Gather your men, put Cubric in charge. In fact, promote him to the rank of captain.'

'But…'

She held up her hand. 'If you don't have the authority, Gundrul, I believe I do in my realm.'

'Not necessary, ma'am. I will conduct the procedure.'

'Good, but make it quick. I want them ready to march on the hour.'

The Council had at first been reluctant to approve Elodi's gamble, and a gamble it was, she could not deny. But she could not afford to delay a moment longer. The Ruuk strolled across the border at will and would soon overwhelm the entire region if she allowed them to capture more ground unchallenged. It had to be now. Wendel and Gundrul had impressed on the Council, while Elodi's plan was ambitious, it could work. But all depended on speed and catching the enemy unaware. If they could free the prisoners being held in Durran Wood, they would greatly enhance Elodi's limited force. And, if in the process of the rescue, they could drive out the evil from the woods, they would improve their position. With the combined forces of Harlyn, Broon, Gundrul's young guards and the freed men, Elodi would feel confident marching on Draegnor. She could drive the raiders out and have the numbers to secure the key crossing points on the border for a while longer. Once they had achieved those objectives, they could take back the mines without fear of reinforcements from the north.

Within moments of the Council's approval, Elodi, Gundrul and fifty-two mounted knights had ridden out of the city to cheers and waving of flags. Behind, Cubric led the Archonian Guard with half of Calerdorn's own force. He was tasked to head for the abandoned settlement of

Durran, just half a league south of the wood. If Elodi had calculated correctly, she and her knights would intercept Bardon's men around noon the following day. From there, a good pace would bring them to Durran shortly after Cubric had set up camp. Elodi's spirit had risen at the impressive sight of her elite force on their fine horses, and the straight ranks of her soldiers proud to march under Harlyn's burgundy banner, alongside the blue of the Archon's guards. But her heart had also ached for their safety in the face of the unknown.

From Calerdorn, she had ridden hard for most of the day and well into the evening along the West Road. They had set off early the following day, reaching the top of the escarpment by noon. From their elevated position, Elodi could see many leagues across the Dorn Plain. A ray of sunlight burst through the heavy cloud. The rare beam shone down on the gray line of the West Road, and to Elodi's relief, four-hundred glistening spear tips of the men of Broon marching under their black banner. She looked to the sky and gave silent thanks to any god who would listen.

Elodi turned to the leader of her knights. 'Captain Aldorman. Have your men wait here. You, Gundrul, and I will ride ahead to greet Lord Broon's men. We don't want them to think they're under attack.'

Aldorman held up his arm. The riders stopped. 'Most certainly, ma'am. I'd wager many of our knights of old would have met a painful death on the end of Broon's spears.'

Elodi looked back. 'Where's Captain Gundrul?'

Aldorman grinned. 'I'm afraid he's not what you'd call a natural on horseback, ma'am. He seemed a little... uncomfortable this morning.'

'Oh dear. He should have said, I assumed he'd be accustomed to the saddle.'

'Here he comes.' Aldorman grimaced. 'Still sore, I'd say.'

Gundrul drew level. 'Apologies, ma'am. It's been a while since I've ridden.' He rose in his saddle.

Aldorman stifled a laugh. 'And how is the rear guard this morning, Captain?'

Gundrul shot him a glance. 'Fine. But I'll be happier once back on my own feet.'

Elodi pursed her lips. 'Gentlemen, I think it's time we ride on to greet our allies.' She nudged Sea Mist and led them down the slope. They had covered only a short distance when she noticed the spearmen of Broon had stopped and formed into squares. Elodi halted. 'What are they doing?'

Gundrul stood in his stirrups. 'I suspect their scouts will have spotted us, ma'am. They're preparing for an attack. I would do the same. Usual defensive procedure in a foreign land, ma'am.'

'Then we shall proceed with caution and make them feel welcome.'

Bardon had been true to his word; his men were undeniably an intimidating sight. His broad-shouldered spearmen looked ready to fight, despite their arduous march. Their armor may have been ancient and battered, but Elodi could tell they had seen combat and survived to boast of their conquests.

She strode beside Captain Ruan and Gundrul along the front rank. Wendel advised her it was customary to inspect an arriving army, especially one crucial to their plan. Ruan was obviously proud of his spearmen, stopping at every opportunity in front of a man with a story to tell. But while the spearmen impressed her, Elodi grew impatient, keen to press on to Durran and meet with Cubric. The longer the prisoners were held captive, the less she believed a successful rescue would be possible.

Inspection complete, they had marched north together to the settlement at Durran, arriving as night fell. Cubric and the combined forces of the realms had already arrived and set up camp. The grim wood was not visible from the village, but Elodi felt uneasy.

She sat with the captains of the four regiments around a flickering candle in the old village hall. Of the four, only Cubric had ever stepped inside the wood. At Elodi's request, he gave them the benefit of his experience. He eagerly offered his advice. 'May I suggest, ma'am, the men plug their ears with mud.'

Ruan spoke first. 'But how would they hear the commands?'

Cubric shuddered. 'Believe me, Captain, once the spirits start whispering, your men won't hear a word of command. Worse still, the spirits will turn them against you, and set your men at each other's throats.'

Gundrul snorted. 'Since when have you ever followed a command, Cub?'

Elodi held up her hand. 'Then it's imperative' — she noticed Ruan's frown — 'vital the men know their orders before we attack.' She turned back to Cubric. 'What of the layout of the wood?'

He rubbed the back of his neck. 'Well, it's barely a league from east to west, and less north to south. It's a small territory to attack. But as you'll know, ma'am, we're up against an unnatural foe.'

Elodi took her cue. 'Captain Cubric is right.' She addressed Ruan. 'I suspect we face a powerful wyke, possibly one of old, and one appearing to grow stronger with every passing year.'

Ruan looked at Gundrul. 'Do you also believe this?'

Gundrul nodded. 'Not at first, but the more I hear about what these scoundrels did at the mines, I believe

Lady Harlyn is right. You've seen the Ruuk firsthand. Yes, they can be a handful when they have the numbers, but they could never organize themselves like what we're seeing here. And let's face it, that rabble must fear whoever or whatever leads them to maintain the discipline necessary to take Drunsberg.'

Elodi felt her shoulders relax. 'Thank you, Gundrul. Then we must assume we'll confront a wyke, so the mud in the ears seems a sensible, if unusual, precaution.'

Cubric smirked. 'We're going to need a freshly plowed field for Gunny's big ears.'

Gundrul snorted, but Elodi noticed Ruan's mouth turn up at the edges. 'So, gentlemen, let us discuss tactics. We know the prisoners would have arrived yesterday at the latest and most likely held in a stronghold at its dark heart. Could you elaborate, Cubric?'

He frowned. 'Ma'am?'

Gundrul grinned. 'Mud in your ears, Cub?' He sighed. 'Lady Harlyn means can you tell us what to expect when we reach the center of the wood.'

'Oh right, I see. Well, I got closer than most' — he glanced to Gundrul — 'and that was *because* I'd blocked my ears. Eventually, we came across a stockade, a poorly made and maintained one I hasten to add, but it doesn't need to be strong. By the time we'd reached it, none of us had the urge to go any farther, and we were in no state for a fight, even if we'd had the strength.'

Elodi's mind raced. 'And what's inside this stockade?'

'Sorry, ma'am, can't say for sure. All we could see was a tower. When I say tower, it's more like a tall, burned-out tree trunk. But don't you be fooled by its appearance. Something inside it made us very uneasy.' He let out a long sigh. 'That's when we withdrew, or if I'm honest, fled.'

'Thank you, Cubric, I appreciate your honesty. Your information has been most useful.'

Cubric stammered. 'If... if I might make another suggestion, ma'am?'

Gundrul laughed. 'Two? In one day?'

Elodi nodded. 'Please do.'

Cubric clasped his hands. 'The longer you stay in its shadow, the weaker you become, even if you can't hear them voices. And with all them winding paths you quickly lose your sense of direction.' He straightened. 'Anyway, I had this idea on the march over. As soon as we're under its boughs, a bowman from each party could shoot a flaming arrow ahead for the men to follow. When they reach it, they shoot another and so on. Then they'll have a target to head for if they become confused. And it will keep them moving forward without delay.' He looked around the table. 'What do you think? We could stamp out anything catching fire so we don't burn ourselves alive... like.'

Gundrul patted Cubric on the back. 'We'll make a captain out of you yet. It'll also keep the men aware of the positions of each other. If any go astray, there'll be other arrows to follow.' Gundrul drummed his large fingers on the small table. 'I suggest we leave a third of our resources in reserve, ready to go if needed, or oversee a retreat if... events don't go our way. Those going in, we'll split into groups of forty and spread them out across the southern border of the wood. Then strike on fast to catch them by surprise and prevent our force from losing their minds.'

Elodi clenched her fist. 'Good, this sounds promising. But note, our first objective is to free the prisoners. So, building on Cubric's tactic, I want torches planted along the route they take in, making it easier to bring the men out. I'm certain they'll be in a bad way and disorientated. We don't want to lose them and leave them behind.' She turned to Ruan. 'If your men can approach from the south, Gundrul and Harlyn's cohorts will attack from the west. And what of my knights, Aldorman? Am I right in assuming they'll be of limited use among the trees?'

Aldorman nodded. 'Yes, ma'am. No horses, not there. For one, the territory isn't suitable, but that's not the problem. These spirits Captain Cubric describes, would likely drive the horses wild. They'd be throwing their riders in no time. So, if I could also make a suggestion, ma'am.'

'I accede to your superior tactical knowledge, Aldorman.' Her captains shifted in their chairs. Aldorman opened his mouth, then changed his mind. Elodi blushed. 'Sorry, what I meant to say was you're better placed than I to determine the best tactics for your knights.'

Cubric glanced at the others. 'Beg your pardon, ma'am, but you use a lot of words us simple soldiers don't hear often.'

Elodi's cheeks grew hot. 'Again, I apologize, and please, do tell me if I do it again. But I want you to know, I do not regard you as *simple* soldiers. We would have lost the realms many years ago without your loyal service.'

Aldorman continued. 'Thank you, ma'am. In my judgment, your knights would be better deployed at the eastern edge. If any of the rascals try to head back to Drunsberg, my men can stop them in their tracks.'

Elodi nodded. 'Yes, Aldorman, that makes for a better use of the knights.'

Ruan leaned on his elbows. 'And what of the north?' Elodi saw Gundrul nudge the man under the table. Ruan added. 'Ma'am. What if they choose to leave north?'

Elodi waved her hand. 'Let them flee back over the border, we don't have the numbers to cover all the ways out of the wood. But if possible, I want to prevent them heading east back to Drunsberg.'

'Does that mean no prisoners, ma'am?'

Elodi exhaled. 'Yes, I'm afraid it does.'

Ruan laughed. 'That won't worry my men. They've all lost a brother or friend to this lot on our side of the mountains.'

Gundrul agreed. 'And trust me, ma'am. The Ruuk didn't take the men from Drunsberg prisoner for their good health. They know our guards are trained to be loyal, and if they can corrupt that and turn them against us...' He sighed. 'If we're to win this battle, I'm afraid we'll have to fight dirty.'

Elodi stood. 'Then so be it. Aldorman? Please take Sea Mist with you. I shall march with Gundrul.' All four pushed back their chairs. She stood tall. 'As leader of the realm, my place is at the front, and that is where I intend to be. I shall leave you to work out the finer points of the preparations.' She turned to leave, then stopped. 'For too long, this dark place has been a blight on our land. Tomorrow, at first light, we will take it back.'

Outside, the cold air reached deep into her chest. Elodi strode in the gloom through the run-down buildings of the village, many without roofs. Through the windows she could see the men of Broon crouching around small fires beneath their shields. The smell of freshly cooked meat filled the air, but she had no appetite. She reached Gundrul's young guards sitting with her own small force. They had taken the hint from Ruan's experienced soldiers and also cooked, but the flickering light from their flames exposed their worried faces at the thought of their first proper fight. She stopped to watch them, unaware of her presence. They would have heard the stories of the wood and tomorrow they would enter at her behest. She knew they would not question her orders and would willingly follow their captains into the unknown. Elodi turned away and walked at pace to the outskirts of the settlement, keeping her eyes straight ahead.

At the gate, she came across two of her men on watch. She nodded to them and whispered. 'I need some space to think.' She pointed to a nearby tree. 'I'll be over there.'

'Don't go too far, ma'am. We can't vouch for your safety beyond the line of trees.'

'Be assured, I won't.' Elodi made it to the tree and stepped around the trunk out of sight. Her legs gave way. She slumped against the tree, covered her face and sobbed. The plan had to work. Elodi saw no other way to defend her people against the growing threat. But if she failed, more than just the lives of those directly under her command would be at stake. It had to work. She shut her eyes tight to stem the flow of tears — it *had* to work.

32. Shadows in the Woods

Had it been two days, three days, possibly more? Toryn lay slumped against the knotted roots digging in his back, but he no longer cared, he barely noticed the discomfort. His stomach had learned to tolerate the fare of stale bread and bitter water. He even welcomed Dohl's daily visit. The old man spoke mostly to himself, but Toryn took comfort hearing another voice that did not whisper dark tidings. But this morning had offered a faint hope. Dohl had spoken of events drawing the *lady's* attention to the outskirts of the wood, distracting her from preparations for some, as yet unknown act.

A shadow appeared under the door. A chill ran up Toryn's spine as a dark shape passed across a crack in the old wood. The bolt shifted. The door creaked ajar. He shuffled back against the earthen wall, squinting into the narrow sliver of yellow light. A large head peered around the edge, tilting as it sniffed the air. Toryn held his breath. Long fingers grasped the top of the door. The light grew as the hand pushed. A stooped figure stood on the other side, with long, scrawny arms and short legs. A cobtroll! It had to be. Toryn's empty stomach clenched. The creature dropped onto its hands and crawled towards him, still sniffing the air. Its rasping breath filled the dank cell with a sickly, sweet odor. Toryn twisted in his chains, shut his eyes and pressed his cheek against the wall. A finger touched his foot. The cobtroll hesitated, then reached out and grasped his ankle. It pulled, gently at first, then with more force.

The door creaked and Dohl sauntered in. 'Chain him up, Dohl, unchain him, Dohl.' The cobtroll's clammy fingers released Toryn's ankle. Dohl grunted. 'What the—? Hey! Get you gone. Go on, hop it. Back to your work.' Toryn heaved a sigh. He croaked a thanks, but Dohl seemed not to hear his gratitude. The man reached into his pocket and pulled out a key. He fumbled with the chain above Toryn's head. 'Untie him, Dohl. Bring him here, take him there. Dress him for a journey. How would they manage without old Dohl?' Dohl lifted Toryn's arms and tore off what remained of his tattered shirt. He took an old sack off his shoulder and pulled it over Toryn's head. The rough cloth irritated his wounds, but it felt thicker and would at least keep him warm.

The old man stepped back. 'Ha! Wouldn't your mother be proud if she could see you now.' Dohl looked Toryn in the eye for the first time. When he spoke, his voice had softened, sounding like Hamar. 'I hope I'm gone before the world changes.' His mouthed curled. '*She* knows, she knows what's coming.' His face changed back to the Dohl, Toryn had come to know. He grunted and tugged on the chain. 'Untie him, Dohl, bring him, take him, Dohl.' Toryn grabbed the ring biting into his throat, stumbled forward and staggered to his feet. His legs felt weak after days of sitting. He wobbled as Dohl slung the chain over his shoulder and hauled Toryn from the cell as if leading a stubborn donkey.

Toryn blinked in the corridor's torchlight. His shoulder scraped against rough, stone walls as Dohl dragged him past doors leading to more cells. The old man stopped, Toryn bumped into him and fell back. Dohl mumbled as he unlocked a gate and heaved it open. More torches lit a short staircase fashioned from dirt and planks. Dohl groaned as he slowly climbed, staying one step ahead of Toryn on his faltering legs. They emerged from underground into cooler, but not fresher air. Ruuk ran in all directions, shouting commands, carrying torches in the

307

gray light of morning or evening, Toryn could not tell.

'You took your time, old man.' Toryn recognized Grebb's voice. 'Get a move on. Put him in the cart.'

'Chain him, unchain him, put him in the cart, Dohl.'

'And make it fast, *Dohl*. There's hundreds of them with big, sharp spears coming for you, *Dohl*. So, buck up. They'll be here in less time it takes you to piss.' Grebb grabbed Dohl's shoulder. 'That means this place will be swarming with the blighters in an hour.' Grebb smirked. 'And trust me, they'll run you through 'til you look like a huckle, then toss you to their dogs.'

Dohl blinked as if waking and trying to remember where he was. He straightened and nodded behind Grebb. 'What about *her*? She'll stop 'em dead in their tracks.'

'Nah, not interested. Brought forward plans to make the move. Unless you're going to stand up and stop them *dead in their tracks* all by yourself' — he yelled in his face — 'I suggest you bloody move!' He tugged Dohl's ragged cloak. 'This way. And make it fast.'

Dohl slumped. He grumbled and shuffled a few steps. Grebb snatched the chain. 'Forget it. I'll do it myself.' He laughed. 'You go and pack your best clothes for the big trip, eh.' Dohl snarled, threw up his arms and hobbled a few steps before jolting to a standstill. His head turned and looked up to something out of Toryn's sight. Dohl cried out as his body shook with a force that should have snapped his bones.

Grebb noted Toryn's shock. 'Don't you worry about him. It's the lady having a quiet word.' Grebb pulled the chain, but Toryn stumbled to a halt as he saw what caught Dohl's attention. Before him rose a gnarled, wooden tower as if spawned by the defiled earth. A circle of torches at its base threw flickering shadows up the twisted structure as it climbed to dominate the surrounding trees. Toryn stared in disgust, unsure its deformity resulted from untold years of wind and driving rain, or the malice of its inhabitant. Flat, dark mushrooms the size of plates grew up the lower reaches, but not the kind you would want to eat. Patches of gray lichen covered much of the walls up to its pointed top of entwined branches. Toryn balked at the abomination formed by the corruption of once beautiful trees, but he could not tear his eyes away from the sinister structure.

More Ruuk arrived at the tower. One led a tall, black stallion. The horse stopped in front, showing obvious disdain for those rushing to form a line behind it. Toryn fell forward as Grebb tugged hard on the chain. 'No time to admire the view, boy. But don't you worry, there'll be plenty more to see where you're going.'

Another approached. His voice trembled. 'She's ready to leave, Captain.'

Grebb stiffened. 'You don't say.'

The squat Ruuk fidgeted with his sword belt. 'What about the prisoners?'

Grebb shrugged. 'Leave 'em. They'll slow us down and I doubt they'll be much use to the enemy by now.'

'Shall I torch the cages?'

Grebb thought for a moment. 'No, leave them to suffer. They'll serve as a message to anyone who thinks they can mess with her.'

The Ruuk nodded at Toryn. 'We taking this one?'

Grebb jiggled the chain. 'Someone seems keen to meet this runt.' He pulled him close and peered into his face. Toryn tried to resist, but had neither the strength or the will. Grebb jeered. 'Can't think why. He looks about as useful as Dohl on a bad day.'

The shouting ceased. The Ruuk forming into line shrunk back as the air chilled and darkened. Toryn's skin crawled, but he noticed the horse was unfazed. His temples throbbed as a door at the foot of the tower creaked open. A tall, cloaked figure stood behind. Toryn wanted to both look and turn away; his eyes stayed fixed on the tower. He squinted. The air around the dark creature either flickered, or his eyes played tricks. The lady turned. It was not his eyes. The air swirled, distorting her outline and leaving tendrils groping into the space about her like dark blood seeping from a wound into water. A cold claw clenched and squeezed his heart. Within the churned air above her, three floating figures took shape. Three hideous beings with burning, black eyes set in gaunt faces, coiled their distorted bodies around each other like eels in a bucket vying for clear water. Long strands of straggly hair thrashed about their misshapen heads as they twitched side to side as if searching for prey. Grebb's hold on the chain tightened as they both froze.

None dared to move as the lady made her way to the horse and rose effortlessly into the saddle. The stallion set off with the three forms, maintaining their vigil over their mistress. Grebb remained on guard. He hissed in Toryn's ear. 'For your people's sake, you'd better hope this Archon of yours is strong. There's three of them kind in this land.' He gestured with his thumb. 'Her on the horse, she goes by the name, Uleva, and from what I've heard, she's *not* the one you need to fear.'

33. DARK DAWN RISING

'Burn it. Burn the whole rotten settlement to the ground.' Elodi removed her helmet and shook out her damp hair. She glanced around the array of dilapidated wooden buildings inside the barricade. The evil may have fled, but the stench still clung to the air. In training, Elodi detested wearing armor, feeling it restricted her movement, but today she welcomed the extra layer of protection. She turned to Gundrul. 'For too long this evil has ruined what was once, I am led to believe, a fair place.' She resisted the urge to spit out the foul taste in her mouth. 'And when it's burned down, take the ashes out of the wood and bury them, bury them deep. Perhaps the trees will flourish once we've rid them of the contamination.'

Gundrul's nose wrinkled. 'And what of the prisoners, ma'am? They're in a bad way. Can't get them to eat or drink no matter how hard we try.'

Elodi's heart went out to the men huddled together in the clearing. 'Get them to the healers at Calerdorn as soon as you can. We can use Ruan's supply wagons, and those they've left behind.' She made a face. 'But clean them first. Who knows what foul purpose they've served.' Gundrul called over two of his men and gave the orders.

Cubric strode towards them. He had a finger in his ear, still scratching out the dried mud. He attempted to smile at Gundrul, but it came across as a grimace. 'My plan worked! Our swift advance must have scared them off, eh.'

Elodi nodded. 'A good plan to be sure, but I don't think we scared them.'

Gundrul held out his hands. 'Look about you, Cub. They easily matched our numbers judging by the footprints. And I'd wager the creature in that tower posed more of a threat than the rest of them put together. No, it wasn't us, it was too easy. Mud in our ears or not, I didn't hear any whispers or feel we were being watched on our approach.' He ran his foot over a deep gouge left by a wagon. 'No, they knew of our attack, but I'd say they left in an orderly manner.'

Elodi sighed. 'Let's be thankful they've gone. But to where?' Gundrul ordered Cubric to give a hand with burning the huts. He watched him leave and turned to Elodi.

'Should we at least search the tower before putting it to the torch, ma'am? Might find something of use.'

Elodi reluctantly let her eyes wander up to the spire. She spun away. 'No. I don't want anyone setting foot inside. It's obviously the source of the corruption about this place, and I fear it still has the power to deprave. If you're right about them choosing to leave, and I believe that to be true, I doubt they will have left anything of use to us. We'll more likely find some sort of trap.' She turned back to the tower. 'Burn it. And do it immediately. I didn't notice it in the trees, but standing in its shadow, I feel we're being watched.' Elodi shivered. 'Please, Captain, torch it now.'

Gundrul saluted. 'This minute, ma'am. I'll sort it myself.' He strode towards the huts and waved men with torches to the base of the tower. Elodi could not help but look back to its crooked top. Despite the growing daylight, the jagged pinnacle appeared shrouded in gloom. Elodi straightened, realizing she slumped as if crushed by the tower bearing down on her shoulders. She found her gaze drawn back to the monstrosity. High above the level of the trees, a crooked doorway opened out onto a small balcony. For a moment, she saw the Archon's Tower with its vantage point of the land. Who had cast their dark eyes upon the world from the top of this hideous tower? Did they possess the same *farsight* as the Archon?

'Ma'am?' Elodi jumped. Ruan stood at her side. 'We followed their tracks out to the east, as far as the edge of the wood.'

She turned her back on the tower, still uneasy in its shadow. 'And what news of Aldorman and his knights?

'Ma'am, we found no sign.'

Elodi's heart faltered. 'Then he must have pursued the enemy.' She thought of Sea Mist, then chastised herself for not considering the fate of her knights first. Behind, the wood of the tower crackled as the fire took hold. She turned, eager to see the demise of the dark spire. With frightening speed, the flames tore up the twisted sides of the building. She retreated as the heat scorched her face. The blaze roared anew as the wood shrieked as it burned. The prisoners cried out as if the flames came for their souls. Gundrul's men ran from the inferno, covering their faces. All stopped and stared at the flames, seeming too bright and hot for the old wood fueling the fire. Then, as fast as it had taken hold, it died. Beneath, the old wood glistened a deep red, glowering like eyes of a mythical dragon of ancient times.

No one moved. The prisoners sobbed. The dragon closed its eyes. The tower fell, folding in on itself as if the force binding the crooked bones in place, finally relinquished its power. Elodi froze as it crumbled. The gnarled pinnacle toppled towards her, plummeting at speed, crashing into the ground a few paces from her feet. Elodi stared at the blackened, twisted trunks pointing straight at her as a finger in judgment of the condemned.

'Ma'am!' She spun around as Cubric approached. 'We found someone.' Behind him, two guards held up a man by his arms. 'This old chap stumbled out of a burning hut.' Cubric recovered his breath. 'He ain't Ruuk, ma'am, but has a bunch of keys on his belt. So I reckon he was in charge of the cells we found underground.'

Elodi regarded the cloaked man slumped between Cubric's men. 'Is he conscious? Can he speak?'

Cubric shrugged. 'Barely. He's mumbling to himself but I can't make any sense of it.'

She walked over to the prisoner. 'Hold him up please, so I can see his face.' They hoisted him up by his armpits and pulled back the man's hood.

Elodi took a step back. His face resembled the knotted wood of the tower. Strands of gray hair clung to his scalp, scarcely able to conceal dozens of crudely stitched old wounds. She cleared her throat. 'Tell me your name.' Her voice wavered. She tried again. 'Who are you? And who do you serve?'

The man's head lolled forward. He muttered, dribbling onto his filthy cloak. 'Who's asking?'

She glanced to Cubric and stepped closer. 'I am Lady Harlyn.' The old man's head turned. 'And your settlement is in my realm. I demand you answer.'

A deep rasp, like a saw cutting through timber, issued from his throat. Cubric's men edged back. He lifted his head and cackled. Elodi held her ground as his gray, clouded eyes sought hers. He sneered. 'You demand? You make demands of me?' He laughed again. 'Dohl of the Wood! You think you have dominion over me? Here in the wood?' Elodi winced as the old man's spine cracked, staring in disbelief as he straightened and stood a good foot taller. His eyes found Elodi, peering through his matted hair. Elodi shuffled back, unable to look away as he held her gaze. His eyes gleamed, briefly changing color, as if another studied her from inside the old man's head.

Dohl thrust open his arms, throwing the guards aside. With a speed belying his age, he lunged at Elodi with outstretched fingers, ready to choke her. Elodi's hand went to her sword, but before she could free it, Ruan crashed into her assailant. But Dohl stood firm. He grabbed Ruan by the hair and hurled the man as if he weighed little more than a child. Elodi drew her sword, stepping back, careful not to lose her footing. Dohl stopped. She stood her ground with her sword tip held at his throat. Gundrul and more of Ruan's men rushed to her aid, circling Dohl with spears leveled. Dohl faltered. He shrank, his spine buckling like the tower as he crumpled to the floor. He groaned into his hands. 'Stay behind and hide, Dohl. Kill the pretty girl, Dohl.' He cried out. 'I've failed. I've failed my lady.'

Elodi gawped at him. 'Lady?' She spun away. 'The message from Drunsberg stated a sorcerer led the raiders, not a woman.' She turned to Gundrul. 'Does this mean we're up against *two* wykes?' She bent over Dohl. 'Who is this lady you serve?'

Dohl sank back on his haunches. He tipped back his head; his pitiful voice carried to the treetops. 'Uleva! Dohl failed. Dohl failed you.'

Elodi tugged at his collar. 'Who is she? Who is this Uleva?'

But the old man ignored her. He slumped forward and whispered. 'Dohl is tired. Dohl just wants to die.'

Gundrul stepped in, drawing his sword. 'Shall I grant his wish, ma'am?'

She stayed his hand. Her voice trembled as she panted, catching her breath. 'No, let him live.' She stared at the tattered cloak, shaking as Dohl sobbed. 'We'll take him to Calerdorn. I want him questioned. But put him in chains. We cannot take the risk he might try such an act again.'

Ruan brushed himself down and came to Elodi's side. 'Apologies for my failure, ma'am.'

Her heart still raced. 'Nonsense, Ruan. I won't hear of it. Who knows what would have happened if you had not

315

intervened when you did?' Her hand went to her mouth; it trembled.

Ruan took her other hand. 'Ma'am?' He led her away from the smoldering huts to the gate in the barricade. She saw him gesture to Gundrul. 'Ma'am, what next?'

'Give me a moment please, Captain.' She stepped outside of the settlement and steadied her breathing. Her eyes still smarted from the heat of the fire, and her nostrils stung from the reek. *Two wykes?* Could there be two of these creatures? How was she supposed to deal with such foes? She heard Gundrul address Ruan. Elodi brushed the soot from her gauntlet and stepped back inside.

Before they could speak, Elodi gave her orders. 'Ruan, once this place is no more, I want you and Cubric to head for Calerdorn and take those poor men to the healers. And deliver that man, Dohl, to Wendel and inform him of his… abilities. We need to know what he knows.' She turned away from the smoke. 'Gundrul. Select fifty of your men and come with me. We shall follow their trail. I trust Aldorman will have turned back from his pursuit once he perceived their strength. I have to know where they're heading, whether they've split their forces, if the wykes are together, or if they have separate objectives.' She sighed. 'I dearly hope it's not Drunsberg. If they held the wood all these years, we don't stand a chance of extracting them from the mines any time soon.'

At mid-morning they emerged from under the shelter of the trees to be met by a pale, gray sky, and the unmistakable stench of Mawlgrim Mire, just a league to the north. According to Gundrul, the tracks suggested many hundreds of heavy-booted Ruuk and two wagons had departed the wood at dawn. It was not the news Elodi wanted to hear. She grew tired, unused to walking under the weight of her armor as they trudged through long, wet grass. She peered ahead, desperate to see Calerdorn's knights accompanied by Sea Mist.

Gundrul held up his hand. He stopped and crouched to inspect the ground. After scratching over the patch with his dagger, he stood and walked back to Elodi. 'The enemy continued east, ma'am. So, I should imagine they drove straight at your knights.'

Elodi closed her eyes. What chance did Aldorman stand against the evil emerging from the trees? If the lady from the tower could grant Dohl the strength to brush Ruan aside with ease, what could she achieve with an army of Ruuk? And if the two wykes had worked together... She opened her eyes, but the bleak landscape had not changed and offered no hope. She had mustered half the strength of her precious few knights, only for them to face an evil from the old days. She trusted they had had the good sense to turn tail and flee, and not harbored noble thoughts of holding their ground for the sake of Harlyn's honor.

Gundrul paced the flattened grass. He waved his arm to the north. 'There are tracks that way.' He took a few steps. 'And more that way. But no sign of a skirmish, and obviously no casualties.' The captain scratched his chin and strode across the grassland. Elodi followed until Gundrul eventually stopped and held up his arms. He called over his shoulder. 'Aldorman formed his line here, two-deep. But they didn't engage the enemy, ma'am.' He strolled a few paces, checked both ways, then walked back to Elodi, deep in thought. Gundrul looked up. 'Your knights split and left in three different directions.'

Elodi trod carefully over the trampled grass. 'Good. I trust they escaped and were not taken captive. I would hate to see them reduced to the state of those poor guards we found in the wood.' She checked the mud churned by horses heading north. 'Would you say more went this way,

Captain?' Gundrul nodded. 'Then we'll follow this lead. Send two scouts after the Ruuk. But they're to disengage once they can determine the tracks don't double back, and we know for sure which way they're heading.'

They did not have to follow the trail of the horses for long. As they approached the brow of a ridge, Elodi recognized a sound she had longed to hear. Sea Mist! Despite her tired legs and weight of her armor, Elodi ran the last few paces to the crest. Below, she counted eight of her knights as they lay strewn across the ground; Elodi noted with a pang in her stomach the horses outnumbered the riders. Sea Mist nickered on seeing Elodi. He tossed his head and trotted to her side. She rested her forehead against his muzzle and patted his neck. 'Shush... shush. You're safe, boy.' But Sea Mist's wide eyes bore witness to the horrors Elodi and her men had avoided.

Elodi took the reins and led him back to the other horses. Aldorman's helmet lay on its side next to a prone body. She heaved a sigh as she saw him move. He struggled onto his feet on seeing her approach. Aldorman took two steps before falling to his knees, clutching his head. She rushed to his side. 'Please, Captain, don't rise. Stay put, there's no need to move.' She kneeled, removed her gauntlets and held Aldorman. His body convulsed as he fought to contain his fear. Gundrul approached; Elodi could not tell whether it was pity or disdain on his lined face.

Gundrul pointed to the next ridge. 'More tracks led that way, ma'am. I've sent two men to round up the survivors and bring them here.'

'Thank you, Captain. See what you can do for these poor men.'

Aldorman sat up. 'What happened? Where did...?'

'Take your time.' Elodi clasped her knight's hand. 'I'm afraid you bore the brunt of the enemy. They left the wood before we arrived.'

She helped Aldorman to his feet. He straightened his armor. His wide eyes met Elodi's. 'Night came. It was growing light when we took our positions, but... but it suddenly fell dark.' He waved his hand in the direction of the wood. 'A swirling, dark fog. Came up so fast I didn't have time to think.' Two more knights emerged over the top of the ridge. Aldorman stammered. 'Is this it? Just ten of us?'

'There are other tracks leading from your position. I suspect there will be more survivors. But what happened here?'

His eyes stayed fixed on the ground. 'Night came. Night came...' He paled, shaking his head slowly. 'No. No, that can't be right.'

'Please try to remember.'

Aldorman looked her in the eye. 'I can, ma'am. I just can't believe what I saw.' He stuttered. 'The night, the fog, there were strange beings in it. Creatures with long spindly arms and legs, dozens of them, moving with unnatural speed straight at us.' He stiffened, trying to stop the tremors wracking his body. 'We stood our ground, ma'am. The horses held their nerve, and Sea Mist, ma'am. You can be proud of him, even without a rider, he stayed in line.' Aldorman ran his fingers through his matted hair. 'But that wasn't the worst of it. What came next spooked them, and I'm ashamed to say if the horses hadn't bolted first, I would have given the order to retreat.'

'You have nothing to be ashamed of, Aldorman.' The hairs on the back of her neck prickled. 'I witnessed only a fraction of this evil in the settlement, and I am not afraid to say it chilled me to the bone.'

Aldorman sniffed. 'Thank you, ma'am. It's good of you to say, but I feel I've let you down. I let those creatures escape.'

'You let no one down, Captain. I'm certain had you tried to hold your position, we'd be lamenting all of your deaths, and for no gain.'

Aldorman managed a few paces to his horse and stroked its muzzle. He turned. 'Behind those stick-like creatures, rode a woman on a horse. Don't ask me how I know, seeing as she was cloaked head to foot, but it was a woman, no doubt in my mind.' He grimaced. 'But then she' — his eyes bulged — 'she raised her arms... a mist rose from the ground.' He clasped Elodi's forearm. 'I'd sooner go beyond the Caerwal Gate and venture into the Lost Realms, than witness that again.' He released his grip. 'Oh, I beg your pardon, ma'am. I didn't mean—'

'Nothing to pardon, Captain. Please, I know it's painful, but can you describe what you saw?'

He took a deep breath. 'I set eyes on it only briefly before we retreated... bolted if I'm being honest, ma'am. The mist about it swirled, masking it somewhat, but it was another lady, of sorts. A dark figure, tall, three, maybe four times the height of a man. When she raised her head, she had long hair like barbed-whips flaying about her.' Elodi felt the blood freeze in her veins. Aldorman gripped the reins of his horse. 'She carried no weapon as far as I could tell, but she didn't have to. Her terrible screams drove us mad.' His eyes closed. 'I can still hear the echo, ma'am. A shriek as if all the demons from under the mountain were baying for our souls.' His head bowed. 'Thought I was ready for the shadow realms until you came along. To see your fair face was—'

'The scouts are back, ma'am!' Elodi turned to see Gundrul striding towards her. He nodded to Aldorman, then spoke to Elodi. 'The bulk of their force turned north about two leagues from here, and there's no sign of them diverting back. Must be heading towards Mawlgrim and the border, or possibly to your fort at Draegnor.'

Elodi's shoulders relaxed. 'Good, at least it will be easier to keep an eye on them if they're in one place. I'll send word to Archonholm. They must hear of this.' She turned to the trees. 'We'll post a watch on the wood in case it turns out to be a trick and they aim to come back.'

Gundrul grunted. 'They'll have to build a new tower.'

'All the same, I don't want them back in that wood while I still breathe.' She looked north. 'I wonder why they came east first? The way north was open, and it's a slightly easier path through the mire that way.'

Aldorman straightened as he tried to regain his authority. 'I'd say they wanted to deliver a message to you, ma'am. They revealed their strength and left you in no doubt we're up against a formidable foe.'

Gundrul touched Elodi's arm. 'Ma'am, could I show you something? It's… over there, at the ridge.'

Elodi frowned. 'Be my guest.' She walked with Gundrul to the top of the ridge; the grasslands beyond never looked bleaker.

Gundrul paced along the ridge. 'I didn't want to say this in front of your captain, ma'am. But my scouts reckon the tracks leading to Aldorman's line were made by one lone horse, one wagon, and about twenty on foot. Their main force didn't engage your riders. They turned north before reaching your knights.' He rubbed the back of his neck. 'It may not be my place to say, but your elite knights fled from a foe they should've easily defeated. Even if one of the wykes led them, they still should have given a half-decent account of themselves.'

Elodi clenched her fist. 'That cannot be true. Aldorman and his men would never flee from a smaller force, wyke or not. I know my knights, Gundrul and I say they would have stood their ground and apprehended them, if events unfolded as you say.' She looked back to the direction of the wood. 'I believe Aldorman came up against a being both dark and immensely powerful.' The woven faces of the drayloks on the tapestry filled her head. 'He's just described to me an entity from the past, a being that came close to overpowering the Archon, let alone a handful of knights.'

Gundrul kept his eyes down. 'But the ground don't lie, ma'am. Not unless the bulk of the enemy's forces had no feet, or' — he turned away — 'the creatures only existed inside your captain's head. But regardless of their size, judging by the numbers we've found so far, the Ruuk have swelled their ranks with your knights. They must have been captured, otherwise we'd have found their bodies, or they'd have returned by now.' He turned to face her. 'I'm afraid at least a third of your horsemen will soon be corrupted in the head and fighting for the other side before the summer's out.'

Elodi shuddered. 'That is most disconcerting.' She eyed the horizon. 'Earlier you said the bulk of the force went north. What of the rest?'

'The horse, wagon and the few Ruuk stayed on course for the east, towards the mountains.'

'And I guess no signs of those creatures Aldorman sighted.'

Gundrul stared at the churned mud. 'No, ma'am, nothing. Besides, these monsters he believes he saw were defeated. The archives tell us only the odd wyke, shroul and droog survived the purges, and we've hunted down and killed most since then. If any of these beasts still live, they'll be south of the gate.'

Elodi's eyes wandered across the grassland. 'I fear that's what they want us to believe.'

34. HOPE AGAINST DESPAIR

Toryn held his throbbing head in his hands. The sickly, sweet liquid Grebb had forced him to drink, still scorched his throat. But his throat was the least of his worries. The dark dreams the Winter Fever had visited upon young Toryn, seemed harmless compared to those he had suffered of late. They took him to murky depths of his mind that he could never have imagined existed. By his own hands, he had committed atrocities, ruthless and terrible acts, that in his dark state, he had enjoyed.

Toryn tried to push the images out of his head. He shifted his aching bones to roll on his side to relieve the sores on his back. The shriek that dragged him out of his nightmare, still echoed in his head. The creature's cry came from times past, fueled by the hurt and misery of the bleak days before the Archon had restored order. Its scream wrenched all hope from the unfortunate ears it fell upon — it could never be unheard.

He brought his hands to his face and sobbed.

'Cheer up, lad.' Two shadows stood at the end of the wagon. 'Your evening has just got better. The good lady, Uleva, wants to see you before she has to leave.'

The other spoke. 'Wait. Do we have to take him?'

'Do you see anyone else? Or should we tell him where to find her and let him go all by himself.' He clipped his colleague around the head. 'Fool! Of course, it's us.'

The second backed away. 'No, not me. I've just eaten. I won't keep my supper down if I have to stand next to her.' He groaned. 'And it will be morning before I get to eat again.'

'Then you'll have to go hungry. Come on! You don't

want to keep her waiting.'

Toryn had no strength to resist as they dragged him from the wagon. The soldiers sitting around the campfire hushed as they drew near. One grinned and slid his finger across his throat. 'Say hello to the Ice Queen from the lads, eh.'

Another kicked him. 'Keep it down, she'll hear you.'

His reluctant escorts took Toryn to the edge of the camp, away from the heat and light of the fire. They stopped and grasped Toryn's arms, holding his sagging body upright. His skin crawled as the air chilled at the threat of Uleva's arrival. Their hands trembled as they drew a sharp breath and turned away. The air shimmered as the hooded Uleva stepped out of the gloom. Toryn twisted away and clamped his eyes shut, dreading what stood before him. She clicked her fingers. His head snapped back to face her; his eyelids shot up into his skull. The touch of her foul breath froze his face. His stomach convulsed as it remembered the stench of a rotting carcass of a sheep torn apart by a wolf. To his left, the Ruuk lost his supper as predicted.

Uleva took a step closer. A faint, blue glow inside her hood revealed a face Toryn did not expect to see: the face of a young woman, both beautiful and terrible to behold. Smooth skin covered her delicate features like fine silk. Toryn's fingers tingled as part of him wanted to reach out to caress her soft cheek. He fought back, stiffening his arm to keep it at his side. But no matter how hard he strained, he knew her large, iridescent eyes of shifting hues of blue, could easily break his will.

Uleva tilted her head forward to behold Toryn. At first, he saw a sadness behind her eyes; a longing to be in another place, another time; perhaps even remorse for what she had become. Her eyes flickered. The window to her past slammed shut as Toryn's shattered, baring his soul. The two Ruuk had long passed out; only Uleva's will held him upright. She reached in, offering immortality and power, great power. If he surrendered, in return, she would grant his many secret desires. The life left in his body, seeped from his fingers and toes, retreating up his limbs into his stomach. It rose to his heart, through his throat and into his open mouth. Toryn knew this to be his soul. Uleva craved it. He took a step towards her, ready to offer her everything. Toryn faltered. His legs stiffened as the last fragment of his resolve drew him back from the gaping maw, refusing to yield what she sought.

Uleva's silken skin puckered. She snatched back her proposal, leaving Toryn as an empty shell ready to collapse. The glow spoiled to a sickly green to reveal the full horror beneath the hood. Two moist, black eyes glistened beneath a large, protruding forehead. Taut, gray skin stretched to bursting point across a misshapen skull as if straining to contain the all-consuming evil within. Uleva's thin, black mouth twisted. She leveled her stony gaze, penetrating Toryn's weakened defenses, seeking to uncover his deepest fears. She found them. Her lips cracked as they stretched into a grin. She raised a skeletal hand, extending her fingertip to Toryn's forehead. He cried out as an icy spike drilled between his eyes. His world turned black.

The whispers had changed. No longer the voices of strangers, he knew the voice — it was his own. And he listened. But as it spoke of his doom, another had joined the conversation. A woman, ever present, watched him from the edges of his nightmares.

The wagon lurched, tossing him about its wooden floor, bruising his bruises and finding more places to cut and open his skin, already covered with scars. The rough sack of his prison clothing irritated his raw skin, but he had grown used to the discomfort and took solace from the little warmth it offered.

Days and nights merged. The wagon moved; the wagon stopped; his captors would light a fire, eat, drink, sing, then sleep. To his relief, Uleva had departed, leaving the Ruuk more at ease, spending longer at rest. His headache had eased, and the dreams less dark, but he knew a sickness lay within, and it spread.

The wagon stopped. Toryn lay back, welcoming the opportunity to be still. Outside, usual preparations for supper were underway. The light of the fire flickered on the canvas and soon the smell of roasting meat wafted in. After the Ruuk had taken their fill, they tossed in a few bones. Toryn scrambled to his daily ration and gnawed on the remnants of meat. The laughter and familiar songs began. He thought of Roold and the men of Drunsberg. What had become of them? He dearly hoped they had survived the torment they suffered in Wyke Wood. He closed his eyes and longed for a sleep undisturbed by dark dreams.

The flap drew back. He bolted upright. A dark, crooked figure clambered into the wagon. Hands fumbled at his ankles and soon the clasps fell away. The visitor grasped his wrist and pulled. Toryn, still dazed from sleep, resisted. 'Fool!' It was a woman's voice, gruff but clearly a woman. She spluttered as if not accustomed to speaking. 'Do you want to stay?' She tugged again. 'Come, while they still sleep.' Toryn did not stop to argue. He stood and staggered into the woman. 'Careful, clumsy bones, you'll wake them all.'

Toryn whispered his apology, but this time stumbled into the canvas. He stretched his back and rubbed the stiff muscles in his legs. The woman steadied him. 'Ready?' She shoved a blanket into his hands. 'Take this.' He wrapped it around his shoulders and followed her out of the wagon.

The embers of the fire rippled in the light breeze, shedding enough light for them to find their way between the sleeping forms of his captors strewn about the campsite. Toryn shivered and pulled the blanket closer. The woman led him away from the camp and light of the fire. In the dark, he struggled to find his footing on damp, uneven ground, but his rescuer refused to slow down. Each time he fell, she tugged on his wrist, dragging him farther from the Ruuk camp. He tried to speak, to ask her name, and where she led him, but she would silence him with a sharp hiss, and press on.

After what must have been two hours of a painful trek, Toryn spied a dark, jagged line between the surrounding hills. He guessed it had to be the Kolossos Mountains against the coming of dawn in the east.

At last, the woman stopped. They stood on the shores of a large lake. She sat and pulled a flask from a pack on her back. 'Here. Drink this.' Toryn gladly gulped down the sweet liquid inside, wincing as the sides of his sore throat scraped together. 'Steady. That's plenty.' She snatched it back. The drink warmed his body, spreading to all parts, easing his aches and pains. But while it helped, deep inside he sensed unease. His limbs felt warm, but his stomach remained cold and numb as if icy fingers clawed at his insides, refusing to relinquish their grasp.

The woman bade Toryn to sit. He joined her on the wet, tufty grass as she took a single sip from the flask. He saw her face for the first time in daylight. Her skin was darker than anyone he had ever met. Deep wrinkles marked her skin like ravines on a mountain range, giving her face the look of an ancient map. But her eyes belied her age. Even in the early light of dawn, her steely, gray eyes shone with a vitality her body lacked.

He spoke his thoughts out loud. 'Who are you?'

She frowned, creasing the lines across her forehead

deeper than Toryn thought possible. She licked her lips. 'Who am I?' She spoke as if asking herself. 'Who am I?'

'Yes. What's your name?'

She snapped. 'Name? I don't need a name.'

He tried again. 'But surely you have one.'

She shook her head slowly. 'No... no name. I don't have to call myself anything. It's just me. I don't need to get my own attention.'

'What do other people call you?'

'People?' She held out her gloved hands. 'What other people? Do you see any?'

Toryn looked about him. 'Well, I'm here. What do I call you?'

She shrugged. 'Whatever you like. There's just the two of us. If you speak, you can only be speaking to me.' She folded her arms as if pleased with her reasoning. Toryn smiled. Despite the old woman's abrupt manner, he already felt at ease in her presence.

He tried to smile against the cold gnawing his gut. 'But you must have a name. I shall call you' — he edged closer — 'Hope. Yes, Hope, because that's what you've given me.'

She threw up her hands. 'Fine. If you must. But don't expect me to remember it, or answer to it, or remember yours.'

'I haven't told you mine yet.'

'Don't bother. If I speak, it's to you.' She frowned. 'But I often talk to myself.' She clapped. 'Got it. If I speak and I'm looking at you, then you know I'm speaking to you. But if I don't, it's only for my ears. Ha! Do you see? We don't need to bother with names.'

Toryn noticed her tattered clothes. 'Where are you from?'

'Why so many idiotic questions? I'm from here, I'm from over there, the other side of that lake. I'm from over the mountains.' She squinted at him. 'Where are you from?'

'Midwyche in Darrow.' He clenched his arms around his middle. The mention of his village expanded the emptiness inside. He tried to see his home, but his clouded mind could only recall the names. 'By the River Tam.' River? But he could not see it. 'There's a bridge, I know. I'm sure I had to cross it to get to the fields.' He rubbed his temples. But as hard as he tried, he could not picture his home. 'And a wood, somewhere, I think.'

Hope shrugged. 'Never heard of it, or the river. And you don't seem so sure yourself, do you.' She peered into his face. 'Tell me, young fellow, where are you now?'

Toryn glanced at the nearby trees in the growing light. 'I... I don't know.'

'Then why does it matter where you're from?' She poked a finger at his chest. 'Don't you think it's more important to know where you are this very moment?' She nodded, looking happy with herself. 'And where you're going? That's more important than knowing where you came from, is it not?'

'I suppose. Then, where are we?'

Hope threw up her hands. 'Haven't a clue.'

'So, where are we going?' Hope shrugged. Toryn tried to reason with her. 'But I thought you said it was important to... forget it.'

She smiled. 'Have already, no need to tell me.' She squinted at the horizon. 'But don't you worry, I'll get you there.'

'Where?'

'Can't recall. I'm sure it will come to me before long.'

He rubbed his bruised elbow, recalling the hard floor of the wagon. 'Why did you rescue me?'

'Rescue? You?'

Toryn pulled a face. 'You found me at that camp. You

took off my chains, somehow, and led me to this place. But you don't know why?'

She scoffed. 'Of course, I know why. Do you think I'm mad?'

'No! I'm grateful, I thought I was done for.' She held his gaze and, for a moment, Toryn sensed another looked back from behind her eyes. 'So why did you help?'

'It's not right, keeping you chained up like an animal.' She turned and spat. 'Nasty creatures. Seen them before, not nice.' She stood and grabbed his wrist. 'Come on. Time to go.'

Toryn had no choice. He found his feet. 'Wait. We have to go to Archonholm.'

She cocked her head. 'Where?'

'Archonholm. You must have heard of it.' Hope stared at him. Toryn tried again. 'It's in the south, close to the gate. Those attacks, the sorcerer at the mines, and that woman, Uleva, the one in the wood. The Archon needs to know about them.'

'Who?'

Toryn despaired. 'Our leader. He has power, the most powerful man in the land. The Archon will know what to do. He has to know what's happening here.'

'But if he's as powerful as you say, he'll already know.'

'Perhaps he does.' He thought out loud. 'Dohl had said men with spears were approaching the wood. I guess the Archon could have sent them.'

'So that's sorted. We don't need to go. Your man in charge has everything under control.'

'But there was that dreadful attack on Greendell. He should be told. And the stone, the Archon is interested in these matters.'

She turned to the hills beyond the lake. 'Where does this leader of yours live?'

'Archonholm. I already mentioned… But, I don't

know exactly where it is. Wait! I have a map.' He ran his hand down his trouser leg. He slumped. 'They've taken it.'

Hope tutted. 'Then we won't be going, will we.' She walked a few paces, stopped and listened. 'Shush! Someone's coming.'

He froze. 'Where from?'

'That way. Six of them. Your captors, I believe.'

His heart raced. 'But there's nowhere to hide.'

She beckoned him closer, seeming calm considering their predicament. 'Take my hands.'

'But…' he heard shouts. 'Shouldn't we run?'

'No time. And like you said, where to? Here, take hold.' She shook off her tattered gloves and gripped Toryn's hands. He stiffened, surprised at the heat emanating from her palms. Hope hummed. Words formed under her breath, her hands grew yet warmer, the air about them rippled like heat rising from a cornfield in summer.

The voices grew louder. 'Fools! She'll skin us alive if we don't find him.' Hope had been right — six Ruuk strode over the ridge, heading towards them.

Another grumbled. 'I'll skin the little runt for making us come this far.' Hope continued to hum her tune. They strode straight towards the spot where they stood but failed to see them. The Ruuk at the front stopped and held up a hand. 'The tracks stop here. Two of them, he must have had help.' He scratched his head and surveyed the ground, almost walking into Toryn. The scout stared through the wavering air, distorting his face. 'I don't get it.' He paced around their spot. 'No sign of camp, no sign of nothing, but there's no tracks leading away.'

Toryn held his breath as another stepped up. 'Well, they can't have flown away or walked across the lake.' He grabbed the first by the throat. 'Not much of a tracker, eh. I'll let you explain to the Ice Queen how you lost him.' He turned to the others. 'And I'll wager a week's rations this fool's tracks won't return from his chat with her ladyship.'

The scout pushed him away as the others laughed. 'You let him escape, chief. It was you and your miserable mob nodding off to blame. I think she'll be more upset by that.' He brushed down his cloak. 'I look forward to eating your dinners for a week when you can't swallow because she's ripped out your scrawny throat.'

The captain held up his hands. 'Alright, alright. We'll tell her a company of knights attacked us if we don't find him. I counted at least forty of those boys in their shiny armor.'

The scout sneered. 'She won't believe you. She knows everything going on in these parts, and she ain't going to be pleased if you lie to her.'

The captain's face paled. 'Then we better bloody well find the whelp!'

The scout pointed. 'They must have continued south east. Can't think they'd have changed direction all of a sudden.' Toryn felt Hope's weight slump against him. He held her firm as she continued to hum, but he could see she grew tired. The air about them cleared a little. Thankfully, the captain had stepped towards his scout. 'Come on, lads, keep looking. They can't have gone far, it's not like we fed him much.'

The scout waded into the lake and stooped. 'Here, chief. I reckon they walked in the water for a while to put us off their trail.' He grinned. 'Ha! They'll have to try harder to fool me.'

'You better be right for all our sakes.' The captain turned and yelled to his men. 'This way you rats, and don't think you're getting a break anytime soon.'

Toryn held Hope upright as his captors set off at pace. And not a moment too soon. The shimmering air shrouding them, suddenly fell away as the last man disappeared around a clump of thicket. Hope collapsed to the ground, releasing Toryn's hands.

He sat by her side. 'How did you do that?' But Hope snored. Around where they had stood, a circle of scorched grass smoldered. His body tingled; it was not an unpleasant sensation, and more desirable to the coldness inside. Toryn had to know. He turned over her hands and examined the palms. Faint, wavy lines covered her skin. They swirled about her palm and extended down each finger right up to the tips. He picked up her threadbare gloves, pulled them over her now icy hands, then placed his blanket over her shoulders. He sat back. She was a wyke. He watched her sleep. She seemed harmless, and his body did not convulse in her company as it had with Uldrak, and worse still, with Uleva.

Hope stirred. She sat and blinked, looking around as if unsure of their whereabouts. Her eyes eventually rested on Toryn. 'Ah! There you are.' She stood and stretched out her arms. 'Coming?'

'To where?' Toryn chose to say nothing of his discovery.

She turned a full circle, stopping to face the west. 'That way.'

'Why that way?'

'I have to show you something.' She scratched her chin as she searched the horizon. 'It's important. You need to see it.' Toryn opened his mouth. Her finger shot up. 'Shush! Don't ask because I don't know, I can't remember.' She grinned. 'But I'll know when we get there.'

35. CALERDORN PREPARES

Elodi had returned to Calerdorn to find the rescued prisoners in better health than she could have wished. But if her spirits rose with their recovery, Captain Roold's account of the battle at Drunsberg, dragged them back down. The old man, Dohl, also troubled her. His transformation from the crooked, harmless creature, into a raging madman, alarmed her. And Wendel had not been pleased to hear of her close scrape with death. But Elodi had little time to worry about Dohl. Reports from her scouts posted around Dorn had filled her with dread. While Elodi and her strike force had focused their efforts on Durran Wood, the enemy had not been idle.

Elodi stood before the giant map and addressed her Council in Calerdorn's Great Hall. 'To the east, the Ruuk hold Drunsberg, but as yet, they have not ventured forth. I have dispatched a division of reserves, led by Captain Cubric of the Archonian Guard to keep vigil. Once we can secure the border to the north, we shall seek to retake the mines.' Elodi ran her hand toward the Kolossos Mountains. 'The wyke, Uleva is heading east, but her destination is not known.' She stepped back across the map. 'Durran Wood is at last free of the evil, and the settlement within destroyed. We shall maintain a watch to ensure it stays that way.' A few heads nodded their appreciation. But that was the last of her good news.

Elodi took a position before the blue sea on the wall map. 'But my primary concern is the situation at Draegnor.' Her stomach knotted. 'We know enemy reinforcements have poured into the fort and surrounding area. And... I believe the wyke who took the mines, who

334

Captain Roold informs me goes by the name of Uldrak, commands the gathering masses.' The room stayed silent. She took a deep breath. 'Members of the Council, judging by the movements witnessed by our scouts, we can be certain they're preparing to launch an attack on Calerdorn very soon.'

Gasps filled the hall. All but Perdew, the longest serving Councilor at the table, leaped to their feet. Elodi tried to speak over them. 'Please, please sit. Let us not panic.' She scanned the faces around the table, suddenly feeling like the Archon as he had reported on the activity behind the gate. Gundrul banged his fists on the table, silencing the room.

Elodi nodded. 'Thank you, Captain. While I agree this is not what we want to hear, I have great faith in the forces I have at my disposal in the city. The defenses may be ancient, but they remain strong, built to last by our ancestors who faced vastly more powerful forces.' Her back straightened as her words took hold. 'I have sent riders to the surrounding villages so more people, and reserves, will arrive over the next few days.'

'But what of supplies, ma'am?' She turned to Perdew. He cleared his throat. 'Apologies for the interruption. But with extra mouths to feed, how long can we hold out should the raid result in a siege?'

Elodi held up a hand. 'No need to apologize, Councilor Perdew.' She tapped her finger on the natural harbor marked out on the map. 'Don't forget, we have the *Celestra* sitting in our dock undergoing repairs as we speak. And while we still hold the port, we can use her to bring grain and supplies from the old docks to the south.'

Perdew shifted in his chair. 'Again, ma'am, I don't want to appear a doom-monger, but do the southern wards have sufficient supplies to spare?'

Elodi smiled. 'I would expect nothing less from you,

Perdew.' She turned to the other councilors. 'I can assure you they are able to supply us. The aforementioned riders also carried a decree to cease sending the levy to Archonholm.' She paused as the councilors murmured.

Again, Perdew voiced the concern of the Council. 'But, ma'am, not since the closing of the gate has Harlyn failed to meet her obligations to Archonholm.'

'Ah yes, but never in that time has the realm experienced an existential threat. This morning, I informed Archonholm I have declared a state of emergency in Harlyn, allowing us to postpone our levy in the current circumstances.' Out of the corner of her eye she saw Wendel grin. She continued. 'Archonholm has already invoked its emergency powers' — she failed to prevent the smile spreading across her lips — 'I am simply applying the same law. I have sent word to the Vice-Archon who will have to accept my decision. Produce already stacked up ready to be sent south, will shortly head to the port of Seransea to be distributed where needed.'

Perdew nodded. 'An astute move, ma'am. Your father would have been proud.'

Elodi's smile faded. 'Let us trust it won't be in vain.' She stepped back to the map. 'We can expect no more help from the Archon. As you are all too aware, the realms face the threat of an onslaught upon the Caerwal Gate. I cannot yet talk about the specifics, but the Archon has plans he expects will give us the upper hand.' She eyed the wide line marking the Draegelan Trench spanning the north. 'We live in troublesome times, but we have to stand as one against the threat. Should Calerdorn fall, the south will be open to the Ruuk. Should the unthinkable happen and the Golesh break through the gate, then Archonholm falls, we will be trapped as a horseshoe between the anvil and the hammer.' She clasped her hands. 'But while the challenges we face may seem daunting, I am certain we will rise to meet them.'

'Has he spoken?' Elodi's footsteps echoed down the corridor as they approached the cell.

Wendel shrugged. 'Dohl has said very little, ma'am, well not to me. He speaks all the time to himself but rarely acknowledges there's anyone else in the room.' He turned to Elodi. 'I don't see the need for you to be here. It's hardly the place for the head of the realm to frequent.'

'A few weeks ago, I would have agreed with you, Wendel. But much has changed in such a short time. The abomination in the wood commanded that poor wretch to end my life.' Her pulse raced. 'In my realm, Wendel. In my realm! I'm sure you'll agree I cannot tolerate such an action. I want him to look me in the eye and tell me what he knows. We must find out where this creature, Uleva, has gone, and what evil deeds she's hatching. I cannot abide the thought of her roaming this land as she pleases.'

Elodi lowered her voice as they neared the guard outside Dohl's cell. 'Whatever came out of those trees drove my knights to the edge of madness. We're not dealing with a troublesome wyke, Wendel. I need to know exactly what we face.'

'As you wish, ma'am.'

The guard leaning against the wall jumped to attention as if he had just woken. Wendel nodded to the young man. 'If you please.' He fumbled with the chain on his belt and found the correct key. The guard turned it in the old lock, put his shoulder to the heavy door, and heaved it open.

Wendel led the way. 'We've scrubbed him clean, although I can't say he appreciated our efforts.'

Inside, Dohl sat on a wooden stool with his head resting between his two chained wrists. Light streamed onto his thin, gray hair from a narrow aperture in the ceiling leading up to ground level. The prisoner kept his head down. Elodi stood before him. 'Dohl? Do you know where you are?' He mumbled into his hands. Elodi continued. 'Then I shall tell you. You are being held in a cell in the walled city of Calerdorn. You have no chance of being rescued, and no one has ever escaped from these dungeons.' She paced the small cell. 'Bearing that in mind, you may as well tell us what you know, and I'll show clemency.' She glanced to Wendel; what that might involve, she had not considered.

'Where?' Elodi jumped. Dohl's cloudy eyes stared straight at her. Her hand rested on the handle of her sword, that Wendel now insisted she carried at all times. His brow knotted. 'Where? Where did you say?'

'Calerdorn. The principal city of the realm of Harlyn.'

'Calerdorn?' Dohl spoke as if trying to remember. He slowly slid off his stool, kneeled and stroked the rough, stone floor. He sat back. Tears streamed down his scarred face. He whispered. 'Calerdorn? Calerdorn?' Elodi looked to Wendel; he shrugged. Dohl's eyes widened like an excited child. 'I'm home.'

Elodi gaped. 'Calerdorn was your home?'

Dohl sobbed, talking to himself. 'I'm home.' He tipped back his head, threw up his hands as far as the chains allowed, and cried out. 'I'm home! My Lord! I'm home.' His arms fell and his head dropped as he sagged to the floor.

Elodi's gasps filled the cell in the sudden silence. She stared aghast at Dohl's crumbled form. 'What do you think he means, Wendel? Did he once serve under my father?' Dohl snored.

Wendel sat back on the stool and rested his chin in his hand. 'I suppose it's possible, but I don't recall a man with his name on your father's staff.'

Elodi crouched by Dohl's side. 'What should we do? We can hardly keep him in chains if he served my father.

Could he also have once been a prisoner in the wood? If so, we can hardly blame him for the wrong Uleva has wrought upon him. Did he have any choice in the matter regarding his attempt on my life?'

Wendel kept his eyes on Dohl. 'But there remains the risk Uleva may still influence the wretched soul.'

'Do you honestly think that's possible? She must be fifty leagues from here by now.'

Wendel raised his eyebrows. 'If she can summon an apparition of drayloks to scare the wits out of Aldorman, I would have thought controlling this broken creature from a mere fifty leagues would present little challenge.'

'Then we should at least make his incarceration more comfortable.' She turned to the door. 'Guard. When did this man last eat?'

The guard entered, keeping his eyes to the floor. 'He had the standard issue of bread and water at midday, ma'am.'

Elodi gestured to Dohl. 'When he wakes, I want him to have a full meal and a glass of ale.'

The guard caught her eye. 'Ale, ma'am?'

'Yes. You heard me, ale. This man is being kept in this cell as much for his own safety. He may yet be worthy of our sympathy and even praise for his past service to the realm.'

The guard glanced at the miserable form on the floor. 'Yes, ma'am. I'll inform the cook.'

Elodi moved to the door. 'And remember. I want him fed as soon as he wakes.' The man saluted as Elodi and Wendel left.

Wendel chuckled. 'You do realize, their prisoner will receive a dinner far superior to one they can expect in the coming days.'

Elodi frowned. 'Is that so? These men perform a difficult and valuable service, they should at least receive one decent meal a day.' She stopped. 'See to it, Wendel. I want their rations increased.'

Wendel sighed. 'That may have to wait, ma'am. I fear we shall all be on prison guard rations should we find ourselves forced to endure a siege.'

Watches placed on the major routes into Calerdorn had yet to see signs of an invasion, but in a way, that fueled the dread taking hold of Elodi's heart. Had the Ruuk attacked immediately after securing the fort at Draegnor, she could have disrupted such a reckless assault, even with the enemy's superior numbers. The delay signaled their intent. This would be no raid, no temporary incursion to steal supplies, or to wreak havoc and plunder settlements at the border. This time they meant to stay. Never in recent times had Calerdorn faced such a threat. Elodi was grateful for her father's tenacity when petitioning the Council to maintain the defenses, despite years of relative inactivity. The walls were in good order, and although ancient, she had functioning siege engines at her disposal. A messenger bird had been dispatched to Archonholm, but she doubted aid would be forthcoming.

Elodi had insisted a watch also be placed on the coast. No Ruuk had ever been known to sail, but in the light of the new weapons and tactics employed, she could not dismiss a surprise attack by sea. The deep inlet offered a safe harbor for a sizeable fleet, whether they be friend or foe. And should the enemy venture as far as Calerdorn's docks, it would stretch her resources to breaking point, defending the city on both fronts.

Scouts to the north reported more Ruuk pouring over the border into Draegnor, no doubt chancing their luck as news of the attack on the Caerwal Gate must have reached their ears. But it was not just the numbers troubling Elodi. Sightings of huge oxen pulling dozens of large wagons, resembling those housing the weapons used at Drunsberg, trundled into Draegnor daily.

Elodi stood on the battlement above the main gate of the city. Her hands rested on the thick stone wall that had protected Calerdorn for a millennium. She looked to the snowy peaks of the Dornan Mountains as she recalled the stories of her realm in its youth. Depleted by the efforts to drive out Ormoroth and his dark hosts from the land, the newly formed Seven Realms feared a counterstrike. But despite their weakened state, her ancestors had undertaken the immense task of constructing a new line of defense. Named in honor of the Archon of the time, the Draegelan Trench spanned the narrowest part of the land separating the frozen north from Harlyn and Broon. One of Elodi's favorite stories from the archives, told of the laying of Calerdorn's foundation stone from the largest rock excavated from the trench. The footings of her ancient city ran deep, but could its current inhabitants honor its splendor in this dangerous time?

Elodi pressed down on the wall as if trying to fortify the stone against the projectiles the new weapons would unleash in the days to come. A gust of wind chilled her face. She turned back to the north. Her ancestors had underestimated the guile of its foe. By his dark arts, Ormoroth harnessed the forces of nature, driving snow and ice against them. For a hundred years, the cold crept relentlessly south, packing the deep trench with snow, until its span became impossible to defend against the numbers swarming across the bridges of ice.

The realms had no option but to retreat thirty leagues south, building fences and watchtowers across a hastily formed border. The dire situation called for a powerful leader and warrior, and up stepped Dorlan at their time of greatest need. Elodi's face flushed as the young girl in her remembered the hours she had stood in front of his portrait in her father's chamber.

Ormoroth's forces soon came to fear Dorlan as stories of his deeds spread through their ranks. The noble knight of Calerdorn patrolled the borders astride his white stallion, Draego, leading the enemy to believe he fought in more than one place at a time. But while Dorlan frustrated the invasion, Ormoroth had waited, growing stronger, not committing his full strength until ready. And when he finally struck, he came like an avalanche, crushing all before its unforgiving, thunderous advance. Untold numbers perished in a single day as Ormoroth obliterated the defensive line, capturing the watchtowers and newly-built fortress at Draegnor.

Yet, despite the defeat, the Seven Realms could still muster a formidable force in those days. Dorlan and his knights held back the onslaught long enough for Draegelan to bring reinforcements from the south. Together, Draegelan and Dorlan formed a powerful alliance the mighty Ormoroth could not take lightly. Both sides suffered terrible losses as they fought to a standstill for every inch of land. After weeks of ferocious battle, Dorlan prevailed and broke through the right flank on the frozen plain at Draegnor. Draegelan exploited the gaps left by Ormoroth's hordes rushing to repel Dorlan, pushing on and forcing Ormoroth to abandon his foothold and retreat behind the Trench. While Draegelan secured the border, Dorlan's army rode on, deep into the ice-bound lands in pursuit of Ormoroth; it was said none returned.

Draegelan himself ventured north seeking Dorlan, but found only a deep rent in the bedrock, blasted free of ice. At this place, the two great rivals fought their last duel. None survived. Of Dorlan's army, only shattered armor and broken weapons remained, strewn about the battlefield as if cut down and scattered by a single sweep of a giant's scythe. It was said, Draegelan knew of the source of Ormoroth's fatal blow, believing the last commander of the Evil One had unleashed a perilous, unworldly force. In the last throes of the battle, unwilling to accept defeat, Ormoroth, in an act of spite, had sacrificed himself to slaughter Dorlan and his brave knights.

Elodi's fingers stung. She looked down to find she clutched the rough edges of the parapet. She may not be facing a force as daunting as Ormoroth, but she had neither Dorlan nor anything like the strength Draegelan had at his command. Elodi turned and gazed out across the darkening plain and imagined Dorlan galloping to the city's aid on his mighty steed, Draego. She shook the frivolous thought from her head.

Below, a mother called out to her children. Elodi watched her progress along the cobbled alleys, visible between the haphazard rooftops nestling between the inner and outer walls. She gazed out to the plain, making a silent vow to do everything within her power to spare her people the ravages of war.

'Ma'am?' She turned. Ruan saluted. He glanced at her bloody fingertips but said nothing.

She placed her hands behind her back. 'Are your men in position, Captain?'

He nodded. 'At Tunduska's Gorge as requested.'

'And you're certain they're *all* volunteers?'

'Yes, ma'am. When a captain of Broon asks for a volunteer, *all* step forward.'

'Your men are very brave, Ruan. Uldrak is poised to strike south at any moment. The Mawlgrim Mire to the east is no place for his heavy weapons as thankfully, it swallowed the old roads years ago.' Elodi turned to the Dornan Mountains. 'The only path to Calerdorn open to him is the pass.' She placed a hand on his shoulder. 'I am heartened by your presence, Ruan.'

'We won't let you down, ma'am.' He saluted and left

the battlement. Elodi watched him descend the stairs. Ninety of his men would attempt an ambush to inflict damage on Uldrak's war machines and slow their progress. They had taken positions at a small fort guarding the Tunduska Bridge in the Dornan Pass. Elodi's ancestors built the road through the mountains for quick passage between Calerdorn and Draegnor. Yet, in these dark times, it would regrettably prove useful to Harlyn's foes. But her forefathers had the wisdom to foresee such a threat and had constructed a small, but strategic defensive position at Tunduska's Gorge. Elodi had made the journey to Draegnor with her father and had admired both the bridge spanning the ravine, and the keep, hewn into the sides of the mountains. But she had wished the builders had not been so capable. It would be wise to demolish the bridge and close the pass, but Calerdorn had neither the means nor expertise to bring down the structure that had stood firm for centuries.

Elodi had bid Ruan's men farewell as they marched tall under the banner of Broon, proud to support an ally in need. She had been both impressed and disturbed at their determined faces as they departed with the knowledge their ambush could likely result in their death. But she had no choice. Commanding an army meant making tough decisions, decisions Elodi could not avoid. And each war machine his men destroyed would improve their odds on breaking the expected siege.

Elodi turned to leave and jumped. Wendel stood a few feet away. She knew the look on his face. He drew up his frame as he took a breath. 'News from Lord Broon, ma'am.'

Elodi straightened. 'Please, go ahead.'

'It's written in the old tongue of Lunn. He's obviously cautious about it falling into the wrong hands. I hope you don't mind, I asked Gundrul to translate. I assumed he could be trusted with its content.'

'Yes, yes, of course.' She gripped the hilt of her sword. 'What does Lord Broon have to report?'

'He states the Archon will lift his invocation on the seas to the east soon.' Wendel cleared his throat. 'The fleet will set sail on Summer's Eve, ma'am.'

'That's four weeks from now!' Elodi found herself staring south. 'Our world will change, Wendel. What we've known for centuries is to come to an end.' Her eyes followed the line of the mountains. 'Things will never be the same.'

Wendel grumbled. 'Then let's hope it's not a change for the worse.'

Elodi sat on the edge of her bed and covered her eyes. She collapsed back and let out a long sigh as the weight of command pushed her down into the soft bedding. But her body refused to let go of the responsibility. Shortly, the Archon would unlock the Caerwal Gate, a gate that had protected them for over three hundred years would be thrown wide open to whatever lay beyond. She pictured Bardon at the head of the fleet and hoped he would make a better sailor than she had managed. The night they had spoken of their doubts for the Archon's plan seemed so long ago, but the doubts remained fresh. If the Golesh had received word from the spies the Castellan believed operated in Archonholm, would Bardon be able to put ashore? If the landing went as planned, what awaited them on the route through the Lost Realms to the old capital of Elmarand? And once the gate opened...? Elodi's stomach sank through her back. The very existence of the Five Realms lay in the balance. She could do nothing to change events at Archonholm, but she had to hold Calerdorn.

Elodi sat up, convinced she would not sleep. She sought for a ray of hope among the gloom. The *Celestra*!

She could be thankful for the fine ship from the glory days of times past. Calerdorn's carpenters had done the city proud, completing the repairs to the satisfaction of Helmsman Horace. He had taken the role of captain and set sail with his crew to Seransea to collect valuable supplies in readiness for the siege. The men and women of Dorn's reserves still streamed into the city, swelling the population two-fold, making the supplies from Seransea crucial. Reluctantly, Elodi had decreed half of the reserves from all over Harlyn come to Calerdorn and the borders. She knew this would create fear in the realm, but should her city fall, the enemy would be free to sack the smaller, weaker settlements to the south. She had watched farmers, blacksmiths, millers and old guards arrive with their makeshift weapons, but all had looked determined, and under Gundrul's command, she trusted would give a good account of themselves in combat.

For days, the sounds of hammers tapping, and ropes straining had filled the city as engineers tested the ancient trebuchets. In the squares and every free space, her reserves honed their skills under the watchful eye of Gundrul, Ruan and Roold from the mines. All around the city, people bustled, preparing for the days ahead, and oddly, it gave them hope. They were not powerless. They could make a stand against the evil seeking to take their realm.

Elodi walked to the window. Outside, the quiet courtyard belied their situation. The watches on the pass, roads and seas maintained their vigil. Nothing could move within twenty leagues of Calerdorn without the knowledge of her scouts, but still Elodi remained uneasy. Aldorman's account of his encounter at the edge of Durran Wood gnawed at her insides. While the city stood a fighting chance against conventional weapons, what could they do against the dark forces sighted at the wood? And what had become of Uleva?

A tap at the door drew her back from the window. *Bardon?* No, of course not; the entire length of the Five Realms lay between them. Her guard called through. 'Ma'am, the Chief Advisor wishes to see you. Shall I grant him entry?'

'Please send him in.' Elodi adjusted her nightgown as she listened to the guard speak to Wendel before the door opened.

Her advisor shuffled in, carrying all his sixty years of service on his shoulders. 'Apologies for the interruption at such a late hour, ma'am.'

Elodi led him to the table. 'No need, I doubt I will sleep this side of dawn.' She picked up a bottle. 'Would you care for a glass of wine?' She grinned. 'Just a little something I brought back from Archonholm.'

Wendel lowered his tired bones onto a chair. 'You partake, ma'am, but I'll decline. I don't think my old head would forgive me come the morning.'

She lifted a jug and poured Wendel a glass of water. 'So, what brings you here at this hour? I don't think I can take any more bad news, well, not until daybreak, if it has to be the case.'

Wendel took the glass. 'I cannot be sure if it's good or bad, but I have spent the last two hours talking… perhaps talking is the wrong word, no, listening to our mystery man in the cells.'

Elodi sat. 'I trust he has eaten well.'

'That he has, ma'am.'

'And the guards are treating him with respect?'

Wendel drained his glass. 'Yes, if reluctantly at first.'

'What has changed?'

'Well, ma'am. The Head Warden is an old Archonian, and he believes Dohl may also have served in his youth.'

'What makes him think that?'

Wendel frowned. 'Something Dohl has been muttering on about. The warden wouldn't give me the full story, but when pressed, he said it relates to a pledge known only to those who've taken it, and he wasn't prepared to break that oath.'

'Well, I admire the warden's loyalty. And as for Dohl, it sounds feasible. Many men would have served from this region. That may explain his longevity in such poor conditions.'

Wendel nodded. 'I'll give him that. But while Dohl appears better physically, he's still muddled in the head.' He leaned back and massaged his neck. 'I found a way to influence his thoughts without having to ask a direct question. He continues to talk to himself, but I believe he's aware of more than we suspect. It's as if another lives inside his head, and dear old Dohl reads these thoughts like a book.' He smiled as if pleased with his tactic. 'I plant a word or two in his mind, and, within a minute, he comes across it, and then off he goes. The words pour out as if recited from a scroll. Quite revealing.'

Elodi leaned forward. 'To what end?'

'As we suspected, Uleva left the wood voluntarily, if earlier than planned, but not directly due to your incursion.'

Her shoulders dropped. 'And I thought we'd achieved at least a minor victory.'

'Well, thankfully they've gone.' Wendel stroked his chin. 'My clerks have combed the archives to find mention of this Uleva, but as yet have found nothing.'

'Ah!' Elodi straightened. 'Now you mention it. Bardon... Lord Broon, informed me of missing scrolls in Archonholm relating to the time of the Archon's victory.'

'You refer to the Lost Years, ma'am?'

'Or the Age of Shadows, as they call it in Broon.' She smiled. 'Yes, I do prefer their name. But that's beside the

348

point. Do we also have a gap in our records, Wendel? I've never had cause to delve so far back.'

He nodded. 'You have to consider the devastation wrought by the struggle. When the Golesh ships extended their raids up both our coastlines, it stretched resources to breaking point. Possibly half of all people in the realm perished. Of those surviving the battles, we know from word of mouth, famine, disease, and sadly, despair, struck down many. I'm amazed we have any records from those dark times at all, and those written, make for disturbing reading.' Wendel's nose wrinkled. 'Not recommended if you're in need of a good night's sleep, ma'am.'

'Then I will forgo the pleasure, it's been too long since I've had an undisturbed night.' She remembered the reason for her question. 'Then am I to assume if this Uleva creature is a survivor from the Lost Years, we are unlikely to find any mentioned of her in the scrolls?'

Wendel grunted. 'That would also be my belief, but I shall continue to search all the same.'

Elodi stared down at her wine. 'Worrying indeed if this creature has endured from those times. She would be at least three hundred years old, and I should imagine she has not been idle in that time.' Elodi lifted her glass and took a sip. 'Does Dohl speak of where she may have gone?'

Wendel sighed. 'He talks of a stronghold in the east but hasn't revealed the exact location. However, I'm not sure we can trust everything this man has to say.' He scratched his head. 'I believe what we witnessed in his cell yesterday before he collapsed, was a rare moment of clarity. He may have lived here once, but there's no mention of him in the records. Although, it's quite possible, *Dohl*, is a nickname from his days as a guardsman, or he's forgotten the name given at birth and made up a new one.'

Elodi finished her wine. 'I think we can forgive him that, Wendel. He must be eighty if he's a day.'

He chuckled. 'If there was a shred of truth to his latest stories, he'd be a lot older, ma'am.' Wendel rolled his eyes. 'He'd be well past three-hundred to be precise.'

'Three hundred?'

'He talks of fighting alongside the Archon. Although it does make for an interesting, if far-fetched tale.'

She almost dropped her glass. For a moment, Elodi wanted to believe him. She would dearly love to hear a moral-raising story from the Archon's last stand. But she knew in her heart that was not going to happen. She sat back. 'Oh, the poor man. He must be repeating the stories from his mother's knee.'

'We can't blame him, ma'am. Most likely a strategy to keep the madness at bay.'

Elodi stood, walked to the window, and spoke to her reflection. 'We have to find a better place for him, Wendel. Father spoke of the incursions into Durran Wood he had sanctioned. But he lost too many men, and eventually he forbade entry. The missing would have been presumed dead, but that may not have been the case for all of them. Dohl must have been one of those lost.' She turned to her advisor. 'This man deserves our gratitude. He must have been in that dreadful place close to fifty years, it's no wonder he's as muddle-headed as he is.'

Wendel rose from his chair. 'I'll see what I can do, ma'am, but I think it's wise to keep him under lock and key.'

She walked with him to the door. 'Thank you, Wendel.' She turned the handle. 'We'll review the situation come—' Her guard almost ran into them.

He pulled up sharp. 'Ma'am. You asked to be kept informed of the prisoner's well-being.' The guard gestured to a wide-eyed warden behind. 'This man says he's taken a turn for the worse.'

Elodi groaned. 'In what way?'

The warden straightened, trying to regain his breath. 'The prisoner's broken free of his chains, ma'am. He's yelling, cursing and hurling himself against the walls of his cell. He sounds in great pain. But that's not all.' He glanced from Wendel and back to Elodi. 'Ma'am, I don't know how to say this but… the prisoner no longer looks like the man we chained up.'

36. WHEREVER YOU GO...

For five days Toryn trudged on after Hope. They had squeezed through a border fence the day after evading Uleva's men at the lake, leading Toryn to suspect they had to be in Noor. If right, at Hope's pace of an impressive twelve leagues a day, they would cross the border into Darrow before long. Hope led him in a mostly straight line, through woods, shallow streams and across the odd deserted road. To the relief of Toryn, the only time she deviated from her course was to avoid a marsh swarming with hornrasps. Thankfully, they were rare in Darrow, but Toryn still carried the scar from an encounter when he stumbled upon a nest while playing with Elrik. The vicious insect, the size of his thumb, had latched onto his arm and it had taken several swipes to dislodge, but not before it had sunk its large stinger into his flesh. Toryn had kept a wary eye on the angry swarm as they had circled the marsh. And for good reason. One sting caused excruciating, but short-lived pain, two resulted in an unpleasant illness, whereas three or more could inflict an agonizing, drawn-out death.

Hope barely spoke to him, being content to mutter under her breath as if having an argument with herself. Toryn soon learned they moved quicker if he kept his thoughts to himself. But he did not mind. He saw more of the land with Hope preferring to travel by day. Despite the fog in his head concealing his memories of home, Toryn could still picture Hamar's map as if under the bedsheets with his candle. He tried to work out their position based on the shape of the mountains, but the squiggly lines in his drawing looked nothing like the real range. The peaks of the mighty Kolossos had gradually dropped below the horizon to their rear and left, meaning they headed south and slightly west. They walked up and down gentle hills, through green valleys with slow, wending rivers heading out to the sea. Toryn wondered if that was Hope's destination. Hamar's stories of the seas had both scared and intrigued him; how could so much water exist in one place?

Hope did not seem as concerned as Hamar in taking routes close to villages and farms, but as yet they had remained unseen. At one point, as they had crossed a high ridge, Toryn thought he saw towers on the horizon. The two tall structures pointed to the restless sky, but as much as he stared, he could not be sure if it was a city, or a trick of the light. If Hamar's map was accurate, it could be Seransea, which confirmed his belief they were in Noor. But as the name hinted, Seransea sat on the coast, and try as he might, he could not spy the sea beyond. He had asked Hope about their location, and tried again to find out their destination, but she would reply with a shrug, *wherever you go, there you are.*

The day before, they had passed a small village with the familiar appearance of one of the many abandoned settlements in the area. Despite the setting sun, the chimneys remained free of smoke, and no inhabitants returned from the fields. Toryn longed for the smell of freshly-baked bread and a hunk of cheese that might help to bring back his memory, but even if the place had been bustling with activity, he doubted Hope would have tolerated a diversion.

The liquid in the flask had kept him going, but he knew his health worsened, and Hope's drink would not last much longer. The coldness had crept up his spine, and now it hurt to take a deep breath. Occasionally, Hope had stopped and studied his face, but she would shake her head, turn away and increase her pace.

As for his guide, she seemed as skilled in the craft of survival as Hamar. How long had she roamed the lands? Hamar had said wykes lived longer than most, but had she spent all her life in the wilds? He wondered if she had known his father, but how could he ask if he did not know the man's name, and she supposedly did not know her own? But Toryn had no doubts that the markings on her hands were those of a wyke. Hope obviously had power. It was no small trick to evade the eyes of their pursuers, and, when he thought back to his rescue from the camp, the Ruuk had laid where they had fallen as if Hope had put a spell on them. The night had been cold, yet none had slept around the fire as he would have expected.

Toryn looked to the horizon. He wondered how many days lay between him and his village. Had news of Hamar's death reached the farm? Would his parents assume he had also perished? But even if the news of the fall of the mines had made it to the backwater of Midwyche, would any know he and Hamar had been involved? He kept his arms wrapped around his middle as Hope trudged ceaselessly onwards. Perhaps when she had shown him what she deemed important, he could head back east and search for Caranach's peak; surely, he would easily recognize the face of the mountain he had grown up longing to visit. Once he lined up the crags he knew so well, he could use the rock face like the stars to navigate home. He would have some explaining to do for Marshal Drakelow's benefit, but he hoped his account would convince the man to send word of the troubles in the north, on to Archonholm.

But what of Hope? Would she come with him? Perhaps she could help bring on the crop through the cold spring. He shivered, trying to picture the farm, but the memory eluded him. If his strange illness worsened, would he recognize the mountain?

Hope suddenly stopped. Toryn looked up, surprised to find the light fading. She pointed to a line of scrub. 'We'll sleep there tonight.'

Toryn stared. He had spent the day watching her back, but now she faced him he swore she had changed. The deep creases on her forehead and the lines around her eyes had softened, and possibly she stood a little taller.

Hope glared back. 'What you gawping at?'

'There's something different about you.'

'Ha! You're right there. My stomach is emptier than it was this morning.'

Toryn laughed. 'And mine.' He took off his pack and set off to find suitable twigs for the fire. He called back over his shoulder. 'Have you remembered where you're supposed to be taking me yet?'

He jumped as she arrived at his side. 'Maybe tomorrow. Who knows, eh? If you have the will, there's a way.'

Toryn clutched his stomach. 'Then could you heal this chill in me? It's getting worse.'

'No.'

'But you said—?'

'If you have the *will*.' She shrugged. 'And I don't, because there isn't a way.'

'But isn't that the other way around to what…? Never mind.' He went back to collecting fuel, hoping a good fire would warm his bones.

37. A WARRIOR RETURNS

Dohl's agonizing cries reached Elodi as she and Wendel turned into the corridor leading to his cell. The warden and three prison guards with swords drawn, formed a line in front of the door. He held up his flaming torch as they approached, yelling above the din. 'Ma'am, I suggest you stay back.' He pointed to cracks in the door. 'I'm not sure how much longer it will hold.'

A puffing Wendel caught up. 'He's right, ma'am. I would advise you leave right away and put more doors between you and Dohl, until the guards have him properly restrained.'

Elodi placed a hand on her sword. 'I won't hear of it. The man is in obvious distress. He needs to be calmed down, not threatened.' More footsteps rang through the corridor as Ruan and a dozen of his spearmen ran to their aid. Elodi held up her hand, bringing them to an abrupt halt. She called down to the warden. 'Stand down. Bring your men here.' The warden glanced to Ruan, then Wendel. Elodi bellowed, surprised at the power in her voice. 'Do as I command, Warden! This man will not respond well to a show of force.'

'Ma'am?' Wendel took her arm. 'Ma'am, are you sure?'

She glared at her advisor and spoke through a tight jaw. 'Let go. This is not the time, Wendel.' She turned back to Ruan. 'Position half your men at the other end of the corridor, and the rest block this exit.' Then to Wendel. 'You can either come with me, or remain with Ruan.' She lifted a torch from its bracket on the wall. 'But I shall approach the man, regardless.'

Wendel stiffened. 'Then I shall come with you,

ma'am, but with some reservations.'

'Duly noted, Wendel, and' — she rested her hand on his forearm — 'thank you.' Elodi spun back towards the cell as Dohl's cries tore at her heart. She raised her voice for all to hear. 'I believe this man will respond better if he doesn't feel threatened. It's no more than he deserves.' The door cracked, spitting splinters across the floor.

The approaching warden stopped and glanced back. He wiped the sweat from his brow. 'He's nearly through, ma'am. I cannot vouch for your safety if he breaks out.' He nodded to Ruan's men taking up their positions. 'And if he has the strength to smash through that door, I'm not sure we have enough men to contain him.'

'Your concerns have also been noted, Warden.' She held firm. 'I'll take responsibility from here. Put out the torches so he can't see the guards.' Elodi lifted her own above her head. 'I want him to see only me.' She took a step forward. 'Position your men behind Ruan's and await further instruction.'

Ruan stepped forward. 'Lady Harlyn? May I accompany you to the cell?'

Elodi remembered his intervention at the wood. 'Very well, Captain, but please stay behind me.'

He nodded and drew his sword, noting her look of annoyance. 'A precaution, ma'am.'

Wendel shook his head. 'Ma'am, when I said you had to be strong and lead from the front, I didn't anticipate you attempting such a foolhardy stunt as this.'

Elodi pulled back her shoulders. 'I can't explain it, but I have to know for sure who this man is, and I believe he may back down if he's not bullied into submission.'

Wendel stared at her. 'You can't think for one minute he fought in the old wars with the Archon.'

'All the same, Wendel, I have to know. I've seen some strange things these last few weeks, so I need to disprove his story, to know this man *isn't* from those times.'

'But…'

'Again' — she held up her hand — 'not the time, Wendel.' Shards from the door burst into the narrow corridor, followed by a loud crunch. The screams from the cell ceased. Ruan stepped forward. Elodi held out her arm. 'Please, stay behind me.' She held her ground as Dohl staggered out of his cell, gasping for breath. Elodi gaped in horror at the powerfully built man before her. With his head bowed between slumped shoulders, and his arms stretched out to the walls, he resembled the tortured souls of old, nailed to the walls of Ormoroth's fortress.

Dohl shuffled forward, keeping his hands pressed to the walls; a dozen hands tightened their grips on swords and spears. But the man was spent, exhausted from his efforts to escape. He tried to speak, but only his rasping breath made it passed his lips.

Elodi held up both hands. Her voice wavered. 'Please, Dohl, stay calm. We mean you no harm. You are safe with us.' Dohl slowly recovered his breath. Elodi edged closer. 'Who are you? Tell me your name? I believe you when you say you once served Lord Harlyn, my father. We want to help you.'

Dohl spluttered and raised his head. 'My name? Dohl…' he spat out the word as if a curse. 'Dohl! Dohl?' He coughed, shaking his head. 'No, not, Dohl. Dorl?' He spoke with certainty. His voice deepened, echoing through the corridors for all to hear. 'Dorlan! I am Dorlan.' He straightened to his full height; a head taller than any man Elodi had ever seen. He stepped into the light. 'And I have returned.'

Elodi and Wendel gasped. Elodi's hand shot out to the wall for support. Before her, stood the very likeness of the noble warrior that adorned many a wall in Calerdorn. Elodi found her lips mouthed a silent, *no*. The man's steely blue eyes glowered between dark strands of matted hair dangling over his face. They met Elodi's. Her heart went out to him. Rage did not consume this man; he was beset with terror.

Beside her, Wendel murmured. 'It cannot be, ma'am. It cannot be…'

Spears lowered, and the wardens gawped at the prisoner claiming to be the hero of their legends. But Ruan held firm. 'Keep your guard! Lady Harlyn is in danger.'

Elodi found her voice. 'Please, Ruan. I do not fear this man.'

The warrior's voice shook as his fierce eyes fixed on Elodi. 'War is coming. I am summoned.' He peered over her shoulder to the armed men in the gloom. He grasped the loose chains still hanging from his wrists. 'And you stand in my way.'

Elodi's heart hammered into her ribs, but she held his gaze. 'Please, could we return to your… room? We need to talk. Do this, and I will command these men to stand down.' Wendel took a sharp breath, but Elodi continued. 'I will honor my word.'

The man jerked upright. His enormous chest expanded. He bellowed. 'He's back!' He staggered forward. 'And I… I am summoned.' His eyes bulged as he watched his fists clench as if belonging to another. He spat out his last words. 'You must flee!' He screamed, lurching forward at Elodi. She jumped aside as the tall man hurtled down the corridor, scattering the bewildered guards like a gale rushing through barley.

'Try this, ma'am.' Wendel handed her the warm mead. 'I think you'll benefit from something sweet.'

Elodi thanked him as she gazed out of the window in her quarters. 'Any more sightings?'

'Not since he burst through the inner gate.' He cursed

under his breath. 'And that's another repair for our over-stretched carpenters.'

She sat on the cool ledge. 'And what is our explanation to the people? Many would have seen his escape, and all would have noticed the likeness. Word will already have spread across the entire city.'

'We are saying it's a cruel deception by our foes, ma'am, to undermine morale. Nothing more. We cannot let them think for one minute there's any truth in this. Imagine if they believed it was Dorlan, and he fled the city at our time of need.'

The mead sloshed out of her cup as she placed it on the sill. 'Did you hear his words? He said he was *summoned*. But by whom?'

Wendel sighed. 'He must speak of this Uleva creature. She has been in his head for many a year, ma'am. Who knows what evil she's planted?'

'But if he believes he is Dorlan, his loyalty would be with Calerdorn.'

'I should imagine Uleva has corrupted any memory Dohl had of the city. He most likely sees us as the enemy now, ma'am. She must be in complete control of the poor man.'

'Then we must assume he's gone back to her.' Elodi clenched her fist. 'And by the Three, I pray when Dohl said *he is back*, he's not referring to a more powerful wyke yet to reveal their hand.' She motioned for Wendel to sit as she moved to the chairs beside the fireplace. 'Who could this *he*, who Dohl tells us is back, be?'

Wendel sat and folded his cloak over his knees. 'Perhaps nothing more than a vague memory, or just another story doing the rounds in his head. Who knows what's going on in his muddled mind? I suppose he could be referring to Uldrak, but we already know about him. I wouldn't lose sleep over it, ma'am. I would be more concerned had he said, *she's* back. Dohl obviously worships Uleva, his lady, but doesn't appear to fear her.'

Elodi looked to the flames. 'Could he possibly be Dorlan?'

Wendel rubbed his hands in front of the fire. 'When he said he'd fought with the Archon, I presumed he meant the current head of the realms. But with Draegelan?' He pursed his lips. 'That would mean he's over a thousand years old, ma'am. Dorlan may have been a great man, but a mortal all the same. He died in the north, along with the rest of his fine knights. Such a tragic tale. No, ma'am, I don't believe for one moment Dohl is our legendary fighter, somehow returned from the dead.'

Elodi sat back. 'I wouldn't have thought it possible to transform an old man into the warrior who brushed aside my men as if frightened children, Wendel.' She drained the last of the mead. 'And he does resemble the Dorlan from the portraits.'

Wendel held up his hand. 'Ma'am, I'm sure Uleva is only too familiar with Dorlan's likeness from the tales. Remember, she's able to conjure apparitions of drayloks, changing Dohl in our eyes to resemble Dorlan would not be beyond her abilities. For all we know, Dohl is lying dead in a field, his body consumed by the evil inside.'

Elodi clutched her empty cup to her mouth. 'I hope you're right, for Dohl's tortured sake. I do wish this poor man could finally be at rest.' She turned to the window. 'But doesn't part of you want it to be him? Imagine that, Wendel, meeting the knight who fought in the early days of our realm, and alongside Draegelan as his equal.'

Wendel chuckled. 'Sometimes, ma'am, I still see the young girl acting out the scenes from your father's stories.'

Elodi managed a smile. 'Sometimes that's where I'd rather be.'

Wendel stood to leave. 'You must excuse this old

man, ma'am. It's been a long time since I last went through a night without sleep, and I don't intend to start now.'

'Of course, Wendel.' She rose and stretched. 'And I too must take to my bed.'

Wendel paused. 'Not wishing to spoil your dreams, ma'am. But if you think about it from Uleva's point of view, what better way to demoralize your opponents than to make us believe our greatest hero has returned, only to abandon us and take up his sword against the realm.'

Elodi walked to the door with him. 'Then we must ensure everyone believes it was a trick. We cannot have the people thinking otherwise. It's bad enough Uleva can reach into the heart of our city with impunity.' She leaned back against the door frame. 'I hope Draego has thus far eluded Uleva.'

'Draego, ma'am? You must be tired. The fortress fell to the—'

'Come, Wendel. Surely, you must remember, the fort was named in honor of Dorlan's horse, and not the Archon of the time.'

'You must forgive me, ma'am. I have too many things on my mind, and it doesn't take much to drive the old stories so deep I can't recall them.'

Elodi opened the door. 'Lord Broon will set sail in a matter of weeks. Just think, Wendel, he could be in the old realms before long.'

'Yes, ma'am, if the winds and luck favor the fleet.'

Elodi's chest tightened. 'I hope he fairs well, and not only for a momentous victory. I dearly want to see him again. He's an honorable man, and one we need to stand shoulder-to-shoulder with if we're to survive these troubling times.'

Wendel stood in the open door. 'So true, ma'am. Your time at Archonholm proved useful in strengthening the bond between our two realms.'

'Is it safe, or even possible, to send a message to Lord Broon?'

'I'm afraid not. The port was closed for so long we've never had cause to send messages to Caermund, ma'am. Therefore, we possess no birds trained for the route. Our only option would be via Archonholm.'

'Then unfortunately, I cannot. I doubt if the Castellan would forward my note to Bardon. In fact, he may even consider it an act of betrayal. Such a pity, I would have liked to wish him a safe journey.'

'Ah, that reminds me. I am informed a rider arrived late last night from the city. He delivered a trunk from one of the Castellan's men. Let me see if I can remember...'

'Would that be a certain gentleman named Tombold?'

'Yes, Tombold. Apparently, you left so suddenly he didn't have a chance to hand over the last of your father's belongings. The rider informed me Tombold has left a note for you in the trunk.'

Elodi blinked away a tear. 'That's very thoughtful of him, a kind act I'm sure the Castellan would not have sanctioned.'

'I'll have the trunk brought up to you, ma'am, but I'll ask them to wait until you've had time to sleep.'

'Thank you, Wendel. I shall sort through his belongings when I have the time.' She yawned. 'Which is unlikely to be any day soon. Good night, or good morning whatever is most fitting.' She closed the door, walked straight to her bed and lay down. She drifted off into a deep sleep dominated by dreams of drayloks, warriors and gigantic war machines demolishing the walls of Calerdorn.

Elodi awoke at midday to words that sunk her heart while raising it into her throat. Wendel stood with a messenger looking uneasy standing at his leader's bedside. He cleared his throat. 'Ma'am, the Ruuk engaged our forces at Tunduska yesterday morning. Broon's men held them for several hours.' He averted his eyes as Elodi threw back the covers. 'Reports claim they have destroyed four machines, ma'am.'

Elodi drew her cloak around her shoulders. 'And the men? What of Broon's men?'

He stepped aside. 'They have withdrawn following heavy losses.' His face paled. 'Captain Gundrul predicts the enemy will be here by nightfall, ma'am.'

38. CALERDORN SHUDDERS

Elodi paced the inner wall above the gatehouse with her eyes never leaving the West Road. The architects of her twin-walled city had chosen the site well, wedged between the Dornan and Calern Mountains lying to the north and south. Shaped like an egg, the walls to the west merged with solid rock abutting the natural harbor. To the east, the strongest defenses faced the open plain. The flat terrain offered an easy route into the city for welcome allies, but also for an army keen to launch a determined attack.

Elodi stamped her feet in the cool, evening air, reassured by the deep foundations that had served her people through both good and bad times. While the wars preceding the completion of the Caerwal Gate had troubled the city, it had been many centuries since Calerdorn had faced the threat of a siege. But most of what Elodi knew of that time was dressed in the cloak of myth and legend. The sight of Dohl's tortured face filled her thoughts.

Elodi stopped.

Only yesterday, she had stood upon this wall and envisaged Dorlan riding to Calerdorn's aid. She shuddered. Could Uleva read her mind? The transformation of Dohl into her hero may have been a demonstration of her power. And what had happened to Dohl? She hoped Wendel was right and the poor man had died, bringing an end to his years of suffering.

Shouts from the outer wall drew her attention away from the crossroads. Below, the artillery commanders bellowed orders as they made ready the trebuchets on the platforms running along the east wall. Elodi trusted their size would give them superiority and therefore damage the enemy's weapons before they could strike back. The ambush of Ruan's volunteer force had achieved more than she could have hoped. In all, they reported four siege engines destroyed, blocking the pass and delaying the progress of Uldrak's army for many hours — but at a cost. Of the ninety volunteers, less than fifty returned.

All but two of Calerdorn's scouts had made it back on their glistening steeds. They reported at least fifteen-hundred infantry and two dozen large wagons had cleared the pass and were barely an hour behind the last returning scout. Elodi feared the bolt-blasting ballistae most, wishing she had such a weapon at her disposal. Smaller than the trebuchets, they would be difficult to target. And if they were the same as those used at Drunsberg, they could launch large arrowheads of fire at the main gate. She turned away, not wishing to contemplate the consequences should their foe gain entry to the city.

Thankfully, Darrow had answered her urgent call for reserves. Two hundred had boarded the *Celestra* at Seransea and were due at Calerdorn late the next day. But again, the doubts returned. Would there still be a city to defend tomorrow? What if Calerdorn should fall? She had summoned half of all the reserves at her command; could the remainder defend their lands alone?

Elodi had left Wendel in charge at the Council to complete preparations for an evacuation of the young, elderly and those who could not hold a sword. Dozens of fishing boats were made ready to sail should the defenses fail before the *Celestra* returned — she dearly hoped it would not come to that. Elodi could not begin to image what fate would befall them should a storm hit once the flotilla reached open sea.

More shouts rose from below as the archers from

Noor took to their posts in among the artillery. But a bow was no match for a fiery bolt. Should her artillery fail, the archers would be vulnerable: a long city wall presented an easier target than a siege engine in the dark. And what tricks did Uldrak have at his disposal? His devilry had defeated the men at Drunsberg, and she had no such power at hand to resist.

Gundrul and Ruan appeared at the top of the steps. Elodi strode to greet them. 'Captain Gundrul, are the fire crews prepared?'

'Yes, ma'am. Every spare hand in the city is clasping the handle of a bucket, ready to dowse any flames behind the east wall.'

'And your men, Captain Ruan?'

Ruan nodded, giving no sign of the hurt the loss of his spearmen at Tunduska must have inflicted. 'Positioned behind the main gate, ma'am, alongside Captain Aldorman and his knights.'

Elodi sighed. 'I wish he and his men had longer to recover from their ordeal at the wood.'

Ruan fastened a buckle on his armor. 'They're fighting men, ma'am, they're ready for duty. Should the Ruuk break into the gatehouse, their front ranks will not live long enough to regret their eagerness to enter.'

Elodi noticed a glance between the two captains. 'Thank you, gentleman, I appreciate your cooperation. Neither of you are of this realm, yet you are as keen to defend her as if your own.'

Gundrul shrugged. 'Makes no difference, ma'am. If one of the five is threatened, all are threatened.'

'Then Harlyn welcomes your loyal service. I have some knowledge of battle strategy, but as you know, my experience in the field is somewhat scarce.'

Gundrul cleared his throat. 'You can include us also when it comes to a large set piece such as this, ma'am.

Until now, our experience is limited to smaller skirmishes.'

'Ah, yes, of course.'

'But may I say, ma'am, I have served under more experienced commanders in less threatening situations who weren't as calm as you before a battle.'

Her face grew hot. 'Then I only wish my stomach would take its cue from my face.'

Ruan nodded. 'And that is how it should be, ma'am. A complacent commander can be more of a threat to his own army than a competent foe.'

Elodi took a deep breath. 'Then you can be assured, I shall pose no such threat to your ranks.' She swallowed. 'How do you cope with this part? My insides are churning.'

Gundrul looked out to the plain. 'Ours also, ma'am, but you'll feel different once the battle starts for real. It's like all the nerves build, ready to burst out when you're fighting for your very survival.'

Ruan shrugged. 'Humor can help, ma'am.' Elodi turned away to hide her mirth; she could not imagine Ruan making a joke. He continued. 'You'll hear it among the old hands before combat.'

'Thank you, Captain. I shall bear that in mind.'

'There, ma'am.' Ruan's flat voice gave no indication he had just spied the enemy. He pointed to the plain. A glittering line of torchlight emerged from behind the Dornan foothills flanking the route. The crews on the wall below fell silent as they stopped to watch the approaching threat.

Gundrul broke the silence. 'Uldrak appears to be a complacent commander, ma'am. That might work in our favor. He shuns concealment and the element of surprise. His army are lit up as if going to a Mid-Winter celebration.'

Elodi watched the line. 'Now that's a gathering I would happily decline an invitation to attend.'

Gundrul laughed. 'There you go, ma'am, you're

getting into the spirit.'

Ruan scoffed under his breath. 'Almost.'

In the gatehouse, men surged to the wall. The shout went up. 'Scout!' A horse rode at speed through the main gate and trotted up the cobbled pathway to the inner gate. Elodi heaved a sigh, relieved another scout had returned, but she doubted they carried anything other than bad tidings. An eerie stillness descended upon the city as the hinges creaked and groaned as the heavy gates swung shut. In the years since the building of the Caerwal Gate, the city had welcomed traders, visitors and the odd stranger. But for the first time in living memory, a rumble echoed through the streets as the main gate was closed, and thick beams dropped into their brackets.

Gundrul gestured to the defenders. 'Would you like to address them, ma'am? Just a few words of encouragement for those about to fight in your name.'

Elodi stuttered. 'Oh, I haven't prepared a speech, I wasn't aware I should—'

'Then may I, ma'am?' He glanced to Ruan and laughed. 'I'm pretty confident I can do a better job than this old lug. His morale-raising words may be a little too... shall we say, flowery for your ladyship's ears.'

She grinned. 'I'm sure it wouldn't be anything I haven't heard before.'

Gundrul smirked. 'I wouldn't be so sure, ma'am.' He turned to face the outer wall. 'But we don't have time for a full address as such. Shall I rouse them with a quick speech?'

'Yes, yes, of course.' She held out her hand. 'Please, be my guest, Captain.'

Gundrul stepped up and bellowed. 'Stand firm! Let's show these bastards they can't stroll into the Five Realms at will. Show no mercy. Spare no force. Strike them down so even their ugly mothers won't recognize them.' Elodi watched the upturned faces of the soldiers about to do battle under her command. While a few nodded their approval of Gundrul's words, others looked too scared to move, but she did not, for one moment, doubt their spirit and loyalty. Elodi hoped she could justify their trust.

Gundrul thrust his sword into the night sky. 'For Calerdorn! And for Lady Harlyn!' He turned back as the defenders cheered and yelled her name. Gundrul nodded to himself. 'That should do it, ma'am.'

Elodi smiled. 'That was… quite poetic, Gundrul.'

He saluted. 'Thank you, ma'am.'

Ruan grunted. 'Worthy of a song, Gunny.'

Elodi fidgeted with her sword belt. 'Then let's also hope for a victory that will be sung in the taverns for years to come.'

'Now's our chance, ma'am.' Ruan pointed. 'They're stopping and setting up camp.' More torches burst into flame, shedding a flickering yellow light far across the plain.

Gundrul clicked his tongue. 'Like I said, complacent. He's trying to intimidate us by revealing his full force.'

Elodi gaped as dozens of Ruuk scrambled over the large wagons and threw back the covers. Thick, tall beams of Uldrak's monstrous engines, reared up in the torchlight and assembled with frightening speed. She could not keep still. 'Remind me. What is the range of our trebuchets?'

Gundrul pointed. 'See the dip in the plain, ma'am? That's where the trial rounds landed yesterday.'

She clenched her fist. 'Ah, then Uldrak appears to know exactly where to set up camp. How long before he'll be ready to attack.'

'An hour, possibly two. It depends on the skill of his crews.'

Elodi scanned the walls. 'Is there anything we can do? A pre-emptive strike before they can set up?'

Gundrul eyed the enemy torches. 'If we send out every defender, they would still outnumber us, ma'am. He's placed spears and archers close to the engines, and foot soldiers ready to rush in and finish those they unhorse. I'm afraid all we can do is sit tight behind our walls and wait. As the battle progresses there may be a time to strike out, but for now' — he turned and leaned on the wall — 'I suggest you sit, ma'am and drink plenty of water. It's surprising how quickly you work up a thirst in battle.'

As hard as she found it, Elodi turned her back on the unfolding doom before her walls, and sat on the low ledge. She looked up to Gundrul and Ruan. 'Can you make your last checks on our preparations, please?' They nodded, reading her desire to be alone. Elodi stared at the clouds flecked with the torchlight of her city and the army desiring its fall. She wondered what her father would have done in her situation. Had she made the right decisions? She accepted a drink from a young woman assigned to the wall. Her fingers gripped the cup as her dry throat welcomed the cool water. She tried to recall the moves taught by her sword-master, but her tight muscles made the swiftness and freedom of her limbs from those lessons, appear a distant memory.

Footsteps on the stairs. Elodi stirred to see Gundrul and Ruan return. She stood as Gundrul nodded to the plain. 'They're moving, ma'am. Just under an hour. His crews are skilled.'

'An hour? Already?' Below, her own artillery burst into action. Ropes creaked as they took the strain to bring down the beams of eight trebuchets into place. The revolving bases groaned as they lined up their first shots, predicting the approaching paths of the enemy weapons.

Elodi's heart quickened as Uldrak's force formed into

dark columns behind his machines. She willed the ground to open and swallow them, but the lines rumbled on, eating up the plain as if whetting their appetite to feast on her city. The black, heavy weaponry gleamed in the torchlight. Elodi's dry mouth resisted her attempt to swallow. She counted. 'I can only see six, the scouts reported at least two dozen.'

Gundrul checked. 'Don't raise your hopes yet, ma'am. Uldrak won't bring them all to the battle just yet. He'll want to take ours out of the reckoning before deploying the rest.'

'Then I pray our aim is true and better than theirs.' Bright flames lit up the walls as the fire balls ignited, hurling their heat into Elodi's face. Her heart pounded faster, remembering the sight of the Archon's retaliation at the Caerwal Gate. Suddenly, it felt very real, as if until now, it did not seem possible. Harlyn teetered on the brink of war, and she was about to unleash the first shot.

Gundrul read her mind. 'This isn't your doing, ma'am. You didn't invite these marauders into your realm. We'll give them what they deserve. And don't be under any illusion they'll show mercy should they capture the city.'

Ruan exclaimed. 'They've reached the outer range markers.' He raised his eyebrows.

'Ma'am?' Gundrul nodded to the wall. 'They're awaiting your command to let loose. Do I have permission to give it?'

Elodi's tongue clicked. 'Yes, please do.' Gundrul turned, picked up a torch and waved it over his head. Immediately, the walls shuddered as the counterweights dropped, and the long beams launched eight flaming orbs streaking into the night. Elodi's fingers dug into the wall as perfect arcs of yellow fire tore up the sky. She held her breath as they reached the top of their trajectory, before plunging earthbound towards their intended targets. As one, they exploded, spraying globules of fire in all directions. Elodi flinched as the sudden brightness lit up more rows of Uldrak's army. Seconds later, the boom thundered over their heads. Her chest swelled, proud of her city's show of power vibrating through her bones. Elodi scanned the line of impact for signs of destruction.

'There, ma'am.' Gundrul pointed to the center. 'One burns.'

'One?' She found the spot. Fire engulfed a black skeleton of an enormous machine, wrapping its flames around the wood and snatching at the crew desperately jumping from the condemned engine. Elodi searched for more victims. 'Just the one?'

'One is a magnificent effort, ma'am. Your men only had a week to practice for real.' The surviving engines crept closer like large, terrifying beasts ready to tear its prey to pieces.

Elodi shuddered. 'How long before they can retaliate?'

'We have the advantage of height, ma'am. We should have time for two more volleys before they can reply.'

'Reply? Such a casual expression for such a daunting prospect.' Again, Calerdorn's defenses spat forth its fire, but Elodi counted only seven arcs. She checked the outer wall. Two men clambered up the frame of an inactive trebuchet to her right. She glanced back to the plain, waiting for her sight to recover from the bright salvo.

Gundrul beat her to it. 'One more, ma'am! We're hurting them.'

But Ruan remained unmoved. 'We make a big target. They still have enough in reserve to hurt us back.'

Elodi groaned. 'Plenty more if the scouts guessed the number correct.' She peered over the wall of flame on the plain. 'Where are their reserve engines? If they incapacitate ours and bring them forward...'

'We have other means, ma'am. Uldrak has committed

all his force to the attack, leaving his weapons undefended at the rear. I see no sign of horses, meaning your knights can counter-strike. Aldorman could launch hit-and-run raids. A sharp blade can damage a rope, cut down the crews, or a well-placed torch can easily disable an engine doused in spilled fuel.'

Elodi envisaged her knights outside the safety of the wall. 'They number barely sixty. I hope it doesn't come to that.'

Gundrul yelled over the next volley bursting from the wall. 'But it's a decision you may have to make. They will not make it easy.'

Elodi groaned. The engines had moved faster than her artillery had calculated, causing the shots to land long. 'None, we didn't hit one!' The opening exchanges reminded her of a game she had played as a young girl with skittles and a ball. She had beaten every child in the city, knocking down all of their skittles while her pieces still stood. But back then, only her childish pride had been at stake, and now she thought of it, had they let her win? Being the only offspring of the lord and without a mother, had they taken pity on her?

Ruan leaned over the wall. 'They're setting up positions, ma'am.' Elodi shrank back.

Gundrul bellowed. 'Take them out! Take them out!' Frantic crews readied their machines for one more unanswered volley. But another trebuchet had become inoperable — just six flaming orbs roared into the sky.

'Ma'am!' Elodi turned to the new arrival as the shots exploded; the shocked face of a scout surveyed the scene below as the sky lit up.

'None hit, ma'am.' Ruan announced.

The man accompanying the scout spoke. 'He's just returned, ma'am, through the postern gate on the north wall.'

Her heart sank at the sight of his gaunt face. She dared to ask. 'What is it?'

'Boats, ma'am.' He struggled to catch his breath. 'I saw them, dozens of rowing boats, packed with Ruuk preparing to leave Inverdorn Bay.'

Her mind raced. 'When was this?'

'I spied them late yesterday evening, ma'am. They left at first light this morning. I tracked them along the coast before taking the mountain pass here. Should the currents favor them, they'll be fast approaching our dock.'

Elodi glanced to Gundrul. 'This is a concern. I've never known them to sail.' She turned to the west, longing to see a storm brewing. 'If there were any justice in this world, the sea would dash them to pieces on the rocks.' But she saw no sign. 'Gundrul? Do we have enough archers stationed at the dock?'

'Not nearly enough to defend a full-scale assault, ma'am. And should they land, we don't have the numbers to prevent them gaining a foothold.'

'Can we spare archers from the main gate?'

Her captain thought for a moment. 'Possibly. It could be half an hour before they commit infantry to the attack. Uldrak will be in no hurry, and from what the guards rescued from the wood say, he'll be relishing the encounter, and imagine he'll want to be first through the gate. But he'll wait until he's silenced our heavy weapons, and possibly has a breach in our wall to exploit.'

'Then give the order for every other archer at the gate to go to the docks immediately.' Gundrul summoned his messenger and issued the order. Elodi addressed the young scout as he stared wide-eyed at the enemy. 'Please go and rest. You have done your city and Harlyn a great service.' She turned to Ruan and made the calculations in her head. 'How many of your spearmen could defend the docks?'

With no hesitation he answered. 'Thirty. It's narrow.'

'Is that sufficient? If the Ruuk establish a position on the quayside, we're vulnerable to more landing, not to mention the loss of supplies from Seransea.'

Ruan nodded. 'It's more than enough. My spearmen will soon run them through.'

'Excellent. Move them now. And please lead them for me, Captain. We cannot afford to surrender the dock. I'd be happier knowing you're at the head.' Ruan saluted and left.

Elodi glanced back to the plain as the enemy weapons delivered their first reply. She watched helpless as the fiery spheres grew larger as they hurtled towards her precious city.

Calerdorn shook as the shots slammed home. Elodi recovered her feet and jumped up to survey the damage. Two had fallen short but sent burning fragments over the wall, starting several fires. Another hit the wall to the left of the main gate, but despite dislodging a few stones, the ancient rock held firm. But to Elodi's dismay, the last scored a direct hit on one of her heavy weapons. Splinters of burning wood lay in all directions, having taken down archers and damaging the next trebuchet along the wall.

She spluttered. 'We have only a few left!' The last of her weapons let fly. Elodi feared Uldrak would count their trails with glee, ready to hurl destruction down onto the city unanswered. But just as she despaired, one of the missiles found its target. She punched the air. 'And another! They've only three remaining.' But her joy was short-lived, remembering Uldrak had more weapons in reserve.

Gundrul guessed her question. 'It will take time to bring the others forward, ma'am.' Elodi ducked as the remaining Ruuk weapons launched another assault. She straightened as they exploded harmlessly on the ground in front of the walls. Defenders rushed to extinguish the fires taking hold. She turned, looking for signs of the attack at the docks. But she had no direct line of sight, and it lay hundreds of yards from her position. She took encouragement from the sky above remaining free of smoke and flame.

Another volley flew from her walls, landing amongst Uldrak's forces behind the machines. Gundrul glanced back to the city. 'I'll send a man to the docks, ma'am. We'll be needing the archers back here before long.' He caught her eye. 'You are aware, ma'am, our trebuchets will be useless against the raiders once they're closer to the walls.' He whistled as his finger traced an arc through the air. 'They can only shoot up and over, and not in a direct line. If they shorten their range too much, they could be more of a danger to us.'

'Ah yes, I suppose that would be the case. Then I trust our archers are up to the task and able to take out the ballistae.'

'If they're using fuel to ignite the bolts, a flaming arrow from our walls will do the same.'

Her jaw clenched. 'That's reassuring.'

'But all depends on how long the archers get a free shot. They'll have their hands full once those brutes deploy their ladders. And if they reach the battlements, they'll overwhelm us all too soon if we can't stem the flow.'

Elodi slapped the wall. 'There must be something more we can do.'

'Your knights could yet save the day, and with the support of Ruan's spears, we may still hold the upper hand.'

Below, her weapons launched another attack, including two of the malfunctioning trebuchets brought back into action. Volleys flew back and forth and, as Gundrul predicted, Uldrak brought two more engines up to his front line. Both sides took hits until the macabre game eventually ran out of players.

Calerdorn's walls had performed their duty and held, but now the attack would focus on the entrance. The enemy edged ever nearer, bringing the gate into the range of the ballistae. Uldrak's feared weapons glistened in the fires like sweating beasts cornering their prey. Elodi's thinned-out archers joined the fray, but their flaming arrows failed to strike home, bouncing harmlessly off the surrounding protective shields. Four ballistae came to a halt, forming a bristling arc opposite the main gate. Behind the shields, dark figures bustled, bringing forward wagons carrying what Elodi suspected was their foul concoction to ignite the bolts.

'Ma'am!' She spun around. An out of breath Ruan stood before her. 'The dock is safe. The threat seen off.' He gasped for air and pointed to the wall. She turned to see lines of archers streaming back to their positions. 'Most are fit for duty.'

She grasped his shoulder. 'Excellent, and not a moment too soon. The gate is about to come under—'

'Ladders!' The shout from the parapet stopped her dead. A dozen archers staggered back, tumbling from the ledge, peppered by black darts.

Gundrul stared. 'Crossbows! They have crossbows? Only our elite forces carry such weapons.' But Elodi had no time to take in the implication. The four bolts pointing at the gate burst into flame.

Ruan bellowed to his men behind the gate. 'Stand clear!' A gap opened as the projectiles unleashed and slammed home. The beams bolstering the gate, buckled but held firm. Of the four, one head pierced the old wood, spraying fire into Ruan's spearman and Aldorman's knights. The horses reared up, Elodi's heart broke as they squealed in anguish.

Ruan yelled above the roar. 'It won't hold long,

ma'am. There's mischief in those flames, it don't burn right.'

'Get them back, Ruan. They don't stand a chance against this devilry. Withdraw them behind the inner gate, we'll have to surrender the main entrance and hit them from the gatehouse parapets.' Ruan yelled his command. His men withdrew in formation, still facing the gate to protect the knights as their horses were happy to retreat from the crackling flames.

The chains rang out as the heavy portcullis of the inner gate dropped shut. Back at the walls, the first ladders clattered against the stone. Archers shouldered their bows and rushed to heave the already laden ladders back with some success. But others reached the top and swarmed through the battlements. The reserves of Dorn and Noor ran forward, but were no match against the battle-hardened Ruuk. Elodi's heart went out to her soldiers as they fell back with mounting losses. She cried out. 'We have to save them!'

Gundrul pointed. 'Help is at hand. Captain Roold and his men are moving into position.' Elodi watched as the guards surged across the parapet, dispatching the raiders with deadly precision. Only days ago, she had believed them to be lost beyond help, yet they fought with a ferocity taking even the Ruuk by surprise. She gasped. 'Such speed. Such strength.'

Gundrul's chest expanded with pride. 'A fine body of men if I may say so, ma'am.'

'An impressive sight indeed. If only we had more.' She noted his impatience. 'The time is now. Go to your men, Captain. Hold the outer wall as long as you can, but Gundrul' — she touched his arm — 'please don't fight a losing battle. I'll leave it to your judgment but retreat to the gatehouse as soon as your position is compromised.'

He saluted. 'I will, ma'am. My men won't let you

379

down. They may be young, but they're disciplined and well-trained. They'll fight for the honor of the Archon and your ladyship with pride.' He turned to leave.

'And, Gundrul.' She sought for the right words. If events were to go against them, the thought they would never meet again was hard to bear. But the words did not come, and time pressed on. She patted his shoulder. 'Good luck, Captain. May the Three be with you.'

39. HOPE RISING

'Over there. See?' Toryn directed Hope's gaze to a gap in the bushes. 'Looks like an old farmhouse.' He clutched his arms around his middle and shivered. 'I'd happily fight a droog to sleep under a roof for once. I've forgotten what it's like to wake up in dry clothes.' Toryn welcomed the opportunity to rest. Towards the end of the day's long trek, they had crossed a deserted bridge close to a small inhabited town. Toryn was certain the river had to be the Great Elda, and the town, that of Buckleburn. The river's source sprang from the icy streams of the Kolossos Mountains, before widening on its way across Noor, eventually reaching the sea at the town bearing its name: Eldamouth. As well as being one of the longest rivers in the Five Realms, it also served as the northern border of Darrow, meaning Toryn had arrived back in his home ward.

Hope clapped her hands. 'Then what are you waiting for? Stop staring and get over there. Check it's empty, and if so, light a fire. That rabbit you caught this morning has been teasing with my belly all day.' She pulled at the two fish dangling on her belt and grinned. 'And these will do for breakfast.'

Toryn removed his backpack and strolled through the scrub. He glanced back and watched Hope as she stood scratching her head. Something was undeniably different, and he wondered if it had come to her attention. He cursed as a thorn scratched his cheek, but thankfully he was right about the building.

The large farmhouse stood defiant against the ravages of time. Thick ivy and other climbers clung to the walls and weather-beaten roof as if trying to claim it for the land. Toryn brushed aside the fronds, put his shoulder to the door and shoved hard. The hinges resisted and creaked, perhaps opening for the first time in decades, but open it did. Inside, piles of dead leaves covered debris from the collapsed roof and ceilings, but enough tiles remained in place to offer some shelter. He stepped into the main downstairs room and almost laughed out loud. It looked like a palace compared to where he had slept over the last few weeks. A small fire in the hearth could make the place feel a little like home and bring warmth to his chilled bones.

He turned to call back, only to find Hope standing directly behind him. She nodded. 'This will do. Barricade the door.' Her eyes widened as she examined her hands. 'My fingers are tingling. Must be nasty creatures roaming these parts.' She yawned. 'I need to sleep. Wake me when supper's ready but… take your time.' He wondered what she meant by *nasty* but decided to let her sleep.

Toryn glanced up from the glimmering embers of the hearth to the stone chimney breast. Skilled hands had built the farmhouse hundreds of years ago, possibly before the closing of the Caerwal Gate. For that, he was grateful. The wind had picked up since sundown, but the thick walls kept it at bay. Sadly, none of the glass had survived, so Toryn had blocked the window with an old tabletop. He wondered about the family who had once sat around the table, large enough to seat twelve. What had become of them? Were they forced to move by disease and famine? Or had they fled from the raiding parties sailing up the Elda before the Archon had changed the seas? Hamar had spoken of the Lost Years, but his account of events, and that of his parents differed. The fact remained, no one knew for sure what happened in those dark times, but none questioned the devastation had set back the Five Realms many generations. Toryn looked to the dying fire — would they see such desolation again?

Hope rolled onto her side and hummed part of a song before drifting back to sleep. Toryn stood, walked to the window and peered out into the night through a small gap. In the gloom, he could just make out an old path leading through what he guessed would have once been a garden full of herbs for cooking and healing. He tried to imagine the children of the house picking leaves to flavor their mother's stew, or soothe cuts and bruises, but brambles had long since choked the garden dead.

Toryn gave up trying to picture the scene and returned to Hope's side, placed a log onto the fire, picked up his threadbare blanket and lay on the floor. The flames took, but he could not stop shivering. He curled into a ball, closed his eyes, and let the dark dreams take him.

Toryn woke in the dead of night. The wind had died; the flames all but spent. Shards of pale silver light speared through the ancient wood covering the window. The westerly breeze must have chased the clouds to the mountains, allowing the moon to gaze upon the land. But with the blanket of cloud gone, the temperature had plummeted. Toryn's frosty gasps filled the air. The moonlight traced his breath as it left his body, drifting across the room like the ghosts of Hamar and his fallen colleagues. Toryn had been both enthralled and terrified of the old man's tale of Hallows Night. In the middle of winter, a gateway opened, allowing the departed to return and spend the longest night together with their loved ones. Toryn's frozen face cracked into a smile. Now he had taken the Oath, he knew Hamar would be happy tilling his field on the Plain of Evermore. Could it be true? Would he see Hamar and Elwold again? Lying in the silent, still night, he believed anything was possible. He puffed out another ghost and watched it curl as it hung in the air before fading to find peace on the plains.

The light outside moved. Toryn jerked upright. *Moonlight doesn't move.* The room grew colder, surely too cold for the season. Hope stirred. Outside, a twig snapped. A shiver streaked through Toryn's already frozen body. He scrambled over to Hope and shook her shoulder, but failed to rouse her. The door creaked. He stood and creeped into the hallway. The door stood ajar, but the fallen joists Toryn had set in place, held firm. The ghoulish light moved along the side of the house. He bent and picked up a rotten banister from the floor. But he doubted even a knight's blade from ancient times would trouble the strange being outside. Ice formed on the inside of the wall, marking the progress of the creature as it made its way along the farmhouse.

The tabletop across the window cracked. Toryn tiptoed back into the room where Hope lay and positioned himself close to the frame. A heavy thud! The beast was huge. He pushed his back into the icy wall, desperate not to let his gasps alert the creature to his whereabouts. It stopped. Toryn held his breath. He craned his tight neck until he could see through a split in the wood. He stifled a moan. A hoof on the end of a long, scrawny leg nudged the wall. The stone shuddered as if remembering a terror of old. The creature crouched, bringing a large head towards the same gap Toryn peered out. His jaw clamped shut. The tabletop moved. A white patch of ice formed in the shape of a claw, spreading across the rough surface.

'Step aside.' He twisted back to the room. Hope stood a few paces from the window. She whispered again, gesturing with her hand. 'Get out of the way. This is not your fight.' He drew strength from her confidence and held up the bannister. She pointed to the hall. 'Get in there. You won't stand a chance.' Toryn did not need telling again. He edged back along the wall, sensing a change in the creature outside — it knew.

Hope bowed her head and brought her palms together. Low at first, barely audible, she muttered a few words. A faint, blue sphere appeared between her palms, warming the room, repelling the creature's icy curse. Toryn blinked as the light intensified.

Hope threw open her arms. 'Begone!' The air burst with a brilliant light. The wood shattered, shooting a thousand splinters at the creature. It wailed, threatening to bring the walls down, and forcing Toryn to his knees. He clasped his hands to his ears, fearing his skull would split in two. Then silence — the room turned black.

Hope panted. 'It's gone.' A warm hand took his. 'It won't dare to trouble us again unless it finds more of its foul kind.'

Toryn blinked in the dark. 'What... what was that?' She led him back to the dying fire. 'Just a shroul. Lucky, eh?'

'Lucky?'

'Oh yes, had it been a shreek, we'd be wraiths in its thrall before dawn is come. I can't fight a shreek, oh no, not one of them. Not at my age.' She shuddered. 'Or a droog. I'm in no mood to face those foul, yellow-eyed worms. The very last way I want to die is kicking and screaming in a droog's putrid stomach.'

Toryn shivered. 'I know of droogs. But what are shrouls and shreeks?'

'Creatures from the past. Shrouls are a nuisance, still nasty. Must have sensed our warm bodies. I see them every winter, but unusual in spring, especially in these parts.'

'And shreeks?'

Hope spat. 'Now they're a different matter, dangerous

and not to be taken lightly. Thankfully, not seen one in... must be years.' She peeked out of the window. 'Worse fates than death await us in the night.'

Toryn staggered forward. He gawped at Hope; her face blurred. His head spun and he collapsed.

Hope kneeled at his side, bringing her warm hands to his face. 'Rest now. Sleep.' She placed his head in her lap, humming as she gently rocked him. The coldness in his limbs eased as she lifted her voice to sing. Toryn's eyelids grew heavy as he let sleep take him — for a moment, he heard his mother's voice as she had eased the aches of the Winter Fever wracking his young body.

Toryn woke as the first pink light of dawn streamed through the empty window. Hope lay by his side, sleeping peacefully. He reached over to cover her with the blanket that had slipped from her shoulders. She sat up and blinked at him. 'You're... let me think. You're Toryn.'

'You know my name?'

Her eyes wandered to the window. 'A voice... from the Song told me your name.'

The words burst from his mouth. 'My father?' Toryn took her hands and turned them over. 'He had markings like yours.'

Her eyes searched for the answer in his face. 'Wait. There *was* another such as me. I had to watch over you when...' Her brow creased.

'When what?'

'He left.' She shrugged. 'I know not why, but the voice tells me I must take you.'

'Where? To my father?'

Her eyes closed, she lay down, mumbling. 'The voice tells me...' She drifted off to sleep before Toryn could find out where the voice wished them to go.

The Hope Toryn knew, awoke several hours later. The coming of the shroul had stirred something within her, and for a moment, she appeared to know him, and his father. But that had soon changed. As she woke, she had jabbed a finger in his face and demanded breakfast. When he had asked about the confrontation with the shroul, she shrugged, having no memory of the previous night. But now he knew more of what lay behind her gray eyes, he found her easier to tolerate. And if his father trusted Hope, he knew for certain he could. But where had his father gone? What had been so important that led him to abandon his son? And... how long had Hope watched over him?

Once they had eaten, Hope had been keen to leave and strode with renewed purpose, heading due south. For his part, Toryn felt stronger and found he could match her pace. But deep down, he sensed the coldness planted by Uleva, still held.

Toryn's foot landed on a firm surface. He glanced up, annoyed at himself for stumbling across a road while deep in thought. Voices! Marching feet! He grabbed Hope's arm. 'Quick, hide us.'

'What?' She held out her hands. 'Where? How?'

'Like you did from the Ruuk. Remember, you used some sort of spell. They walked straight...' he glanced back to the road. 'Never mind. No time.' He dragged her behind a tree.

She moaned. 'What the——? You can't do that, you could have——'

'Shush!' Her eyes widened. He remembered her words and placed his hands on her shoulders. 'The voice, the one from the song, tells you to shut... to be quiet.' His words caused her a moment of confusion, but she nodded as the request appeared to register beyond her reasoning. Without protest, she leaned against the broad trunk, slid down to crouch, and mumbled quietly under her breath.

Toryn peered out from behind the tree. Close to forty men and women marched in two lines, armed with a variety of weapons ranging from swords to spears and the odd farming tool. He heaved a sigh. They were not Ruuk, but the reserves of Darrow. He watched their set faces, young and old, including a number who could have served in the Archonian Guard. But they marched north, not south. Apart from the Archon, only the ruler of Harlyn had the authority to muster the reserves. Had the forces from Wyke Wood mounted an attack elsewhere in Dorn? But despite the power Uleva had, surely it was not beyond the skill of the Knights of Calerdorn to contain her. What had prompted Lady Harlyn to summon her reserves from the far reaches of the realm?

Toryn took a step. He should join them. Harlyn obviously needed all who could carry a sword. His shoulders dropped. He had no sword — it had shattered during his first taste of action at Drunsberg. And what difference could he make? He was an Archonian Guard in name only. A guardsman without a sword. A guardsman because of a rash decision made in an emergency by Roold.

Toryn returned to the tree and slumped beside Hope. He listened as the reserves marched off to answer the call of Lady Harlyn. What could he do? He glanced over to Hope. She held her finger to her lips, looking pleased with herself for staying quiet. He tried to smile back but achieved no more than a grimace. But he could not deny Hope had powers, even if she appeared to be unaware of their nature.

Toryn stood. He had another important task, perhaps ultimately more critical to the safety of the realm. The Archon obviously placed great value on the Singing Stones; Hamar had spoken of the threat of death to those revealing their location. But was the Archon aware of the destruction of the stone in the cave? This would be his mission. Toryn clenched his fist. He was the son of a powerful man, yet had wasted his life digging holes and building fences. But no more. He would make his father proud and deliver his message to Archonholm. It was a risk he had to take, regardless of whether the Archon would discover his secret. Whatever Hope wanted to show him would have to wait. This had to be more important.

Toryn waited for the two supply wagons following the reserves to trundle out of sight. He turned to Hope and held out his hand. She stared at his outstretched fingers, then back to his face. He tried to remember her as she had been at the farmhouse, but right now he found it difficult to imagine she could be anything other than a forgetful, old woman. He wriggled his fingers. 'Come on, it's safe.'

She scowled, meeting his gaze. 'I'm comfortable here.'

'You must' — he felt a tinge of guilt as he remembered a game he had played as a child — 'the voice says you must come with me to Archonholm.'

40. LADY HARLYN RIDES OUT

An explosion rocked the city. Elodi flinched and twisted away as night briefly became day. She steadied herself, grasping the wall as another projectile erupted, throwing her against Ruan. Elodi rushed back to the parapet and gaped in horror at the burning buildings between the twin walls. A line of bucket carriers formed, but as the man at its head hurled water at the fire, it flashed white, roared, and to Elodi's despair, the violent flames consumed the man and those close by him. She spun away, unable to watch their flaying arms, but even amid the din of the battle, their cries pierced her heart.

Ruan peered over the wall. 'Same fire as from the bolts, ma'am. There's nothing we can do to quench it.'

Elodi threw up her arms. 'Our heavy weapons are spent. Uldrak brings more forward. We cannot sustain too much—' The second volley of bolts crashed into the main gate, hurtling burning wood and glowing metal across the cobbles. Elodi cried out, feeling the blow as if a battering ram had slammed into her chest. The city lay open. Only the portcullis stood between her people and Uldrak's army.

Elodi stared, open-mouthed, frozen for a moment. She had failed. She had let down her people, leaving them vulnerable to the hate-filled Ruuk bent on revenge. Elodi gazed to the east, longing to see signs of the dawn. *Rise up! Send these demons back to the darkness.* The Archon's plea she had witnessed in his dazed state, hammered home. He had not been calling for reserves; in his madness he had begged the sun to rise. Now she understood. But he had faced a far greater foe and did not have thick stone walls to shield him. How had he endured for so long? Yet endure she must — it would be another hour before dawn, and a rising sun would not save her city.

But as quickly as her dread had risen, part of her yelled back. *I'm not finished yet!* She straightened and closed her visor. Archers raced to the gatehouse parapets, forming lines ready to greet their uninvited visitors. Elodi yelled to Ruan. 'To the gate!' They ran down the stairs, taking them two at a time, stumbling as another salvo erupted over the inner wall. She skidded to a halt and turned to take the last flight. At the gate, Ruan's spearmen formed a semi-circle, five deep with their spears lowered. 'Join your men, Ruan!'

'And you, ma'am?'

'I have to destroy those weapons. We cannot hold out if he brings more into range.' She whistled for Sea Mist. 'I'm going out with my knights, it's our only hope, I don't know any—'

'Ma'am!' For the first time since she had met him, Ruan looked shocked. 'You won't last one minute. They'll be pouring through the gate. You'll never get out.'

She yelled above the commotion. 'There's more than one way out onto the plain.' She referred to the postern gate to the south. 'We can ride out and strike in the dark. They won't see us until it's too late.'

Sea Mist galloped across the cobbles with his head held high. She whispered. 'I'm sorry, Misty, but I need you to be brave for me.'

Ruan stooped with his fingers locked and hoisted Elodi onto the saddle. He reached up and grasped her forearm. 'Ride true. Strike fast, ma'am.'

Elodi returned the guard's grip. 'May the Three be with you, Ruan. Hold the gate as long as you can. This isn't over yet.' She squeezed her knees and Sea Mist trotted to meet Aldorman, who had guessed her intention. She greeted him. 'I ask a great deal from you and your knights,

Captain. But the very survival of Calerdorn is at stake.'

Aldorman sat tall on his horse. 'All have made their vow to you, ma'am. All are ready to honor that promise. And' — he leaned forward — 'I wish to make amends for my failure at Durran Wood.'

'Nonsense, Captain. You have nothing to make—'

'You can't be serious, ma'am!' She turned as Wendel hobbled across the yard. He steadied himself with a hand on her saddle as he caught his breath. 'You're surely not contemplating going outside, ma'am?'

'That I am, Wendel.'

'But this is madness. Please, ma'am, I beg you, for the sake of the realm.'

'This is for the sake of the realm! If the city falls, so does Harlyn.' She adjusted the bridle. 'I am superfluous here. Ruan and Gundrul are in command at the vital points of the city, I shall take command on the plain. Father taught me to lead from the front, and I intend to do just that.'

Wendel held up his hand. 'Please, ma'am, there's something you must—'

Elodi gathered the reins. 'It will have to wait. Now please step aside, Wendel. We shall speak later.'

He stood back and patted the horse's neck. 'I dearly hope we do, ma'am.'

She nudged Sea Mist and set off across the yard to the street leading to the concealed South Gate. He hesitated as another explosion shook the city. 'Steady, boy, steady.' Aldorman drew level as another missile struck the inner wall. Elodi yelled. 'They're moving closer.' She spurred Sea Mist on. 'Not a moment to lose, Captain. To the gate!'

The sky glowed a deep orange, lighting the faces of her people who stopped and stared as the knights rode by. Elodi met their wide eyes, desperate to reassure them the city was not yet lost. But this would be the first time she had ridden into open battle. The foe outside had fought many, often among themselves, and would cherish the opportunity to humiliate a leader of a realm. Her jaw clenched. But Uldrak had made the mistake of underestimating her resolve. And for that, she would make him pay.

Elodi and her knights reached the narrow postern gate, surprising the guards who maintained their watch. She ducked and guided Sea Mist through the tight bend and out of the city. Outside, the narrow stretch of land between the mountains and Calerdorn was strangely quiet, shielded from the fiery glow and noise of the battle by the southern stretch of the wall.

Elodi turned and faced the knights streaming out of the gate. She looked along the line, making eye contact with every one of them. She rose in her saddle. 'Knights of Calerdorn, we don't have long, our time is short. You know the long history of your order, founded by Dorlan' — her heart skipped a beat — 'no less. In dire times, our knights have shown great bravery and ridden to defend the realm. I don't have to tell you this is such a time.' She turned to the east. 'Stealth and speed are the key. We'll split into four corps and seek out their heavy weapons. Destroy them and move on. Trebuchets first, then, if we have the resources, the ballistae next. Keep moving, keep burning, don't let yourself become trapped.' She steered Sea Mist to face the plains, drew her sword and held it high. 'For the Five Realms! For Calerdorn!' Elodi kicked on and cried. 'And for Dorlan!'

Heat coursed through her veins as Elodi led her knights to battle. She had spent the night watching events helplessly from the wall, but now she could make a difference. This was her moment. She rounded the curve of the wall to be slammed in the face by the heat and cacophony of the conflict. But she held her nerve, driving

Sea Mist onwards to meet the challenge. Instantly, she picked out the artillery raining death onto her people. To her left, the bulk of Uldrak's forces swarmed at the base of the outer wall, scrambling up the many ladders scaling the defenses. More thronged at the breached gate. Of Uldrak, she could see no sign, assuming he remained focused on breaking through the inner wall's defenses.

Undeterred by the greater numbers, she spurred Sea Mist on with her sword drawn, hurtling towards the unsuspecting crews of the war machines. She would make them regret the day they came to Calerdorn. How dare they bring death and destruction to her people. They would soon feel the cold steel of her blade twist in their guts.

Elodi yelled against the din as she rapidly closed the gap on her target. She fixed her eyes on the tall, gangly structures hurling their fire at her city. She counted four, including another, possibly brought forward from Uldrak's reserves. The monsters had crept closer, so every volley now crashed over the inner wall. Her eyes lit up. With Uldrak's infantry now committed to the ladders, they had left their machines unprotected.

Her knights divided into four. Elodi waved her sword, directing each corps to its destination, choosing the furthest machine for her cohort. Cries from the closest trebuchet signaled the first strike. She glanced back to see a knight ride down a Ruuk carrying the torch ready to light the projectile; instead, he fell, setting the platform ablaze.

Elodi urged Sea Mist on. The crew of her objective spotted the attack, but had little to defend against the onslaught of her horses. The heavy jackets protecting them from the heat, afforded the Ruuk limited movement. They leaped from the platform, drawing their swords to little avail. Sea Mist charged down the first, swerved past a second, then onto the wagon stationed behind the weapon.

Elodi dipped, scooped up a torch, turned and launched it onto the wooden base. The crew had been careless, soaking the deck with spilled fuel. Instantly, it flared, sending a blast of defiant heat back at her. She ducked and watched the flames eagerly take hold. Behind, her knights mowed down those left standing, then circled about to finish the job in hand.

Elodi drew Sea Mist to a halt and quickly surveyed the scene. To the rear, Uldrak's reserve machines sat in wait, but without the squads to operate them, they posed no immediate threat. Back at the walls, the ballistae were on the move. Elodi made her decision. She stood in her stirrups and circled her sword above her head. 'To the main gate!'

The four cohorts wheeled, formed a line, and drove at the rear of their foe. As she drew near, Elodi spied a company of crossbowmen rapidly forming a wedge to face them. She dipped, placing her head close to Sea Mist's neck. 'Stay with me, boy. Stay with me.' A hail of darts brought down three knights at her side, but she rode on, determined to charge them down before they could reload. Sea Mist tore up the ground, covering the distance in no time. Elodi braced herself for the impact as her knights smashed into the lightly armored formation. Sea Mist stumbled but held his course through the line, taking out half a dozen Ruuk. She twisted and turned, raining blows onto the heads of those grabbing at her legs, attempting to drag her from her saddle. Elodi fought off the last assailant with a kick to his throat, before Aldorman drew level and finished him with a swift blow.

She gasped for air. 'The ballistae! We have to reach them before they get into the city.'

Aldorman nodded. 'Leave them to us, ma'am. You should head back.'

'I shall do no such thing. The job's not done.' Elodi

rose. 'To the gate!' She patted Sea Mist's glistening neck and yelled in his ear. 'Ride! Ride for Calerdorn!' He kicked on, surging ahead as if he alone would save the day. Elodi's eyes widened, taking in every Ruuk, every formation, and every probable outcome in a second. She had never felt more alive, more energized, and more driven to serve her realm.

'Spears!' She called back. A wall of spearmen, three-deep, rushed to block their dash for the gate. In the growing light, Elodi could see fear in their eyes beneath their crude, metal skull caps. And fear her they should! She lowered her sword as they leveled their spears, keen to impale the bellies of her horses. Without a word from Elodi, Sea Mist accelerated and leaped as if hurdling a hedge in a field. A handful of her knights made the jump, but others in the front rank met their end on the spear tips. Sea Mist landed heavily on the other side, but Elodi clung on, steering him around to slam into their rear. With renewed vigor, she and her knights slew and scattered the last of the spearmen.

Elodi glanced about her. Less than forty knights remained saddled with most carrying an injury, or missing part of their armor — but it had to be enough. She yelled, despite her hoarse throat. 'One more push! Clear the gatehouse.' Elodi drove on. Ahead, the rear ranks spun about on hearing the thunder of their hooves. But they were no match for Calerdorn's finest, and many fled, chancing their luck on the ladders. The way soon opened. To Elodi's relief, the ballistae had pulled back, unwilling to risk damage from the hail of arrows from the gatehouse battlements.

Elodi reached the gate and slowed Sea Mist. Many lay dead in the narrow pathway between the main and inner gates, but in the midst, a dark shell of shields, riddled with hundreds of arrows, edged forward like a giant beetle.

Elodi knew Uldrak had to be inside.

Lady Harlyn rode into the city with her sword held aloft. The keen blade glinted in the orange light of the rising sun at her back — this had to be a good omen. The archers on the wall cheered, focusing all their shots on the shields, but to little avail. Her knights formed up behind. She had Uldrak trapped. If her defenders could hold the gatehouse, she could cut off the head of this evil army and send them leaderless back over the border.

Elodi bellowed. 'Now, Misty. Now!' Sea Mist dashed forward, leading the remaining knights directly at the shields. The well-trained horses knew what to do. They quickly closed the gap, reared up and pounded their hooves down onto the shell, exposing the innards of the beast. The archers spied the breach and unleashed a volley of a hundred arrows to pierce the wound. Many inside fell. The shell cracked and split wide open.

Uldrak stood isolated; trapped between the inner gate and the Knights of Calerdorn.

Elodi poised to strike. Sea Mist froze. The air chilled, sending a shiver through all in the gatehouse. A dark figure rose from the strewn bodies. He raised his hooded head; a thin, gray sliver of a mouth twisted into a grin. He thrust out his arms. Sea Mist backed away as the air shimmered and closed over Uldrak, forming a shield. The stunned archers rallied, releasing another volley. But the arrows burst into flame, disintegrating as they struck. Uldrak took a step towards Elodi, waving his arms in a swirling pattern, twisting and distorting the air.

Night returned to Calerdorn. Elodi staggered back. The fighting ceased as friend and foe, gawped up at a churning, black cloud descending over the gatehouse. Elodi could only stand and stare as Uldrak raised his hand and circled his gray fingers as if plucking an apple from a tree. His fell voice echoed across the city, bringing despair to all who heard, as he proclaimed their inevitable doom. Sea Mist stumbled, determined to hold his ground. But Elodi had no words of comfort. Uldrak's voice penetrated her armor, her head and her heart. She shrank back in her saddle, suddenly afraid and ashamed as she sought protection from Sea Mist's neck.

Uldrak reveled in her humiliation, smiling as he pointed to the cloud. Her eyes obeyed. At its center, it bulged, oozing its dark contents like blood seeping through the dressing of a fetid wound. A funnel formed, spinning faster, descending as it sought the ground. The air howled; the horses screamed and reared up. Sea Mist bolted, throwing Elodi from her saddle. She crashed onto the pathway as the funnel struck. Cobbles flew in all directions, taking down many on the parapets.

Silence.

The funnel vanished. Elodi gasped for air as she staggered to her feet. A few paces ahead, gray smoke rose from the damaged cobbles. It billowed to three times her height, folding in on itself to take the shape of a gangly beast. Two moist, black eyes formed and glared straight at her as it unfurled its ragged wings. Dazed, she pitched forward, clutching her stomach, unable to take her eyes from the horror.

A shreek!

An abomination from the old world, a creature from the nightmares of her childhood, slowly stretched out its scrawny limbs, straightened its spine, and loomed over her. It lowered its head. Elodi's insides turned to water. Her legs buckled as its dark, roiling eyes revealed the full horror of its soul, threatening to trap hers for an eternity.

But Elodi was not ready to accept defeat. Deep within, a fire grew in her belly. She was the leader of this realm; this was *her* domain. No foul beast would take it from her without a fight. Elodi forced her legs to straighten, pushing back against the great weight bearing down on her shoulders. She took a step and met the glare of the creature, determined not to let its hatred crush her spirit. She raised her sword and leveled the tip at the shreek's chest. The heat within grew. Her blade glowed brighter in the sun's early light.

Elodi cried out. 'Begone, foul beast! Leave my city!' Its large head tilted, then pulled back. She lunged, thrusting her sword at the creature's gut. The shreek retreated, its body rippled. She gasped. *An illusion.*

Elodi drove forward, swinging her sword to slice through the apparition. The air erupted, hurling her against the wall, forcing the air from her lungs. Thankful for her armor, she slumped against the stone, blinded by the light, and left gasping for breath. Elodi blinked hard and regained her sight. The shreek had gone. Her head throbbed and her vision faded, but not before she saw four Ruuk scuttling out of the gate carrying their defeated leader.

Elodi let out a long sigh. Her city was safe... for the time being. She lay back her head and surrendered to the fatigue.

41. A Victory Stolen

'If this is what victory feels like, I would hate to suffer a defeat.' Elodi stared aghast at the plain scattered with the fallen.

Wendel limped to join her, trying to avoid treading on the dead. 'A victory all the same. How is your hand, ma'am?'

Elodi wriggled her fingers. 'The pain is easing. And what of your ankle?'

He winced. 'Such a foolish thing to do. Didn't see the stairs.'

She grimaced as the acrid taste of the battle clung stubbornly to the air. Elodi stepped over the charred body of a trebuchet crewman. 'Is it wrong, Wendel, that I... I enjoyed killing these poor devils?'

Wendel took her hand. 'No, ma'am. It's not wrong. Many change in the heat of battle. You did what you had to do.'

She released his hand and spun away. 'But I'd never felt more alive. For a moment, I didn't want it to end. That isn't who I am, Wendel.' She turned back. 'Or is it?'

'I've not experienced combat, ma'am, but your father spoke of it. If you'd ridden out to face the foe as your usual caring self, you wouldn't have lasted five minutes. I don't think for one moment you'd *enjoy* killing, away from the field of battle. But mortal combat is another matter entirely.'

Elodi stared with regret at the prone bodies of the horses killed by Uldrak's spearmen. 'But last night, we fought as wild animals.'

'Yet this morning you're feeling guilty. Believe me,

ma'am, had we lost the city, these fellows would be *enjoying* putting your unfortunate people to the sword. And it would not be a swift death.'

'I appreciate your efforts, Wendel. But I for one fear I may have to become a wild animal again before too long.' She tore her eyes from the horses. 'And what of the casualties?'

Wendel frowned. 'Not good, I'm afraid, but let's face it, the city came to the brink of falling last night, it's a wonder any survived that onslaught.' He glanced over his shoulder. 'But on the bright side, we gained those bolt-throwers. They could prove useful if the enemy return.'

'We're finished if they return anytime soon.' She tried unsuccessfully to hold back the tears. 'Twenty-four, Wendel. Just twenty-four knights returned.'

He rested his hand on her shoulder. 'But you, Aldorman and his knights saved not only the city, but secured the realm, ma'am.'

'For now, at least.' She turned to face the wreck of the main gate. 'How is Aldorman?'

'He's strong, he'll pull through. But Ruan may take longer.'

Elodi had regained consciousness to find the gatehouse beset by bodies, so badly burned, she could not tell friend from foe. She had stumbled into the city to find Ruan seriously injured by fragments of the inner gate, destroyed by Uldrak's last desperate act.

Elodi turned back to Calerdorn. Smoke still billowed high into the gray morning. Wendel saw her grief. 'We can rebuild, ma'am.'

'And make improvements, and fast. We cannot let this happen again.'

Wendel surveyed the blackened walls. 'The city has stood for a thousand years and I'm sure it will stand for a thousand more. And all thanks to you, ma'am.'

'Not just me, every man and woman played their part, many paying with their lives.'

'All except me.' He patted his leg. 'I could have ruined it all. If I'd had my way, I would have stopped you riding out and winning the battle.' Wendel groaned. 'I'm getting long in the tooth, ma'am, too old for this game. I feel it is time for me to make way for a younger mind.'

'Nonsense, Wendel, don't be hard on yourself. If it were not for your counsel over the years, Calerdorn would not have been in any state to defend itself.'

His eyebrows raised. 'Kind of you to say, ma'am.'

'Your greatest weapon is your mind, honed by many years of experience. That is why I need you by my side.' She turned. 'Ah yes. Before I rode out last night, there was something you wanted to tell me. Can you recall?'

'I…' Wendel blushed. 'I was about to say' — he scanned the clouds as if seeking the right words — 'I trusted your leadership, ma'am. And how lucky Harlyn is to have you at the helm at such a time.'

Elodi felt her cheeks flush. 'Oh, I see. From your expression I thought it was important.' She took his arm. 'I'm so sorry, that came out all wrong. What I meant—'

'Morning!' They turned to see Gundrul's broken, white teeth grinning from his soot-caked face. He strode to greet them. 'And if I may say so, ma'am, your heroics at the gate will be the stuff of song and legend before the day is out.' She extended her hand. Gundrul took her forearm in the manner of a guard greeting a colleague. He squeezed. 'No man I know could stare a shreek in the eyes, let alone take it down.'

Elodi looked away. 'It was merely an apparition, Captain.'

'All the same, ma'am, must have been real enough to scare the wits out of the men and horses.'

She noticed blood seeping through his shirt at the

shoulder. 'You're wounded.'

Gundrul shrugged. 'I've had worse. I'll have it checked later.'

'Let's hope Ruan recovers. I'm informed it's serious.'

He laughed. 'It will take more than a six-foot plank in the gut to stop that old dog. He'll pull through.'

Elodi turned back to the scene of devastation. 'Fortune favored us. The enemy had the numbers and equipment to make matters far worse had they been patient.'

'As I said before the battle, Uldrak is a complacent commander, ma'am. He committed his men too early to the wall, and didn't use all his resources.' Gundrul smirked. 'Ha! Too keen to take the prize for himself.'

'Hmmm.'

She turned. 'What troubles you, Wendel?'

He stared out to the road. 'How many war machines did our scouts count?'

'I believe dozens, certainly close to thirty.'

Wendel frowned. 'We know Ruan's men accounted for the destruction of four at the pass.' He turned back to the city. 'I can see four ballistae and the burned carcasses of eight trebuchets.'

Elodi scanned the smoking skeletons of the weapons her knights had destroyed. 'Then where are the rest? There should be at least ten more.' She turned to Gundrul. 'Wendel tells me you witnessed the enemy flee.'

'That I did, ma'am. And they didn't stop to recover the engines left on the plain, or heavy wagons for that matter.'

She strode towards the line of the smoking remains. 'Did he bring them this far?' She turned. 'Wendel, have our scouts check the tracks immediately.'

'Already on the task, ma'am. We should see them return within the hour.' He peered up to the sky. 'There's

403

rain in those clouds. I suggest we make our way to the hall. The Council will be eager for updates on what immediate action we must take.'

Elodi let out a long sigh. Gundrul smiled. 'And you thought the battle was the hard part, ma'am.'

Reports from around the city did little to ease Elodi's pain. She ached to her bones and wanted nothing more than to retire to her quarters and sleep for a week. But parts of the city still burned, bodies needed to be removed and buried, and hundreds more injured required urgent attention. Elodi grieved to hear many had lost their lives when Uldrak's apparition had erupted, right at the moment the battle was won. The Ruuk had eventually overrun Gundrul's young guards on the outer wall, but the Archonians had reformed and successfully defended the inner parapet. Once Uldrak had collapsed, exhausted by his summoning, they had quickly routed his demoralized force. But to Elodi's regret, they had failed to snatch Uldrak from those carrying him from the city.

Elodi slumped back in her seat as the last of the council members filed out. She turned to Gundrul. 'Where is Wendel? I thought I'd asked him to stay.'

He grinned. 'Allow him some slack, ma'am. He needed to take a… short break. Four hours is a long time for a man of his age to go without, well, you know.'

'I see. Well I trust he can stay the course for the coming months.' The door opened. Wendel hobbled in.

He blustered. 'Ma'am. A message from the scouts.'

Elodi's heart sank. 'Your face says it all. Will I live long enough to see the day when you bring good news?'

Wendel arrived at the table and regained his breath. 'Alas, ma'am, it is not to be this day.' He grimaced as he sat. 'It transpires half the force crossing the border did not commit to the attack.'

Elodi's hand went to her mouth. 'Half? Where are the rest?'

'Heading east, ma'am. And...'

Elodi slumped. 'And? And what?'

'News from Captain Cubric at Drunsberg. It's dated three days ago. He reports sighting large wagons entering Drunsberg' — he took a deep breath — 'from the south.'

Elodi sprang up. 'From the south! How is that possible?'

'He believes the wagons were too large to enter via the Drunshead Gate. They must have traveled through central Dorn, then onto the Northwest Road.'

Elodi ran her hands down her face. 'And all the while we were occupied with our so-called siege.' She strode to the window and looked out across the smoldering town. 'Was all this a ruse, Wendel? We focus all our strength here and allow them to march straight through the middle of our realm.' She leaned on the stone and rested her head in her hands. 'Twice! Twice when I thought I had a victory, they pull the rug from under my feet.' Her jaw clenched. 'All of those deaths, and for what? Such a hollow victory, and one dearly bought.' She sat on the wide sill. 'But if the attack intended to deceive, I don't understand why Uldrak didn't sit back and keep us holed up behind our walls.'

Gundrul walked to the window. 'I'd also add arrogance to Uldrak's growing list of shortcomings, ma'am. I don't doubt he was under orders to keep us occupied, but I suspect he had the desire to take the city for himself. He brought ladders which leads me to think he had every intention to seize Calerdorn.' He grunted. 'I expect this Uleva creature will be angry with him for wasting so many for no gain.' He patted her shoulder. 'So that makes it a victory by my reckoning, ma'am.'

Elodi sighed. 'Thank you, Captain.' She turned to Wendel. 'Does Cubric elaborate on the content of these wagons?'

'He does, ma'am.' Wendel held her gaze.

'And?'

'Shortly after their arrival, he states the ground beneath their feet shook.' Wendel limped over to the window. 'Captain Cubric is situated half a league from the mines. The rumblings can only mean activity in the deep seams.' He groaned and rubbed his shoulders. 'It appears the attack on Drunsberg was not just to deny us the ore. They obviously have grander plans and intend to execute them using our resources.'

Elodi slapped the wall. 'We cannot let that happen! They're already better equipped than us. If they gain access to the ore and, we can assume they have the smithies and expertise to build, that puts us in a very precarious position.' A cry went up outside as a smoldering roof collapsed. 'Can you smell the smoke, Wendel? Captain?'

'Ma'am?'

'I can't, not anymore. It's been only two days and already I'm accustomed to the stench of death and ruin. And from what we've learned, this is only the prelude.' She turned her back on the town and leaned against the cold stone. 'I trust there's no news of Lord Broon's fleet sailing yet?'

'Not as yet, ma'am. According to his last dispatch, it may be another week.'

Elodi pursed her lips. 'And, I assume, we've heard nothing more from him?'

'We cannot be sure if he's attempted to send another message, ma'am. If the Ruuk hold positions south of here, their hawks could have brought down Lord Broon's birds, and also those from Archonholm.'

'We have to know what's happening, Wendel. If the Archon opens the Caerwal Gate, where does that leave us? If he's successful, he can spare us reinforcements, but should he fail' — the blood drained from her face — 'how long before we have a war on all fronts? The current foe we face is bringing us to our knees, but what seeks to break through the gate? The primary threat has always been from the south. What force will they bring to the field of battle?'

Elodi watched the people bustling below, sorting and removing rubble. Were they merely clearing the way for more dead to line the streets? She faced the room. 'Captain Gundrul, please go to the main gate and enquire on the progress of the repairs. Then go to the infirmary and check on Ruan and Aldorman, and whether they need more supplies.' Gundrul saluted and left.

Elodi walked to the table. She waited for the door to close behind Gundrul, but still lowered her voice. 'I haven't mentioned this to anyone, Wendel, and I would appreciate... insist you keep this to yourself.'

'Ma'am?'

'Lord Broon and I witnessed' — she drew up — 'witnessed an unsettling incident while in Archonholm.' Wendel raised an eyebrow. 'We saw what I can only describe as the Archon suffering a... for want of a better word, breakdown.'

Wendel frowned. 'Is he unwell?'

She sat at his side. 'We saw, what I would call a waking nightmare, reliving the last moments on the Gormadon Plain. Then, he tried to throw himself off the balcony of his tower.' Wendel gasped. Elodi continued before he could speak. 'Thankfully, Bardon reached him first, and I helped to pull him back.'

'But this is... what would have happened if you'd...?' He turned away. 'Is he recovered?'

'The Archon insisted we need not be concerned, but I'm not so sure. A Palace Guard informed us he spends most nights in a state of turmoil, as if fighting demons within.'

Wendel closed his eyes and sighed. 'He is under a great deal of strain with the responsibilities of the position, ma'am.'

'That was Bardon's opinion, and one, I can only now appreciate. But if our forces take Elmarand in the south, and' — a shiver ran up her spine — 'the Archon chooses to open the gate. What if he is too weak to face the Golesh?' She clutched Wendel's arm. 'What if he devised the whole plan while in a state of confusion?'

Wendel sat in silence for a moment. 'I trust his advisors and generals would have scrutinized the details.'

'And how many people in Archonholm have the backbone to question his strategy? From what I've seen, even the vice-Archon is reluctant to confront him.'

Wendel brushed at a mark on his robe. 'You may have a point there, ma'am.'

'And we have yet to receive a reply from my last dispatch. We don't know if the Archon is aware of our plight.'

He groaned as he straightened. 'I shall dispatch another bird, ma'am. Only this time I'll send it on the *Celestra* to be released from Seransea, she's due out this evening. Hopefully, our feathered messenger will avoid the enemy hawks. I shall take the precaution of requesting dispatches are sent to the old port, ma'am.'

'Thank you, Wendel. Ah! Those poor reserves. What are they to think of me? I bring them all the way to Calerdorn, only to send them back. But I cannot abide to think of vast swathes of the realm left so perilously under-defended.'

Wendel smiled. 'I don't think you need have any concerns about what your people think of you after your exploits last night, ma'am. Already they're saying you single-handedly defeated half the Ruuk, sent the shreek scurrying back to the underworld, and then chased their commander out of Calerdorn.'

Elodi sighed. 'Are all our beloved legends such a poor representation of the truth?'

He nodded. 'I should imagine, but there's value in the legends, ma'am. People take heart from such stories.'

'We shall need more than stories to survive these dark times. I feel every decision I've made has done little to secure our survival. Have I put the future of our realm at risk, Wendel? Is our thousand-year history about to come to an end under my watch?'

'Nonsense, ma'am. You've done everything you can. You did the right thing by concentrating our forces here. Had you tried to spread them across the realm, the enemy would have picked us off one-by-one. Who knows, perhaps they did plan to take the city. They came with the numbers and weapons to do so. I think you can take the praise for holding Calerdorn. Imagine our position should we have lost the city and the port?'

'I know, but it doesn't prevent the nagging doubts. What if I'd done this, or what if I'd done that, would we be in a better state? Is our current predicament an improvement on last week? They may yet still pick us off one-by-one.'

'You must stay strong, ma'am. I know you've only had the title for a short while, but the people love and trust you. Your intervention at the gatehouse has elevated your status, and not only with us. I'm pretty sure the Ruuk will be more wary of you now, ma'am. But this is just the beginning. Show them why you continue to deserve it.'

'I must, indeed.' She clenched her fists. 'Now I have to decide whether to commit our depleted and tired forces to re-taking the fort at Draegnor, or to head east and extract the enemy from *our* mines.'

'That will not be an easy decision to make, ma'am.'

42. THE POWER IN THE STONES

'A Singing Stone?' Toryn stared at Hope.

She removed a bone from her teeth. 'A what stone? No, these stones go by another name, but that's where I have to take you.'

Toryn held the fish to the flame as Hamar had taught him. 'If it's as you say, a tall, straight rock, warm to the touch, that's what Hamar showed me.' He ached to lay his icy hands on another. And perhaps it could bring Hope back as the woman he had witnessed three nights ago at the farmhouse.

Hope held up a bone between her fingers. 'Would you look at this? Something this small stuck in the wrong place can kill you. Ha! Even this great leader you speak of, could be brought down by this most insignificant of things.' The fire hissed as she flicked it into the flames. Hope turned as if she had just heard Toryn's words. 'You say you've seen one?'

Toryn checked the sinking sun and pointed over his shoulder. 'Down that way I think, east, I reckon two or three days from here.'

Her lips pursed. 'Oh no, not you and this old man of yours.' She took another bite and spoke with a mouth full of fish. 'The likes of you couldn't get anywhere near one.'

Toryn's jaw clenched. 'And we saw another destroyed.'

Hope choked and spat out her supper. 'Destroyed! Not possible.' She poked the fish spine at his face. 'You must speak of another stone.' She scoffed. 'Nothing can *destroy* an Echo Stone.'

'Echo Stone? You said you didn't know the name.'

'Did I call it that?'

Toryn sighed. 'Yes, just now.'

'Echo Stone.' Hope repeated it slowly several times. 'That does sound familiar.'

'Do you know what they are?'

She glared at him over her fish. 'If I can barely remember what they're called, how do you suppose I know what they are?'

'Yet, for some reason, you have to show me one.'

'Precisely.' She wiped her hands down her sleeves. 'Clean this up and we'll be on our way.'

'But the voice, remember? The voice says we have to go to Archonholm.'

She shook her head. 'Oh no, you're not fooling me with that trick again. No, we go later. The voice insists I take you to the stone.'

Toryn gave up. 'Which way?' It wouldn't hurt to delay by a day or two. And besides, he wondered if he would reach Archonholm if the illness chilling his core, persisted.

Hope shrugged. 'It's not far.' She waved a hand over Toryn's head. 'Down there... I think.'

As the light faded, a solitary star twinkling in the gap between the clouds, caught Toryn's eye. He wondered if it had a name. It deserved a grand name, an ancient name, one worthy of its tenacity to deliver its faint light to their dark land. Were others he knew looking up to the star at this moment? But as he tried to remember their names, a thick cloud smothered the starlight.

Earlier, they had passed close to a village, close enough to hear voices from an inn. But the raised voices did not sing. Harsh words drifted across the still air, but whether in debate or in fear, Toryn could not tell. He longed to leave the damp fields, to stroll into the tavern, and warm his numb fingers and toes by the fire. But Hope had kept on, appearing to care not for the comfort of a soft bed under a roof, or the company of others.

Toryn glanced up. If only the clouds would clear, he might recognize the animals and ancient gods in the stars and know for certain how far they had come. But he rambled on, accustomed to wet feet and soggy clothes clinging to his tired body. But Hope had grown stronger. Her bent spine had straightened more, making her ragged clothes look too small. Her stride had lengthened and quickened to the point, Toryn felt the slower and older of the unlikely pair.

Hope spoke of times past, but not as if telling a story, more as if reminding herself. If Toryn asked a question, she would silence him with a dismissive wave of her hand and retreat into her own thoughts. He learned to stay quiet and listen, hoping to hear something he could understand. But little made sense. She murmured names that may have been people, cities, rivers, mountains or places beyond the sea, or perhaps existed only in her head. At times, she would stop, raise her hands to the sky and sing a verse or two in an unfathomable language. One caused the ground beneath Toryn's feet to tremble; another cooled the air until his breath became visible; and one particular song raised the hairs on the back of his neck, making him homesick for a place he had yet to visit.

'Ah!' Hope stopped. 'We're close.' She peered at a wood a short distance ahead. 'Yes, in there.' He stared into the evening murk, relieved to see the familiar outlines of elms and oaks, and not the tall, harsh spikes of the dreaded Wyke Wood. Toryn shivered and followed Hope, looking forward to the welcome touch of a Singing or Echo Stone. He pulled up. What if the evil that had destroyed the stone in the cave, had discovered the one Hope believed lay within the wood? But she kept on undeterred towards the trees. Toryn followed. Both he and Hamar had sensed the ill as they had approached the damaged stone in the cave. But this time he felt good, better in fact than he had for many days. The stone had to be near.

Hope stopped at the tree line. Toryn tried to see what awaited them inside, but could see nothing in the darkness beneath the heavy boughs. Without asking, Hope took his hands as she had when evading their pursuers. She closed her eyes and spoke in a low voice. Toryn recognized a pattern of repeating words as if she called upon another. He closed his eyes, welcoming the heat emanating from her hands. Hope's words lulled him from the chill night. The cold released its grip on his limbs as he drew sweet, warm air deep into his lungs.

Faint at first, a single female voice answered. Toryn's scalp prickled. Deep down, he instinctively knew it came from a far-off place, and from a different time. Tears filled his eyes as his spirits soared, but for what reason he knew not. Another, then another voice joined the first, harmonizing, weaving their song around each other. Hope replied. She spoke, but it sounded to Toryn as if another sang with her.

'Keep your eyes closed, Toryn.' She released one hand and placed the other on his shoulder as she led him forward. He took three steps, feeling as if he walked through a warm waterfall, washing him clean of the world he left behind. 'Now you can open them.' Toryn obliged and gasped.

They stood at the edge of the wood, but not a wood with dark trees as before. Silvery trunks and branches glowed under a thousand stars gleaming in a cloudless sky. His mouth dropped open as his eyes wandered across the star-speckled ceiling of this new realm. They shone with an intensity, true and bright, as they must have done at the time of their birth. Toryn blinked away tears, keen to let the starlight flood into his soul. Hope smiled. 'You should close your mouth. The wood is teeming with fireflies, starwings and leaflaps.' She laughed. 'And while they are beautiful to behold, I cannot vouch for their taste.' Toryn studied her face for the first time since entering the wood. To his astonishment, she now appeared many years younger in the starlight.

Hope raised an eyebrow along with her hand. 'This way.' She led him through the glimmering trees, shedding a faint light on a path winding its way deep into the wood. A gentle breeze brought the leaves to life, rustling as if joining the distant voices of the song echoing through time. About them, insects buzzed in abundance, some with gossamer-thin wings flickering with all the colors of a rainbow, others with bodies glistening as if a faint star shone within.

Hope touched his arm. 'What we seek lies at the center, but we cannot tarry long. The way is open for only a brief time.' Toryn turned and followed a path leading them one way, then another, even doubling back. They walked for what seemed like centuries happening in a blink of an eye. How long it took, Toryn had not a clue, but the path eventually reached a clearing. A spiral of smooth steppingstones led up to a low mound of lush grass glistening silver in the starlight. At the center of the mound, stood a black rock pointing to the night sky. Toryn's feet tingled as he stepped onto the first stone. He walked behind Hope as she glided around the spiral to step onto the mound.

Hope held his hand, took him to the stone and placed it against the smooth surface. He tipped back his head and drank in the warmth emanating from the rock and surging up his arm. She sang a greeting, and the stone replied pulsing slow and strong as if an echo of the land's beating heart deep beneath their feet.

Toryn watched the transformed Hope. Her gray eyes

shone with an ancient wisdom set within a youthful face of dark skin as smooth as the surface of the stone. Whether it was a trick of the starlight or magic, her clothes looked different. The tattered rags had gone, replaced by a thin cotton shift, shimmering like the air she had drawn about them on the ridge. Toryn checked his own clothing and laughed. The baggy, itchy cloth of the prison cell had gone, replaced by the same fine cotton worn by Hope. He blinked hard, convinced he must be dreaming. But he was most definitely awake, more awake than he had ever been in his life.

Hope noticed his bemusement and smiled. She circled the stone, running her fingers lightly across its surface as she sang softly. Where she touched, it glimmered, releasing specks of light. The lights floated briefly before fading like sparks from a fire. Hope completed her circuit and stood opposite Toryn. 'Shall we sit?' She gestured to a patch of grass beside a stream. The urge to sleep welled up as soon as he sat on the soft ground. Hope stroked his cheek. 'Lie back and let it take you.'

But Toryn resisted. 'There's something I have to know.'

Hope raised her hand. 'Now is not the time. You must rest, as must I. A dark force has done you great harm, far beyond my powers to heal in my present state. Sleep, and this place will undo the wrong.'

Toryn could not hold back a moment longer. Despite the questions forming in his head, he lay on the soft grass and let the night take him to places he longed to see.

Toryn sat, unaware of how long he had slept. Above, the stars shone with such intensity he felt sure he could feel their light settling on his face. He ran his fingers across the warm grass, stretched and took a deep breath, relieved the coldness inside had gone. Pictures of home flooded back as the fog in his head had cleared. He stood and felt the aches drop away from his body.

Hope appeared at the edge of the clearing. Toryn watched in awe as she gracefully skipped across the stones to the mound. She stepped up and held out her hands. 'Here, eat. You'll find these most nourishing.' He reached out and took a handful of berries and gratefully placed them in his mouth. As they burst on his tongue, the sweet juice seemed to reach every part of his body.

Hope laughed. 'You should see your face.' She stepped closer and ran her soft hand across his cheek and down to his chin. 'Ah! I see the stone has healed. You are free of the seeds of evil. And' — she looked deep into his eyes — 'stirred the latent power within.' Hope nodded to the ground. 'Have you not noticed? You are taller.' She touched his shoulders. 'And broader.'

Toryn glanced down. He assumed Hope stood lower on the slope, but her feet were on the same level. 'Ha! So, I am. By almost a full hand.'

Hope's eyes shone. 'The power focused here can help and nurture in more ways than one.'

Toryn beamed. 'And how about you? You're... younger, so much younger.'

She held out her arms and ran a hand up the smooth skin of her forearm. 'That I am.'

'Will you stay this way? Or will you change back when we leave?'

Her eyes wandered to the stone. 'Alas, I believe I will change. My life is a long walk in and out of thick fog. Of my past, I have little knowledge. The stones rejuvenate but it is short-lived. I will soon return to my confused state once back in the land governed by time.'

Toryn finished the last of the berries. 'Where are we? We must be in Darrow, but Hamar never spoke of a place like this.'

'This wood lies in our land but is not *of* our land. It exists outside of time, not ravaged by the elements that age and mar the world in which we live.' She walked to the stone. 'These were set long before we came into this world, but by whose hand, I know not.'

Toryn enjoyed the warmth growing under his hand as he rested his palm next to Hope's. 'What is their purpose?'

She interlocked her fingers with his. 'I can only guess, but I believe they protect the land from a force craving to corrupt all that lives. They number seven, stretching far to the north, south, east and west. Each has—' She gasped and withdrew her hand. 'You are right. One is no more. Now I have rested, I feel the pain in this stone.' Hope bowed her head. 'How did I not know of this? I appear to grow weaker as the power in the stones wane.'

Toryn felt her loss. 'That must explain how Hamar and the guards could find them.'

'They have long remained hidden from the mortal world. This does not bode well.' She placed both hands on the stone and closed her eyes. Her hands glowed as she whispered a few words. In the following silence, Toryn thought he heard a faint reply. Hope sighed, letting her hands drop. She turned to Toryn. Her eyes shone briefly like starlight. She smiled. 'The Foundation Stone, the most powerful, lies far to the north. The exact location eludes me, but I can still sense its power. We stand by the second stone, untainted, hence the old knowledge is required to enter its domain.'

'And you have this *old* knowledge?'

'Apparently so, but much I have forgotten, and my time here has yet to reveal what I seek. And I will not know what I seek until I find it.' The few lines on her forehead deepened. 'A shadow lies across my past, a shadow I suspect created by myself for my protection. And for that reason, I cannot recall why.'

Toryn took her hand. 'I never got the chance to thank you for rescuing me. There was a woman in the wood, Uleva. Is she part of the force seeking to destroy these stones?'

Hope shuddered. 'I know not the name.' She walked to the edge of the knoll. 'But it is an evil name, one bestowed upon her by the wrong this stone resists. They are the Ul-dalak.' She turned back to Toryn. 'This woman, Uleva, must serve the dark powers of this world.'

'The Song? Ul-dalak? The more you tell, the less I understand.'

'Then allow me to explain. Standing beside this stone sheds a little light into the shadows concealing my past, sufficient perhaps for me to answer some of your questions.' Hope guided him to sit. She dipped her fingers along with Toryn's in the cool water. She spoke above the sound of the babbling stream. 'The water, air, rock and even the trees, resonate with the echo from the Song of Creation, sung at the dawn of time. Every newborn creature, every object made, every event, becomes part of the Song, adding its own verse.' Hope tilted her head. 'Listen carefully, and it's still possible to hear. Yet many are unaware of the harmonies flowing through the land. As mortals leave childhood, they soon become distracted by the hardship of day-to-day life, and thus, the wonders of the world are lost to them. But the echo remains, and while it's ever changing as the passage of time adds more, the original, very first verse sung, still lies at its heart.'

Toryn's face tingled. 'It's true? The Three Maidens are real?'

'Whether it is as the tale maintains, or if it came from a desire for order, I do not know. But I hear three voices in the early verses of the Song.'

Toryn's pulse quickened. 'Have you heard the first?'

'No, not as yet. Of my past I can recall, I know I am

from an order who seek the first verse, sung by pure voices, unsullied by the evil that followed. We believe if we can recite the first lines once more, completing the circle of creation, we can be forever rid of the dark forces, shutting them out, and thus removing their influence.'

Toryn wriggled his fingers in the cool water. 'Back at the farmhouse, you remembered something about my father. Could he also serve the same powers as you?'

'I believe he must.'

'Can you hear his voice? In the Song?'

'I'm afraid I cannot. He is lost to me.' Hope saw Toryn's shoulders slump. 'He may yet live, but in a dark place beyond my skill to locate.'

Hope cupped her hands and lifted them from the stream, letting the water trickle through her fingers. 'If your father is one of my kind, I believe you too can hear these voices, the echoes from a distant time.' She led his gaze up to the stars. 'All that has gone before is woven into the Song; joy, sorrow; kind acts and cruel acts; creation and destruction. Past, present, and what has yet to come, make themselves known — if you know *how* to listen.'

Toryn laughed. 'My mother! Hamar said she couldn't hold a tune to save her life, but I thought she sang when I had the Winter Fever. I must have heard voices from this song of yours.'

She caught his eye. 'And maybe other times?'

'At the stone. I woke to the sound of a voice like a Maiden. But later, in the dark wood, I heard harsh whispers, barely what you'd call singing.'

'Alas, there are other voices, those of the Ul-dalak, the Dark Verses sowing discord to corrupt the Song. But beware, much of what you hear are false verses, that at first, sound pure, yet they will entice you to places to entrap and darken your spirit until eventually you'll be lost and in its thrall. The one you name Uleva is one such follower.' She glanced down to the stream. 'And I suspect, she could have once been one such as me.'

A shadow passed over Toryn. 'When I first saw her, I thought I sensed a sadness in her eyes, even remorse.' He shuddered. Uleva's moist, black eyes filled his vision, and despite the proximity of the stone, Toryn feared they would eagerly suck the life from his flesh and bones. He shook the image free. 'But it soon passed, and she changed...' he turned away.

Hope took his hand. 'You are strong, Toryn. Most would not have survived such an encounter. These creatures wield a most deadly power, and we must find a way to resist, or they will soon be victorious.'

Toryn stiffened as the reality of the world outside found him. 'I saw another wyke, Uldrak, poison the rock beneath our feet, and Uleva conjure witches from the air.'

Hope stood and dried her hands on her shift. 'I know not this word, *wyke*. But Uldrak must number among the ranks of the Ul-dalak. They are able to bring things from the past to the present, things that should never see the light of day again. The Ul-dalak also unmake objects, and indeed people, if they locate their origin and alter their verse.' Her head dropped. 'I believe I have witnessed such callous acts. A man can be plucked from his time if his birth can be *unmade*.'

'Do you have such power?'

She nodded. 'Yes, but not to such an extent. That is how I hid us at the ridge. I recited the verse from the previous day to bring it to the time in which we stood. Our pursuers would therefore see it as it would have been prior to our arrival.' Her brow creased. 'But compared to pulling spirits from the distant past, mine was a mere jester's trick, I wouldn't know where to begin to resist the force threatening these stones. And you saw how I could maintain my deception for only a short time.'

Toryn climbed to his feet. 'But the Archon tells us he holds back the dark forces with his gate. Is that not true?'

'Apparently not. There are ancient powers still roaming this land. If a more formidable enemy lies behind this gate, it must stand firm.'

Toryn stared into the stream. 'Then we are in danger. At the mines, I heard of an attack on the gate. Should they break through, we'll be trapped in the middle of two evil foes. Could they be in league with each other?' He looked back to the stone. 'And if the power in these grows weak, how will we fight back against such a destructive force?'

'Then we must petition this Archon for aid. We cannot allow another stone to fall.'

Toryn straightened. 'Hamar, my old friend, says the Archon has immense power and commands the largest armies in the land.'

'Then come. It is time to leave. Please refill my flask from the stream, it will give us strength for our journey.' She walked to the edge of the grass and placed her foot onto the first stepping-stone. 'You must take me to his city but beware I will diminish by dawn. I believe the old woman you see is a disguise to protect myself from the forces that would otherwise sense my presence.'

'Won't it be morning outside?'

'Not yet. No time has passed since we entered. It will still be twilight, as cold and wet as we left it.'

Toryn's heart sank. 'Wait. Did the stone reveal your name? I would like to know what to call you.'

A wry smile spread across her lips. 'Sadly, no. I am named by the Song, but it's kept from me by the shadow obscuring my past. It matters not. I have grown fond of the name you gave me. Hope will suffice for now.'

Stepping out of the timeless wood had felt like a slap

in the face as the cold, wet evening begrudgingly tolerated their return. With every step, Toryn's memory of the mystical land slipped farther from his grasp is if it had been a dream. He had turned back to see a dark wood bearing no resemblance to the one they had entered. And as hard as he had tried, much of the time spent among the trees evaded recall. And if the sudden cold was not enough to dampen Toryn's spirits, the clothes they had worn in the wood had vanished, leaving them in their dirty rags as before. But he noticed they were tighter; he had at least retained his taller, broader frame, serving as proof he had not imagined all that had happened in the wood.

Toryn fixed his eyes ahead. He had done his best to lead the straightest route to Archonholm using Hamar's map etched in his mind. In the rare moments the sun had broken through the low cloud, he would take a bearing and head south and slightly eastward. Towards the end of the second day since leaving the wood, the setting sun had shed its red light on a dark line to the east: the jagged peaks of the Kolossos. Toryn had quickly sought for signs of the mountain he knew so well, but suspected Caranach still lay some distance to the south. However, their progress had slowed as they had ventured farther from the stone. Hope had fully reverted to the bent-backed, muddled old woman. Like Hamar, Toryn had stayed off the well-trodden paths and roads, hoping to avoid the odd, rare traveler. But now he pondered whether to march into a village, demand to see the marshal, and insist on an escort to take them to Archonholm. But who would believe two bedraggled strangers dressed in clothes fit for a dungeon? Worse still, strangers who spoke of magic stones and dangerous verses from a song.

The unfamiliar birdsong caught Toryn's attention. He peered up between the leaves to see a small, yellow bird perched on the twigs at the top of a tree. It sang with a vigor belying its diminutive size. More joined the brightly-colored bird in the treetops. They huddled together as they sang to each other as if sharing the events of the day. Toryn listened, recalling Hamar's tale of the Three Maidens teaching birds different parts of their song. If true, it must have been beautiful to hear, judging by the evening chorus in the wood.

For a precious moment, Toryn forgot his worries, losing himself in the birdsong as the scent of the blossom-laden trees took him back to the first of the summer evenings of home. He let out a long sigh as the last warmth of the setting sun bathed his face.

Hope tugged at his sleeve. 'You've stopped. I thought we were in a hurry?' Toryn nodded, and without a word, walked on, leaving the moment behind. He knew with every step they drew nearer to the Caerwal Mountains and the gate. But what had happened since the attack? He shuddered at the memory of Captain Bulstrow's violent end; it seemed such a long way off as he stood beneath the fragrant blossoms of the trees.

Toryn watched the birds nestling together on the crowded branches, taking pleasure from the arrival of summer. If the Golesh had broken through, surely these trees would already be charred stumps, and the skies empty as the birds would have fled north. He listened again, trying to identify the birds whose songs he knew. Despite their predicament, Toryn grinned to himself. Not so long ago, he spent his days building fences while dreaming of the world beyond his borders. Yet here he now stood, having walked half the length of the land, and on his way to deliver a vital message to the Archon. But what he would say, and how much use Hope would be, he could not tell. Thankfully, he had at least three weeks to contemplate his message before they arrived.

Toryn glanced up and noticed they had left the cover

of the trees. To the east, the Kolossos Mountains loomed tall, and, as the last light waned, Caranach showed its pink-tinged face. Toryn stopped to gaze upon the west face of his old friend, taking comfort from the part of the world he knew remained true. The lines of the familiar face revealed they stood due south-west of his farm, by perhaps a league or two. He had left only seven weeks ago, but it felt like a lifetime. The urge to see his home, and especially his mother, surprised him. He imagined strolling up the path to find her tending the herbs in the small garden outside the kitchen window. She would run and fling her arms around him. Then, stand back and gaze in amazement. He heard her voice exclaim, *well look at you, haven't you grown.*

'We going that way now?' Hope nudged his arm.

'That's my home.' He pointed to the peak. 'Between here and Caranach.'

She shrugged. 'How nice for you. Are we visiting your folks?'

'I… I don't know.'

'Why not? Don't you want to go home?'

He turned away. 'I do, but we have to head south.'

'Suit yourself.' Hope stared into his face. 'Am I still going with you?'

'Yes.' He sighed. 'The voice says so, remember?'

Hope nodded as if she did not care. She glanced over his shoulder and grimaced. 'What a hideous mountain.'

Toryn felt obliged to come to its defense. 'It's the tallest in the land, well, the land we know.' He puffed out his chest. 'And I intend to climb it one day.' He slumped. It sounded ridiculous when spoken out loud. The parts of the journey causing the most difficulties had been mountain pathways and ravines, not to mention tripping over tree roots. How could he possibly scale Caranach?

Hope scoffed. 'Can't see why. It's the last place in this

land I'd want to call upon.' The clouds returned, cloaking the mountain from view. She smiled. 'There, that's better. The gods have drawn the curtain. Now we can't see it.'

Toryn looked at a clump of trees on the ridge opposite. 'It'll be dark before long. We'll camp over there for the night. Then it won't be long before we'll need to find a way into Kernlow.'

43. One Summer's Eve

The work to repair the gatehouse had gone at a pace surpassing Elodi's expectations. But restoration of her once beautiful city would take many months, possibly two years to complete. She had ridden out to the plain to give thanks to the workforce who had the unenviable task of clearing and burying the enemy dead. As the sun began its descent, and the men and women returned to safety behind the walls, Elodi chose to stay a while longer and give Sea Mist a chance to gallop across the cleansed land. But if she thought the rare moment to spend time alone would clear her head, she was mistaken. As Sea Mist gladly sped through the cool evening air, Elodi's decisions of late, clouded her mind. Rightly or wrongly, she and her Council ruled out taking back Drunsberg. Captain Cubric had reported no signs of their foes venturing forth, so she had been satisfied to leave them holed up inside the mine for the time being. Besides, until she knew of events at the Caerwal Gate, she was reluctant to commit a large force anywhere other than Calerdorn. But no word had yet been received from either Bardon or Archonholm.

Elodi glanced back to the towers, standing tall against the reddening sky. *Consolidate, always secure your position.* The words of her father had much to do with her decision. Calerdorn was vital to the future of her realm. A strong city would provide the foundation for all actions in the near future. And while she still had the service of the *Celestra*, she had hope. As long as she could secure supplies from the south of Harlyn, she could hold their position, or at least put up a fight to make the creatures of Nordruuk think twice before launching another raid.

The ground rose. Elodi looked up, surprised she had

ridden so far from the walls. She slowed, turned Sea Mist, and let him stand. To the north, the red-tinged peaks of the Dornan Mountains drew her eye. The occupied fort at Draegnor beyond, had split the members of the Council. Ultimately, Elodi had cast her deciding vote as its head to rule out an attempt to recapture the old fort. It pained her to leave it in the hands of the enemy, as it left a wide part of her border open, but she was unwilling to take it back at a cost of depleting her army. After a long debate, they reached a compromise. They dispatched a small force to keep watch, while informing the Ruuk they could not expect to have a free reign over her realm. Should they ride out, they were to withdraw and defend the narrow pass at Tunduska's Gorge while waiting for reinforcements.

Elodi nudged Sea Mist, and he readily set off. The saddle rose as his head and neck lowered and his stride lengthened. Elodi tilted with him as his power surged. She cried out, not caring who would hear. 'Ride, Misty, ride!' He shot forward, streaking across the plain as if barely skimming the surface. Rising in the saddle, she yelled her defiance into the wind. They sped towards the city. Elodi's heart swelled as Calerdorn's towers loomed ever higher into the evening sky. They had stood against far greater foes in the past, and Elodi vowed they would endure under her rule. Harlyn would not fall. Let the full force of the enemy come. Let them break on the solid walls of her city like waves on the impregnable cliffs of Dorn. Let them—

Her eyes fell upon the small pile of stones commemorating the knights lost in the battle. Sea Mist eased to a canter, bringing Elodi back to the reality of her precarious situation. While they could rebuild the walls of Calerdorn, the gaps in her ranks could not easily be filled. But the forces at her command had proved themselves once, and she believed they could be victorious again, if used wisely. A single wrong move could spell the downfall of her realm.

One at a time, with an eye on your next three moves. Her father's advice on playing the board game, *Squares*, came to mind. As a young girl, she had sulked for hours following defeat, but her father asserted she would learn nothing if he let her win. Now she appreciated why he insisted she played both him and Wendel when she detested losing so much. But she could recall every move the first time she had beaten her father at fourteen. At times you had to sit back and wait for your opponent to reveal their strategy. Later, you might take the game to them with an unexpected move, catching them on the hop, letting them make the first mistake. The hardest part was to balance caution with boldness.

Until now, her foes had been in control. Even when she thought she had taken the initiative at Durran Wood, Uleva had been one step ahead. But unlike *Squares*, if the Archon failed, Elodi would face two opponents on the other side of the board, and both would command many more pieces. And what of Uluriel? Did the woman who drove the Archon to the brink of defeat, still live? Uluriel had pushed the immense forces of the Seven Realms to the brink of destruction; she could only hope if Uluriel had not perished in the last battle, at the very least, the conflict diminished her powers.

Elodi looked back to the memorial. As soon as she could, she planned to build another, fit to honor all the two hundred and eighty fallen. But that would have to wait. The living took priority, and her forces had to rebuild and prepare for the darker times she knew lay ahead.

Gundrul had been right about Ruan. Within ten days he was back on his feet, and in only seven more, he had reported fit for duty. But Aldorman had yet to rise from his bed. His wounds had become infected, along with many others, leading the apothecaries to suspect the enemy had used poisoned blades and arrows.

Sea Mist's hooves clattered on the road as he took Elodi back to the gatehouse. The walls still bore the stains of Uldrak's devilry, but much of the rubble had been cleared and the gaps had begun to fill. The evening workforce at the gate cheered as she entered. Elodi waved but still felt uneasy with the adulation as it only added to her sense of responsibility already weighing heavily on her young shoulders.

'Ma'am!' Gundrul strode down the cobbled road. He pointed to the sky. She glanced up to see a bird. A message! It had to be from Bardon. Elodi urged Sea Mist across the stones and up into the city.

Still panting from her ride, she took two steps at a time to the top of the East Tower. But Wendel had beaten her to it. He glanced up from the small roll of paper as she burst through the door. She gasped between breaths. 'Do we need Gundrul to translate?'

He nodded. 'Perhaps best to confirm, but from the little of the tongue, Ruan taught me from his sickbed, I think I can read it well enough.' Wendel's nose wrinkled as he re-read the note.

'Well?'

'Bardon is true to his word, ma'am. As it had been four weeks since his last dispatch, I took the precaution of spending the day in the tower in readiness.' He handed the paper to Elodi. 'Such big news from such a small note.'

She scanned the strange words before her. 'Has it sailed? Has the fleet sailed, Wendel?'

He nodded. 'Yes, ma'am. They departed a day ahead of schedule.' He took her hand. 'If the winds have favored Lord Broon, they will make landfall in the Lost Realms early tomorrow.'

44. A Voice From Afar

At first, Toryn could not be sure, but as the light of the new day grew, the Archon's blue banner could be seen flapping high in the sky, far to the south. Hamar had said you could see it from ten leagues, but they had to be at least twice that distance from the city. Toryn smiled; perhaps not all Hamar's tales were as tall as the Archon's Tower.

Toryn sat back on the rocky ledge jutting out from the hillside and let out a long sigh. They had made it. He and Hope had trekked virtually the entire length of the Five Realms to stand within reach of their goal: the great fortress city of Archonholm. Just the sight lifted his spirits. Archonholm had been the foundation of the realms north of the Caerwals as Toryn's ancestors had searched for fertile lands to feed their growing numbers. And since the days of the war, the city had served as the guardian against the evil amassing on the other side of the gate, not content with conquering the lands south of the mountains.

Toryn lay back and inhaled the clear, blue sky as he listened to the birds. He watched them flutter overhead and whistled along, taking heart from their eternal melody. It had taken the best part of three weeks to wend their way through Kernlow's golden fields of wheat and barley, before giving way to the green vineyards of Gwelayn. The wide plain rose to deliver them to Farrand; the southern-most realm. Once through the ward of Tamarand, they had finally reached Holm. At first, the open skies to the east exposed by the end of the Kolossos Mountains, had unsettled Toryn. He had lived his life with the ever-present ridge protecting him from the bitter easterly winds, and for most of his journey had been be a useful guide. But their abrupt end suddenly made the world a bigger, more daunting place.

Now another feature dominated where the mountains ended — the Great Foranfae Forest. Toryn climbed to his feet and found his eyes drawn to its expansive green canopy. The trees stretched from close to where he stood on the east slopes of the Menon Hills, right out to the horizon, dominating the ward of Holm. Of all the regions of the Five Realms, Foranfae numbered among the few as yet unexplored. Even Hamar had limited knowledge, although it had not stopped his dear friend pondering what terrible wonders were hidden within. Hamar reckoned a power lay in its trees, only the Archon could muster. Toryn speculated whether a Singing Stone stood at its center, but he had not the time to consider the mysteries of the forest — his objective lay south.

Toryn looked back towards Archonholm. He gasped. As the morning haze lifted, what he had first taken to be clouds, turned out to be the snow-crested peaks of the Caerwals. As far as he could see from east to west, the sheer line of the mountains rose reassuringly high and impenetrable.

Toryn turned to find Hope standing at his side. As before, she had changed as they progressed through Kernlow, leading Toryn to believe a Singing Stone had to be in their midst. Her eyes had cleared and Toryn saw a glimpse of the Hope from the timeless wood. She gazed at the mountains, and Toryn thought he saw a flicker of recognition. Her eyes widened; her mouth gaped. Toryn took her hand — it was cold despite the warm day. 'What is it?'

Hope's head shook slowly. 'An unfamiliar voice… in the Song.' She searched his face as she struggled to come to terms with the change. She mumbled. 'A great power, a very, great power.' She took a step away from Toryn, twisting her head. 'It's everywhere. All around.'

Toryn's heart sank. 'The Ul-dalak?'

She wavered. 'I… I'm not sure.' Her lips trembled. 'I cannot tell. It could be one of my Order, but… different, strong… such power. It comes from—' She tilted her head and frowned. 'Far away, far to the south, many leagues yonder.'

'The Archon. It has to be, he must be of your kind.'

She continued as if not hearing his reply. 'Over mountains, tall mountains, like a great wall.'

Toryn stared at the horizon. 'But it cannot be, that's beyond the gate, outside the Five Realms. Nothing could—'

'No!' Her head turned as if trying to find the meaning from the mountain wall. 'It's a warning… or a threat…'

Toryn shivered. 'From the old realms? What does—?'

Hope clung to his arm, gripping so tight it hurt. She gasped. 'We're in great danger. Your leader is in peril. The Archon cannot hear. He does not listen.' Hope stiffened. She whispered through her clenched jaw. 'It's found me. It sees me.'

Hope clutched her head, screamed, then sagged into Toryn's arms. He staggered back, gently lowering her to the ground. He scanned the ledge, convinced unseen eyes were upon them, but they remained alone. Hope's chest rose and fell rapidly, but as he cradled her crumpled body her breathing slowed, and she drifted into a deep slumber. He wiped away a trickle of blood seeping from her ear, constantly checking for signs of their watcher. Hope needed to rest, but while they stayed on the exposed ledge they were vulnerable. He had no choice but to move her to a sheltered spot. Toryn scooped his arms beneath and gently lifted her so not to disturb her sleep. He checked his footing and carried Hope to a thicket down the slope.

Once under cover, he placed her on a soft bed of undergrowth and stepped back. To his relief, she slept peacefully and appeared to have suffered no harm from the encounter. Despite the shelter from the bushes, Toryn could not shake the uneasy feeling of being watched. He looked out to the forest. The climbing sun warmed the thick canopy of the Foranfae, enticing the trees to release the cool night air still trapped beneath its boughs. Toryn watched the mist rise and thought back to the tale of the Three Maidens. If the Gods truly raised the peaks of the Kolossos to save the world from the falling sky, the unprotected forest would have been flattened had the Evil One succeeded. Now, the threat came not from above, but from the south, and more recently, the north. Who would save them this time? Did the old Gods still watch over them? Or had they abandoned the world as the tales told, leaving mortals to fend for themselves. Toryn guessed they were long gone, and the destiny of the Five Realms lay in the hands of the Archon. But Hope had claimed he was in peril.

She stirred. Toryn turned to find the old, confused Hope from the grasslands of Dorn. He held out a hand. She took it without question, and he led her out from the bushes and down the slope. He turned before their path dipped below the ridge to look once more to the towers of Archonholm. His joy on seeing the Archon's banner deserted him. The journey was the straightforward part. The real challenges lay ahead.

Hope stumbled and stopped. She stared at Toryn as if unsure of her young companion. Her brow furrowed. 'Where are we going?'

Toryn placed his arm around her stooped shoulders. 'Remember the voice from the Song?' She nodded. He pointed south. 'It says we must go to Archonholm. We have to deliver a vital message to the leader of the Five

Realms.'

'Oh, I see.' She took a step. 'We better get a move on then. Mustn't keep him waiting.'

To be continued…

Book two: Age of Shadows

Thank you for reading *Song of Echoes*. I hope you enjoyed it. If you did, it would be great if you could write a review or mention it to your friends.

You can also sign up to my newsletter at www.frontrunnerbooks.com/sign-up.html

Printed in Great Britain
by Amazon

29816930R00249